Into the Northlands

Book 1
of
The Master of Fate

William Price Jr

Lanasia
Ulheim
The Northern Keep
Ironheartshaven
Melesorna
Oonograd
Oueld
Alvaro
Velaross
Tordenia
Sylvai Vale
Varrik
Dagon'ay
Delsemoria
Darez

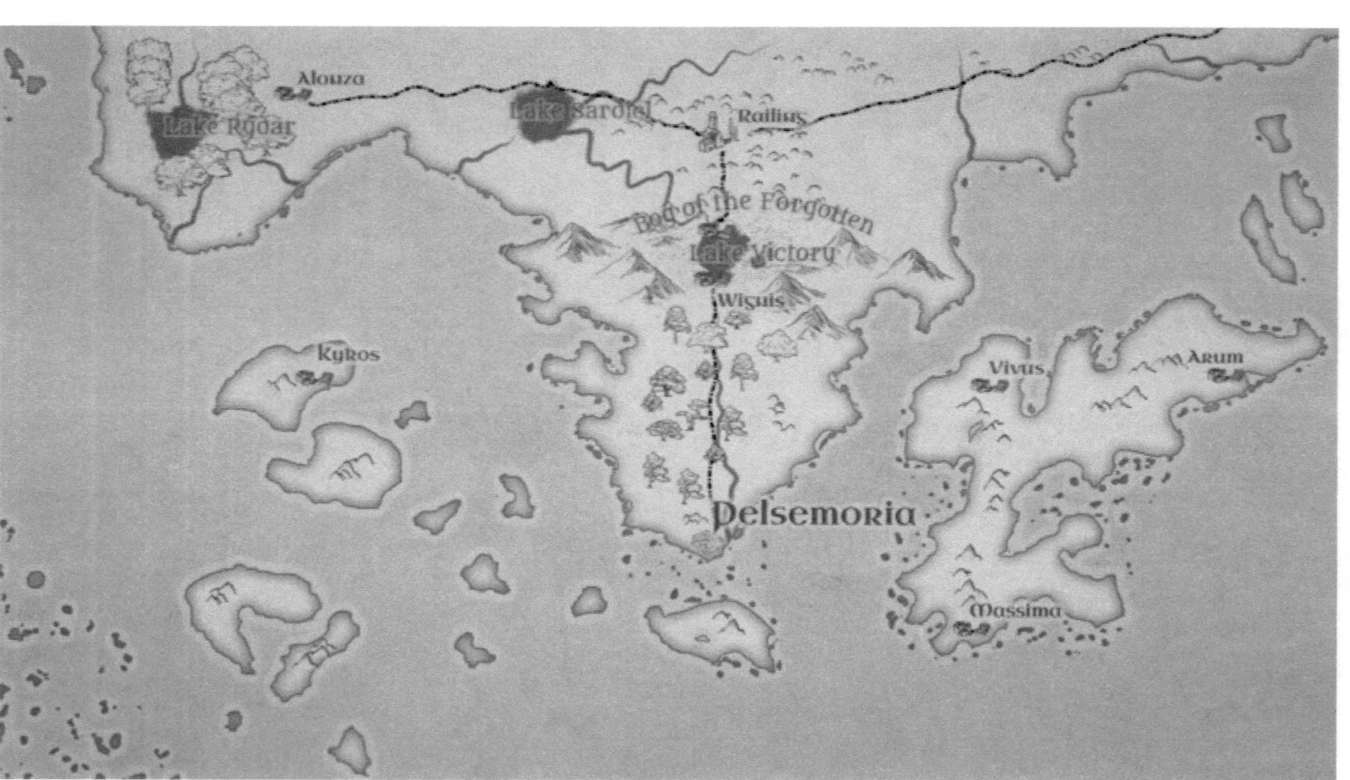
Alouza
Lake Ryoar
Lake Sardiel
Railius
Bog of the Forgotten
Lake Victory
Wisuis
Kykos
Vivus
Arum
Delsemoria
Massima

I

The Imperial Prefecture

Chapter 1

Every day, no matter the grey veil covering his fallen world, nor the bleak sight of his decaying home, Tomas Fidelis spent most of his time sitting and staring at the ruined Pelsemoria. As a shepherd to a flock of shaggy, emaciated sheep, Tomas had great opportunity for contemplation- an unending, mournful meditation on the despair of his life since the Black Duke destroyed everything he loved. Many low hills surrounded Pelsemoria; where once these grassy knolls offered the citizens a pleasant retreat from the bustle of capital life, now these mounds offered only a better vantage to see the bitter reality of a fallen Republic.

Often Tomas would bring with him one of the books he had saved from the Forum Biblitheca, the great library in the heart of Pelsemoria. In the days following Kyla's Madness, the great curse unleashed upon the Capital by the Black Duke's demonic daughter, Tomas had struggled to save as much of the invaluable knowledge within the library as he could- still only a fraction was spared from the ensuring flames. Before the murder of the Emperor and nearly all the Electors Council, Tomas had been a gifted student with a love of language, history, and non-Human cultures. Books and their knowledge gave themselves freely to Tomas, and the destruction of the Forum Biblitheca had wounded the young man nearly as much as the many other horrors of the night of Kyla's Madness.

Despite the all-too-brief comfort his books could bring, Tomas nevertheless still found himself looking up from those old pages, his mind drifting into the past. Staring through the distance of years more than miles, the shepherd saw Pelsemoria in its grandeur. He did not see ruined towers, reaching to the veiled sky in supplication; rather he saw mighty towers and monuments to the glory of the Republic. Tomas did not look at buildings, burned and broken with gaping doorways moaning their death or empty windows staring into broken streets; he saw welcoming homes filled with the elite of the Republic and the servants who tended their needs. The shepherd did not look upon a crumbling wall, grinning a toothless smile at an uncaring world; he saw the mighty defenses of the Pelsemoria, invincible capital of the mighty Republic. Tomas did not see his blighted home filled with desperate survivors; he saw a gleaming city, heart of the world- beautiful, powerful, and eternal.

Tomas would enjoy the sights of the past for as long as his mind could sustain the illusion. His hilltop was the largest of its neighbors, and so it offered vantage not only of the dead city, but also of its surroundings. From his place, as near to the sheep as he was to the present, the shepherd could look out towards the north and the dark forest that pressed ever closer to his home. For a decade, the woods had moved silently, hungrily, eager to claim the crumbling stones that had once commanded the civilized world. Or, Tomas could look south, past the thundering cliffs, and let his gaze drifts along the jagged coast of the Nassinal Sea. Tomas rarely looked upon the old port; the skeletal docks with their rusted chains, rotted ropes, and broken ships could offer him only a grim reminder of a lost mercantile tradition and a defeated fleet. The sights all around the young shepherd worked constantly to pierce his desired illusion of a happier past.

In addition to the city, Tomas would often think of his father, Alessandros. The shepherd had always been proud of his father, even to the earliest days he could remember. Alessandros was, in his son's opinion, the very epitome of a Republic soldier. Because his father had been a humble man, he would not speak much of his accomplishments in the Emperor's service; his wife, Cara, had no such reservations. Tomas' mother spoke often of her late husband's campaigns. The young man could recite, word for word, the tales of his father's actions and adventures. Tomas" mother even insisted that on the very night the shepherd was born, Alessandros was leading the rescue force that saved the 13th Legion from the bloody uprising of Reydia the Deranged. It was after that very mission, in fact, that Tomas' father had earned the greatest honor possible for a soldier of the Republic: assignment within the Praetorians.

The Praetorians; First Company of the First Legion. Personal guard to the Imperial Family and sworn defenders of Pelsemoria. This assignment meant a knightship for Alessandros and an educated upbringing for his son. Thus it was that Tomas enjoyed the great benefits of cultured life within the greatest city in the world. He was the son of an officer in the most honored position within the Republic.

And then one day a man named Rogan Eigenhard, a mercenary in the service of the Black Duke, assassinated the Emperor. Rogan Eigenhard, who had been banished forever from the noble House Eigenhard of the distant Gwyndd Islands and hunted for years by the authority of the Republic. Rogan Eigenhard, the mercenary who sold his sword to the Shamashi, desert rebels in constant warfare against their rightful rulers, House Parano. Rogan Eigenhard, the murderer who had found his true calling in service to the Black Duke as both assassin and consort to villain's daughter, the only creature in the world whose corruption could rival his own. Rogan Eigenhard, who murdered an Emperor and destroyed the Republic, all in service to his evil master.

Only one member of the Elector Council had survived that day. Only one witness lived to reveal the truth of Eigenhard's crimes. Balshazzar of Tordenia, ruler of the western provinces in the Emperor's name, spoke the truth he had witnessed with his own eyes. Eigenhard had waited until the Council had assembled, having gathered to hear charges leveled against his master, the Black Duke. Eigenhard then, through bribery and the darkest magics, smuggled into the chamber his assassins and, sealing off any escape, slaughtered all those who could speak out against his vile lord. Leaving only the Emperor, who stood defiant before the Redwood Throne, supported by his most loyal Preatorian, Alessandros Fidelis. Eigenhard called forth his lover, the Black Duke's insidious daughter Kyla, dark priestess of a Sylvai cult. This demoness drew forth the flames of Underworld itself and immolated the Emperor and Tomas' father. Thinking themselves save, Eigenhard and his foul bride retreated to their master, but Emir Balshazzar revealed their treachery and threatened to gather the full might of the Republic's Army.

Plans formed by the surviving leaders for the arrest of the Northlanders and, most especially, their Black Duke. The night before Calonar would face justice, though, the unholy Kyla again summoned her infernal power. With Eigenhard assisting, she unleashed an unnatural lust upon the unsuspecting Capital. Reports of the most horrific acts of carnality caused nightmares for the survivors years after the fact. Those men and women unable to reach their loved ones instead lay with friends, relatives, even non-Humans. Some few unfortunates even forced themselves upon animals. Tomas, a mere child at the time, had been somewhat fortunate, in that Kyla's witchcraft had no purchase upon a child's innocence. Despite this, he had still been forced to watch the effects of the spell all around him. On the night of the Madness, called so by the survivors, Tomas had been staying at the home of his friend Elpidius. When the magic struck the house, he was forced to watch, huddled in a corner with his friend's younger sister Cecilia, as the adults around them engaged in acts of carnality that no child should ever witness. Worst of all for young Tomas was the sight of his own mother, half-dressed in the colors of deepest mourning for her fallen husband, writhing in passion with Elpidius' father. Elpidius himself, being a few years older than Tomas, had not been spared the Madness and had run off into the night, caught in its horrid affects.

So it was that having stripped the people of Pelsemoria of their Emperor, their defenders, and even their dignity, the Black Duke retreated back to his Northern Keep, from whence he continued his campaign to dominate the crumbling Republic. In the wake of the attack and ten years of onslaught from marauders, traitors, and the dark agents of the Black Duke, Tomas and his neighbors have tried desperately to hold on to some shadow of their lives, even against the pressure of the approaching, inevitable darkness.

Lost as he was in his memories on the day that would begin Tomas Fidelis upon the path of his destiny, the shepherd sat with yet another book in his lap for some time before strange sounds echoing in the nearby woods penetrated his illusory thoughts. Standing up, his book on ancient Khepric hieroglyphs forgotten, Tomas looked about, as the clang of steel against steel, as cry and moan and curse, as the destruction of flesh and the embrace of weapons, reached his hungry ears. For the past decade, the young man had come to learn such sounds, to recognize them.

Hurrying off, giving his starving sheep no more than a moment's thought, Thomas made a dash for the sounds, his pulse quickly picking up with a blend of excitement and fear. The shepherd did not know why the sounds of battle so attracted him; he did not think at all, but rather let his body respond to a deep-seated instinct.

The woods were surprisingly mild in the early winter afternoon. A gentle breeze danced through the branches of the trees overhead, pushing at the unyielding mist, but unable to fully banish the worst of the winter chill. On any other day, at any other time in history,

Tomas could have taken great pleasure in idly walking through this wood, passing amongst the trees with no sorrow weighing upon his heart. On this day, though, in this time of history, Tomas ran as fast as he could over the uneven ground, cursing the trees for hindering his movement and sight.

The young man leapt over a large root rising above its brothers and gave a startled yelp as his feet came down on something surprisingly lumpy and slippery. Tomas hit the ground with a thump, more startled than hurt. Standing again quickly and rubbing his backside, the young shepherd looked back to see on what he had landed.

Looking back at him were the dead eyes of a Xeshlin raider. Burning red eyes still cursed the uncaring world, for all their lifelessness. Ghostly pale skin still reflected even the dim light of the veiled sun. Layered armor of leather, dyed so dark a red as to be nearly black, enveloped a well-muscled frame that bore a network of crossing scars, deliberately forming the strange slashing marks of the Xeshlin language. The raider's throat was open, and the dark blood which bore the curse of his race still flowed freely from the mortal wound.

The Sylvai who had killed this Xeshlin was small as all its kind were, more than a head shorter than Tomas, and lean with little outward indication of gender. Its complexion was paler than a Human, yet glowed in healthy radiance compared to the ancestral enemy lying beside it. The warrior was dressed as Tomas had heard they did when preparing for battle. Thick leather armor dyed in various woodland colors was strapped to its lean frame. No helmet rested on the warrior's head; rather, a thin leather headband held back the thick mane of long white hair with a series of the strange glyphs of the Sylvai language decorating it. Resting near the warrior's still fingers lay a short, slightly curved blade stained with Xeshlin blood. A second blade, barbed and serrated as the Xeshlin preferred, was sheathed within the Sylvai's ruined heart.

Death was nothing new to Tomas, nor to any of the other survivors still scratching out a life from the ruins of Pelsemoria. Most of them, the young man included, had seen many of their closest friends and family cut down by starvation, disease, or the jagged blades of Xeshlin raiders. Even so, something disturbing stared up from within the opalescent eyes of this dead Sylvai and her Xeshlin murderer's. Despite the centuries-old hatred between the two races, and the oceans of spilled blood between them, now to include their own, these two mortal enemies seemed at peace. A look of calm reflection showed on the creatures' faces, smiles even rested on blood-stained lips.

Tomas' eyes drifted across the rugged glade. Scattered about were more bodies. A Sylvai here, a Xeshlin there. Some alone, some in pairs. Most were adorned with cuts and lashes, others bore the feathered shafts in their torsos: colored feathers for Sylvai arrows, and black ones for Xeshlin. More than a dozen bodies had fallen in this small, unimportant corner of the forest. The non-Humans seemed as though to be already fading into the tangled maze of roots and fallen branches, as though the wood was eager to absorb these creatures.

But then, Tomas' gaze fell upon something that did not belong. A piece of shining, Human steel. The Shepherd investigated and found a Praetorian. Still wearing his gold-trimmed breastplate, with his gladius still clenched in a righteous fist, a warrior of the First Company lay dead, with two arrows in his throat, one bearing colored feathers, the other black.

Tomas was jolted back to reality and looked about, trying to listen for the sounds that had drawn him into the woods. The sound of steel-on-steel echoing through the trees again pulled Tomas into a run, the thought of the danger into which he could be running once again failing to manifest in the shepherd's mind.

After only a brief time, Tomas could make out voices to accompany the metal strikes. At first these were only sharp cries of pain or curses in Velish, the common tongue of the Republic, and the strange singing language of the Sylvai; but gradually the sounds changed into commands and shouts of encouragement and challenge. A jolt of excitement and recognition shot through Tomas' body as he finally caught sight, though the dense wall of trees, of the dark blue and gold of a Praetorian uniform. The sight was quickly lost amongst the trees but was more than enough to compel Tomas further.

The shepherd may very well have continued running, right into the melee ahead had he not been brought to an abrupt stop by a smaller struggle erupting suddenly just in front of him. Exploding from the foliage off to his left, Tomas was surprised nearly to the point of terror when another Sylvai warrior rolled along the ground. This Sylva, distinctly female despite its armor hiding the swell of chest and curve of hip, had obviously not intended to be on its current course as, even though Tomas spoke not a word of the Sylvai tongue, still made clear from grunts of pain and a barking manner of speech its unhappiness with the current predicament.

After rolling only a few feet, the Sylva used its momentum to regain its feet and stood with bow in hand and an arrow already set, its own mane of thick white hair writing about its head and reaching past its waist. Its ears twitched then, bringing head and body around to point the missile directly at Tomas' heart. The young man froze in mindless terror as he took in, not only the barbed arrowhead directed at his frantically-beating chest, but also at the small insignia sewn onto the Sylva's armor: two crossed, four sided diamonds, one blue, the other grey: the heraldry of the Black Duke.

Shepherd and Northlands warrior stood, staring at each other. The Sylva's face betrayed no emotion, as though considering where exactly in Tomas' body its missile would be most elegant. Before the warrior could complete its decision, however, those ears again twitched and the Sylva turned in response, this time releasing the arrow before azure eyes even locked upon the approaching target.

The charging Praetorian grunted as the arrow plunged into his shoulder, penetrating the leather strap and drawing fresh blood. However, the wound and obvious pain could not stop, nor even slow, his attack. The Human warrior charged at his Sylva counterpart, swinging his short sword and roaring. The Sylva spun and deflected the Praetorian's sword-arm with its bow, dancing back and drawing another missile. With one, impossibly smooth motion, the Sylva knocked the arrow, drew, and released. The missile flew for less than a second before burying itself in the soldier's hip, below the last iron segment. With a short scream the Praetorian dropped to his knee, still holding his blade and snarling at his killer in defiance. The Sylva maintained its look of calm indifference as it slowly drew the last of its arrows and knocked, drawing the bowstring back while taking careful aim at the Praetorian's heart.

Tomas looked about desperately and spotted a small stone near his feet. Moving as fast as he could, the shepherd ducked and, picking up the rock, launched himself at the Black Duke's servant, roaring all the while with as much courage as he could muster. A look of surprise crossed the Sylva's face as it glanced azure eyes at Tomas, yet the arrow remained locked upon the obviously more dangerous Praetorian. That was a mistake that would cost the Sylva dearly.

The shepherd hurled his stone at the servant of the Black Duke, hoping against his terror that his aim was true. His silent prayer was answered as the rock struck the Sylva's bow just as it released, sending the shot arching over the feathers rising form the Praetorian's head. The Black Duke's servant spun just as Tomas reached it and struck the shepherd on the back of the head with its bow. Then, spinning in place, the Sylva struck with the other end of its bow, catching Tomas in the neck and cutting off his breath. Not bothering to follow up the attack, the Sylva raised its bow in both hands to block the attack it knew the wounded Praetorian had already launched.

As Tomas knelt on the ground, struggling for breath, he watched through watering eyes as the Praetorian broke the Sylva's bow with his first strike and hesitated not a moment before striking again with his blade. The Black Duke's servant tried to dance out of danger, but the Praetorian ignored his blood and pain, pressing the attack and forcing his opponent to draw the short Sylvai blade at its hip- the flawless metal of near-mirror polish contrasting sharply with the dull grey of the Praetorian's gladius. Although an accomplished archer, the Black Duke's servant could not match the Praetorian in blade-skill, nor could its slight body match his raw Human strength. Within only a few strikes and parries, the Praetorian's gladius was buried hilt deep within the Sylva's chest, bringing a gasp of blood from the Sylva's lips.

They stood there, the two warriors, locked in an embrace only one could survive. Finally, the Sylva dropped its brilliant sword to the ground and put a hand on the Praetorian's shoulder, azure eyes already going dark and turning to look at Tomas. No accusation emerged from those eyes, the shepherd thought, only surprise and disappointment. With no more than a sigh, the Sylva dropped lifelessly from the Praetorian's gladius, its landing made gentle by the moss of the forest floor.

Finally regaining some control over his breath, Tomas limped over to the Praetorian, starting to feel the effects of having run so recklessly over uneven ground. The soldier was leaning against a nearby tree, wiping clean the Elder blood from his blade before sheathing it in the short scabbard hanging from his right side. He then reached up into his gold-etched armor to where the other arrow still rested and felt at his shoulder. The hand came back covered in fresh red blood.

"Damn," the Praetorian grunted.

"Are you alright?" Tomas asked softly.

"Been better."

The shepherd reached up to pull the arrow free but was startled when the Praetorian drew back with a hiss. "Don't," the veteran advised while breaking the shaft. "You'll only make it worse if you just pull it out." The Praetorian looked Tomas over. "That had to be the biggest combination of bravery, luck, and sheer stupidity I've ever seen."

"Thanks."

"That wasn't a compliment. What in Underworld are you doing out here?"

Tomas kicked a stone at his feet. "I was tending the sheep on the hills," he explained, gesturing vaguely toward the hill upon which his flock was still grazing. "When I heard the sounds of the fighting…"

"You thought you'd come and take a look?"

"Something like that."

The Praetorian shook his head, the two large feathers on either side of his helmet swaying as though in emphasis. "Dumb, really dumb. You've got no business on a battlefield." He shook his head and tried to stand straight but his legs buckled and the soldier collapsed.

Tomas grabbed the Praetorian's arm and helped him to rise, turning in the direction of town. "What do you think you're doing?" he demanded.

The young man shrugged. "You need help, so I'm helping you back."

The Praetorian shook his head weakly. "No. The fight's still going on. I've got to link up with my squad."

"You're in no shape to fight," Tomas insisted. "You wouldn't last two minutes."

"Duty, honor, and loyalty," he replied, quoting the motto of the Legions.

The shepherd shook his head. "Look. You just said I've got no business on a battlefield and you can't walk without my help. I'm heading home and it looks like you're stuck with me."

Any further arguments by the Praetorian were cut short when Tomas set off and his new companion had to fight not to cry out in pain with every movement. Despite the assistance the shepherd provided, it was clear that each step was agony to the Praetorian. The arrow that protruded from the man's hip was no doubt a source of almost unbearable pain but somehow, he continued on, all but ignoring the blood loss that stained his blue tunic. Once again, Tomas was filled with pride for the defenders of what remained of the Republic, for never once did the Praetorian cry out or offer the slightest complain, despite the pain that he must have been feeling. The young man should have known little of war and the injuries a warrior could pick up on the battlefield, but after a decade enduring the constant raids of a dozen different warlords and probes by the Black Duke's forces, Tomas had seen more than a man of any age should of blood and misery. The shepherd knew the slow walk to the settlement and help would be endless to the wounded Praetorian, a misery that would grow increasingly harder to fight the further they walked.

"Maybe we should stop," the young man suggested.

"No," the Praetorian gasped. "Home's not getting any closer and I'm losing blood fast."

"So… who were you fighting?"

The soldier grimaced as they left the trees and the sun pressed down on his face. "Not really sure. We stumbled into something. Xeshlin raiders were probably scouting, getting ready for another attack."

Thomas grimaced. Since the Legions had abandoned the Capital, Xeshlin raids had been an increasingly-common tragedy. The cursed-ones appeared at least once a year to take slaves and spoils, to burn and rape. In each raid, the Praetorians had fought the raiders off, but the losses had mounted. In recent years, the First Company had seemed to be making progress, with fewer and fewer Xeshlin reaching the survivors, and fewer still getting away. "And the Sylvai?" Thomas asked.

"Scouts. The Black Duke uses Sylvai mercenaries to scout possible targets."

"But you stopped them, right?" the shepherd asked, a quiet desperation gnawing at his soul. "You stopped the scouts." The thought of the Black Duke's forces attacking, adding to their misery… it was almost too much to bear.

"We were lucky." The Praetorian took a deep, gasping breath. "This time. We've spotted Calonar scouts here and there for the past year, but they've always retreated from us, never engaged."

"What about now?" Seeing the trickle of blood that seeped from the veteran's mouth as he struggled to speak, Tomas changed their course slightly so they would avoid the worst of the hills. Their trip would take longer, but the new path would be easier on the wounded man.

"Now wasn't about us. Seems like the Xeshlin and Sylvai were both scouting the Capital and ran into each other. Their hatred wouldn't let them retreat. The First Company came in halfway through the fight."

"We were damned lucky today," the Praetorian continued, almost to himself.

"Why lucky?" Tomas asked.

"We were tracking those Xeshlin, trying to sneak up and ambush them. The Sylvai got to them first. Most of us just wanted to let them fight it out, to take the survivors, but the Captain ordered a charge."

Of course, Tomas thought proudly. Even though the Republic and nearly all its forces had abandoned Pelsemoria, the First Company would never abandoned their centuries-old oath to protect the citizens of the Capital. The Praetorian commander would never allow non-Humans near the people he has sworn to protect, and no Legionnaire worth the name would let someone else fight his battles for him. They would naturally charge. The survivors were proud of their heroes, whether patrolling the surrounding hills and forests or attacking the merchants that risked their souls doing business with the Black Duke.

"How many were there?" Tomas asked.

"No way of knowing," the Praetorian replied. "Once a Sylvai gets in among the trees, he disappears. And the Xeshlin," the veteran grunted as he stumbled over a stone. "Xeshlin can find a shadow to hide in on a cloudless day. Given the chance, no sane man ever fights a Sylvai in a forest or a Xeshlin on a sunless day." He threw a hostile glance upwards, to the tree-shrouded canopy and its veiled sky beyond.

"But you still went after them?"

"That's our job," the soldier shrugged.

"How did the battle go?"

"I couldn't tell you. We moved into the trees, the Captain had us spread out, and things got out of hand pretty quickly. Everybody was fighting everybody."

"Was that their plan?" Tomas guessed. "Draw you into their battle, and then jump you once you were spread out?"

The Praetorian nodded. "A couple of us were afraid of that, and even tried to warn the Captain, but he overrode us."

"What do you think?"

"Doesn't matter what I think. We had our orders."

Thomas sighed. "So, once again Humans get caught between the Sylvai and the Xeshlin."

The veteran nodded.

"Did we win?" Tomas asked.

"I don't know. The fight started, me and two other guys got separated. A couple of Xeshlin jumped us, killing my friends. I managed to kill one of them, but the other snuck up behind and gave me this," he nodded towards the gash in his side. "Luckily, that Sylva showed up and killed the last Xeshlin. That's when you appeared."

"So the fight's just started?"

"Maybe a quarter-hour before I ran into you. Time moves differently in a fight, so it's hard to tell." The Praetorian cast another glance behind, towards the thick trees.

Reading the glance and the implied thought, Tomas continued onward. "What good would it do for you to go back," he asked. "What good would you be in a fight you couldn't survive?"

"Surviving isn't the point," the Praetorian replied. "If there's a job to do, you see it done. A soldier doesn't leave a battle while his teammates are still fighting… especially if he can still hold his weapon high."

"*Could* you hold your weapon high right now?"

The Praetorian shook his head "Don't be reasonable with me right now, squirt. I know in my head that survival is better for the cause, but that doesn't mean my heart understands."

Lost in the conversation, Tomas did not notice his friend Elpidius approaching. The red-haired older boy was very nearly on top of them before the pair became aware. This happened more often than not, Tomas realized, for even as Tomas was solidly built, muscles the gifts of his late father even as sharp mind were those of his mother, Elpidius had obviously been gifted with the sleek agility of his own father.

"Afternoon El," Tomas said, feeling little need to explain the wounded soldier he was half-carrying. Over the past miserable decade, the two young men had felt their friendship grow into a brotherhood only shared suffering can form. They had always been close, their fathers having been the best of friends despite a difference in military rank, and their mothers having been blood relation.

"Tomas!" Elpidius gasped, winded by his excitement. "What's happening? I saw the herd and found your book lying on the hill but you were gone!"

"A battle," the shepherd replied.

"Battle!?! Who? Where?"

"Another probe," Tomas explained. "The First Company stopped them."

"More Xeshlin?" Elpidius guessed.

"And scouts of the Black Duke."

Elpidius moved to duck his shoulder under the Praetorian's free arm to help, but a gasp at the movement of his wounded shoulder and the still-present arrow stopped him. Instead, Elpidius wrapped his long arm around the Praetorian's waist. "They're getting closer, aren't they?"

Grimly the Praetorian nodded. "If the Calonar patrols are pushing this close to the settlement, then it's only a matter of time before the Black Duke sends another large force."

"Will we have to leave?" Elpidius asked. "Like everyone else?"

"That's up to the elders," Tomas declared. "If the threat is real, then we may have to abandon Pelsemoria just to survive."

All three of them breathed a sigh of relief as they passed through the crumbling remains of the once magnificent city walls. The rolling hillsides through which they had been forced to navigate gave way at last to the decaying streets, already yielding to the pressure of time. Despite the uneven stonework, the trio were able to increase their pace a bit. Tomas said nothing as they continued their odyssey, it being obvious to the shepherd that the Praetorian was growing weaker and the need for haste was growing. Finally, with a few sharp breaths marred by a wet echoing that suggested deeper wounds, the Praetorian's eyes rolled back into his head and he sagged to the street. The two friends, caught off-guard, could not stop, but merely slow, the descent.

"Is he gone?" Elpidius asked flatly. Death had become such a common visitor to the survivors of the capital that her arrival no longer carried much force.

In response, Tomas put his ear very near to the Praetorian's mouth. After a moment, the young man could make out the faint movement of the soldier's chest and the bubbling hint of breath. "No," he said. "But we're almost out of time."

The two worked to release the straps holding the Praetorian's segmented armor and sword in place, taking care as best they could not to disturb the arrow nor worsen the soldier's other wounds. Once freed from his arms and armor, the two young men had an easier time lifting the Praetorian. "We have to get him to Father Konrad as fast as possible," Tomas insisted.

"What about his things?" Elpidius asked.

Tomas glanced about. "Leave it," he muttered.

Chapter 2

Father Konrad was the only clergyman who still

tended to the people of Pelsemoria. During Kyla's Madness, Konrad
had been forced to engage in an almost bestial carnality with several
of the Sisters of Purity. Even those most holy of women were not
spared from Hell-spawned powers of the Black Duke's insidious
daughter, stripping their pure vestments and falling upon one
another and the helpless Konrad without a thought to their sacred
vows. No one in the Church or the community blamed the old cleric
for his actions, not even the Sisters whose chastity he had violated
forcing them to leave their Order. This forgiveness did not, however,
prevent the priest from blaming himself. Within a week of being
freed from the affects of the Kyla's Madness, Father Konrad had
renounced his vows and left the Church, intent on absolving himself
of the sins forced upon him by the dark magic of the Black Duke's
vile daughter.

Once the majority of Pelsmoria's citizens had begun leaving the
Capital and, worse, when the ordained clergy abandoned the
survivors, Konrad found himself the only one left with any training
by the Holy Mother Church. He saw staying as not only a necessity,
but his duty. He tended to both the physical ailments of the survivors
as best he could, as well as their spiritual welfare. The ensuing decade
of woe offered a kind of redemption for Father Konrad, and he had
worked tirelessly to earn it.

Tomas and Elpidius made their way as quickly through the
Capital as possible without doing more injury to their Praetorian
charge. They skirted the worst of the ruined buildings, cutting
through vacant home and shops when possible to make up time.
When forced over collapsed columns celebrating lost glories, the
teens struggled to hoist their dying protector, fearing new damage to
his already-failing body. Father Konrad kept his small home like all
the survivors in the old Sylvai Quarter, in the northeastern corner of
the old Capital.

Once the looting and raids had tapered off, the remaining citizens had been forced to move from their old homes to somewhere their meager resources could still maintain. They consolidated in the old Sylvai Quarter out of necessity, as the houses built there had once been the poorest and least maintained section of the Capital. Because of this poverty, the Quarter had been, for the most part, left alone by raiders. The Sylvai themselves had run off just as the Madness had begun to sweep through Pelsemoria, leading some to believe that they had been warned ahead of time. Ironically, the same fences and guardhouses that had once been put in place to keep control of the Elves now were used by the Praetorians to defend their charges. This combination of factors forced the survivors to seek refuge in this most unappealing of Pelsmoria's districts.

Despite how important Father Konrad had become to the remaining citizens of Pelsemoria, he insisted that he had no need for any of the remaining rooms or buildings. Instead, the old cleric maintained a small makeshift hut resting against one of the remaining sections of the city wall. Even for the Sylvai Quarter, the hut was pathetic, with walls made of wood and stone debris, and a roof of straw and thatch that sank against the winter weather. He had a small area sectioned off with debris to contain his chickens, keeping them inside with himself during the night. No one know how the holy man maintained his large collection of animals, chickens and pigs and the sheep Thomas was supposed to care for. No matter the difficulties, Father Konrad always had supplies which he happily shared with the other survivors. In those hard times, the old holy man was often the thin line keeping hunger and disease at bay.

As the two young men approached, Tomas called out for the priest. "Father Konrad! Father Konrad, we need you!" The young man continued to shout out the priest's name, hoping they were not too late to save the life of the brave Praetorian. Finally, Konrad appeared from behind the crumbling section of wall behind his home, clearly unsurprised by what he saw. His old brown eyes took in the blood-stained soldier and the two exhausted looking teens. Not a single moment of uncertainty could be seen on his wrinkled old face. Instead, Konrad merely nodded and moved as quickly as his many years would allow him to join the trio inside his home.

Relieved beyond all measure, Tomas nearly sobbed as he and Elpidius dragged the unconscious Praetorian into the cleric's home and dropped him as gently as their weary bodies would allow on the examination table that Konrad had in the back room where he tended to the sick and wounded of his flock. The priest entered, rolling up the sleeves of his stained and fraying robe as he crossed to a basin of water and washed his dirty hands.

"Tending your garden, Father?" Elpidius asked.

The old man smiled slightly and nodded. Finishing with his washing, the priest crossed the room without drying his hands and leaned over the Praetorian.

"Is it too late?" Tomas asked hoarsely.

Konrad shook his head slightly. "He lives." There was a common joke that during his many years in the Church, Konrad had given one sermon too many and finally run out of words. Ever since the fall of Pelsemoria, the cleric had not given a single sermon or speech and never used more words in any conversation than was necessary. Even in times of crisis, the old priest maintained his same calm expression and quiet voice. Konrad leaned in closely and put his ear to the Praetorian's bared chest. "Elpidius, on the shelf, a red pouch with grey powder, beside it is a very sharp knife."

As Konrad inspected the Praetorian's wounds, he was forced to squint his failing eyes in the dim light of the room. Looking up, he glanced back at where the two friends stood. "Thank you," he said softly to Elpidius, taking the offered knife. "I need light."

Elpidius glanced about and grabbed a burning candle from a small table. Moving briskly, he carried it to the table where Father Konrad was working to carefully cutting free the Praetorian's tunic. "Thank you," he said without looking up. As Konrad pulled the blood stained blue cloth away from the soldier's wounded hip, he pointed back at a large chest resting in the far corner of the cramped room. "Tomas," he said. "Bandages, wrappings, and the jar with the green herbs." The shepherd moved quickly to gather the items.

Dipping the finger into the bag, the cleric then ran the powder-covered finger across the soldier's lips and handed the bag back to Elpidius. "Water," the cleric requested.

Tomas returned with the items Konrad had requested and laid them out on the table beside the Praetorian. Konrad barely nodded his thanks while dribbling water in to his patient's mouth. "Good Tomas. Now, needle and thread." The shepherd looked about for the items.

Konrad handed the jar over to Elpidius. "Three leaves," he instructed. "In a small bowl, fill it with water and stir gently." Elpidius nodded and grabbed up a nearby bowl. When Tomas returned with the needle and thread, he noticed that the Praetorian's eyes were fluttering and his breathing became stronger, though harder and more uneven. With a sudden jerk, the soldier started kicking his arms and legs wildly, knocking the bandages off the table and threatening to overturn it.

Father Konrad glanced at Tomas. "Hold him, please."

Tomas roughly grabbed the Praetorian's shoulders, even his injured one, and forced him back to the table, straining to keep him in place. "Is this normal?" he asked.

The priest nodded slightly and reached out a hand for the bowl that Elpidius brought up. "Help him, Elpidius."

As the two young men struggled with the kicking soldier, they threw concerned looks at each other. "Uh, Father?" Elpidius grunted. "Are you sure this is ok?"

Konrad nodded again as he began to spoon the contents of the bowl into his patient's mouth. "The powder gave him a surge of energy, enough to help him fight to live. This potion will still his muscles and quiet his pain with a deep sleep. Then we will see to his wounds."

"We?" Elpidius asked.

The priest nodded. "I will need assistance." Within moments, the Praetorian became calmer and stopped thrashing. Konrad handed the bowl back to Elpidius. "Boil water," he instructed. "And clean the bandages. Tomas, hand me that knife."

The young man complied and watched in fascination as the old cleric cut into the soldier's hip, taking great care to cause as little damage as was possible to finally remove the arrow.

Once the sylvic missile was out, Konrad handed it to Tomas and then picked up the needle and thread. "Tomas, go into the other room, burn the arrow and draw the poker out of the hearth."

When the shepherd returned from his tasks, he saw Father Konrad holding his needle in the flame of the candle. "What are you doing, Father?"

"We must take care keep the wound clean." the priest replied.

"What do I do with this?" Tomas asked, raising the red-hot poker.

Konrad unrolled a clean white cloth and carefully placed the needle on it, then turned back and took the poker from Tomas. "Hold him," he instructed.

The young man pushed down on the Praetorian's chest, fearing what was to come. Father Konrad's face stayed neutral as the crossed to his patient and carefully positioned the poker over the hip wound. Never losing that look of neutrality, the priest stuck the poker into the wound. Despite the Praetorian's deep sleep, the soldier still bucked against the pain, but somehow Tomas held him still. Konrad pulled the poker out of the first wound and circled around, positioning it over the shoulder wound. The stench of burning flesh, so much like the pork that filled much of their diet, filled the room and nearly made Tomas retch for the knowledge of what it truly was. Finally Konrad pulled the poker from the Praetorian and handed it back to Tomas. The old priest put his hand on the young man's shoulder and nodded. "There are many that cannot watch that. Well done."

The young shepherd nodded weakly and considered passing out.

Elpidius entered the room with a steaming pot of water. "They're as clean as I can get them, Father," he said.

"Thank you Elpidius," the cleric replied. "Now, make sure that pot stays full of hot water. Tomas, use the wet towels to clean the blood from the wounds as I sew them up."

The sun was already slipping behind the western hills by the time the work was done. Tomas and Elpidius exited Konrad's home, rubbing their eyes and silently praying that they did not look as horrible as they felt but knowing that they probably did. They were exhausted, with blood covering most of their clothes and limbs that refused to obey their orders. Father Konrad emerged soon after them, cleaning the last of the Praetorian's blood from his hands and breathing in the crisp air of early winter.

"Will he be alright?" Elpidius asked.

The cleric nodded. "Thanks to you two. He is sleeping now and will take some time to fully heal, but he will live." Tomas shook his head. "Those wounds looked bad."

"He may never run as fast nor shoot a bow as quickly. Still, he will live where he would have not."

The small group had only a few moments to enjoy the rest and satisfaction of saving the life of one of their honored protectors before Kineus, the son of Gregor the old harbormaster and a good friend of both Tomas and Elpidius approached at a hard run. "Tom! El!" the young man cried through his heavy breaths. "Riders coming in! There's been a battle! The Praetorians just returned from a fight!" Although older than both Tomas and Elpidius, Kineus acted much the younger. His boyish looks blended with his blonde hair and constant youthful exuberance to give him a perpetual energy that his friends frequently fought to keep up with.

"A battle?" Tomas asked in mock surprise. "You don't say."

Father Konrad looked at Tomas in mild reproach then raised a hand in greeting for another of his young flock. "Yes, Kineus, we already knew of the battle. Tomas and Elpidius helped to rescue a wounded Praetorian."

Elpidius cleared his throat. "Actually, Father, Tomas did the rescuing. I just ran into him on his way back."

The old priest nodded, gently stroking his grey beard. "Your honesty is commendable Elpidius, even if your intentions towards your neighbor's daughter are not."

"So, have any of the Praetorians talked about what happened?" Tomas asked, trying to spare his friend from the scrutiny of the cleric.

Kineus nearly bubbled with excitement. "Two of them are answering questions at the Inn! Let's go before we miss everything!"

Tomas looked back at Konrad. "Father?"

The cleric patted Tomas on the shoulder. "Go. I must stay and tend to our patient. Bring me news of what the Praetorians say."

"Come on!" Kineus demanded.

"Oh, and Thomas?" Konrad called out.

"Father?"

"When you have a moment, perhaps you could round up the sheep?"

Chapter 3

It took only a few minutes for the three young men to navigate the maze of narrow streets for them to reach the center of their community. The Sylvai never bothered to create the organized grid of city blocks for their district that Humans tended to construct, and their architecture was frequently inconsistent. Streets often ended in cul-de-sacs and houses were built wherever it seemed appropriate to the Sylvai, even in the middle or even over top of the streets. The people of Pelsemoria had lived for years now within the old Sylvai Quarter, and still they were not accustomed to the street design. Many still grew lost if they attempted to use a short cut versus a well-known route.

Tomas and his friends were among the only people who had an intimate knowledge of the district layout. Kineus because of his endless energy, Elpidius because he always sought places where he and whichever companion he currently found himself with could remain undisturbed, and Tomas because he never forgot any of the lessons his father taught him, one of the most important being about knowing your home terrain; each member of the group contributing their own part to the collective whole that made the friends the undisputed masters of the Quarter's layout.. The three friends zipped through the broken district, ducking through alleyways and crossing through empty houses, cutting a trip of a half hour into only a few minutes.

Near the center of the Sylvai Quarter rested the Inn of No Name. This title was a long-standing joke to the people of Pelsemoria, as it certainly did have a name, but one in the unpronounceable Sylvai language. Humans did not bother with the Inn of No Name, just as they did not bother with the Sylvai themselves. The Capital boasted some of the finest inns to be found in Lanasia, with accommodations that could rival those of the wealthiest of the Noble Houses. To stay within the Inn of No Name was a dark stain on anyone's reputation, as it meant you could not afford a proper room in a proper inn.

Since the collapse of the Republic and the retreat of Pelsemoria's surviving residents to the Sylvai Quarter, the Inn of No Name had become the center of their dying community. Meetings were held their, and ceremonies. These were the few weddings and celebrations that still occurred, but most commonly the Inn of No Name hosted funerals and the transmission of bad news. For this reason, when the survivors took possession of the building, they unofficially renamed it the Inn of Lost Hope.

Entering the inn, the three friends spotted the elite Praertorians and the crowd around them almost immediately by their black cloaks and deep blue tunics, still gilded in gold and silver and proudly displaying the Republic eagle on the chest despite the collapse.

"What did we miss?" Elpidius asked of his younger sister, Cecilia.

Cecilia, seeing Tomas, blushed as she always did, bringing a burning color to her pale face that nearly matched the faded red dress she was so fond of wearing. The young woman was reminded by Tomas' mere presence of the night in which they had been forced to watch something together that was meant only for those many years older. Mumbling something about having chores to do, she left, her calloused hands twisting her frayed gray apron. The girl, now plainly approaching full womanhood as her rigid tomboyish figure was blooming into one of subtle, yet still feminine curves, hurried off to the back of her father's inn so quickly that her raven black hair flew about, trying to catch up. Ever since the night of Kyla's Madness, Cecilia and Tomas had been extremely uncomfortable around each other. Tomas liked her, quite a bit actually; many restless nights passed with Tomas searching for the words that would close the gap between them. Before the night of Kyla's Madness, Cecilia and Tomas frequently played together and spent much time in each other's company; some, in fact, thought it was Cecilia who was Tomas' best friend, not Elpidius. There had even been one incident in which Tomas' father had caught the two of them in the garden about to exchange a first kiss. Alessandros had spoken of the incident with Cecilia's father, but had kept the children's secret the mothers. The two old friends had long since decided that, if Tomas and Cecilia still showed such an interest in each other after growing up, they would be married.

The Praetorians' words drew Tomas' thoughts and eyes from Cecilia's retreat. "It's true," the taller of the two soldiers was saying, resting his clearly wounded leg by seating himself on a chair near the fire. "We fought them and won."

"How did he hurt his leg?" Tomas asked Macharus, another of his friends.

"His squad was fighting Xeshlin raiders," the younger man with coal-black hair replied. "But then a group of soldiers wearing Duke Calonar's colors ambushed them all."

"I tell you once and for all its true," the unwounded Praetorian, a centurion, was saying, handing his comrade a cup of thin ale. "We'd been tracking another Xeshlin raiding party, but were ambushed by the Sylvai. It was a bloodbath."

The wounded Praetorian drank deeply. "More like a trap," he grunted. "Those damned Sylvai had to have been tracking us, the same as we were tracking the Xeshlin. The fight broke out and Underworld followed. It was insanity."

The centurion nodded gravely. "We think the Sylvai wanted to track us, but couldn't help an attack on the Xeshlin, you know how much they hate each other. By the time we arrived, both sides were heavily engaged. We hoped to clear them all out."

"Should've blasted retreated," the wounded Praetorian said in his ale cup. His friend put a hand on his shoulder, silencing the protest.

"They… the Sylvai, they were Walkers, had to be." This revelation caused a great stir among the crowd, the implications being shouted back and forth.

"What's a Walker?" Kineus asked his friends.

Macharus leaned in to his friend. "Walkers are the warriors of the Sylvai," he said. "I learned about them from my teacher back when we were still in school. One of the Black Duke's ancestors made an alliance with the Sylvai warriors who live in Wildelves Wood. They became the Walkers."

Colin, the only blacksmith left within Pelsemoria and frequent voice of reason in such unreasonable times, spoke up then, his deep voice carrying throughout the cavernous common room. "A Walker you say? That can only mean the Black Duke has again joined with the Sylvai warlocks."

"I thought the current Duke Calonar was Human?" the old harbormaster Gregor asked. "What would he be doing making deals with the Sylvai?"

"Everyone knows the Black Duke consorts with witches and pagan clerics," Colin replied. "It's no surprise that he's making deals with the Sylvai and their Walkers."

The wounded Praetorian tried to stand, saying, "The Captain had left for Velaross several weeks ago, to get better news and try to get help from the Holy Knights against the Xeshlin and the Sylvai. He returned just this morning, but our scouts had spotted the Xeshlin and we had to move out. We haven't heard what news the Captain brough, but we should know something soon."

A rustle of excitement ran through the common room of the inn as Colin restrained the soldier, gently pushing him back into the chair. Dunnalban had been a nobleman before the collapse of Pelsemoria. Although he had never been in an actual battle, his training and education were second to none. If any man could have convinced the Church to help, it would have been Lord Dunnalban.

"What about the Xeshlin and the Black Duke's soldiers?" Colin asked. "Are they all dead?"

"As I said," the wounded Praetorian said with some annoyance, "the battle degenerated into a running brawl. We were scattered across half the damned forest. We," he gestured to his companion," we were going to try to regroup, but then got ambushed by a half-dozen Xeshlin." He rubbed the still-bleeding wound. "Bastards had us, until…"

Both soldiers looked uncomfortable, glancing at each other and blushing as though in shame. Finally, after much prodding, the centurion spoke. "Until we were rescued."

"By the Praetorians?" a member of the crowd asked.

The wounded man shook his head. "By a Sylva."

The crowd grumbled, uncertain what to do with this revelation. The wounded praetorian held up his hand. "A Sylva. An old one. Female. We were surrounded and disarmed. The Xeshlin were talking back in forth in that cursed tongue of theirs, and then…" He shook his head.

The centurion looked out the stained window, towards the distant forest. "And then, the tress came alive."

"What?" Colin the blacksmith demanded.

The wounded Praetorian nodded. "The damned trees, they just… came alive. Branches and roots, the whole thing, the forest came alive and killed the Xeshlin. It ripped them apart. And then…"

"And then she was just… there," the centurion added. "She was standing there, singing in the Sylvai tongue. When the Xeshlin were dead, she looked at us and smiled. She *smiled*!"

Again, the crowd muttered amongst themselves, whispering the word "Speaker."

Kineus gave a curious look to Thomas. The shepherd only shrugged.

The wounded Praetorian raised his voice above the worried din of the crowd. "After, she said, 'If any of your people are interested, the King has offered sanctuary to all the people of Pelsemoria.'" 'The King' was said through clenched teeth.

The Praetorian's words caused a roar of commotion.

"King? Do you think she meant the Black Duke?"

"Is there a new king?"

"Will he try to extend his control here?"

"She said the people of Pelsemoria! They know we're here!"

"What about the sanctuary?"

"I'd rather die than live under the Black Duke's rule!"

"What about Velaross?"

"Yes! Surely the Holy City will fight him!"

"And Frostfront! Or even Ironheartshaven! Someone must stand up to the Black Duke!"

"SILENCE!!" The roar cut through the commotion instantly, as all eyes went to the figure standing in the doorway. Despite the collapse of Pelsemoria, Lord Dunnalban still kept his uniform pristine. His sculped leather armor was still oiled and polished to the point it reflected light. The golden Republic Eagle upon his chest so exquisitely engraved that it seemed as though it could take flight at any second. All his medals still hung from his torso, even the ones he had awarded to himself after the fall of the Capital. Under the arch of his arm, the officer held his blue and silver helmet, the tall horsehair crest showing obvious signs of care. Even his boots, though caked with mud from a long day of fighting, still showed signs of a recent polish.

Asinu Dunnalban, commander of the 1st Company, looked about those gathered in the inn with little less than a sneer. It was commonly known that Lord Dunnalban thought little of the people he had sworn to protect. From his point of view, only those people who could display their achievements deserved recognition for them.

Walking over to the wounded soldier and his centurion, Dunnalban said crisply, "Return to the camp, tell them I will return shortly."

Nodding, the two Praetorians stood and gathered their gear in preparation to leave. Dunnalban stood in place with his well-trimmed eyebrows raised expectantly. Seeing this, the centurion, showing obvious irritation, nudged the younger soldier and, raising himself to attention, raised his fist to his chest in the traditional salute; the legionary beside him quickly followed suit. Nodding his satisfaction, Dunnalban returned the salute and said, "That's better. Let us not lose our military baring and courtesy for some trivial wound."

The Praetorians finished gathering their gear and walked out, muttering something under their breath that sounded like, "God knows he'd never get wounded; what with all that 'planning' and 'coordinating' he's always doing during a fight."

Without a thought for the people in the inn, Dunnalban turned to leave, having little time for the common folk. "Lord Dunnalban!" Gregor called impatiently, "Your soldiers said you would have news for us from the north. Is this so?"

With a haughty expression only practice could produce, Dunnalban regarded Gregor. "I hardly see what use you would have for such information." he said.

"We may not have as much use with the news as you, Captain," Colin replied evenly. "However, we would still much appreciate knowing what's going on."

"Very well," the nobleman said with growing exasperation and waning patience. Stepping into the middle of the common room, thus ensuring all eyes were on him, Dunnalban began. "Following the night of Kyla's Madness and the destruction of our beloved city, the Black Duke Calonar did indeed crown himself king. He is currently working to extend his reach through political and military means. To try and add a source of legitimacy to his kingship, Calonar has even married off that sluttish daughter of his to none other than Rogan Eigenhard himself. Eigenhard has been named the Black Duke's heir."

"What of the Republic?" Tomas called out.

His face flushed with anger, Dunnalban snapped, "I haven't finished! Do not interrupt me again, boy!" Collecting his thoughts, the captain continued. "The Republic is gone. The whole of the continent is embroiled in civil war. There are perhaps a dozen petty noblemen trying to establish their own territories, each insisting that they are the true, lawful rulers of Lanasia. The Republic Army has been reduced to hundreds of small bandit and mercenary groups led by various warlords and Velaross has recalled all her knights to the Holy City.

"The Black Duke," Dunnalban said, with a mocking laugh, "insists that he, in fact, is not next in line for the Redwood Throne, but that he intends to create a new, better empire in which each race will be equal, with himself ruling, of course."

The Common Room filled with nervous laughter. In other words, Tomas thought to himself, the Sylvai will once again rule over us all. It would be the old Sylvai Empire all over again.

"Good captain!" Elpidius called out, "What of Velaross? Surely the Holy Mother Church will send her knights and soldiers to stop the Black Duke."

With something that was barely less than a snarl, Dunnalban replied, "The Church has allied with Calonar."

A shocked silence filled the room, so much so that the crackle and pop of the hearth fire seemed unbearably loud. Finally Gregor stood up from his stool. "What of the Inquisition? Of all the factions in the Church, at least they must stand up against the coming darkness!"

Dunnalban shook his head, "Shortly after the night of Kyla's Madness, Eigenhard traveled to Velaross with Calonar's daughter. Through bribery or threats or the powers of that evil priestess, the Lords Cardinal were coerced into recognizing the Black Duke as a legitimate ruler, as a king in his own right. Death warrants were issued for the leaders of the Inquisition. The survivors fled with whatever loyal priests and knights remained to the west coast, where Emir Balshazzar offered them sanctuary.

"As things stand now, the Black Duke is very nearly in a position to lay claim to a new empire, one centered around his Northern Keep. Calonar has secured complete control of the Northlands, including Ironheartshaven and all the towns along the Oolaug River and south to the Sentinel Mountains. Most of the communities in and around Ulheim are also under his control, though Frostfront remains free. Alvaro and the Gwyndd Islands remain free, though both are currying favor with House Calonar, attempting to enter alliances with him so as to avoid being conquered outright. The

Black Duke's ambassadors have signed alliances with both Velaross and the villages within the Sylvai Vale, gaining him not only the full might of Holy Mother Church but also the power of the Sylvai as well. He is currently negotiating with Baron Amuna of the City of All Sins. Duke Parano still controls Daivic and Oneld, though the deep desert of the Endless Sands is as lawless as ever and there are hints of a rebellion brewing amongst the Khepri, thus House Parano will be unable to confront House Calonar. Emir Balshazzar rules Tordenia and Sorania and is closely allied with most of the Western Empire while Czar Nicalos holds Medesorna and all of Kessia. With Ironheartshaven and now Velaross supporting him, and the Gwyndd Islands and Alvaro licking his boots, only Balshazzar, Parano, and Nicalos have the strength to stop the Black Duke and even then, only if they unite."

The captain placed his helmet back on his head in preparation to leave. "Now, if you have no other intrusive questions, I have duties."

Despite the repeated requests by the town elders to stay and share more of what he'd learned, Lord Dunnalban departed the inn, leaving a concerned chatter behind. The Captain had brought a great deal of very dark news to the people and had done nothing to quiet their fears. It seemed to all those assembled that nothing could stop the Black Duke from conquering all of Lanasia. After making his apologies to his friends, Tomas hurried after the officer, catching up to him in the rubble-strewn street as the nobleman readied his horse to leave with the two wounded Praetorians.

"Excuse me, sir," he said humbly. "I was hoping to ask you a question."

Turning to look at Tomas, and obviously disappointed by what he saw, Dunnalban sniffed in dismissal, mounted his horse and departed without another word.

"Don't mind him, kid," the wounded Praetorian said. "Some officers just spend too much time polishing their own brass."

"I just wanted to ask a question," Tomas insisted.

"We all have questions," the centurion said. "Not too many of us have answers, though."

The shepherd sighed. "If there are no armies strong enough to defeat the Black Duke alone," the young man asked, "and the remaining Noble Lords will not unite, then surely there must be some other way to stop the Black Duke."

The wounded Praetorian snorted, "If there is such a way, boy, it's beyond us."

"What of the Praetorians? What will you do now?"

The centurion pulled himself onto his waiting horse. "The First Company is sworn to the defense of Pelsemoria and its inhabitants. We'll stay here and defend the city and its people to the last man."

"Is there nothing more we can do?"

The Praetorians settled themselves into their saddles and looked off into the distance. "Against the evil of the Black Duke's armies from the north," the centurion finally said, "and the Xeshlin in the south, there's nothing any mortal man can do."

Without another word, the two soldiers rode back down the ruined street, following after Lord Dunnalban as the Captain headed back to their collapsing barracks. Standing alone on the road, Tomas could only stare after them, a thousand fears crushing in on him at once as a storm crashes itself upon a sinking ship. Finally though, as dawn must inevitably break over any storm, an idea, so insane and unlikely that it must work, presented itself to Tomas, and with it, the first spark of renewed hope.

Chapter 4

The world had gone quiet. Wooden signs offered muted objections to the light breeze from the Nassinal Sea that struggled against the winter chill. Dark clouds had been gathering in the north, from even further than the Majestos Mountains. The approaching wall of grey, streaked with blue lightning, threatened a harsh storm that would finally and forever banish hope of an early spring. Birds overhead squawked their warnings, fleeing south for a hoped-for safety. The scurrying animals, scratching the lives amongst the crumbling city, retreated into their dens, awaiting what was to come.

The people of Pelsemoria sensed the storm's approach. Shutters were closed and latched. Animals were brought in. Prayers were said to an absent god. Adults hurried about their final tasks and rushed children into the questionable safety of broken homes. Voices were hushed and words short. What feeble and likely futile preparations were made, and then the people waited, waited for what was to come.

Tomas had never returned to the inn or his flock of sheep after the Praetorians left for their crumbling barracks. Nor did he return to the inn or Father Konrad's hut. As his friends and neighbors sought shelter against the coming weather, no one knew to where the young shepherd had gone. Finding that her son was not resting in his bed, Tomas' mother had asked as many of her friends as she could rouse to assist in the search. Elpidius found the young shepherd, knowing where his friend would go.

Walking up to the cathedral was always painful to anyone with courage to do so. Indeed, the sight of the desecrated building was so hurtful that of all Pelsemoria's remaining inhabitants, it was only Tomas who still visited. Even Father Konrad, with his renewed sense of purpose and faith, found the current condition of this house of God to be heartbreaking. Of all the great wonders of the Capital, the cathedral had been greatest. Golden spires had once reached the heavens themselves and formed a crown upon the top of the great building. Often compared to Humanity's quest for the paradise of the hereafter, the spires could be seen from any point in the city as a gentle reminder that any sin one might commit would be seen by God and his Holy Church. Stained glass windows once adorned the walls and arches of this most holy place, each larger than the largest man and depicting everything from the great history of the Church to portraits of the various saints. The most beautifully and painstakingly carved oak formed the pews that held the faithful while the altar itself had been a lovingly crafted masterpiece of marble, jade, and ivory.

After a decade of looting and desecration, the cathedral now resembled little more than a condemned warehouse; the gold and jewels and valuable stonework had all been stolen. Empty holes stared out of the building in place of its beautiful windows. Hollow rooms echoed the loss of sacred artifacts. After ten years of abuse and neglect, only a mournful collection of broken stone and rotting wood remained.

Despite all this, however, Tomas still came; every Godsrestday, Tomas came and prayed. After meeting with the small group that sat with Father Konrad and prayed in the early morning, the young shepherd gave the remainder of the day to God, sitting in His house for at least and trying to understand and obey His will.

Sure enough, Elpidius spotted his friend sitting in one of the few remaining pews, eyes locked on the space where the altar had once been, his mind lost in memory. Elpidius never really understood why his friend dwelt so much on what was. Sure the time before the fall of the Republic was better than the one they lived in now, but Elpidius had always felt it was much healthier to try and find happiness in the now, not the then. Besides, the young man thought, this building could in no way now be called a church. The stained glass that once depicted the holiest of people and places now resembled twisted mockeries best suited to the lowest level of hell. Of course, there were many in their small community who believed that they did now reside in the infernal realm.

Sitting down next to Tomas, Elpidius eyed his friend nervously. "Your mother asked me to find you. She said you never came home last night." Elpidius never let his eyes wander to the hole that was once the central shrine. Even a man like him, who had only a passing familiarity with God, felt a sting in his heart over such a desecration.

Tomas eyes, however, never wavered.

Elpidius shifted nervously, "Look Tom, I don't mean to be rude, but you're not going to go mad or anything are you?"

His gaze still locked, Tomas finally spoke. "Do you remember the stories the teachers used to tell us?" he asked.

"Which ones?" Elpidius replied, relieved his friend had spoken.

"The ones about Cyras Darkholm."

"The Trickster-Mage? Not really. You know fairy tales were never my thing."

Tomas broke his stare and looked at his friend. "He was always one of my favorite characters. All those stories about how, in an hour of greatest need, when a group of heroes most needed a miracle or a town cried out for a savior, Cyras Darkholm would appear and save them only to vanish again afterwards. Stories of those people brave or desperate enough to seek out Cyras' tower and the Trickster-Mage rewarding those that made it by answering any one question or fulfilling any one wish.

"The stories said that of all the greatest archmages who have ever lived, Cyras was the wisest and most powerful. Among great wizards, he was the greatest."

Looking confused, Elpidius said, "But didn't our teachers say there probably never was a Cyras Darkholm? That different wizards from different times probably took the name and did all those things?"

"But what if there *is* a Cyras Darkholm, just as the legends describe him?" Tomas insisted.

"He'd have to have been alive for hundreds of years!"

"Exactly! If there really was a Trickster-Mage, he would have to be the most powerful wizard who ever lived. How else could he have lived so long?"

"Tom, what are you getting at?"

"According to all the old stories," Tomas said, his eyes returning to the former alter, "Cyras would answer a single question, or grant a single wish to anyone brave and lucky enough to find him and ask."

"So?" Elpidius insisted.

"If I could find him, I could ask Cyras to tell me how the Black Duke can be defeated!"

Elpidius sat there for a moment, staring at his friend. Then, without changing his expression, he hit Tomas on the back of his head. "That has got to be the stupidest thing I've ever heard of!" he snapped. "What makes you think *you* could find Cyras Darkholm?"

Rubbing his head, Tomas replied, "By doing exactly what the stories say to do. The legends say *exactly* how to find him."

"Don't they say something like, 'seek a place that cannot be found, listen for a sound that cannot be heard, and yearn for a home that does not exist.'"

"That's it. The Ballad of Bard Amuna, the first man to set foot in the tower of Cyras Darkholm."

"Didn't Amuna say that the tower couldn't be found by anyone who was looking for it?" Elpidius asked.

"Don't you see, El?" Tomas demanded. "The entire ballad says the same thing in a number of different ways about the Trickster-Mage."

"What's that?"

"Darkholm can never be found by the people looking in the wrong places or for the wrong reasons. Only someone looking not for himself but for someone else can find he one place in the entire world that could never be called home by any man of good heart."

"Which is?"

"The City of All Sins."

Elpidius burst out laughing. "You? In the City of All Sins? That's ridiculous!"

Standing in a huff, gathering his dignity about him, Tomas turned to leave.

"Wait Tom, please wait." Elpidius rose and caught his friend. "I know we live hard lives here, but the City of All Sins is a cesspool. Anyone entering that place is automatically excommunicated. They say the people there engage in the worst forms of debauchery, even taking chemicals that cause hallucinations. They still have gladiator fights, with slaves and exotic animals! For God's sake, there's a reason that it's called the City of All Sins. What in the world makes you think that Cyras would be there?"

"Bard Amuna wrote his ballad after he found Darkholm's tower. Before he died, he built the City of All Sins and founded House Parano. Why do you think that, of all places, Amuna built his city in the heart of the Endless Sands?"

"I don't know, and I don't want to know," Elpidius declared. "It isn't for people like you and me to go to such places or know such things. People like us are meant to do exactly what we're doing here, surviving."

Tomas started walking towards the exit, followed closely by Elpidius. Once he reached the broken doorway he stopped. "Someone has to do something El," he said quietly. "I can't stand another minute of sitting in this godforsaken ruin wishing to the stars for a better tomorrow. By God," he said, grabbing Elpidius by the arm, "given enough time, the Black Duke will rule all of Lanasia! If all it takes is my life to stop him then so be it!"

Elpidius called after Tomas as the shepherd once again turned to leave. "And what if it takes more!?!" he demanded.

"Then I'll give more," the shepherd replied darkly.

From the cathedral, Tomas made his way to the home of Father Konrad. Of everyone left in the community, there was no one whose advice meant more than his priest. As caught up in the moment as he was, the shepherd gave little thought to the time as he rushed through the pre-dawn light and thick mist that promised even more rain towards Father Konrad's small hut.

So it was that when Tomas knocked politely on Konrad's door, it was only a few moments before the priest answered, showing little surprise at the presence of his guest. Leading the young man into his house, the old cleric offered his young friend a seat at his humble table, poured some stew for them both from his small cook-fire, and sat across from Tomas, regarding the young man thoughtfully as he eat his dinner. "You seem unusually energetic this evening, Tomas," the priest finally noted.

"I was in the cathedral, Father," Tomas replied. holding his bowl of thin stew without taking a bite. "I was just sitting there, not praying or even thinking, just sitting."

"You have the look of a man whose had a… thought."

"I think God has spoken to me, Father."

At any other time, with any other two men in Pelsemoria, such a statement would be the cause of some distress. Typically when a man claims that God has spoken to him, that man is viewed with a great deal of skepticism; there had, after all, been a growing history of madness throughout their small community. These two men, however, were kindred spirits. They both had a deep faith that left within them no doubt of the validity of the Creator speaking to someone's heart.

The old cleric set aside his dinner and steepled his fingers in front of his mouth. "You think God has spoken to you." Konrad said introspectively, not as a question, nor a statement, but merely a consideration.

"While I was sitting there, I felt His will. It was as if He lifted a veil from my eyes and showed me exactly what He wanted me to do."

"How can you be sure it was the Lord and not something else?"

Tomas shook his head vehemently. "I couldn't have been just my imagination, Father. It just couldn't."

"I wasn't suggesting it was, Tomas." Father Konrad took a long drink of his tea and refilled it. "However, we are no longer living in the seat of all the world's power with the safety of the Church all around us, protecting us."

"I don't understand, Father," the shepherd admitted.

Konrad leaned back in his creaking seat, staring at the ceiling. "Do you recall the tale of Sir Talius Ironheart's knighting?" he asked.

Tomas thought for a moment. "I think so. On the evening before he was to be knighted, he spent an entire day and night in prayer, trying to hear the Voice of God. One hour before dawn, a spirit appeared before him and tempted Sir Ironheart to turn away from his vows."

The priest nodded. "You always did have a good memory for the old stories, Tomas. But do you understand the lesson behind that story, the warning?"

The shepherd shook his head.

"There are dangers in reaching out to the immaterial, Tomas. God is infinite and eternal. For those of us who truly wish to understand His will, we must try and push the limits of our mortal minds to reach some small degree of the infinity in which God dwells. It is, of course, impossible for any mortal being to fully understand the will of the Lord, but we have been endowed with the ability for prayer, which is the conduit through which God may speak with us in a way that we can try and understand. Most people pray and live and die without ever really trying to touch the mind of our Creator. If you really believe that you can be one of the few who can try and reach His will, you must beware the dangers."

"I still don't understand, Father. Are you saying that God doesn't want us to understand His will?"

Konrad shook his head. "No, Tomas. It's nothing like that. Haven't you noticed that the most satisfied you've ever felt, the most triumphant, was after a difficult trial? The rewards we value most are the ones which come the hardest to us. God made us this way. He wants us to be competitive, to struggle for what we want. For a mortal to touch the Mind of God, even for an instant, is the ultimate prize. Some holy men work their entire lives to be granted just one small glimpse into the eternity God created. That would be wonderful. But as with all rewards, the Lord has put a price on it so that it would be valued all the more."

"When someone prays," he continued. "When he really prays. When he calls out to God, asking for understanding or forgiveness, then that person is opening himself to the dangers of the immaterial. You see, Tomas, there are things in this world and the next that you and I could ever understand. Humanity was not the Lord's first creation, we were the last. There were beings and constructs here before us that we supplanted."

"You mean the Sylvai?" Tomas agreed. "The Uldra and the Khepri and all the older races."

Konrad shook his head. "No. There are things even older. Creatures that defy our understanding. Beings outside of this world, that were banished from Arayel but who hunger to return.

The old cleric stood and set his half-empty stew bowl near the fire, stirring the embers back up. "We are the most favored of all God's creations," he said, "and that makes these older creations jealous. That jealousy causes these entities to attack us in any way they can and at every opportunity." He looked closely at Tomas. "They will do anything to break back into Arayel, and Humans make very tempting doorways."

The priest returned to his seat and held up a finger in warning to his young student. "For a mortal to try and touch the mind of God before his death, he must find within himself the strength and peace to let go of these shells into which we've all been placed." He placed a hand on his chest. "To have only the barest glimpse of what knowledge the Creator holds, one must cast his mind out, into the nothingness between infinity and eternity, where these older creations exist."

"Are you saying that it could have been a demon that spoke to me? A creature of Underworld?"

Konrad shook his head. "Tomas, no one, not me, not the Lords Cardinal themselves, can tell you whether it was God who spoke to you or whether it was something malevolent. That answer can only lie within your soul."

"But how do I know? How can I tell the difference? I was so sure."

"What happened specifically?"

Tomas considered and finally started eating his stew. "Well," he said through a mouthful, "I was sitting in the cathedral, not really thinking about anything in particular. I started wondering what will happen now that the Black Duke is sending his Sylvai to search the forest, now that we know that Calonar knows that we're here."

"And what do you think will happen?" Konrad asked.

The young man shrugged, finishing the small meal. "If the Sylvai have found us, if they've realized people are still living in Pelsemoria, then we'll have to leave this place before the Black Duke can send a large enough force to defeat the Praetorians."

"Not a very appealing prospect," the cleric admitted. "Despite the condition of the city, Pelsemoria is still our home, and life as a refugee is never easy."

"Still, if Calonar has found us, then we must leave. It's either leave or live under his rule."

Konrad shrugged. "Would that be so bad?"

Tomas stared at the cleric in open-mouthed shock. "Father, how could you even suggest that? The Black Duke had the Emperor and his entire family assassinated! He worships dark gods and encourages the practice of witchcraft and rogue wizardry! If the Black Duke conquerors all of Lanasia, nothing will be the same."

"But we would survive, Tomas. Velaross has sided with Calonar. If the Holy Mother Church is willing to live under his rule, who are we to argue?"

"Father Konrad, you know as well as I do that the Lords Cardinal were replaced by men specifically chosen by servants of the Black Duke. Any decision they make is suspect."

"But still dogmatic law." The cleric held up a hand, silencing Tomas so he could finish. "Please don't mistake me, Tomas," he said. "I admit that I'm just playing a devil's advocate here. Part of living, though, is accepting that which is unavoidable. Neither you nor I have the power to halt the coming changes. Whether we like it or not, the Republic is dead. That death has created a vacuum that must eventually be filled."

"By the Black Duke?" Tomas almost spat.

"Lanasia needs a strong leader, Tomas. We are a collection of very different peoples with very little in common. Even Velish, the blessed language of the Church, is not universally spoken by the people of this land. It was always the strength of the Republic that maintained the peace in Lanasia. With the Republic now gone, war and misery now envelop all our nations. If the Black Duke is the only man that can bring to an end all this conflict and reunite the kingdoms of Lanasia, then are we really sure that we should fight him?"

Tomas was silent for a time. Staring into his tea and considering what his priest had said. It was not often that Father Konrad said so much, and when he did it was cause enough for anyone in Pelsemoria to stop and listen. His words, though, said everything that Tomas' heart railed against. Finally, with the calmness that he felt in the cathedral, the young man spoke his mind.

"Father," he said, "there are many things I don't know. I don't know why the Emperor had to die. I don't know why civil war had to envelop Lanasia. I don't know why so many of our friends and family had to die. I do know something, though. I know that all the misery pressing down the people of this land, all the tragedy we have been forced to endure and all the strife that burns through the dead Republic is the result of the Black Duke's actions.

"You are right that there is a vacuum now that the Republic is gone. You're right that this void must be filled and that peace will not return to us until it is. But the Black Duke is not the man to do that. Any man that would assassinate an entire family, raise his own daughter as a harlot, and employ the darkest of magics just to further his own ambition is not the man to lead us to a new Republic."

The shepherd put down his wooden bowl and stared into the hearth embers. "Elpidius said we need to find happiness in how things are, not in the way we wish they were. But I say that my own happiness is incidental compared to the happiness of the people of Lanasia. Joy cannot be bought from terror. Peace cannot be found in viciousness. Justice cannot be forced by tyranny.

"It seems as though nearly everyone in the world is ready to lie down and accept Calonar as the next Emperor. The only men willing to fight him are the ones who want the Republic for themselves. But

are any of them really any better than the Black Duke? If peace is to
be won in Lanasia, then it must be won by people who want it for
each other, not just themselves."

"Are these your words," Konrad asked. "Or God's?"

"Mine," Tomas declared calmly. "God only pointed out the way
that I can help."

"Is that what you want to do? Help?"

"Yes, Father. I just want to help everyone."

"Not just the people of Pelsemoria?"

The shepherd shook his head. "Everyone. Even the people who
now live in the lands of the Black Duke. If I'm right and Cyras
Darkholm does hold the answer to how Calonar can be defeated and
peace restored to Lanasia, then someone must first find the
Trickster-Mage."

"Forgive me Tomas, but the stories outside of the history of the
Church have never been overly familiar to me. Why is it, do you
think, that if the Trickster-Mage has the ability or the knowledge to
bring peace to Lanasia that he has not done so already?"

"The stories are clear, Father," the young man replied.
"Darkholm will never act until the need is dire enough to force
someone to quest for him."

"And you think that the situation now is dire enough?"

"With all my heart and soul."

"Do you think you can really find Darkholm?"

Tomas stood and walked to the shuttered window, listening to
the approaching storm's angry rumbling. "I don't know," he
admitted. "Nothing gives me the feeling of inevitable success. I only
know this is the right course."

"What will you do if you can't find him?"

"I will never stop looking," the shepherd swore. "As long as I still
breathe, I will never stop. Once I leave, I will not look again on my
home until I have the answers I seek."

Father Konrad stood and crossed to stand behind his young
student. Putting a hand on the shepherd's shoulder, the cleric
nodded. "It seems that you've already made up your mind to leave
on this quest. What did you come here for if not to seek my council?"

Tomas turned to face his priest. "There is a tradition among the
Holy Knights," he said. "It is a tradition going all the way back to Sir
Ironheart. Before beginning a quest, a knight will seek out his priest
and make one last confession and seek absolution for his sins before

setting out. I just thought that, although I'm by no means a Knight of the Holy Church, I should still seek absolution before I leave. Just in case."

Konrad shook his head and stepped back. "I'm sorry, Tomas. I no longer have the endorsement of the Church. I cannot hear your confession, nor can I grant you absolution."

"You left of your own choice to perform penance for your sins. I remember Cardinal Alton telling you that any day you wished to return to the Church, you would be welcome. There is no one I trust more with the protection and care of my soul than you, Father. Even if not officially recognized by the Church, you *are* still my priest. You have said many times over the last decade that you are only waiting for God to give you a sign that He was ready for you to resume your duties."

The young man dropped to his knees and put his hands over his heart in the traditional pose for confession. "Let this be your sign, Father. Let this show you that your flock needs their shepherd."

The cleric stood there for a few moments, looking down on the devout young man. Finally, Konrad slowly crossed to a large cabinet that dominated the far wall. Opening it reverently, he pulled out the soft velvet cloth with the holy emblem of a golden flame above a pool of water decorating it. Lightly placing a kiss on the traditional raiment of a priest, Father Konrad put on the symbol of his responsibility and crossed back to where Tomas still knelt and put a hand on the young man's head.

"Do you have sins to confess?" he asked, beginning the rite of confession.

"I have sinned, Father. I seek forgiveness from God."

"Then confess now before the Lord God and his Holy Church."

"I have lusted in my mind and heart for the flesh of a woman."

"Have you made advances towards this woman?"

"No, Father. Though I often wish I had the words to."

"A sin of the mind is still a sin. Confess to this woman your feelings before you leave and seek absolution from her. Forgiveness from God will follow."

"I have battled one morning ago with a Sylva and gloried at her death."

"Was her death at your hands?"

"No, Father. I assisted the soldier who killed her."

"'Do not hate those who would take arms against you,'" he said, quoting the Teachings. "'Instead pity them that they must turn away from God's light.' Wait until the Lord presents you with another of her race. Do this Sylvai one favor and seek no reward. If a reward is offered, then you must refuse it. Then you will be forgiven."

"What if the Sylvai serves the Black Duke?"

"Do not question the design of your Lord. He will lead you to one of the Elder Race. You will do as I say if you truly seek forgiveness."

"I will, Father."

"Are those all of your sins?"

"No, Father. I also hold hatred in my heart for others. I see the colors and heraldry of the Black Duke and hate those who wear it."

Konrad nodded. "Hatred is from Underworld and the beings who reside there. It is the temptation of the Demon-god Ramalech and its minions to turn us away from God's light. Let your heart be free of this hatred before you begin your quest. Your mission must be of God, not his adversary. Let no hatred into your heart for as long as your quest. Keep your intentions pure; as long as you do, your Lord will always be with you."

"Father, I also claim to have heard the Voice of God in my soul, though I cannot prove it was anything other than my own pride that spoke to me. I fear Underworld's temptation."

"If you feel you have been given a task from on High, you must fulfill it. If you feel you must leave, you must do so in the service of others, not to take war to your enemies. Keep your fear of Ramalech and his whispers close; do not be tempted into hate. If you must quest, ensure that you do so in the name of God and to help not only those you love, but those who you do not even know. If you do all this, then regardless of whether your quest has come from God, something of God will come from your quest. Are those all the sins that weigh down your soul?" Konrad asked.

"No, Father. There is one last sin, the worst of them all."

"Confess now."

Tomas lowered his head even further. "I look about and see the suffering of our people and our home. I see death, and misery, and doubt. I have seen all these things, and I have prayed to God to deliver us from this life and this sorrow, instead of trusting to his eternal reward that waits us after death."

Father Konrad removed his hand from Tomas' head and knelt down beside his young friend. "Tomas," he said gently, putting a hand on his shoulder. "Prayer to our Lord is never a sin. The Teachings are clear that He loves us and is there for us always. Asking for His help in the dark times of your life will never be seen by our Father as sinful. Look always to the Lord whenever you feel lost or uncertain, and He will show you the way. The true sin in life is not asking for our Lord's help; it's not acting when that help is given."

Tomas looked up into his priest's eyes. "Then I have your blessing to begin my quest?"

"Tomas Fidelis, I grant you leave, by the grace of our Lord and the authority of His Holy Church, to quest. You will search the world for as long as necessary. Your quest will not end until you find the Trickster-Mage Cyras Darkholm, or God calls you home."

Konrad lightly pulled the young man to his feet. "Perform the contrition I have named and forgiveness shall be yours, in the name of the Creator, His Work, and His Holy Church. Amen."

Chapter 5

"When a Druug comes at you," Luigino Mariano instructed, "he'll charge with his head low. It's what they do. They always grab for the upper chest, so the secret is to spin just an instant before the attack lands and cut along their backs."

Tomas had left the home of Father Konrad and traveled to the Inn of Lost Hope where the wounded Praetorian he had saved the day before was recuperating. The sky still rumbled, dark clouds hiding the stars, but instead of harsh winter, the air carried a scent of the springtime sea, as though the winds had shifted and were once again pushing against the northern storm.

It was not only to check in on the wounded Praetorian that Tomas paid his visit, though. Because his planned course would lead him through Ulheim, he would eventually encounter the great beasts. Logic told the young man that he would need the advice of someone who had fought them. With his father dead, that left only the Praetorians, and luckily Tomas knew one.

The wounded soldier, still weak but clearly on the mend, had struggled to rise from the bed Elpidius' father had provided. Unable to, Tomas helped prop the soldier into a sitting position. "Now once you manage to get yourself a blade, you've got to use it as it's meant to be used," Mariano continued, breathing heavily but steadily.

"I don't understand," Tomas admitted, sitting on a small stool next to the bed.

He reached over to where Tomas had laid his equipment. The shepherd had made a point of retrieving Mariano's weapon and armor before leaving Father Konrad's hut, bringing them back to the wounded Praetorian. The relief and gratitude in the old soldier's eyes had made the minor effort more than worthwhile. While the segmented armor was priceless in such hard times, the complex armor being beyond the abilities of their sole remaining blacksmith, the sword's worth to Mariano was even greater. The gladius had long been the symbol of the Republic soldier, and the gold etched hilt that marked the weapon of a Praetorian did more than offer a means of identification. The sword of a Praetorian was not forged until the soldier began his advanced training. It was sized perfectly for the one man and no other. Should a potential Praetorian fail in his training, the sword was destroyed and the metal sold off to be used for anything other than a weapon. On the day the soldier was granted his blue uniform and gold lined armor by the Emperor, that Praetorian gave up his own blood to the weaponsmaster so it could be mixed with the water and oil that would cool the blade after its forging. The people of Lanasia said a Praetorian's sword was an extension of his very soul. No two comrades in arms were ever closer, it was said, than a Praetorian and his gladius.

Drawing his blade, the wounded Praetorian raised the short sword, letting his young friend admire its design in the gentle candlelight gleaming from the flawless blade. "Well, take the gladius here. Now, this is a stabbing weapon, not a slashing one. Notice that unlike the swords other people use, the real power of the gladius is at the tip. If you must slash with it, use the very end of the blade and even then, only to disable. The design of this sword is for a man to put his whole body into a thrust. When you do it right, a thrust with a gladius is unstoppable."

"Why the lower back?" the shepherd asked.

"Druug have a lot of muscle," the veteran replied, "and it can be real hard to cut through all that. A bigger man could do it with a little effort, but you aren't finished growing just yet, so you need to rely on speed to beat a grey-skin. The lower back of a Druug is the easiest area for a blade to penetrate. Plus, a Druug has a lot of arteries in his lower back, so it doesn't take much damage to really get them bleeding."

"So stab them in the small of the back," Tomas mused.

Mariano held his hands up. "No, no. Don't try to stab them; not unless you've got one of these." He again held his weapon aloft. "I've seen many a blade break off in a Druug's body. Never stab with a common blade. Most swords have an edge, and they've got them for a reason. Use the edge to slash, only use the point on a soft spot to finish something off. If you have to stab a grey-skin, go for the throat.

"There's a reason the Legions have kept using our gladius instead of changing to a longer blade like the ones they use in other parts of Lanasia. For one, you only need one hand to wield it. The gladius was designed so that a man could use it but keep his other hand free or carry a shield. Don't forget in a sword fight that you have your other hand. When someone swings their weapon at you, catch the attack with the edge of your blade, then punch him."

"Punch him?"

"Or kick him; gouge his eye, use a dagger with your other hand to kill him. Do whatever it takes to be the only one still breathing."

"Isn't that dishonorable?"

"If it bothers you that much, then after the fight's over and you're the one who's not dead, lie to everyone bout how honorably you fought. Remember, kid: stories are just that, stories. A real fight gets real ugly, real fast. The most important part about a fight is winning it. Dying for your principles is never as good as living for them."

Tomas smiled at the praetorian's half-joke. "Well, I guess all I need now is a sword."

"Don't be too quick to pick up a sword," the veteran warned, sheathing his weapon. "Once you do, you'll find it's damn hard to put it down again. Some men never learn how to put a weapon away once they've drawn it."

"What does that mean?" the shepherd asked.

"Think about it. So, you plan to go through the mountains towards the City of All Sins?"

"They always say that the shortest distance between any two points is a straight line."

Mariano chuckled. "Actually, you'd be surprised how often the quickest way to your objective is to go around the obstacles. Ulheim can be pretty dangerous. You might want to think about going around, through the Sylvai Vale and up along the coast towards Oneld. You could take a boat from there upriver all the way to the City of All Sins. It would take a little longer, but would be a lot safer."

Tomas shook his head. "I can feel myself being pulled to the City of All Sins by the shortest means possible. The fastest route there is north through the Sylvai Vale, but then to Frostfront and across the mountains."

"Well," the veteran warned, "the army doesn't patrol those roads anymore. After ten years, you can bet the grey-skins have infested the mountain passes. Once you get up into Ulheim, you stay away from any roads. Druug may not be very bright, but they are smart enough to realize that Humans travel on roads. And stay high; Druug hate the snow. All their territories are in the valleys and passes; if you stay to the highest points, you should avoid the worst of them."

The soldier pulled a map of eastern Lanasia from his bag. He drew his finger along Tomas' proposed route. "You'll have to time your trip just right," he advised. "It's actually a good thing that you waited until the new year started and winter is just gearing up. It gives you more time to get to the mountains.

"Take your time as you move north. If you head into the mountains too early, the weather up there will still be warm enough for the Druug to be wandering around. Too late, and you'll get snowed in. You don't know misery until you've had to winter in Ulheim. Take plenty of provisions and don't stop for anything once you get in there. If you think a Druug pack is tracking you, start crossing streams. The grey-skins have horrible eyesight; they use their noses to hunt. If they pick up your trail, crossing water will buy you time. The best thing is to find a skunk. Have the little guy spray you down and the Druug won't want anything to do to you."

"What do I do if the grey-skins trap me in a ravine?"

"Start praying. You can't outrun a Druug, so don't try. You might be able to outfight one, if there's only one; unfortunately, Druug hunt in packs. Your best weapon against the grey-skins is your brain. You're smarter than the smartest Druug, so outthink them." The Praetorian folded up the map and handed it to Tomas.

The shepherd took the rolled up parchment with a surprised look on his face. "You're giving me this?"

The veteran nodded and leaned back into his bed. "You're dad was one of the best commanders I ever had. A lot of the guys feel the same way. Most of us served with him. In fact, it was your dad's endorsement that got me and a few of the other guys into the Praetorians. We had a lot of respect for that man, and I figure that earns his son a few favors." Mariano chuckled. "Besides, I can just tell Lord Dunnaban that I lost it in the fight."

The young man nodded his thanks. "I'll try not to get any blood on it."

Mariano grinned. "Don't worry. Humans have been traveling through Ulheim for centuries. Just keep your head and you'll be fine."

Tomas stood and tucked the map under his belt. "Thanks for everything. Wish me luck."

Mariano shook his head and took Tomas' hand. "Soldiers don't say 'good luck.' We say 'good hunting.'" Once the door was closed, the veteran shook his head and sighed. "Good luck, kid."

"So you're really going then?" Cecilia asked, her eyes solidly on the worn peasant shoes everyone in the city had taken to wearing. Tomas grunted an acknowledgment as he continued collecting his things together.

Cecilia had arrived to the cramped quarters the shepherd shared with his mother just a few minutes after Tomas. She said nothing, instead silently watching the drama around her while she stood in a corner with her arms crossed and head down. The young woman had made no comment when Tomas had told his mother his plans.

Cara had not taken the news well, sobbing uncontrollably and running out of the house. Cecilia had watched as Tomas began packing the few possessions he still had, some clothing, mostly. "What will you do for food?" she asked, finally raising those midnight black eyes to her childhood friend.

"I have my bow," Tomas replied, not looking at her. "I can hunt for what I need along the way."

Cecilia stood in silence, watching as Tomas struggled to fold his clothes into a small enough bundle to fit in his bag. After his third attempt, she walked over and, without meeting his gaze, folded the clothes herself. "There are a lot of people here who will miss you," she said.

Watching her, Tomas replied, "There are a lot of people here I will miss; some more than the rest."

As Cecilia finished packing, they both desperately searched for the words that they both ached to say but never could. Tomas then put the bag over his shoulder, his conversation with Father Konrad replayed in his thoughts. Finally, he found the words he wished to say. "You know," he said, finally catching her eyes. "I spent a long time trying to build up the nerve to ask you for that kiss. I was furious at my father when he interrupted us. We got into so much trouble that, after that night, I just couldn't figure out how to ask you for another. Then the night of Kyla's Madness happened…"

Cecilia blushed furiously, recalling the night they had spent together watching as all the adults lost themselves to their lusts. Putting his hand on her cheek, feeling the warmness, Tomas continued. "But you know what, I don't regret that kiss at all. I only regret that we saw the darker side of lovemaking before we were old enough to appreciate the more beautiful side."

Cecilia's eyes, shut after Tomas touched her, now snapped open, staring up at him in surprise.

Tomas smiled. "I've had fantasies about being with you for years. To be honest, there have been times when I wished the Madness would have happened now, when you and I could have been together with such total freedom. But you know what, Cecilia? I realize now that you mean enough to me that I'm glad we weren't forced into the Madness like everyone else. If ever you and I were to be together, I would want it to be as tender and loving as you are."

Cecilia tried desperately to speak, but her voice failed. With a sad smile on his face, Tomas raised Cecilia's face with a light hand on her chin, and gently met her lips with his. The young man had meant it to be a chaste kiss, but as her breath and pulse quickened and she brought her hands to his chest, their kiss intensified and their arms went about each other's bodies. Finally breaking their kiss, Tomas touched his forehead to hers and said, "I will come back, Cecilia. I swear I will come back."

Finding her voice, the young woman whispered, "Then let me give you something to warm the cold nights ahead." Her hands went to the front of her dress.

Sometime later, Tomas walked downstairs, preparing for his departure. Stopping in surprise, Tomas saw his father's sword sitting on the small table by the door and a traveling bag beneath that was the same type the Praetorians used. The young man would have recognized his father's gladius anywhere. Tomas lifted the sword reverently with one hand and sheathed it in its short leather scabbard, also adorned with a golden eagle, which had lain beneath the blade. It was only then the young man noticed a small pouch lying on the table with the sword and a note beneath the pouch.

"My son," the note read. "Every mother both dreads and yearns for this day. I have raised you as best I can and now must trust you will be the person your father and I have hoped you would become. I wanted so much to be there to see you off, standing at the doorway waving goodbye even as I did for your father so many times. I was afraid my tears would keep you from your quest, though. Your father often said it took every bit of his sense of duty to carry on despite the tears I would shed at each of his departures. So I leave only this note to tell you all the things a mother needs to say to her son when the day at last comes when he leaves home.

"This sword kept Alessandros safe throughout his many adventures; in his will he said that as soon as I thought you were ready, I should give it to you. You have shown me tonight you are a man in every way that matters, so the sword is yours. I pray it will protect you as it protected him. I have spoken with the rest of our community, the purse has what little money your neighbors and I could scrape together. The Praetorians have left some supplies that should help you, as well; your friend among them convinced our protectors to give you whatever they could spare. We will all pray for you.

"I am so proud of you, Tomas, please come back to us safely."

So, with his father's sword belted to his waist and the hopes of his community slung on his back, Tomas Fidelis left his home. The clouds had broken in the night, leaving no hint of their stormy threat. The morning's sky promised a hopeful journey, with a welcoming breeze pushing up from the sea, encouraging the young shepherd north. There were not well-wishers, no cheering people. The world still slept in the early morning, dreaming of hope and the bright day to come.

Chapter 6

Tomas had always been a private person. He had friends, this was true, but after a decade of watching the people he cared for suffer and die on the whim of this warlord or that disaster, it simply no longer paid to allow the heart to attach itself too tightly to any one person. The young man more often than not took greater comfort in the company of his books and the heroes of the past than in any person still living. The characters in those stories of so long ago would never age, never die. Tomas would never wake up one morning and find them murdered in the street, or given in to despair, or lost to some new pestilence. The shepherd would never have to bury those who had already been dead for centuries.

Because of his typical isolation from the rest of his community, it came as something of a shock to the young man that after only two days walking along the old Sylvai road, he found himself feeling terribly lonely. The shepherd tried thinking about the history of the road, a highway thousands of years old, built in the height of the Sylvai Empire, whose stones were worn smooth by centuries of travelers. He tried focusing on the solid construction, still in good repair all these generations later. But he could not. Tomas missed the bright optimism of Elpidius, never letting the darkness of the times sour his own happiness. He missed the innocent brilliance of Macharus, always tinkering with something in his endless drive to build. Tomas missed Kineus who lost his entire family years ago and seemed forever determined to look under every rock and building until he found where they had gone. The shepherd missed the quiet comfort Father Konrad offered. And Tomas missed Cecilia; he missed her soft eyes and even softer voice.

At night when the young man sat in his small camp, braced against an old Sylvai wall. He traced his path along the map given to him by his Praetorian friend and tried to ignore the quiet night and the crumbling Sylvai ruins nearby. These were the hardest times, when his loneliness would well up in his heart, and it was with some difficulty that Tomas forced it away, thinking only of his oath and quest. He would find Cyras Darkholm and gain the Trickster-Mage's help in defeating the Black Duke and all his unholy forces, or he would die trying; there would be no compromises.

Tomas' isolation was made all the worse at the emptiness of the Imperial Prefecture. Once the heart of a continent-spanning Republic, the lands around Pelesmoria once housed magnificent villas, expansive vineyards, and picturesque villages. As he walked north, the shepherd found only the decaying memories of Pelsmorian culture. The villas were all abandoned, looted corpses with gaping windows and doors moaning their long-fled families. Thorny encroachment was reclaiming the vineyards, strangling generations of taste and tradition. Worst of all were the villages, though; these offered mute testimony to the violence of the last ten years. Dark stains and burnt homes spoke of wrath and greed. Mossy bones and crumbling walls testified to murder and misery. And in the center of each dead community, the authors of this suffering left their signature.

Tomas could not help but stop, the first time he came upon one of the Xeshlin *Olins*. In the center of every dead community, every desecrated chapel, every violated home, was the monument to suffering, the hideous shrine, of the Cursed Ones. The raiders of Davenor, taking advantage of the Republic's death and Pelsemoria's destruction, always left behind one of their *Olins* after an attack. Made of the darkest basalt stone, these small monoliths born carvings venerating the Dark Empress, the unholy unifier of the Xeshlin. Like a goddess of evil, of suffering and spiteful delight, the Daughter of Ramalech was made to appear beautiful, as only the worst suffering, the most taboo sins can be beautiful. Nude and reveling in the her victim's desecration, the Dark Empress blesses her Xeshlin for their offerings of pain, mutilation, and violation. Around her image were the despairing victims of her slavers, with their names carved in the hideous language of the Cursed Ones. Dark lines Tomas' mind refused to identify bore glyphs, foul spells that blighted the land. There were no bodies, though; those who fell beneath poisoned Xeshlin blades became part of a sacrificial feast while those who survived were taken as slaves. Which fate was worse, the shepherd did not know.

After eight days on the road, Tomas finally encountered another traveler on the deserted Sylvai highway. During the Republic, this highway had been one of the most traveled in the world, with caravans, envoys, immigrants, and voyaging to and from the great Capital. So many walked upon these pavestones that the occasional Sylvai glyphs had long since been worn away. This was the great artery of Lanasia, connecting its heart with the rest of the Republic. It had once been so widely traveled that many proposals had been put forward by the Elector Council to widen it and restore the old Sylvai hostels, now to be manned by the Legions. Due to the cost, however, none of the emperors had been willing to allow the projects to go forward.

Now, with Pelsemoria a forgotten ruin, the highway was slowly succumbing to nature's encroachment. Tree branches stretched over the highway. Stones were coming loose, carried away by scavengers of many species. Grass poked up form the sides, and cracks had appeared in any section of the road that had seen Human repair. The road, like the Republic itself, was not just dead, but decaying.

It thus came as something of a surprise to Tomas when he spotted another traveler on the road, moving north as he was. The shepherd had resigned himself to his isolation at least until he reached Wignis, the next town on the highway north from the capital. As Tomas looked on, the traveler, wrapped in a dark blue cloak against the morning chill, was pulling fruitlessly at a large wooden cart that had become trapped in a deep rut, formed by a missing stone on one side of the old Sylavi road. The person, a woman Tomas could tell from the small sounds of exertion she made during her labor, could make no progress in her efforts, but nevertheless continued.

The young shepherd moved towards his fellow traveler, his deep sense of chivalry making him unable to see a woman struggling at anything without offering assistance. As he approached, he at first though she was a child, as she barely came to half his own height. Her movements, and voice, though, gave evidence of maturity. "Hello, there!" he called out, not wanting to greatly startle the stranger.

The hooded woman turned slightly towards the approaching Tomas. Her face was obscured by the hood of her blue cloak, but she kept her small hands visible. "Greetings, fellow traveler," she replied in a voice that seemed light, yet mature. An accent danced among her words, hinting at an origin of somewhere in central Lanasia, yet whose exact point remained elusive.

"Can I be of some assistance?" Tomas asked.

"Whatever assistance you could provide," she replied, "would be greatly appreciated." She stepped back from her cart, giving Tomas room, and kept herself obscured in her dark blue cloak.

Tomas looked over the cart for a moment before spotting the problem. A rear wheel had become stuck in a small hole. "This will only take a moment," he smiled. "Then we'll have you on your way again." The small woman bowed slightly at the waist. "I give you my thanks, young sir. I feared I would be trapped for some time."

The young man grabbed a large branch and set it in the hole against the wheel, then put his shoulder under the frame of the cart and set himself to push. "Your accent is strange," he grunted, working himself to the best advantage against the weight of the cart. "You're not from these woods, are you?"

"No," she replied, finally pushing back her hood. "I am from a village in the plains to the south of Ulheim."

"You're a long way from home," Tomas said as he set himself again for a renewed effort. Busy as he was with his relief efforts, he did not bother more than a glance at the grey dress that concealed much of the small woman's generous curves. "What brings you here?" he asked.

"Duty," she replied. "I had duties here that are now nearly complete. I have only one last before they are finished."

"Duties?" Tomas asked politely, resisting the urge to curse against the stubborn cart. "What duties could require you to travel so far from your..." The young man's words trailed off when he looked up and saw, at last, the full face of the creature he was helping.

She was old, yet still carried the looks of youth and beauty only recently left behind. Slight lines along her round cheeks and around her generous mouth did little to mar her timeless beauty. Of course, all those of the Elder-blood appeared deceptively beautiful, despite the passage of the years. The conservative tailoring of her grey dress did little to hide the generous curves of hip and breast, suggesting motherhood. A great flowing mane of pure white hair spilled out from her hood, to cascade gently past her waist. Her only adornment was a golden pin, a rose in full bloom, on the collar of her dress. None of this was first to register in Tomas' mind, though. What he noticed first were her azure eyes, shining opals the color of a cloudless winter sky; the eyes of a Sylvai.

Tomas halted his labors and stood straight, his hand moving of its own accord towards the hilt of his father's sword. The Sylva noticed this with her glowing azure eyes and sighed. "Was your offer of assistance only valid on the condition I be one of your own race?" she asked.

"What is a Sylva doing so far from the Vale?" he demanded, the steam of his breath coming less from the morning's chill than his burning intolerance.

The Sylva raised an eyebrow. "With the collapse of your Republic, we of the Elder Race are no longer imprisoned within our own lands. We may once again go where we please." She stepped to the side of the cart, the soft half-boots on her small feet making hardly a sound on the old Sylvai stones. "As for your questioning my being in this one particular place, out of gratitude for your prior civility, I will again answer." The Sylva pulled back the canvas covering the top of her cart. "I am fulfilling my last duty as my family's Speaker."

Tomas looked in the cart and was stunned to see the body of another Sylva. Unlike the living one standing before him, the fallen Sylva had a blade belted to her slender waist and wore the leather armor so favored by her people. Although some effort had been made to wipe the mark away, a slight stain of blood remained at the corner of her lips. On the breast of the Sylva's armor, the young man could not help but note the two crossed diamonds sewn there, the symbol of House Calonar, of a soldier in the service of the Black Duke. It was then Tomas realized he had seen this warrior Sylva before; he had been a party to her death less than a week past.

"You are her priestess?" he asked.

"I am her Speaker, her connection to the Wyld. I saw to her well-being for as long as she journeyed. I now take her home to be lain to rest alongside her kin in the manner of our people, sending her spirit to rest in the Eternal Forest. It has always been my responsibility to see to the needs of her body and her spirit. I work now to tend to this one final duty."

Tomas stepped away from the cart and back onto the highway. "Your responsibilities are none of my concern," the shepherd declared. "She served an evil man and you served her. I will waste none of my time helping you." He turned to leave.

"I do not blame you for your behavior," the Sylva said. "Most would react in the same manner. It is not a common thing to help those that cannot help you in return."

Tomas stopped then. The words of Father Konrad rang in his mind, the advice he had given to his young charge only a few scant days ago. A Sylva was in need of his help. God had indeed led him to where he could pay the penance for his sin, and He had done so much sooner than the shepherd would have ever thought possible... or convenient.

As the Sylva returned to her labor, struggling to free the cart from its prison, she was briefly startled when assistance came once again. She spared only one glance behind to see that Tomas had returned, then wordlessly worked with the young man to free her cart and fallen friend. Between the two of them, the cart was freed and again on the road, ready to resume the journey north. The Sylva stood beside her charge, looking up at the much taller Human. "My thanks to you," she said.

Tomas held up his hand. "Please," he said, "don't thank me. I was ready to leave you here, and would have."

"Yet you did not," she pointed out.

"I only didn't because I was commanded to help you, as penance for a sin."

"I thank you anyway," she replied, bowing much deeper than before.

"You're traveling north?" Tomas asked.

"I am. This is the only road still safe for a cart to travel upon."

The young man glanced at the cart, careful not to let his eyes fall on the warrior laying within. "You have no supplies," he noted. "No food, no water. How is it you plan to walk, burdened by this cart all the way to the Sylvai Vale?"

The Sylva shrugged. "There is water in these woods, and some food. I have no doubt the journey will be difficult, but it must be done."

Tomas sighed deeply, wishing desperately that he could ignore the voice that was speaking to him from the deepest corners of his soul. "Your route will continue north along the highway all the way to Railing?" he asked.

"Yes," she replied. "At the crossroads of Railing, I will turn west towards our Vale."

"I also go to Railing," he noted. "And from there west towards the Vale. I have food and water enough for two as easily as for one, to say nothing of my bow here. There's an old saying that two people make a road shorter."

"Again you offer assistance to one you hate," the Sylva said. "I must ask why."

"I seek to hold no hatred in my heart," he replied. "No hatred for Sylvai, Uldra, or my own kind. By traveling with you, by helping you in your task, perhaps I can learn to free myself from the whispers of Ramalech."

The Sylva gasped and made a gesture before her heart. "I would ask that you not speak the Demon-god's name. It is a most terrible curse to my kind."

Tomas nodded. "Forgive me."

The Sylva bowed and moved to pull the cart. Tomas hesitated momentarily before making a move to help. His newfound companion held up a small hand to stop him. "She is my burden," she explained. "My responsibility."

"As you wish," the shepherd replied and began walking beside her. "My name is Tomas, by the way."

"I am Palsilyagathalexia."

"Palsiya... what?"

The slightest curve of a smile flittered across her full lips. "You may call me, Alexia."

"Alexia." Tomas bowed. "I wish I could say that it's a pleasure to meet you."

Alexia laughed a bright sparkle of a laugh, one that pushed away the morning chill and replaced it with the promise of spring. "Perhaps someday it will at least become a pleasant memory."

"I can only hope so."

Much of that day and the next were spent in silence. Alexia did not seem put out by the lack of conversation between them. Instead, the Sylva often looked about with a pleasant smile on her soft face at the forest they passed through while Tomas struggled with the conflict raging through his soul. Despite the young man's problems, he was true to his word. The rabbit he took with his bow in the morning was shared equally with the old Sylva, as was the water he collected from small, cascading fall of a nearby stream. When the sun began to sink behind the trees and winter cold pressed in with the night, the shepherd set up a small camp and offered Alexia his blanket.

"Thank you, Tomas," she smiled. "But I think you need it more than I."

The young man held the blanket out. "No offense, ma'am. But I'll be plenty warm beside the fire. A woman of your years has more need of the extra warmth than I do."

The Sylva raised an eyebrow as she took the blanket, her opalescent azure eyes twinkling at Tomas' chivalry. "'A woman of my years?' You use interesting words."

"I meant no offense," he insisted.

"I took none," she assured him, accepting the blanket and wrapping herself snugly within. "To deny my age would be childish. We all age during our lives until we die. Since the Owl and the Wolf have yet to visit my door, I still age."

"Owl and wolf?"

"The Harbingers of the White Lady. It is said amongst my people that when one's time is near, a wolf will howl on the same night that an owl visits one's roof."

Tomas added more wood to the campfire. "I thought the Sylvai didn't age," he said. "I thought that you were young and beautiful forever."

Alexia laughed, a small hand going almost of its own accord to her long white hair before resting on the small golden rose pinned at her collar. "So, in one breath I am a woman of many years, and in the next I am young and beautiful? It is rare when a female of any race may claim both."

The shepherd blushed. "I didn't mean... that is..."

The Sylva settled deeper into the blanket as she laughed slightly at the young man's discomfort. "Worry not, Tomas. Your words flatter me, even if you yourself are uncertain of their meaning." A growing smile decorated her lips as the young shepherd awkwardly arranged himself opposite her from the fire. "I must say, though," she noted with a bright twinkle in her azure eyes, "it has been some time since I earned so many compliments from such a handsome young man."

Tomas just shook his head, having no idea how to respond.

Chapter 7

"Why?" Tomas asked, looking at yet another Xeshlin *Olin*. "What made them like this?" He and Alexia had come upon another empty, decaying village, and another monument to the Cursed Ones' evil.

Alexia refused to look upon the monolith, keeping her opalescent eyes averted as they passed by. The pair had silently agreed that, though the day wore one, they would not sleep in this unholy place. "They are consumed by a generational sin," she said in a soft voice.

"Generational...?"

The Sylva nodded. "During the darkness of the Uldra Uprising, when the Elder Race faced extinction, some turned in desperation to forbidden powers. One such was Kelinva. She made packs with the prisoners of Underworld, even with its king. Her master revealed secrets of Shadow and Soul to her, gifting her unholy might."

"The Dark Empress..." Tomas breathed, the memory of her Invasion of Lanasia distant, yet still a source of nightmares.

"Eventually," Alexia nodded. They continued on, past the *Olin*, and she continued her tale. "First, she fought for the *Sy'lva'n*, before her kind were Marked. She tried to use her master's power to save us from the Uldra. But our mothers saw the vile corruption she brought. They understood that Kelinva offered not freedom, but a horrid slavery to Underworld itself. Thus was made the Mark of the Xeshlin. Kelinva and all her followers were cut from the Wild, from life itself, to prevent her corruption from spreading."

"You denied her access to magic?"

"More," Alexia countered. "They could not heal their bodies, they could not create art or music. They could not feel love. Their bodies and souls were drained of color, and their eyes bled fire. Kelinva took her followers south, to Davenor, and their forged an empire of hate and vile pleasure. She became what your people call the Dark Empress."

"Why not kill her?" Tomas asked. "The Xeshlin Invasion almost destroyed Lanasia. If your people had just killed her..."

"I do not know. The decision was made by our last Empress. She commanded that Kelinva be spared and gave no explanation." Alexia looked to the cloudy sky, then closed her opalescent eyes and sighed. "I belive life is better, that we who suffer age and death should not be so quick to kill. But," she sighed again.

"How many suffered because the Dark Empress was allowed to live?" the shepherd asked. He did not mean to sound so accusational, so spiteful, but the generational animosity still burned in his soul. He gestured to the nearby, now-fallow fields. "The Battle of Bloody Fields was fought somewhere out there," he reminded the Sylva. "How many thousands had to sacrifice their lives to defeat the Dark Empress' Invasion?"

"Yes," she nodded. "The Elder Race made many mistakes in our history. We caused much suffering that the others, particularly Humans, have born the worst of. This is one reason that so many of us now serve. We try to atone, to help heal to wounds we caused."

The early winter weather was pleasantly cool, without threat of bad weather. Only a chill in the early morning and evening reminded the two companions that winter had recently arrived. One more blessing of the location of the capital had been the mild climate and typically easy winters. The scent of aspen filled the woods around them and buoyed both their hearts. Often as Tomas and Alexia continued their journey, they would pause in their conversations to gaze about in contentment at the trees and shrubbery and animals.

These mild sounds of nature that filled the air also filled Tomas with a deep sense of peace. The rustle of leaves from a startled rabbit's run or the harsh calls of birds overhead that could quite easily have unnerved many raised in such a city as Pelsemoria only served to sing a soothing song in the shepherd's soul. The dead silence that had surrounded the old capital had become such an integrated part of the young man's worldview that he could not help but often fear, along with most of the others that haunted the ruins of the old capital, that all of nature had died along with their Republic. The knowledge that their fears were wrong and that nature had not only survived the collapse but was, in fact, flourishing, was almost enough to banish the sorrow of Pelemoria's death. He even found himself telling Alexia of his life there, not with sorrow or accusation, but with nostalgia.

"This Captain Dunnalban seems to be quite the fool," Alexia noted as Tomas spoke of the Praetorians one day.

The young man nodded. "I often wonder why it is the Praetorians still follow him. Unlike all the other army units, the First Company stayed in the capital to defend us. They're loyal, brave, and selfless, but it's no secret to anyone except Dunnalban that the Praetorians have almost no respect for him. How is it that men in such dark times could still muster the discipline to obey the orders of a man they consider undeserving of loyalty?"

His companion shrugged slightly, shifting her grip on the cart. "I suppose it has much to do with the military mind," she replied. "The soldiers of your army were trained for more than a year before being allowed to join their legions, and the Praetorians trained further still. In all that time, they were told not to question orders, not to undermine the authority of their superiors. Habits like those can be very difficult to break."

The young man lifted a low branch to allow Alexia to pass beneath. "If it was up to me," he said, "Dunnalban would have been forced to step down a long time ago."

"Change often requires a new voice, Tomas," she said. "Change is difficult and often dangerous. It is not a thing that people readily welcome, and yet we would wither and perish without it. I have noticed that in times of crisis, it often takes a single voice crying out from a mountain to force change and stave off disaster."

"Well, this is a time of crisis," Tomas muttered. "And things are changing."

"Are they?" she asked pointedly. As always, it was Alexia who initiated their breaks. She set down the cart handle and took a deep breath. "Your republic has fallen, as all empires must. Most members of the Elector Council have perished, and all but a few of the great Houses have been destroyed." She glanced around, accepting the water Tomas wordlessly offered, briefly raising the waterskin to her lips. "Rather than adapting to this new world in which you have found yourselves," she continued after drinking, "Humans are instead warring with one other to take control of an empire than may no longer exist."

"Are you trying to say the Republic can never be rebuilt?"

Alexia drank again, deeper this time before returning the waterskin to her young companion. "I am saying that perhaps there is no need for it. Everything has its time, Tomas. And that time must inevitably pass. Perhaps the time of empires has gone. Perhaps the world would do better without them. The Sylvai have done well without our *Im'peri'a*." She stepped lightly to a nearby root, arching high from the ground, and sat. The old Sylva arranged the folds of her grey dress and blue cloak about her matronly body, pushing back her hood to let the cool breeze dance about her pristine white mane.

"How can you say that?" Tomas asked curiously. "Since the Sylvai lost their empire, you've gone from the rulers of Lanasia, great and powerful and feared, to being almost completely isolated in your Vale with no real power or influence."

Alexia closed her opalescent eyes and breathed deep, holding her left palm flat against the living root as though drawing something from it as the fingers of her right hand drifted along the golden rose pinned at her collar. "While it is undeniable," she said softly, "that our worldly power has waned over the past centuries, I could argue the reach of our influence."

"I don't understand."

She opened her azure eyes and smiled. "Since the time when first you Humans arrived on Lanasia and lost the *Iel'an'asi* War, it has been the task of the *Sy'lva'n* people to guide you, to help you grow as a race into something more than what you are now. First, we tried ruling you, treating you as favored pets. With the uprising of the Uldra and your kind's abandonment of us in that dark time, we realized that ruling you was not the way to help you. So, we instead let you rule us, treating you as though you were children nearly ready to enter the world. This past millennium of your rule has shown that this too, is not the way for Humanity to achieve its true potential. Now we must again change our method of helping you."

"By ruling us again?" Tomas asked somewhat pointedly.

Alexia smiled again and shook her head. "No, Tomas. As I said, we have no need for empires, nor any real desire for them."

"What about the Xeshlin?"

She shrugged and sighed, rubbing her hands together. "Well... there are exceptions to every rule. Every family has its... outsiders. But for the most part, the *Sy'lva'n* have realized that ruling is not the way, nor is being ruled. We will now try something new."

"What?"

"I have no idea," she admitted wryly. "My nephew has some ideas, but I worry at his youth and idealism." Alexis looked around the forest. "We, like you, are a people waiting for someone to appear and show us the way. We of the Elder Race are simply able to wait without becoming bored and doing war with each other."

"So, what happens to Humanity while you wait?" the shepherd asked.

"The same thing that always happens when any child reaches a crisis," she replied, a tinge of sadness mixing into the smile on her lips. "You will rage, and you will fight, and you will suffer. Then, you will change. Perhaps you will change into something wonderful."

"What if we don't?"

"Your change is inevitable. The only real questions are how long it will take for the change to finish and what you will change into." She closed her eyes once again, but this time her aging face seemed to pass under a shadow. Alexia's expression grew distant, as though she were studying an intricate tapestry. "Something approaches," she said in a whisper nearly lost on the breeze.

Tomas looked around, seeing nothing but the woods. "Where?"

"Distant," Alexia replied in the same soft voice, "but drawing nearer. History is growing restless, as restless as Lanasia herself. A storm builds to the south, seeking something here... someone." The Sylva opened her eyes and let her opalescent gaze rest on Tomas. "Change is needed to prepare."

"Is there any way to control what we change into?"

Alexia stood and put an affectionate hand on her young friend's arm. "Yes, but it will take more people like you."

Tomas blushed. "I'm not so special."

She stared at him, her azure eyes seeming to slip past Tomas' own, as though she were running a light finger over his very soul. "In that, my young companion, you are wrong. You have forsaken all that is known to you, risking your life in a quest to try and bring light to your home. That is special." She cocked her head slightly, her smile taking on a hint of mischief. "And disruptive...?"

There was nothing Tomas could say to that, so they walked on, speaking instead of unimportant things and enjoying the sights of the forest around them.

The old Sylvai highway swerved around the forest that surrounded the Imperial Prefecture, taking care not to disturb the largest of the ancient trees. During their Empire, the Sylvai had built their villas, vineyards, and villages to accommodate the trees rather than uproot them; the great redwoods were never cut down for Sylvai construction. Even with the collapse of their Empire, though, the tradition continued in the new Human Repubilc. These trees held a special significance to the people of Pelsemoria, no matter their race. Some of great trees, the oldest being more than a thousand years old and towering hundreds of feet in the air with trunks wider than a building, had stood as silent witnesses through the entire history of Humanity's Republic; they saw the greatest moments of the noble Majestos Dynasty and the coming of the Heroes of Fate, along with the darkest times of the Xeshlin Invasion and the night of Kyla's Madness. They were the silent record of everything suffered, accomplished, and lost.

"You often look to these ancient trees," Alexia noted one evening as they sat at their small fire.

"They're the symbol of the Republic," Tomas replied. "The Rosewood Throne was crafted out of one that had been felled by lightning the night Sharl Majestos was crowned."

"Interesting," she smiled, the opalescence of her azure eyes twinkling. "Your ruler sat on the dead remains of the symbol of your empire."

Tomas threw a look at his companion. "It's a Human thing," he said.

"As are so many odd customs," she replied with a sparkling laugh.

"These trees are the largest in the world," the young man noted, gazing up to the distant branches. "A professor at the Pelemoria University compared their heights and widths to the trees on other continents and confirmed it."

Alexia nodded. "All that remains in this world of the Eternal Forest," she said somewhat sadly.

"The what?"

"The Eternal Forest is the fount from which the *Sy'lva'n* people sprang. Our histories tell us the *Sa'kai*, the first of the ancient races, formed my people from the living branches of the Eternal Forest. Even as the Uldra were formed from the stones of the tallest mountains, we were formed from these swaying leaves. The Forest was once an unending sea of trees and life resting in the center of the single continent in the heart of *Ar'ae'el*. After the Disaster at Nassinalia, when the continent was broken, the sea filled the vast plain, destroying the Forest's physical form. This small section of woods is all that remains now."

"Why do you call it the 'Eternal Forest?'" the shepherd asked.

"The Eternal Forest was not only where we of the Elder Race lived. It was also where we died. It was the focal point of the Winds of Life. It was a gateway through which one could travel freely from this world into Otherworld and back. The Eternal Forest now only exists in that realm, and Otherworld itself was twisted by the Disaster at Nassinalia; its connection to this mortal world now harsh and unpredictable." She gazed up at the red trees surrounding them before closing her eyes. "Some small spark of that power still rests in these ancient trees," she said in a whisper. "Not so much as they once had, but still..."

"Is that why this forest was always inviolate during the reign of the Sylvai Empire?"

Alexia nodded. "To us, it would have been the blackest heresy and the greatest tragedy to have harmed the Eternal Forest. In fact, it was once a tradition amongst our kind to plant a new tree at the birth of each child along with the *vay'en*, to give the young one a personal connection to the Eternal Forest and the Winds of Life."

"What's a vayen?"

"I believe Humans call it the 'after-birth,'" she replied.

"Why bury that with a baby tree?" the young man asked.

"It strengthens the bond between the child and her *Saw'am*, her protector-spirit. It also provides a great deal of nourishment to help the child-tree in its delicate youth. For as long as the *Sy'lva'n* lived amongst these trees, it has always been our most sacred task to care for them in their youth just as they care for us in ours."

"Until Luddig Majestos banished the Sylvai to your Vale," Tomas added glumly.

"That was the price," she said. "In return for the safety of our woods, we agreed to leave your republic and live only in our Vale."

"But there are still Sylvai across Eastern Lanasia. Most cities have a least a small Sylvai Quarter."

"The detention was eased after a few centuries, and we of the Elder Race were allowed back into the world, making ourselves useful to you. We remained under strict control, of course."

"Why didn't you fight the restrictions?"

Alexia shrugged with a sigh, pulling Tomas' blanket around her slight shoulders and adjusting the collar of her dress, pausing briefly to adjust the golden rose pinned at her collar. "To what end?" she asked. "We were already a defeated people; the Uldra saw to that.

Had we fought against the Humans, the Uldra may have used that as an excuse to eradicate our species. I have noticed that you Humans speak of the Uldra Uprising as though it were a speedy thing, a few battles, glory all around, and a happy conclusion. In truth, the campaign of the Uldra lasted for nearly a millennium; an entire generation of my people was lost to that darkness. Both the Sylvai and the Uldra were pushed to the point of extinction; this is why there are so few of both our kind left. Had we of the Elder Race tried to fight the restrictions imposed upon us by your second emperor, we would have been destroyed; we, instead, chose life."

"Life in bondage rather than death in freedom?"

"Living in bondage is still living. And where there is life, there is hope."

"I think I would rather fight," Tomas announced.

"Humans are quick to battle injustice or any wrong committed against them. But you must understand, my young companion, that a *Sy'lva'n* lives for a very long time. Our lives are easily a thousand years, quite often longer; I myself have lived for nearly twelve centuries. For a Human to sacrifice herself is one thing, a loss of perhaps a few decades. For a *Sy'lva'n*, the loss is of centuries. We are not so quick to give that up."

"Maybe that's why you lost," the shepherd noted. "The Uldra were willing to throw away everything to defeat you, but the Sylvai held back. You didn't want to die."

"In a battle between one who values life and one who does not, the advantage goes to the one who does not."

"So, nothing is worth dying for to a Sylvai?" the young man asked.

"I did not say that, Tomas. For a *Sy'lva'n*, the greatest gift we can give is the offering of our lives, but we only do so when we must."

Chapter 8

The cool mist that filtered down from the treetops did little to spoil the pleasant mornings. All around the two companions, the sounds of life echoed throughout the ancient forest through which they traveled; sounds of birds and deer and creatures of all sizes that gave little notice to the companions traversing through their eternal home. Tomas smiled up at the wonderful light that filtered through the trees, highlighted as it often was by a refreshing mist. It looked to the young man as though a rainbow had been shattered and its pieces spread throughout the trees by God Himself in some expression of natural art.

One morning as they broke their small camp, Tomas looked over at his friend to ask some unimportant question when he noticed her doing a very peculiar thing. The old Sylva seemed to gather the mist from all about her and hold it in her cupped hands. Even more than the mist, the multicolored light itself seemed to gather, rebuilding itself into a glimmering sphere that mirrored her opalescent eyes. Alexia called the water and the light to her hands and held high the gentle sphere, almost as though giving thanks to God, before holding her hands against her mouth with closed eyes.

When Alexia finished, she looked over at Tomas, and smiled again that soft smile of hers at his bemused expression. "One should always be grateful for the gifts one is given, whenever they are given," she said by way of explanation.

A thought entered the young man's mind then; it was a thought that he could not help but voice. "Alexia, are you a witch?"

It was strange, Tomas thought, that no matter what question he asked, Alexia never seemed surprised or offended. No matter what topic the young man brought up, often without warning, she would respond as though expecting the tangents in his conversation.

"I suppose," she replied without hesitation, "that would depend on who you ask."

"I don't mean to be offensive," the shepherd assured her. "It's just that you do so many things the Church teaches is witchcraft."

"Does not your church also teach that witchcraft is an evil thing that must not be allowed?"

"Yes."

Alexia smiled and continued on down the highway. "In that case, were you planning on gathering enough green wood to perform a proper burning?"

Tomas smiled a bit at her comment. "I've thought about it," the young man admitted lightly. "But the wood around here is too wet right now for a proper bonfire."

"Again, I must give thanks for this gift."

"I notice you didn't answer the question," the shepherd pointed out.

"I did," she corrected. "You were simply unsatisfied with the answer."

"Would it bother you terribly to expand a little more on your answer?"

"It would not bother me at all." Alexia lifted up the cart once again and resumed their journey. "If I am not mistaken, the current incarnation of your religion believes in Underworld, the infernal realm of the Demon-god."

"We do," Tomas replied. "The Teachings tell us that Ram… that the Adversary works to tempt us away from the Creator's Plan at all times through our lives, and that if he is successful in leading a man or woman into a sinful life, our souls will descend into the maelstrom of Underworld rather than ascending into Overworld to join with God."

"Humanity gained much of this belief-system from the Uldra and their worship of the one they call the Allfather. They too believe in living a just life, avoiding temptation, and earning passage into the paradise of Overworld.

"We of the Elder Race, however, believe differently. We know the Demon-god is a prisoner of Underworld and, like all prisoners, eager to escape. We do not consort with the creatures of Underworld for fear of offering them purchase in *Ar'ay'el.* As for morality, it is our belief that if a person has lived a just life, leaving the world a better place than it was when first we opened our eyes to it, our souls go to join all the others in the Eternal Forest of Otherworld. If our lives were not as they should have been, then we are born again with a new chance."

Tomas helped guide the cart back to the road but stood aside as Alexia took up her burden. "Then there are no consequences?" he asked. "No final price to be paid for evil deeds?"

Alexia pushed back her hood and let her long white hair spill about her slight shoulders. "It is interesting to note that what one considers an evil deed can often be viewed in many different lights."

"For example?"

"The Uldra Uprising is perhaps the best example of this," she replied simply.

The young shepherd pulled one of his waterskins from his sack and offered it to his companion; the Sylva drank lightly before handing it back. "In that great conflict now more than a millennium past," she said, "the Uldra tribes rose under a single leader and attacked our *Im'peri'a*. They burned our cities and killed the *Sy'lva'n* wherever they found us. To us, these were evil acts, malicious and brutal with no justification. To the Uldra, their acts of barbarism were perfectly acceptable ones of vengeance for the hardships they had endured under our *Im'peri'a*. Two points of view, Tomas; tell me, which one was correct?"

Tomas drank from the skin. He nodded as he put the water away. "There can't be a simple answer," he agreed. "From what I've read, the Uldra killed women and children as well as the warriors of the Sylvai. They burned temples and destroyed public works. All things that mark evil men. But they did have some justification."

"Indeed. The Uldra suffered much under the rule of my people. They were slave labor, and their blood sports were the delight of the nobility. But did the *Sy'lva'n* acts of cruelty in some way give the Uldra the right to do the same or even worse?"

"I don't know. I'm trying to think of what I would do in their place, but I don't think… I hope I wouldn't go to such an extreme. Fighting for your freedom is one thing, but slaughtering everyone you find in the name of vengeance is another."

"No one, living or dead, would like to think of herself as being capable of great evil, but in truth, we all are. There is no person walking on the face of *Ae'ae'el* today that is incapable of evil. As mortal creatures capable of thought and creativity, we all possess the potential for great evil. It is true there are those who embrace this darkness within themselves, becoming the worst sorts of villains. It is also true that life can be a very difficult thing, full of hardship and pain. These things can force a person into performing acts of utter cruelty that the rest of the world decries as evil.

"Take your republic's legionnaires. Once they were the loyal defenders of your empire. There was a time when a single company of your soldiers would stand against an unstoppable foe in defense of a simple village. But they were not always so; in fact, they began as little more than a loose collection of mercenary groups and bodyguards of the wealthy. It was your first emperor who gathered them together and began a process that took centuries to complete. And now that your republic has fallen, the army has once again degenerated into what it once was, a group of mercenaries and bodyguards."

"But not all of them," Tomas argued. "Some of them stayed true to their oaths. Some of them held to their honor."

Alexia nodded. "And so it is with any group. For the most part, a person, be she Human or *Sy'lva'n* or Uldra, will live her life by whatever means she must to survive in the world, no matter how cruel she must become. But in every generation, there are always a few, a very small few, who battle against the darkness. Where all the world would descend into barbaric anarchy, there are a very few who stand tall and hold to the ideals of goodness."

"We could certainly use someone like that now," Tomas muttered.

The Sylva again let her azure eyes drift to Tomas, seeing past the surface. A soft smile of trust and hope glided across her face. "Perhaps there is such a one," she barely whispered. "Perhaps he is just in need of the right events to compel him to act."

Tomas did not hear. He simply shook his head and sighed. "I don't understand what all this has to do with whether or not you're a witch?"

Alexia laughed. "You are so full of ideas, my young friend. Your mind is so open and yet it amazes me how often you do not perceive the underlying message in a conversation."

"So what's the message?"

"What is a witch?"

Tomas shrugged. "According to the Teachings, a witch is a man or woman who makes a pact with Rama… with the Adversary in exchange for power."

"In that case I am most certainly not a witch. We of the Elder Race would never consort with any being of Underworld, let along the Demon-god itself. Not even the *Xesh'lin* would cross that horrible line, despite their varied debaucheries."

"The only reason I ask is that I've noticed you doing things that I've heard witches do."

"Do you have a specific example?"

"Well, just now. With the mist. You looked so reverent when you held it against your face. And you talk about nature like it's a living thing."

"She is. She is all around you, suffused with the Winds of Life. Trees and birds, insects and animals. Even the wind and the mist. All are the Wyld in one form or another. All have their place in the world and all influence both this world and Otherworld, the realm of the *saw'am*."

"Saw am?"

Alexia stopped and looked around, gesturing to the woods surrounding them. "What compels a tree to grow? What lifts the birds above us into the sky or teaches a fish how to swim in the sea? The *saw'am* are the spirits of the Wyld; they are all around us and in all things. Your Church often collects all things mystical together and calls it 'God.' There is some truth to this, as there is a spark of the divine in all things, even as there is awareness in the world that we mortals cannot fully perceive.

"I respect the spirits of the Wyld, the *saw'am*, and I offer thanks when they present their gifts. It is the way of the *Sy'lva'n* to do this, but most especially for a Speaker. Since the fall of our *Im'peri'a*, we Speakers have returned to the knowledge of our ancestors, embracing once again the knowledge we once nearly lost."

"Is that what a Speaker is, then?" Tomas asked. "A wizard of nature?"

The Sylva laughed again. "I respect the Wyld and give Her thanks for what She gives, but I do no worship her. Rather, what you call 'worship,' is not something most *Sy'lva'n*, do. Rather, we venerate the *Sa'kai*, the oldest of ancients who have passed into Overworld and from there guide us."

"So it's true the Sylvai still worship your old pagan gods?"

She nodded. "We have many of what you call gods. Many names for the same thing."

"The same thing?"

"By whatever name you call the quintessence of life, it remains the same thing. There are beings, very old and very powerful, who came before the *Sy'lva'n*. We call these the *Sa'kai*: beings who first resided here on *Ar'ay'el*. One of those became the Demon-god. We *Sy'lva'n* were, in fact, created to help defeat that creature. Once our creators had banished the Demon-god to Underworld, they themselves passed into Overworld. Still, though, we venerate our creators, guides, and masters."

Tomas was silent for a little while, puzzling over what his friend had said. So much of what Alexia believed passed close to the Teachings, so close to what he understood as the truth of God and His Creation. Much of it, though, echoed with Father Konrad's warning of strange, ancient powers and their hunger for Humanity. Tomas did not know what sense to make of these similarities and differences, how to find the truth. His head ached as possibilities folded themselves in on one another. Finally, he stood straighter and shook free the conflict. "Well," he said, "at the very least you've convinced me you're not in congress with the Adversary."

"That is a great comfort," Alexia laughed.

"No kidding," the young man noted while looking around the woods. "I'd hate to have to start a fire in this damp mess."

"Your concern is touching," the Sylva murmured.

They sat on opposite sides of their campfire that night, as they did every night. After nearly two weeks together on the old Sylvai highway, Tomas and Alexia had developed a pattern that brought familiarity to their trip. It was on this night, however, that Tomas at last found the will to voice a question that had nagged at his mind for many days. "Alexia," he hesitantly asked, "how is it that you're able to laugh so often? In fact, I've noticed it's rare that you're not at least smiling."

The Sylva was smoothing a bed of moss, clearing any stones. "I long ago realized that there is too much joy in life not to revel in it," she remarked.

"But your friend has died," he said, sparing a glance at the covered cart which Alexia slept beside. "I would think that you would mourn her."

The Sylva sighed, sitting and wrapping Tomas' blanket around herself. The light from their small fire seemed to make her lustrous white hair glow, accompanying the slight twinkle of gold coming from the rose pin on her collar and the opalescence of her azure eyes. "You Humans still have so much to learn," she sighed, resting her back against the cart. "Death is not something to fear or bring sorrow. The White Lady comes for us all at some point. She is the destiny of all things living."

"Don't you miss your friend?"

"I miss her company, of course. She was my Walker and I her Speaker, a relationship beyond Human understanding. We have traveled together for so many years they often blur together in my memory. We shared in uncounted joys and sorrows, victories and defeats. Friends and lovers entered our lives and drifted away, but Walker and Speaker are bound forever. She was the truest companion I have ever had, and her company and conversation are something I often yearn for in my remaining time in this world. But if you mean to imply that I should miss her presence, then you clearly do not understand how the *Sy'lva'n* view death."

"Tell me."

Alexia cast her azure eyes about the trees surrounding them. "Look around you," she said. "What do you see?"

"Trees," Tomas replied, looking around their camp. "We're in a forest."

"Yes. Here there are trees, animals, insects, flowers, and bushes. There is grass and stones, water and wind. All about us there is life. Everywhere in this world, we are surrounded by the living. And for as long as either your race or mine has walked *Ar'ae'el*, there has been life. The wind blows through the branches overhead, and the sun shines down on the flowers at our feet. Everything that lives must eventually die, but when it does, all that energy and life does not simply vanish. Nothing that lives can really die. It simply changes.

She plucked at breast of her grey dress. "These bodies that we wear are laid to rest in the ground where they can return to *Ar'ae'el* and replenish her. From what has passed, new life can be born. Our bodies will one day be reborn into new forms, flowers perhaps, or the trees or the wind or the rain. Is that not a pleasant thought? Would it not be wonderful to be reborn as the wind?"

"But what about the soul?" Tomas asked. "Does that get reborn as well?"

"Our spirits, our memories and knowledge and feelings and dreams are set free of mortal constraints to live in the Eternal Forest."

"I thought the Eternal Forest was destroyed after the Disaster at Nassinalia?"

"The mortal form of the Eternal Forest was sundered," she replied, "even as our mortal forms will be. But its true form exists still, even as our own true forms will live on in Otherworld, in a reality far removed from our own and yet as close as the air we breathe. It is within the Eternal Forest that we are rejoined with all those who have come before and await all those who will come after. We once again know the joy of friends and family and lovers. But in the Eternal Forest, that joy lasts an eternity."

Tomas smiled at the thought; it was a pleasant one after all. "So your friend... you Walker waits for you in the Eternal Forest? She waits for you to join her?"

Alexia smiled and nodded. "Yes. I find her traveling there first so very proper; she was the Walker, after all; she spent her life wandering. I only ever followed behind. She waits now, along with all those who I have ever loved. They all wait for when I can set aside this mortal shell and enjoy what awaits us past the mists of time."

"You speak as though that time will be soon."

Her azure eyes closed and her face once again took on a distant look. "It will," she calmly replied.

"I don't understand."

Alexia glanced calmly at Tomas, the opalescence of her gaze unwavering. "My time is drawing close. I can feel my many years pressing down upon my soul. The White Lady approaches, to journey with me across the mist between worlds."

"You're going to die?" Tomas asked, for some reason shocked by the thought.

"Yes, very soon now. I will perhaps see the coming spring."

"How could you know that?"

"A Speaker knows. *Sy'lva'n* live for a very long time. Often your race has thought us to be immortal, perhaps even gods, but we are not. We remain virtually ageless for much of our many centuries, but there comes a point in our long lives when our bodies begin to slow, when the weight of living begins to press down upon us. I feel my time approaching."

"Does it frighten you?"

"Somewhat," she smiled. "Any journey brings with it a sense of anxiety. But there is no pain, no discomfort. Only a sense of weariness that grows a little more with every new day. I look forward to my journey, despite my fear. I yearn for my last voyage and the easing of all my worries."

"I'm sorry."

"Why? You and I only just met. In the length of your admittedly brief life, my presence will be as nothing at all. As you said when first we met, I serve one who served your enemy. My duties are none of your concern."

"I'm sorry for my words. You're a good person and a noble one as well. You know your end is near and you're willing to spend the last of your days carrying your friend home for a proper burial. That's something only a very few would be willing to do."

"You give me more credit than I am due. My companion and I are from the same village. We will be laid to rest beside one another. We have traveled together; we have lived, loved, fought, and suffered together. I am simply completing our travels together in the most logical way."

Tomas looked up into Alexia's eyes. "I am sorry, despite your words."

"Why?"

"I'm sorry I couldn't have known you before now. I'm sorry our time together must be so brief. I'm sorry your companion served the Black Duke. And... I'm sorry I helped kill her."

Alexia only paused a moment, no hint of surprise or shock betraying her calm face, before finally answering. "It was her time," she whispered. "Whether it was the sword of a praetorian or the weight of her years, she and I both knew that soon we would pass together from *Ar'ae'el*. Do not let her death weigh at your soul, my young friend. I have known her for as long as she has lived. She and I were often of one mind on a variety of subjects. Were she to have met you in any other situation, I have no doubt she would have felt the same fondness I myself feel."

Tomas stared into the fire, the tears in his eyes making the light of the flame dance in beautiful patterns. "What was her name?" he finally asked. "What was your friend's name?"

The Sylva smiled again at her young friend. "If only.. Her name is *Aebre'seph'rava'asya*. Humans call her Raven."

They were quiet then. Words were meaningless and useless. Only the healing power of time would ease what they felt. If only, Tomas thought, there was time.

Chapter 9

"I do not recall the name of this place," Alexia admitted.

Tomas stood beside her, looking down into the broad valley. Stretching before them was a rolling countryside decorated with more rocks and boulders than a man could count in a dozen lifetimes. It was barren compared to the forest they had left behind only the day before. Majestos Wall, the mountains which formed Pelsemoria's natural northern border, rose both to the east and west. This wide valley was the only interruption of the great range, as though some great finger had drawn a line across its center. In the center of the great valley was Lake Victory, the vast body of water marking the halfway point between the capital and Railing, with a single, small island in its center. Wrapping around that lake was the Bog of the Forgotten, cite of the greatest battle in history. On the northern and southern sides of the enormous lake were small towns, each only a dock with a few shops and homes pressing around it, meant only to give travelers a brief rest before ferrying across.

The highway they followed was like a grey stain that rolled and dived amidst large stones on its way north. "Wignis," Tomas replied in near-awe of the valley's history. "It's called Wignis."

Alexia nodded. "Yes, I recall now. The group my companion and I were accompanying crossed Lake Tragedy on our way south, passing through the town on our way."

"Victory," Tomas corrected.

"Excuse me?"

"The lake, it's called Lake Victory, not Lake Tragedy."

"According to your people, this place is Victory. According to mine, it is Tragedy."

"I guess that makes sense," the young man admitted. "This is where the final battle of the Uldra Uprising was fought. It was here the Sylvai Empire was destroyed."

"It was also here, I believe, that your first emperor was coronated."

Tomas grinned at his friend. "So which was the tragedy?" he asked. "The victory of the Uldra or the coronation of Sharl Majestos?"

Alexia smiled. "Neither," she replied. "My people refer to this as Lake Tragedy because it took the deaths of nearly thirty thousand *Sy'lva'n* and twice that of the Uldra to finally halt their onslaught. *Sy'lva'n* from across Lanasia gathered here on the command of the last Empress: the last of our warriors and nobility, our mystics and clergy, an entire generation, all to feed Uldra hate. Not until this entire valley was flooded in blood could the mountain-people finally feel their vengeance was complete."

"You make it sound like the Sylvai sacrificed themselves to stop the Uprising."

"Would you imply our actions were something other than a sacrifice?"

"History says that the last Sylvai empress sent her entire army north of the capital to delay the Uldra long enough for her to escape."

"*Human* history," she pointed out. "The Elder Race knows the truth."

"Which is?"

"In those dark times, the entirety of the Uldra were united. They were joined together by the desire to avenge themselves against my people for the hardships they had endured during our long reign. They could not have stopped until that vengeance had been sated. This is the nature of revenge, Tomas. Once the target has been destroyed, another is found, and another, and another. Once the Uldra had destroyed Pelsemoria, they would have turned on some other city. Eventually they would have turned on you Humans, despite your alliance. After all, both *Sy'lva'n* and Uldra share the same Elder blood; we are both children of the *Sa'kai*. Despite this kingship, still we have visited countless horrors upon one another. Your Human blood keeps you separate, and attacking what is separate from ourselves is always easy. Once a creature or race has so very much bloodlust within it, only a flood can quench it.

"Annakarala, the last ruler of our *Im'peri'a*, commanded everyone we had left, any who could wield spear or spell, to face the Uldra horde on the shores of this lake in the hopes that so much blood would at last satisfy the vengeance of the Uldra. The Empress herself led the initial charge and was the first of the *Sy'lva'n* to fall. By the time the sun set on that most horrible of days, more than a hundred thousand lay dead on this field. But the Uldra were at last sated."

"I guess that would count as a tragedy," Tomas admitted.

"War is only ever that." The aging Sylva cast a glance south, her opalescent gaze clouding over. "Unfortunately," she said, "war is sometimes all that can halt the darkness."

"You mean it's a necessary evil?"

"Yes, Tomas. War should only ever be a last resort, but is all too often the first of the unscrupulous."

"You say that, but your companion was a warrior."

Alexia let her azure eyes drift back to where her companion lay in the cart. "Yes. And she disliked it. But as you say, Tomas, war is a necessary evil."

"You never mentioned what your patrol was doing so far from the Black Duke's lands." Tomas mentioned.

"You never asked."

The young man smiled and shook his head as he often had to. It seemed that an hour could not pass without Alexia making him feel foolish without feeling insulted. It was a rare gift that his companion seemed adept at using. "Well, I would like to ask now," the shepherd said, bowing slightly. "What was it that your group was doing so far south?"

"Our mission was twofold. Our primary objective was locating the warlord, Vagris," she replied.

"Vagris? I've never heard of him."

"For your sake, I am glad you have not. Vagris was once a colonel in your republic's army. He commanded a legion near the Sylvai Vale. After the death of your emperor, he and many of his men found their time more profitable and entertaining in raiding the nearby villages instead of protecting them, though he still referred to his actions as protection. Vagris has made life very difficult for the people living in and around the Sylvai Vale, but in the past year, reports have filtered to the Northern Keep that the warlord is expanding his territory past Lake Sardiel and Majestos' Wall into the many villages within this area. Unfortunately, his stays in these communities are brief, making an assault on his force difficult. The patrol my companion and I were traveling with was one of several tasked with tracking the warlord and his army down so that the army of King Cylan Calonar can destroy him."

"The Black Duke doesn't like competition I take it?"

"Would you rather such a man as Vagris continue his raids?"

"You said twofold," Tomas pointed out. "What was the second objective?"

Alexia paused then, for the first time in their short association, not offering an immediate, if perplexing answer. She looked at Tomas. "I would prefer not to explain," she admitted. "The second aspect of our mission was of some secrecy and, I fear, shall need to remain obfuscated for now."

Tomas had little desire to debate with Alexia. During the weeks they had been traveling together, the two had made an unspoken agreement not to discuss those things that were likely to result in argument. Tomas knew Alexia and her friend Raven had served the Black Duke willingly. The young man also knew from several comments she had made that Alexia believed in the cause her lifelong friend had died for. Perhaps in time Tomas could show his friend the evil Calonar had brought to the world, but it would take much too long and would likely destroy their emerging friendship, so he left the subject alone for the time being.

"I think I have enough money for a room at the inn and the ferry in the morning," the young man said, absently hefting the purse he had been given before leaving home. He then squinted at descending sun. "I'm just not sure how the people will feel about allowing a Sylva and her dead kinsman staying in their town and riding on their boat."

"As I said, our group passed through here on the way south," Alexia pointed out. "The townspeople were neutral, but generally friendly. They seemed to care little for my race one way or the other. I should think their attitudes would have changed little over only a matter of a few weeks."

"I guess there's only one way to find out," Tomas said.

Wignis was much like any other moderately prosperous town in that part of Lanasia. The buildings were built close together with wide cobblestone streets and thatched rooftops casting long shadows in the fading light of the setting sun. With the forest more than a day's walk away and the abundance of nearby rock, the use of stone was more present than wood in the town's architecture. Despite this, however, one still gained a sense of warmth and welcome from the open windowsills and doorways of Wignis. Of course, that was in ordinary times, not the present. Now, doors showed recent signs of being knocked down, burn marks scarred the walls of numerous buildings, and the dock that the ferry would normally rest at was nothing more than a ruined pile of useless stone and lumber.

Upon entering the small town, both Tomas and Alexia were uncomfortably surprised to find by just how much the attitudes of the people had changed over a matter of a few weeks. Shouts of "Sylva witch!" echoed from building to building within moments of their arrival.

Alexia raised an alarmed eyebrow at their reception. "We would have perhaps been better off had I left my hood up," she noted.

"No use crying over spilled blood," Tomas replied, looking about anxiously.

"I believe the expression is spilled milk."

The young man eyed the crowd gathering around them, clearly blocking their path. "Not if these people have anything to say about it." His hand drifted to the hilt of his father's sword.

Alexia placed a hand lightly on her young friend's sword-arm. "There would be little gained by an aggressive reaction on our parts," she whispered. "Little gained except perhaps our deaths."

"There are only a few dozen of them," Tomas noted with feigned enthusiasm.

She looked at the young shepherd evenly. "For your sake, I hope that was a failed attempt at humor."

Before Tomas could think of something a little cleverer to say, the leader of the mob strode up to them, hefting a large cudgel. "So, you damned Calonar lackeys thought you'd come back and bring more misery on us!?!"

"I better not get killed because someone thought I served the Black Duke," Tomas muttered.

"Such a fate would be ironic," Alexia noted.

"Sir," the young man said, taking pains to sound reasonable. "I'm not sure what grudge you bear, but I can assure you that I am no servant of the Black Duke."

"Lies!" another of the townspeople called out from behind them. Tomas and Alexia turned and saw that a pox-scarred man was standing beside the cart, holding the canvas up and showing the dead warrior beneath. "This one still wears the Duke's symbol!"

"Our situation grows worse," Alexia noted.

"You couldn't have stripped that damn patch off before we came into town?" Tomas demanded.

"My apologies for a lack of foresight," she replied. "But our energies would perhaps be better spent on divining a solution to the current situation."

"You damned Sylvai brought nothing but death with you!" the leader roared.

Alexia stepped forward. "Good merchant," she said, bowing deeply with her small hands covering her heart. "I know not what tragedy has so incurred your wrath, but I assure you that it is not of our creation. Your community was most welcoming when last my eyes beheld it. I cannot imagine any action of mine that could have caused your hospitality to turn into such bitter hatred."

The leader struck Alexia across the face with the back of his hand, knocking her violently to the ground. "Be silent, witch!"

Tomas quickly knelt down beside his friend. At the sight of the blood flowing freely from her small mouth, a terrible rage filled Tomas. He spun to attack the crowd, his own life unimportant compared to the injury they had inflicted on her. Fortunately for the rash young man, Alexia grabbed his shoulder with more strength than the shepherd would have guessed she possessed. "No!" she snapped in a harsh whisper, pulling herself up beside him. "They feel nothing but hate. They will kill you. Do not answer their rage with your own."

A rock flew from somewhere in the mob, striking the Sylva in the head and sending her back into the mud-covered and debris-strewn street. Alexia let out a brief outcry of pain as more blood trickled from her temple. She started to rise but realized that the mob would only strike her down again, and so remained on the ground.

Reason gave way to righteous rage, and Tomas drew his father's sword, letting the light of the setting sun shine off the perfect blade. Seeing the gladius with the golden eagle of the Praetorians, the mob took an instinctive step back. There was no man or woman alive in Lanasia who did not know of the awesome reputation of the Praetorians and feared it. No citizen of the Republic would ever rashly charge against a man who wielded the gladius of the First Company. "Do you see this?" the shepherd demanded. "Look carefully at the blade of my father. I swear the next one among you who harms my companion will feel its kiss."

The leader once again stepped forward, letting the point of Tomas' sword dig slightly into his chest. "There has already been blood split on this ground," he growled as a point of red appeared on his chest. "The gladius has already cut into the people of this town."

Tomas held steady his father's blade, despite the small trickle of blood that began to seep out of the merchant's shirt and down the sword. "What do you mean? What happened here that caused such hatred?"

"Not three days past; a group of men carrying the blades of the Republic entered our town. They rounded us all up in this street, in this very spot. The leader, a man they called Vagris, had heard that there had been a group of soldiers serving the Black Duke that had passed through our town. He had heard that we had done business with these soldiers and let them go on their way. When we said that this was true, that we wished to remain neutral, he killed a third of our men and let his soldiers have our women. He stole everything of ours that held any value and destroyed everything that didn't. He threatened to return if ever we allowed safe passage to anyone in the service of House Calonar."

"If this Vagris did these things then its Vagris who deserves your wrath!" Tomas insisted. "Not us!"

The merchant leaned even closer towards Tomas, forcing the young man to lower his blade or drive it fully into his chest. "If the Black Duke had never sent his soldiers here, Vagris would never have had an excuse to attack us."

Alexia rose to her knees. "Men like Vagris have little need of excuses. He would have taken what he wanted no matter the reason. You must believe that we are only interested in helping you. You have nothing to gain by harming us but risk losing your decency if you do. Do not allow Vagris to destroy everything you are, everything you have built."

The leader ignored Alexia, instead nodding at the golden Imperial Eagle that adorned Tomas' sword. "It was a blade like that, Praetorian Eagle and all, that stole the life of my daughter after Vagris himself had finished with her." Tears of grief and hatred flowed down the man's face. "She hadn't seen her thirteenth spring."

The image of so young a girl being brutalized by a man who had once served in the honored First Company was unthinkable to Tomas. The Praetorians were all that was good and decent and noble. Tomas blinked away tears, shaking his head. "It can't be," he insisted. "No Praetorian would ever do such a thing!"

The leader of the mob turned slightly and pointed towards the ruined dock. The crowd parted, giving Tomas and Alexia a clear view of what the large man was pointing at. Resting at the top of a large pile of rubble, driven into the wood so that the hilt pointed up towards the sky and the golden eagle pointed to the ground, rested a gladius, its blade stained with innocent blood. Tied to the hilt was a scrap of cloth fluttering in the breeze, as though even in death, the blade's final victim could not escape it.

"That blade came from Vagris himself," the leader said. "It bears my daughter's blood. He drove it into the wood, tying a scrap of my daughter's dress around it. Before he left, he said that he would return, and if that blade was moved or tampered with in any way, he would destroy our homes, kill our men, and sell our women and children to the Xeshlin."

Tomas stared hard at the blade, unable to see anything but the blood. Some citizen of the Republic had been cut down by a gladius. Tears ran freely from the young man's eyes, and he did nothing to wipe them away. Alexia put a comforting hand on his arm. The shepherd looked down into her soft azure eyes and saw the truth. Those men who had once sworn to defend the Republic now picked at its bones.

Their gaze was broken when two men grabbed Alexia and pulled her to her feet. "By God, I swear to you that you have nothing to gain by this!" Tomas insisted, trying desperately not to let the horror of what had happened here enter into his mind. "I do not serve the Black Duke. I quest to bring these wars to an end."

The crowd muttered and several torches burst forth in the fading light of dusk. The leader of the town looked deep into Tomas eyes for some time. Sincerity shown through the young man's eyes with such power that the townsman could not help but concede the truth of Tomas' words. "Any man that can still call on God clearly does not serve the Black Duke," he finally said with a low voice. "Any man that can still call on God has not seen the horrors of this world. You may leave and live to see the truth."

Tomas sheathed his father's blade. He nodded his thanks even as the men that had grabbed Alexia began dragging her towards the cart. "What are you doing?"

"You may go. But the Sylva bitch will burn." The merchant raised his voice. "She will burn for our dead!" The crowd roared its approval.

"But why!?!" Tomas yelled. "She did nothing to you!"

"If she had never come here, my daughter would still be alive!" the leader roared. The crowd roared their fury, cursing all Sylvai and those who traveled with them. "These Calonar soldiers bring nothing but pain and misery!" the large man roared again to the accompaniment of the mob. "They think their Black Duke's power makes them invincible! They think the world centers around the Northern Keep! It's time they felt the pain that we feel!"

Tomas knew then that words were useless. The crowd wanted blood, and only blood would satisfy them. He wordlessly spun and made to charge the men who were dragging his friend to her fiery death, his hand once again going for his father's sword. Two men grabbed Tomas' arms and held him in place. Seeing this, Alexia shook her head. "You have your life, and it is only now beginning." Somehow, despite the roaring of the mob and the distance that now separated them, the young man could hear his friend's voice as clearly as though she were whispering right into his ear.

The men began tying Alexia to the cart as others lay kindling and broken bits of lumber down in preparation of the fire. "You knew my time was coming," she said then, once again as though whispering into his ear. "Nothing can prevent this tragedy. Let my death give them some solace. I beg you; do not let yourself die for the sake of one whose life is over anyway."

The shepherd clenched his teeth and blinked tears from his eyes. He made a small effort to break the hold the two men had on his arms, but his friend's words seemed to drain the strength from him.

Alexia smiled and looked at her young friend, love shining in her opalescent gaze. "Go, Tomas; eyes as young as yours should not see what must happen here." Torches were brought forward. "Please, go and live."

A strange thing happened then. The sorrow Tomas felt gave way to something else. A fire sparked within his heart. That spark then erupted into a great rage that burned his soul and summoned back all his strength and will to fight. "NO!" Tomas roared. He kicked the man to his left, catching his captor off-guard and freeing his arm. Spinning then, Tomas struck his other captor, knocking the smaller man to the ground. The sword of his father leapt from its sheath and danced in an arc that sliced through three members of the mob. Torchlight gleamed off Alessandros' gladius as one townsman after another fell to Tomas' awkward swings. As surprised as they were, there was little to stop Tomas from reaching the side of his friend. The torchbearers fell with only brief screams.

Alexia made no effort to stop her young friend. His entire soul blazoned with resolve Instead of berating her companion for his foolish heroism, the Sylva flexed her hands once freed of the rope and spoke words of ancient power. Neither Velish nor Sylvish, nor any tongue spoke in common purpose: words of long-dead civilizations and near-forgotten mysteries sang forth from the Sylva's clenched teeth. Alexia's azure eyes grew brighter still, the characteristic Sylvai opalescence giving way to an arcane light of sapphire brilliance that mocked the villager's torches. Some unfelt wind, imperceptible yet undeniable, surrounded the Speaker, her lustrous white mane rising and glowing as though it were a living, wrathful thing. The golden rose, pinned as always at her collar, no longer reflected the weak light of the villagers' torches, but instead burned with its own golden arcane fire. The entire world took a very deep breath.

The mob rallied itself and pushed forward, their minds filled only with the blood of their families. The ground beneath their feet suddenly split, with thick green vines rising like the tendrils of some vengeful, chthonic god. They lashed out, wrapping around the screaming mob and lifting them. Ivy that had peacefully climbed along stone walls detached and struck, whipping tools and torches from hands. Alexia chanted and waved her arms and the living world obeyed.

Despite the power of the vines and the speed with which they moved, several townspeople made their way to Tomas and Alexia. Tomas ducked beneath a thrown pitchfork and swung his father's blade again, cutting down a woman who approached with a butcher's knife raised high. A large man grabbed Alexia by the shoulders, meaning to lift her in the air, but the Sylva twisted suddenly and thrust her arm back into the man's middle. The air rushed out of the attacker's lungs even as Alexia spun again, driving her knee into his groin. She then grabbed his head over her shoulders with both hands and pulled him around her, sending him to the ground. The threat defeated, Alexia resumed her mystic song, the arcane chant echoing off the burn-marked walls.

Occupied as they were, Tomas and Alexia did not notice until it was too late the several torches that had been thrown onto the cart. With surprising speed, the flames spread, enveloping the body lying there. Alexia saw this and screamed in horror. Tomas leapt onto the cart, intending to save Raven's body from the flames. The young man dropped his father's blade and grabbed the dead Sylva but a large rock caught him in the temple. The world spun. The shepherd fell off the cart, into the very teeth of the raging mob.

Alexia pointed at her friend and spoke a single word. A burst of wind, a thousand times stronger than the strongest storm swept across the mob, sending screaming people tumbling away from the reeling young man. She looked on in grief as the wind she summoned to save her young friend also fanned the flames that were destroying Raven's body. Another of the crowd grabbed the small Sylva then, pinning her arms in place. The priestess threw her head back, knocking her captor in the mouth before spinning and kicking the man in the knee, sending him screaming to the ground.

Tomas struggled to stop the world from swaying. He shook his head and swung his fists with all the energy he could summon. Laughing at his efforts, the mob swarmed at him again, heedless of the magic his Sylva friend could summon. They stopped laughing, though, when a deep sleep came over them and they each toppled to the ground under Alexia's power.

The Sylva stood beside her friend and faced the mob. Tomas could feel her small body trembling, as though the constant effort to use her Speaker skills was draining the strength from her. Sweat poured down her face and her great mane of white hair no longer flowed in her invisible wind, but instead was matted against her head and back. The light from her eyes and from the golden rose seemed to flicker, to falter. The words and gestured that had danced so freely only moments before began to tumble, tripping over themselves. Alexia's tone became fearful, almost panicked. Again and again Alexia called to her magic, forcing back the surging mob with spells of wind and light and sleep and fear. But each time, with each exertion, the effects grew weaker. The vines no longer held townsmen fast, but rather could only push at them. The ivy's strikes drew fewer flecks of blood, less cries of pain and alarm. Tomas struggled to help, but his wounds and his untested body withered against the unending tide of mindless rage.

Finally, another pitchfork flew out, but Alexia saw it too late; her desperate gestures and words came too late to stop the missile. The world slowed in Tomas' mind's eye as he saw the weapon arching straight at Alexia's heart. Before his mind could even understand what had happened, Tomas threw himself in front of his friend, taking the pitchfork in his middle.

Tomas heard only Alexia's agonized scream before the entire town was on them. The mob surged forward, driving into Tomas and Alexia and sending the two friends to the ground. Blows landed. Blood spilled. Bones cracked. Tomas lost sight of Alexia in a blur of red. More blows, more blood, and more bones. Pain flared through his mind, tensing every muscle and forcing a scream of agony from his lips. Dimly he was aware of the screams of his friend but was powerless to help her.

After an eternity of suffering, he was lifted into the air. The mob carried him, ignoring his weak attempts to fight, and then he was thrown. The bitter cold of water hit him and threatened to drag him down into darkness. Tomas felt his will to fight slipping away. The pain of living seemed too much to bear as comforting warmth filled him. *Just let go*, the warmth seemed to say. Tomas was not inclined to argue.

Another splash brought the young man's head slowly around where he saw Alexia drifting down beside him, a red cloud drifting sleepily from his friend's unmoving body. Her eyes were shut and her face at rest. But in her hand was clasped Alessandros' blade.

Unwanted strength forced its way into Tomas' body and banished the welcoming thought of eternal sleep. The fire of determination burned what remained of his mind. A reserve of willpower fueled a renewed sense of duty. Even if he lacked the strength to save himself, Tomas would never lack the strength to at least try and save his friend. The young man ignored the warmth that wanted so much to carry him down, instead forcing his muscles to move, to swim.

Tomas clawed at the water, demanding it yield, pulling himself to Alexia. He then fought to the surface, gasping a lung-full of air. Battling not only the bitter cold of the lake as it slashed into his mind, body, and soul, to say nothing of the agony of his many wounds, the shepherd drew strength from somewhere deep within to make for the shore, as far from the town as he could manage. With the very last reserves of his strength, Tomas felt ground beneath him and pulled his friend from the freezing water and into a small grove of trees.

Tomas felt his life once again drifting away. The intense shivering that had raked his body slowed and stopped. He fell to the ground but did not feel the impact. The unbearable cold around him gave way once again to comforting warmth. Contentment wrapped around him and gently cradled him, whispering the joy of surrender.

Chapter 10

Something anchored Tomas to his mortal body. The pleasant warmth he was sinking into slowly retreated, or was forced away. The aches and pains of the brutal encounter in Wignis began making themselves known again. He moaned and tried turning about as though to push away the hurt that so afflicted him. He wanted nothing more than to sink into the warmth, but something would not let him.

A soft voice filled with caring and gentle compassion caressed the shepherd's mind. "Peace, Tomas," the voice said. "Rest and be healed."

Even as the voice said the words, they became reality. Peace wrapped around him like a comforting blanket. He found he could rest and dream. He dreamed of childhood and friends. He dreamed of finding Cyras Darkholm and defeating the Black Duke. He dreamed of returning home in triumph. He dreamed of Cecilia, of her warmth, her smile, her scent wrapped around him. He even dreamed of Alexia.

In dreams of his Sylva friend, he seemed to be lying on the ground or perhaps suspended in mid-air. Because it was a dream, Tomas accepted what was happening. In his dreams, Alexia moved her small hands above his body, a soft golden light drifting along his flesh. In his dreams he was aware of bones becoming solid, of cuts and bruises healing, of life returning.

There was no fear in his dream. Days and nights passed but time was all the same to Tomas. Even when he realized that his wounds did not stay healed, he did not fear. He did not fear when he saw worry and intense concentration play on Alexia's face. It seemed to Tomas that he heard the howling of a wolf.

Sometime during the endless dream, he dimly heard Alexia say. "You will not have him." Tomas opened his eyes and saw that Alexia was not speaking to him but to a white owl perched overhead, staring down at them. "He will live through this and fulfill his destiny. No matter the cost to me, he will live." Again in his dream, she bent low over Tomas and let her golden light drift across his body.

Tomas finally awoke in the morning, what morning he did not know. The young man sat up and looked down at his naked body. There were numerous small scars and he was as sore as he could ever remember being, but he was alive. He looked about and saw they were still in the grove beside the lake into which he had pulled them. The memories of his dream faded despite his efforts to hold on to them. His clothes, torn and burnt, were folded near the small campfire. He dressed and looked around.

Alexia sat with her back against a tree. The blue hood of her damaged and soiled cloak was raised, concealing her head. It was then that the memory of what had happened returned to Tomas. He stood and flexed his hands, realizing that he had forever lost his father's sword before memory restored itself in the young man's mind. He looked about and saw where the gladius lay waiting beside Tomas' folded cloak along with the map his Praetorian friend had given him and the purse from the survivors of Pelsemoria.

With careful steps, the shepherd walked down to the nearby lake and brought back to their small camp some water, making brief note that they were much further from Wignis than he would have thought possible. It was odd, he thought as he worked to gather a morning meal, finding mushrooms and nuts and little else. Alexia had slept so late. In the weeks they had traveled together, she was always awake longer than he and always the first to rise. No doubt the battle and whatever it was she had done to keep him alive and heal his wounds had taken a great deal of effort.

With their small breakfast prepared, Tomas resolved to wake her. He moved up beside her still form and knelt, drawing back the hood. The young man gasped and nearly fell backward as icy fear grabbed his heart and squeezed. Alexia's face was crossed with a hundred new wrinkles. Where once she was a woman of mature beauty, now she looked all her twelve centuries and more. Her flowing mane of snowy white hair hung drab and lifeless. Her hands were skeletal and limp. Her once-full figure was hollow and sagging. Tomas felt grief crashing in upon him as the reality of his friend's sacrifice tore his soul.

Alexia sighed and her azure eyes fluttered open, their opalescence faded to almost nothing. She smiled gently through wane lips and looked up at the young man kneeling over her. "I will not, it seems, see the next spring," she whispered weakly with fading breath.

"How long?" he asked, tears standing in his eyes.

Alexia sighed and tried to straighten, but then gasped and slumped forward. Tomas shot to her side and eased his friend to the ground. She closed her dimming eyes. "Hours, perhaps. Less. My eyes will not see the dawn."

"Not for me," the shepherd whispered. "Please, God. Not for me."

The Sylva reached a skeletal hand up and held it against his cheek. "Yes, for you. You cheated Fate, Tomas. It was my time that night. I was meant to die in the fire, but you defied Fate and saved me. You traded your life for mine. You cheated, my young friend, so I cheated as well. I have balanced the scales and given you back your life."

"I was ready to die."

"It was not your time to die. You still have much ahead of you. It was not for you to give your life for me. There are others who still need you." She looked closely then at Tomas, the opalescence briefly glowing again as her azure gaze saw past the surface, past the present, and into the truth beyond. "This is your power, Tomas," she said, "your gift."

"I don't understand."

Alexia took a deep, shuddering breath. "They can't touch you. They can't... control you."

"Who?"

Her gaze lost what remained of its opalescence, becoming unfocused, her eyelids fluttering. "They... the brothers... Fate." She forced concentration, forced herself to speak. "They'll try to... they'll want you to... Trick you. Maneuver you. But they can't *make* you..." Her eyes again drifted shut.

The tears that had only a moment ago stood in the shepherd's eyes now flowed freely. Alexia looked up at her friend. "Did I not explain... death is not sadness? Soon my Walker and I will be together. Along with all our family and friends. Someday you will make the journey. When you do, we will be waiting."

"There's so little time," Tomas sobbed.

"That is the way of life," she replied, her voice losing strength and her breathing becoming labored. "There is only ever... as much time as we need. Never… as we want. But perhaps I have the time…"

"For what?"

"To repay your kindness."

Tomas shook his head. "I told you before that I couldn't accept any repayment."

Alexia again put her hand on his cheek, looking up at her young friend with great affection. She struggled to rise to a seated position but could not. Instead, Tomas cradled her in his lap. "You have made my last days pleasant," she said weakly. "I was not forced to die… alone in that town… as was fated. You can thwart destiny, dear Tomas. I would have suffered in the fires… but instead I slip through the mists in the company of a… good and decent man. What more could any lady want? If you cannot accept… repayment for your kindness… accept a gift from a dying friend."

"It would honor me," he said without hesitation.

"First I must ask you… one more favor… one you must do after…"

Tomas thought he knew what she would ask for. "I swear I will take you home to be buried with your kin."

Alexia smiled. "No, Tomas. Again, your nobility shines through. You would put yourself through great trials… only to fulfill a friend's last request. There is something of the old heroes in you, Tomas. Some believe… the time of heroes has passed. Perhaps you can bring it back. If I were forced to name only one regret… it would be that I will not see your deeds."

She took a deep breath, seeming to struggle just to gather the strength to speak. "No, Tomas," she finally said. "Your path does not lie along mine any further. Besides, what matters is that *Ar'ae'el* benefits from our lives."

"I don't understand," he admitted.

"Bury me here, Tomas, among these trees… in this valley that carries… so many memories. Put me to my rest here in the lands where… so many of my ancestors lie. Lay me beside a sapling that has just sprouted. Let my body nourish it. Swear to me that you will do as I ask and accept my gift."

The shepherd took his friend's hand in his and brought it to his lips. "I swear, Alexia. I will do as you ask. I will bury you here and I will treasure your gift for all my days."

She smiled then and reached with a shaking hand to the small pin that adorned the front of her dress, the golden rose that was her only adornment. "This has been with me since I first left my mother's house," she gestured for Tomas to take it. The small pin, a rose in full bloom, still caught the faint light of the morning sun. "It has been the one and only thing to endure our many adventures. Take it."

Tomas accepted the gift from his dying friend. He held it lightly in his hand, wishing hard to find the words to express his gratitude. Alexia smiled again. "You cannot wear it on your hand," she laughed ever so lightly. The dying Sylva took the pin and, within trembling hands, attached it to her young friend's collar. "There," she said. "It fits."

Tomas took his friend's hand and looked into her azure eyes through his tears.

"And now for your gift," she whispered.

The young man put an uncertain hand to the pin on his collar. Seeing this, Alexia smiled. "There is more," she breathed. She drew him closer and put a hand to Tomas' forehead. Chanting softly in the language of magic, she reached her other hand up and put it against her young friend's heart. Something passed between them. It was warm and soft, like the embrace of a loving mother. A glow passed from Alexia into the soul of the young man kneeling before her.

"There," she smiled.

"What?" Tomas asked.

Alexia let her arms drop. "Give it time. You will learn … in time."

"No matter what it is, I'll treasure it. I promise."

"That is more than… a gift for you… also for… old friends."

"I don't understand."

She smiled. "They will."

Alexia looked then, and saw something new in his soul not been there before. "I was wondering," she whispered. "Was there one last thing…?"

"Anything," he replied.

"I had a child… You remind me of him. He was noble, as you. He was brave and foolish... like you." Tomas smiled through his sorrow at her soft jibe. "He was sincere and just…"

"Where is he now?" Tomas asked.

"With my Walker… waiting..." Seeing Tomas' eyes cloud, she smiled and brought his head low to place a light kiss on his forehead. "Now, now. Bad enough… you mourn an old *sy'lva*. No grief for my…"

"What can I do for you?"

"Help me…" she gestured and Tomas lifted her, placing her seated back against the nearby tree. Alexia then smiled up at him and said, "When my son… when he was young enough to still need… a mother's comfort… to keep back the monsters of the night. I would sing for him. I would very much… like to sing now, Tomas. Let me sing you into a peaceful sleep with… a song to keep away the monsters."

Tomas smiled and laid his head in Alexia's lap. She gently ran her fingers through his tussled hair and began a soft melody that soon brought a great lassitude down on the shepherd. Although her voice was, at first, weak, as the song continued, Alexia seemed to draw strength from the singing. She sang in her native tongue and brought contentment to the young man. Her song caressed his soul and rose among the distant branches. The wind quieted to hear, and the lapping waves of the nearby lake sang along. Alexia's breath steadied and the voice deepened, her song unbroken as it found a quiet place within Tomas' mind. Sleep tugged at the young man, pulling shut his eyes as Alexia's soft voice drifted on the breeze, joining the wind in its journey.

Tomas did not wake until the next morning. He leaned up from where his head had apparently rested in Alexia's lap the entire day and night. He looked up to see her eyes closed and her head resting against the tree behind her. The shepherd did not need to check to know her heart beat no more. He kissed his dear friend lightly on the forehead and held her close one last time.

In front of a small sapling, nestled in a small grove in the heart of the valley that held so much sorrow for the Sylvai, Tomas laid his good friend Palsilyagathalexia to rest, as she had wished to be. He stood there for a long while, wishing his friends Alexia and Raven well on their journey to the Eternal Forest and asking them to be patient until the day came when he could rejoin them.

The sun shined down on the small field. The wind sang through the branches overhead. Everywhere there was life. The road called to Tomas, and he waved one last farewell to his friend before carefully tying his father's now unsheathed blade to his back and resuming his quest.

Chapter 11

Tomas needed almost a week to walk around Lake Tragedy. He was often forced to take large detours thanks to the Forgotten Bog, named for the thousands of nameless dead forever resting beneath its murky waters. The young man made his way as best he could through dismal swamp, following solid ground however it meandered and frequently forced to double-back when it ended. Land that appeared solid would frequently give way beneath Tomas' feet, sending him cursing into the cold water. His path twisted and turned even more than the many rivers and creeks which wound their way down from the mountains and into the swamp. His misery knew few limits as he doggedly pressed on through, foraging for food as possible, but often forced to subsist on the cranberries growing wild throughout the Bog. The floating red fruit often gave the marsh a look as though it swam in blood, a thought Tomas found appropriate given all the lives lost within its shallow waters. The Forgotten Bog was a place of death and mourning, Tomas decided.

At long last, the young man caught sight of Placidus, sister community to Wignis. Because he no longer traveled with a Sylva, he was not greeted with the same animosity as before, though many in the small village did cast cautious glances at Tomas' unsightly appearance after weeks of travel through the Forgotten Bog; travelers too poor to afford the ferry were not unheard of, but still uncommon.

Tomas inquired of this from a few men loading supplies into a wagon. The shepherd was surprised to learn the warlord Vagris had yet to attack this community. The people had been nervous when his bandits had ferried across, having seen in the distance the flames and heard the screams from their sister-village. Offering no resistance, though, and an offering of supplies in exchange for mercy, Vagris had seemed content to leave their homes be. Rather, one man admitted, it seemed as though the warlord was in a greater hurry to be elsewhere, some place to the north.

Though he chafed at the cost, Tomas decided that too much time had been lost in the Forgotten Bog, and so he decided to make some up with a horse. The animal required most of the silver the people of Pelsemoria had provided, leaving only enough to replace the supplies lost in Wignis, but Tomas reasoned that he could sell the animal once he had covered sufficient distance.

Now mounted, it was only a single day before he left behind the rocky valley surrounding Lake Tragedy and entered the woods which bordered Railing. Though in no way comparable to the ancient red trees near Pelemsoria, this new forest was a welcome relief from the lake and all its sad events. Tomas was reminded of what Alexia had said of the Eternal Forest. Was there some truth to her words, he thought? The Teachings spoke of the Paradise awaiting all those of the true faith. The Church taught that so long as people lived a humble and dutiful life, the Lord would reward them with an unending life in which there was no pain, no loss or sorrow, and all those who went before you waited. Could it be the Sylvai believed the same thing the Church taught? For centuries, the Lords Cardinal had proclaimed that all beliefs of the Elder Race were heresy; but was it heresy to simply call Paradise by another name?

Tomas smiled at a thought that sprang into his mind just then. When the time came and he would travel to what lay beyond death, he would love to sit in on the endless debates between Alexia and Father Konrad. The two of them were equally devout, believing in apparently the same things, just with different names.

Many Church leaders had warned against the dangers of experiencing the ideas of non-Humans. Was Tomas falling into the dark pit of heresy? He thought of his friend. Her smile, the light of her soul, her willingness to sacrifice herself for him. There were the acts of a good person, a person of faith and kindness. If there was any justice in Judgment, Tomas decided, then Alexia would find the Eternal Forest.

Tomas needed another four days before he reached the town of Railing, the town that marked the traditional boundary of the Imperial Prefecture. Alessandros had once taken his son with him on a trip there. From his admittedly idealized childhood memories, Tomas recalled the village to be a very pleasant place. While in no way comparable to the splendor of the capital, Railing still seemed to radiate a welcoming warmth. The streets had been cobblestone with close buildings of stone and wood. The front doors and windows were all open, allowing the pleasant scents of spice and pastry, fruit and perfume to fill the air. Carts and wagons filled the streets, but there had seemed to be a subtle order to the movement around the very young Tomas; there was no pushing or shoving, and he could not remember any harsh words being spoken.

Railing was the town families retired to. Many in the army and the government worked their whole lives to afford a home there. It was where many yearned for in their deepest hearts when the cold of the world pressed in on a troubled life. Friendly neighbors waving hello walked along pleasant streets. The town was long considered a second heart of the Republic, the crossroads of the old Sylvai highway system, where any traveler was welcome to stay as long as needed, then wished well on their journey. Railing was a home for anyone who needed it.

Tomas found something else entirely.

The dark birds were his first warning. A more experienced man, more traveled and more accustomed to the horrors of the world may have spotted other warning signs sooner, the lack of any sounds so close to a large town, or the absence of field-hands or other laborers. For Tomas, though, the birds were the first warning. Due to the thickness of the woods he was traveling through, the shepherd could not see for more than a mile in any direction, except further along the twisting highway. Once the trees started to part, revealing the first glimpse of Railing, Tomas' initial sigh of relief at the thought of a warm bed was almost immediately overridden by his view of the sky. Although it was still early afternoon, a great shadow moved over the forest. Wave after wave of birds were in constant motion around the village; for no one second was the shadowy mass stationary as it hovered about in search of food.

Fear was pushing at Tomas as he looked up at the sky. The closer the shepherd moved towards the town, the more he could make out the harsh calls of the darkness swarming above him. The birds' dark symphony sent deep chills down his spine, but something compelled him onward. It seemed as though the flock was trying to force Tomas away from the town with their cries, a wall of harsh noise pushing at him; but he would not be turned aside. The horse beneath Tomas was having much the same reaction, shaking and making frequent attempts to turn away despite the young man's constant urging.

Tomas' pace increased without his thinking about it, the dark flight of the evil birds drawing the young man quickly down the highway. It was not until, at the very edge of the town where the paved highway joined the cobblestone streets of Railing, that the flies added their weight to the testimony of the birds. Mistaking Tomas for a part of their grisly feast, the insects swarmed onto the traveler with a vengeance. Suffering through the enthusiasm of the flies and the birds' announcement of his arrival, Tomas continued on towards the town center. As distracted and frightened by the birds and the bugs as he was, the shepherd did not even notice the signs of recent fire on nearly every house he passed in his hurry to get to the town square. It was not until he entered the town proper, past the outlying houses that stood ominously open and quiet, that a new wall replaced the cries of the birds filling the sky and the insects buzzing all around him; this one a wall of stench.

Coming to a dead stop, the young man retched as the unmistakable odor of rotting meat filled his lungs. Tomas' horse reared, throwing him to the ground, and bolted back south, away from the awful horror that unfolded ahead. Instinct screamed at Tomas to do the same, to turn aside from the cursed place and never return, but a numbness filled the shepherd's conscious mind. He stiffly rose back to his feet and continued on, some morbid part of his soul demanding to see what lay ahead.

After Tomas had emptied his stomach, he managed to look up and spy the fading traces of what must have been several large fires that had only recently burned themselves out. Wisps of smoke could barely be seen amidst the dark birds overhead and the acrid smell of burnt wood added a spice to the horrid odor of decay in the air that brought tears to Tomas' eyes that complemented his writhing stomach. Despite the protests screaming from his soul, Tomas still picked himself up and pushed forward, desperate to discover just what had happened in this once peaceful community. Upon finally reaching the town square, Tomas wished, for the rest of his life, that he had listened to the birds and the bugs and the smoke and his horse and his soul and stayed far away from the dead town of Railing.

The best estimate Tomas could make was that the population of this town had been two or three thousand men, women, and children. They had a small militia, but traditionally depended on Republic detachments for defense from any serious threats. Commerce was the primary concern of this village; trade was what most citizens worked towards. The last thing any of Railing's inhabitants would have wanted was a fight. In the myriad rebellions that had occurred through the history of the Republic, it was only Railing's unwavering loyalty to the Redwood Throne that had always kept them safe. The dozen men wearing the blue and gray uniforms of House Calonar crucified in the village square gave mute evidence that Railing's loyalty to the Republic had ended.

Tomas could only stare in open-mouthed shock at the men wearing the Black Duke's emblem. It seemed as though everywhere the young man looked, he could see tunics with two crossed, four-sided diamonds sewn onto the breast. Mutilated corpses in blue and white were strewn about the town center, but the bodies decorating the crosses above had the gold braiding on their left shoulders marking them as officers. The common men of the garrison the Black Duke must have forced upon this peaceful town had clearly not rated as high nor warranted the special attention that the officers received as they had simply had their heads placed on stakes in a circle around their leaders with their dead eyes looking on at the failed leaders.

As for the townspeople, it was obvious that whoever had attacked Railing had felt little need to waste time making examples of them. The people of Railing lay where they had fallen, where they had been cut down. Men, women, and children all lay as they had died. There had been no mercy.

With tears burning in his eyes, Tomas desperately ran throughout the small town, ignoring his tears and his heaving stomach and calling to any possible survivors. Everywhere he went, the young man saw only more horror. Everywhere he looked the young man saw doors kicked in, stores looted, men and children cut down, and women who had obviously been violated before being butchered themselves. Fire had burned through most of the homes, and some still smoldered. A few men and even a great many mothers had improvised weapons in their hands, but it was clear this had done nothing to save them.

Stopping suddenly in his desperate search, Tomas' heart turned to lead in his chest. There, lying in the doorway of a cobbler shop was the body of one of the invaders. Tomas wanted nothing more than to leave and somehow try to wash away the memory of what he had seen here, but somewhere in his mind, the small parts that still functioned despite the horror around him, a voice spoke, a voice of mercy and music, of kindness and forgiveness. If any justice could one day be found for the people of Railing, the voice said, the identity of the invaders would need to be uncovered.

The body lay on its side; one arm crossed over the head and covered the face. Tomas knelt down over the murderer and, shaking in a mixture of fear, revulsion, and rage, pulled back the arm. Tomas saw that he had taken a knife to the throat. At a glance, Tomas could tell the man was a common type of mercenary as to be seen in any part of Lanasia. His armor was a simple chainmail shirt, expensive but common, marking him as a murder of means. He did not carry a crude axe or spear, instead a scabbard still hung by a belt around the raider's waist, looking to be for a shortsword. No regalia or heraldry adorned the man or his equipment, despite the suggestion of resources otherwise unavailable to criminal scum. Tomas could find no identifying marks of any kind, until he pulled up the tattered sleeve of this monster's shirt.

On his left shoulder was tattooed a red eagle with outstretched wings and a sword clasped in its talons, the traditional mark of a Republic legionnaire. This creature had once served in the Legions. The young man staggered back, his mind reeling at this revelation. Unable to believe what his eyes were showing him, he stumbled back into the street, spotting yet another of the raiders. This one as well he inspected and again, found the mark of the Legions. Running again throughout the small town, Tomas found several more armored men, each of them bearing the emblem of the Republic army. These were not petty raiders: runaway peasants or highwaymen. These were not ragged murderers, petty mercenaries, or undisciplined killers. These men were professional soldiers, defenders of the Republic.

Wignis. The words of the outraged mob that had threatened both Tomas and Alexia intruded back into the young man's thoughts. Men wielding the blades of the Legions and bearing their mark, charged with defending the people of the Republic, but now nothing more than ravaging monsters. Every oath they had taken, every day of training, every tradition of honor, had all been cast aside.

Could it be that an entire legion had turned to such violence in response to the fall of the Republic? Had a local garrison commander heard that Railing was taken over by the forces of the Black Duke, then moving against the beasts of House Calonar would not only be acceptable, but commendable. But whatever group it was that had attacked Railing had clearly not cared to distinguish between the loyal villagers and the occupation forces. It could not have been a group made of nothing but soldiers. Tomas could not accept that.

The shepherd could look no longer at the traitors around him. Instead, he continued his search of the small town, crying out to any that might be hiding and assiduously avoiding the sight of any fallen warrior. As time passed, his pace slowed as the truth made itself unavoidable. There had been no survivors, no mercy. The young man could not avoid the thought that such meticulousness was the trademark of the Legions. Only they went out of their way to destroy an enemy so completely. Any common mercenary group seeking only the spoils of pillaging a prosperous town would have cared little for escaping women and children. Only a disciplined unit from a trained Legion would have thought to kill any possible witnesses.

Time seemed to stop for Tomas. He found himself on a street he had traveled before, so many years ago. On this street he could still pick out the spice merchant's shop, and the candlemaker's. The young man even remembered one shop in particular that his legs seemed determined to visit again. In the bakery that Tomas recalled from his trip of so long ago, the young man found the shopkeeper, a pleasant, grandfatherly kind of man who had given the young boy a small tart in exchange for a smile. Now, that kind old man was only a pile of meat, cut to pieces in front of his own store. In the baker's hand was a baking knife with caked dough and dried blood covering it. Within the shop, the bodies of two very small children lied in a corner, unmoving. On a large display table, its previous, sugary contents scattered across the room, was the body of their mother, sprawled and still showing the signs of several attackers, several monstrous violators, her face locked in horror. In the back of the shop where delightful treats had once been made was the young woman that must have been the baker's eldest daughter. Tomas remembered her being a very cheerful girl with a bright smile, only a year or two older than he, dressed in a light pink dress with flowers decorating her hair. Now, the young woman's body, covered only in a few tattered pink rags, lay bent backwards over a different counter, the evidence of her abuse still covering her entire body. The girl's empty eyes were turned towards the doorway in which Tomas stood, her mouth a silent scream echoed by the gaping hole in her throat.

Stumbling outside the shop, the horror of everything around him pressing in on his soul, Tomas looked to the town center. Once a small monument to a famous, forgotten general stood there, a stone pillar decorated with unremembered glories. Now, the pillar held a new marker, a new monument to a murderous victory.

The garrison commander the Black Duke had forced upon the people of Railing was tied to the pillar, suspended by his wrists with his limp legs dangling in the feeble breeze. The man's head hung limply, blood staining his face. Metal wire had been used to secure him to the pillar in the town center. His arms had been broken either before he had been lashed to the stone or during the process. His torn and bloodstained uniform of blue and grey held an officer's rank, and numerous metals had been torn from the tunic and instead decorated his flesh, along with the crossed diamond symbol of House Calonar which had been carved into the man's chest.

A sudden rage filled Tomas. His lips curled back in a snarl of hatred and he gripped his father's sword so tightly that his knuckles turned white. The young man did not remember pulling the gladius free of its improvised sling. With a roar, the shepherd launched himself at the Black Duke's officer. Again and again he hacked into the body with his father's sword. Despite the burning in his shoulders and the tears flowing from his eyes, he kept swinging. With each cut he screamed, "It's your fault!" "Damn you!" "Why can't you leave us alone!?!" But no answer came from the body.

Driven finally to exhaustion, Tomas was forced to stop, taking a few steps back before falling to his knees. Panting from the exertion, the young man finally noticed the blood that covered both his sword and his hands, blood that he feared would never wash off. A wet, tearing sound pulled Tomas' gaze back to the officer. With a sickening series of snaps, the torso tore free of the arms, falling away from the stone pillar and landing on Tomas, driving him to the ground. The young man shrieked in revulsion and terror, pushing the dead remains away and scrambling back. After a few moments, a soft voice, more a silent song within his soul than actual words, guided Tomas' gaze up. He looked up to the pillar and the ruined mess adorning it. The sun had broken through the dark clouds of smoke overhead, its light reflecting off the wedding ring resting on a lifeless hand.

Tomas, surrounded by the people of Railing and covered in the blood and gore of the man who had caused their deaths, wept. He wept and desperately tried to wash the blood off his hands in a polluted gutter. He wept for the people since there was no one else left to weep.

Strengthened by thoughts of Alexia, Cecilia, his mother, and everyone in Pelsemoria who was praying for his successful return, Tomas was eventually able to rouse himself from the emptiness that pressed in on his soul. For a very brief time, the young man thought about digging graves for every innocent that had fallen in this senseless tragedy. Eventually that silent voice in his soul forced him to an unpleasant truth. It would take much too long to even burn all the bodies. If the fires set by the invaders that had turned nearly every building in Railing into hallow tombs could not destroy the remains of their victims, then no blaze the young shepherd could build would be enough. It would have to be left in God's hands to prevent a pestilence from spreading to any of the other communities in the area. Fortunately, Railing was bordered by hill country keeping it somewhat separated, even from the neighboring Kordenel Counties. The nearest settlement was days away, even on horse, a horse he no longer had.

So it was that Tomas could offer only what prayers he could think of for the souls of the fallen, even those souls that had served the Black Duke. He was torn briefly by the thought of praying for the eternal souls of men that would willingly serve House Calonar, but finally, Tomas was forced to admit that their judgment was not in his hands. Alexia had proven to him that not all those in service to that evil man were evil themselves; as with all people, their Judgment would be based on their individual actions, not the actions of their masters. If they were to be damned, it would be by God's decree, not his. Prayers for those who die before their time are often just empty words, but if those words could help to bring some peace to the spirits that would now haunt this place, then Tomas would say them. After all, the words cost him only a little breath, and unlike those who had fallen, the shepherd had some to spare.

Tomas stood outside the dead community, considering his options. He found himself at a literal crossroads of his quest, staring at the convergence of all roads and highways of Lanasia. The crossroad was marked in the traditional manner of the old pagan myths with a mask facing in each direction in honor of the old Sylvai goddess Tryviana, patron of crossroads and journeys. The eastern highway would lead to Alvaro, Velaross, and even up into the Northlands. The western highway led around the Sylvai Vale, into Ulheim to Frostfront and on towards Daivic in the lands of Duke Parano. From those far western lands, the shepherd could turn north along the great Harun River and press on towards the City of All Sins, where he hoped to find Cyras Darkholm. Of course, nothing said the young man must travel along one of the old Sylvai highways. There were many smaller roads and wagon trails that led north towards the Keep of the Black Duke; there was a dark part of Tomas' soul that told him vengeance could be found in the north, but walking into the lands of the Black Duke was not something any sane man should ever do. The western highway branched off towards Velaross. It was the right thing to do, the young man knew. Even if Holy Mother Church had been forced into an alliance with House Calonar, there were bound to still be at least a few men and women of pure faith there who could help Tomas and the people of Railing. The final choice was the highway that led south, back through the town and home to Pelsemoria.

Tomas took a deep breath and squared his shoulders. He would not go home, not so early in his quest. Nor would he go north. He had no doubt that someday he would be in a position to do something about the Black Duke, but now was not that time. That only left Velaross or the City of All Sins. What an irony, the young man thought. Should he turn to the light of the Holy City for help, or should he turn to the darkness of the home of sin for the Trickster Mage? The only thing driving Tomas to the City of All Sins was a hunch, he decided. Something in his heart, some quiet, clear-thinking part of his soul seemed fixated on the road east. Finding help in the Holy City would be difficult, and the Church was unlikely to spare anyone to travel all the way back to Railing after so long. Sill, that quiet part of Tomas insisted that the path east was correct.

With a renewed sense of purpose, Tomas turned away from the City of All Sins and the beginning of his quest. The road east now called, into the Koredenel Counties.

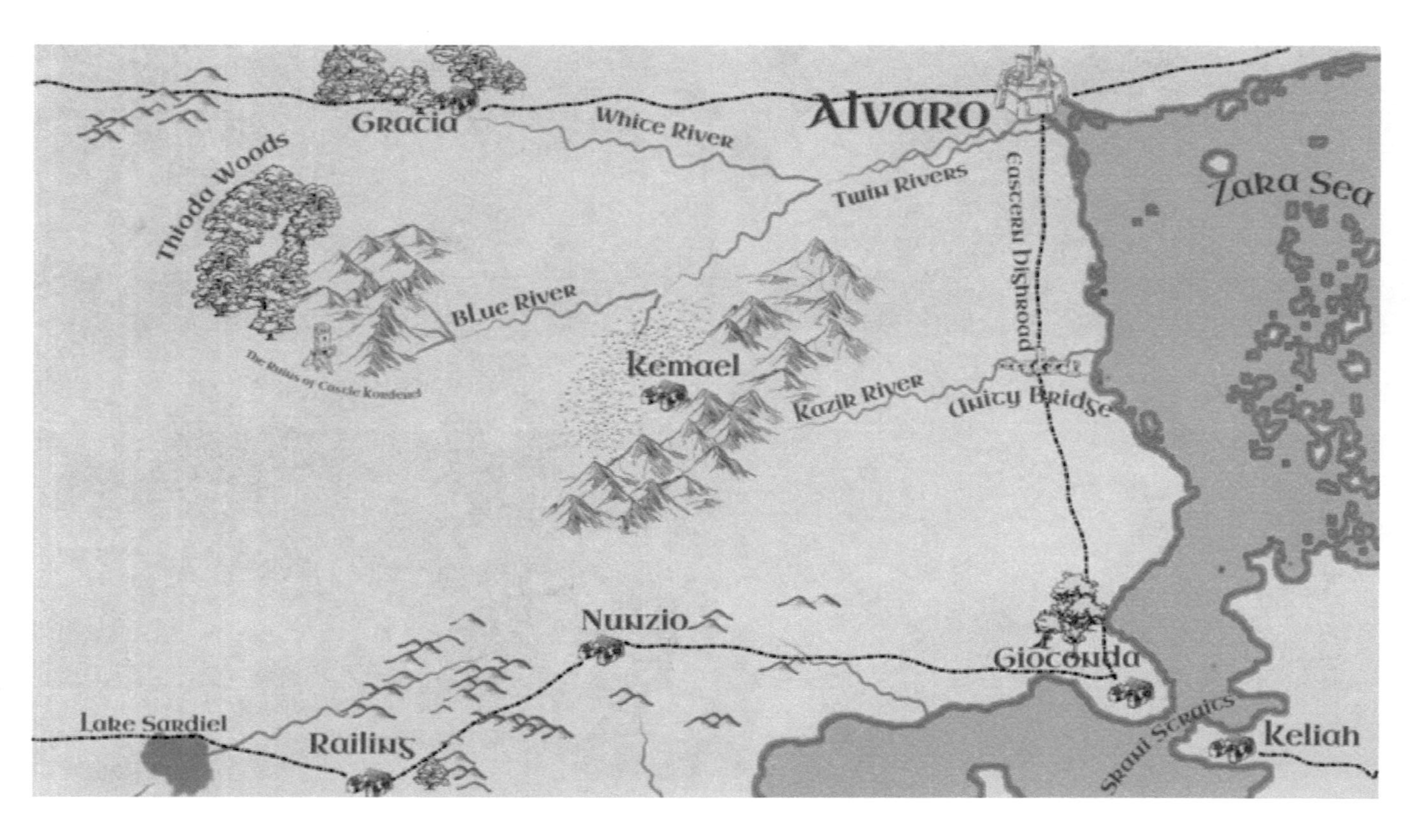
Gracia
Thioda Woods
White River
Alvaro
Twin Rivers
Eastern Highroad
Zara Sea
Blue River
The Ruins of Castle Kordead
Kemael
Kazir River
Unity Bridge
Nunzio
Gioconda
Lake Sardiel
Railins
Skaui Scraics
Keliah

II

The Kordenel Counties

Chapter 12

The forest that had so welcomed Tomas was gone. The young man had left those woods behind days ago. Instead, he now traveled through the rolling hills and endless grasslands of the Kordenel Counties. It would be some time before he saw trees again, Tomas knew, for Kordenel was a place of grasslands broken only by scattered hills and mountains. It really was a shame; the shepherd had enjoyed the company of the trees, even before meeting Alexia. Out in this plain, there was nothing to keep the sun from beating down on Tomas' head and shoulders, and he quickly became burnt. There was little game out amongst these green hills, at least little that the young man had any hope of hunting without a bow. Out here, in this wide-open sea of grass that could easily reach a man's waist, broken only by the grey stretch of Sylvai road, the endless sky and strong winds were Tomas' only company. Within the forests he had, the air was calm and pleasant, but out here there was nothing to block the winter wind as it blew across the continent on its way towards the sea. The loud waving dance of the grass soon irritated Tomas to the point that he gave serious thought to taking his sword to it, if for no other reason than to silence at least one small area.

How he missed Alexia. The Sylva's laugh and bright soul could have lit a darkened room in the dead of night. Where was she now when he most needed to see the joy in life? How would she have responded to the tragedy Tomas had witnessed at Railing? Surely in her long life, she had seen similar acts of barbarism, but would she still have the smile that seemed such a permanent part of her features? Surrounded by such death and horror, could even Alexia's bright soul maintain its shine?

Tomas had so many questions after what he saw in Railing, but no answers were available. He had now seen the worst of men, he knew. Men who had sworn to serve the people, to protect them, were instead stealing from them. Instead of serving the people, they were satisfying their darkest hungers at the people's expense. Why? What could so drive the Republic's soldiers to do such things? Where were God and His Church to stop it? Why did the good people of Railing have to suffer and die on the whim of a warlord that lacked the honor and courage to fight the darkness that threatened to swallow Lanasia?

Breaking from his habits of more years than he could count, Tomas no longer spoke to God before going to sleep each night. In fact, during those endless days in which he struggled through the rolling hills and pasturelands, the shepherd had not prayed once since leaving Railing. Tomas did not consider his thoughts to be any real kind of crisis of faith. He still believed in God and could find no doubt about His presence in the world. However, more often than even he realized, the young shepherd found himself questioning the Creator's plan.

For as long as he could remember, the Church, to include Father Konrad, had always preached of God's plan. Anything bad that happens to you, Tomas was always assured, had to be taken with anything good. It was all a part of the Creator's master plan. God loves us, Konrad often said, and is looking down on us from Paradise. If some sadness must befall us in life, then it was a small price to pay for an eternity in the glow of God's love.

But what Tomas had seen in Railing forced him to question that. What plan could possibly have warranted such brutality? What possible purpose could there have been for the people to not only have been killed and all their possessions stolen, but to have been treated with such utter lack of basic decency? Why did the baker's have to be abused so terribly? Why his daughter?

Did God love us? Tomas wondered this at night when the ghosts of the past came to haunt him in the winds and the grasses. Could it be that perhaps the Creator has no real love for His creations? Were we just some minor diversion, some way to pass the idle moments in eternity? So many questions nagged at the young man's mind, with no answers making themselves known. Tomas could only struggle through his thoughts on the lonely road with no one to help him through his turmoil, hoping that God would make His purpose known.

It took more than two weeks of walking up and down and around the hills of that area, but finally Tomas did reach the next village and without any serious incidents. The sight of the stone and brick buildings surrounded by strong fences brought a sigh of relief to the young man, even as the smoke rising from the chimneys and the smell of fresh bread nearly brought tears to his eyes. Tomas saw wide fields spreading as far as he could see that slept in anticipation of the coming spring, and herds of cattle that were grazing in complete contentment. The shepherd's pace picked up as he entered this small village, whose name he could not remember.

Nunzio. The name came like a near-forgotten memory. Tomas could not think of anything significant about the town. Looking about, it seemed, in fact, that Nunzio's only outstanding feature was a lack of outstanding features. Many children ran up to the young man, eagerly asking him a flood of questions that sounded much akin to the chirping of a nest of baby birds. The villagers regarded him from their walls and doorways with idle curiosity, neither threatening nor fearful. He was a diversion to the quiet life of a farming village, nothing more.

Finally breaking through the children's insistent questions, Tomas was able to get directions to the home of the elder and so made his way to the large house near the northern edge of the village. From the older man, one of the more prosperous farmers named Uberto, the shepherd learned that the warlord Vagris was attacking any and every town that allowed the soldiers of House Calonar safe haven inside their homes.

"Railing had signed a treaty of free-passage with the forces of the Black Duke in exchange for protection just a month ago," Uberto told Tomas once they had been seated at his kitchen table. The elder was a short man with think black hair that was nearly finished turning grey. His short beard did little to hide the many creases on his leathery face, but his eyes still sparkled with a hint of youthful hope.

The village's blacksmith, Rinaldo, nodded. He had already been in the home of the elder, having been invited for dinner. "It didn't take long for word to spread around these parts about what happened," the thick-bodied man said. "Vagris must have heard as well. Apparently, the protection of the Black Duke isn't all they say it is." Upon his arrival, the two village leaders had insisted that Tomas join them. After making only the most perfunctory objections, the young man tore into the food, nearly ecstatic over the prospect of eating something other than his meager scavenging over the past two weeks.

"We were considering such a treaty," Uberto informed Tomas. "We reached a decision just yesterday to accept the Calonar's offer. However, with the news you bring, it seems obvious that the Black Duke's protection doesn't outweigh the danger."

Rinaldo nodded. "I think we should call a meeting," he suggested. "Let the young man tell his story."

The knowledge that this village, unlike Railing, might be spared the shadow of the Black Duke brought some sense of peace to Tomas. It was not much, he realized, but it was probably the best result he could hope for after the slaughters at Wignis and Railing.

"What of you, son?" Rinaldo asked Tomas.

The young man shrugged, drinking deeply of his fourth cup of fresh milk to help wash down the delicious bread. "If you think it would help, I'd be happy to talk with the others. I just worry over the lost time."

Uberto clapped Tomas on the shoulder. "Don't worry, my boy. After what you've gone through, I think a few nights rest in warm company would do you a lot of good."

Tomas nodded. "I guess that means I just need a place to sleep. If there is a barn or something, I'd be grateful."

Rinaldo shook his head. "Out of the question," he insisted. "After the others hear your story, I'm sure they'll rethink allying with the Black Duke. We owe you a large debt for keeping us from making a serious mistake that might have cost us dearly."

The elder nodded. "We have a small inn here; just a couple of rooms above the common house. I'm sure I could speak with the innkeeper about putting you up for a few nights. It seems the least we could do."

"Sir, I wouldn't feel right about taking advantage like that. There must be some way I could repay your generosity."

The blacksmith shook his head gravely. "Lad, consider the warning you've brought us more than payment in advance. Besides," he added brightly, "you know as well as we do that no true son of Holy Mother Church can turn away a man on a quest."

Tomas nodded with a grin on his face. Since the time of the Heroes of Fate, on the commandment of their leader, the Holy Knight Sir Talius Ironheart, no son or daughter of the Church on a quest from God for the good of others could be denied the help of any community. Ironheart had established the standards by which any hero would be judged for generations and was thought to be the best example of what a Knight of the Church should be. It was he, as all men knew, that forged the Heroes of Fate into what they were. Ironheart had, just before his death, decreed that God would forever curse any man or woman who denied a reasonable request from a true servant of God on Quest.

"I guess in that case," Tomas shrugged, "I can hardly turn you down. But I insist that I only stay a day or two."

Chapter 13

Tomas was as content as he had been in many weeks. The meal the innkeeper, an older man named Donato, had provided was as delicious as any he could remember eating in a very long time. Apparently his wife, Agata, was a master chef who could perform miracles in her kitchen. A feast to rival that of kings was laid out before Tomas. Servings of chicken and warm brown bread along with heaping portions of soft cheese and delicate pastries threatened to overwhelm the young shepherd. Every time Tomas tried to assure his amiable hosts that he had already eaten with the village elder, his objections had been overridden and even more food heaped upon his plate.

Serving him was Donato's daughter, Fiametta. She was a pretty girl with long brown hair that glowed vibrant brown in the light of the hearth and a pleasing figure to look at despite the conservative dress and apron worn by most peasant women in the south. Fiametta insured that Tomas' wine cup was always topped off and the nearby fire was kept plenty high for the honored guest of her family. The young shepherd frequently caught himself glancing at Fiametta whenever she leaned over to fill his cup. Her hair would often spill over one shoulder, to tease aginst Tomas' face, accidentally giving a pleasant view of her modest bosom. When this happened, a scent of kitchens and homes and the comfort of close company filling the young man's heart, oddly pleasing him even more than the glace at exposed flesh. As Fiametta would stoke the fire, the light danced around her lean frame and silhouetted a tantalizing shadow. The young woman would glance behind when her work required her to bend over, a soft smile and heavy-lidded eyes welcoming Tomas' attention. Even when Tomas had no need of drink or food or fire, Fiametta found plenty reason to be near his table, if only to wipe up a spill the young man not made. Tomas did not complain, however, since the girl had a bright smile and sparkling laugh that sent tingles down his body. Fiametta was welcome company, Tomas decided; she agreed with nearly all his opinions and listened with breathless anticipation as the young man related stories of his life in Pelsemoria and so far along his adventure. She was warmth after so many hard, lonely weeks.

The arrival of the elder Uberto and the blacksmith Rinaldo, accompanied by three men appearing to be of middle age, forced Tomas to finally end his pleasurable meal. The men pulled chairs around Tomas' table as Fiametta took the last of the empty dishes away, bringing back several more cups and a pitcher of wine along with some fruits and nuts for them all to enjoy. Learning the council had arrived, Donato reappeared out of the kitchen and drew up his own seat.

Pouring himself a cup of wine, Uberto nodded to the three men Tomas did not know. "Tomas," he said, "this is Fausto, our most prosperous merchant." The elder on the far left, a large, blocky man with the squint and soft hands of a money counter nodded. "Carmine, whose family owns our largest vineyard." The middle man, lean but tanned from years of work in the sun, smiled. "And this," he finished, pointing to a large man with iron grey hair but more muscle than his frame should have been able to hold up, "is Brizio, our tanner."

Tomas nodded to each.

Carmine the winemaker, took a brief drink of the wine and grimaced. Turning to Donato, he narrowed his eyes at the innkeeper. "Couldn't afford one of mine?" he asked with mock disappointment.

The older man shrugged. "Not at the prices you're demanding."

The winemaker leaned back in his chair and crossed his arms over his chest. "Uberto here has told us your story," he told Tomas.

The shepherd shook his head. "No words any man can speak could do justice for what was done to the people of Railing," he declared. "What I saw there has haunted me ever since."

The tanner, Brizio, grimaced. "It's unfortunate," he rumbled, "that someone as young as you should be forced to witness such evil."

The young man looked deeply into the giant's eyes. "I think it would be unfortunate for anyone of any age to see what I saw."

"Are you sure?" the merchant Fausto asked. "Are you sure that it was because of the presence of the Black Duke's men that the town was attacked?"

Tomas shook his head. "I have no way of knowing, sir. Not for certain. All I know is the soldiers and officers loyal to House Calonar received special attention, much more so than any other in the village with the possible exception of the young women."

The men all shook their heads and muttered at the thought of a warband ravaging their small community and violating their women. "Gentlemen," Tomas said then, "all I can tell you is this: Railing was the most prosperous town in this part of Lanasia, with the obvious exception of Pelsemoria before its destruction. That the town has gone these past ten years without suffering nearly as much as so many other communities says something. The local warlords all know the value of a prosperous town, and whoever wins this civil war will need the revenue of communities like Railing to maintain control. That the town was destroyed just days or, at most, weeks after signing a treaty with the Black Duke should also say something; the warlords that abound in Lanasia today may be too cowardly to engage Calonar directly but will not hesitate to destroy any town or village that openly sides with the Black Duke."

"Your words do little to comfort us, young master Tomas," Uberto noted.

"I'm not trying to comfort you, sir. I'm trying to make sure that I will never again have to see done to any community what was done to Railing. I have been in this village for only a day, and already I can tell you that its destruction would do me much harm."

"It seems we have few choices," Fausto remarked.

"Four," Brizio grunted. "We can join with House Calexto of Alvaro or House Calonar of the Northern Keep. We can join with one of the nearby warbands, or we can try and remain neutral."

Donato shook his head, glancing around his small inn. "I don't like any of those options," he said. "We are not as prosperous as Railing was, but we still have much. Our allegiance would mean much to whomever we give it."

Rinaldo rubbed his chin with one hand as he stared at the low wood ceiling. "If we join with any one warlord or minor noble, all the others would take action against us to deny their enemy our support."

"And," Carmine added, "the moment we declare our support for anyone other than Calonar, Velaross will withdraw any possible support and protection they might otherwise be willing to offer us. That would leave only Alvaro, which I doubt would be quick to defend us if we are attacked by the Black Duke."

Fausto nodded. "It sounds as if the safest course would be to side with Calonar. He is the only one strong enough to offer protection."

"Like the protection he provided Railing?" Tomas pointed out.

All the men were silent. The young man shook his head and drank deeply from his cup before speaking again. "Do you gentlemen know about the Emperor's death?" he asked.

They all nodded. The news had been circulated for nearly a decade, after all. Fausto clasped his hands on the table. "Were you actually there, Master Tomas?" he demanded.

"I was in the city at the time, sir," the young man replied.

"But a child, yes? And were you actually a part of the actions that led to the death of the Emperor and the destruction of the capital?"

"As I said, sir, I was in the city. I saw the Imperial Palace burnt to the ground; a building that dated back to the Sylvai Empire and it was gone in a matter of hours. I saw the effects of Kyla's Madness; our entire city under the power of Calonar's daughter, making people do unspeakable things to each other. I saw my home destroyed by countless raids and the lack of help from anyone." Tomas leaned in very far over the table then. "And, gentlemen, I saw my father's lifeless body on the floor of the chamber of the Electors Council. I saw Rogan Eigenhard's sword stained with my father's blood.

He took a deep breath, bringing to the surface memories normally forced into the furthest depths of his mind. "I was there, gentlemen. My father had convinced my mother to allow me to visit him in the palace that day. My father, a Praetorian centurion, brought me with him to see the wonders of the Imperial Palace and the wise men who had once made up the Electors Council. I watched as Eigenhard had his Halvan witch, Kyla, set a man aflame and destroy the council chamber. I watched, hidden by my father and safe from harm, as the assassins under Eigenhard's command slaughtered the council, the Imperial Family, and the Emperor himself. I watched as the Praetorians rushed to try and stop the attack, and I watched as they fell. It is only by the grace of God that an explosion forced my head down, so I was spared the sight of Eigenhard murdering my father.

"I have never before told any man what I saw that day. Even my own mother thought that I was rushed to safety along with the other children once the attack began. I tell you this now because I fear for this town. I fear for you all more than you can know. You say there is no other way but to ally with one of these evil men who now war against each other over the scraps of the Republic? Brizio said you had four options. Ally with the warlords, ally with Alonzo, ally with Calonar, or *stay neutral!* Do not think that you must take sides! Why choose between what you hope will be the lesser of two evils? Your village is very far from Alvaro and Velaross but still close enough for trade. Neither of those two powers would tolerate you siding with the other, so do not side."

"Any alliance, no matter with whom, will draw an attack. That much is certain. Alvaro would offer much for your loyalty but lacks the strength to defend you so far from its walls, and House Calexto lacks the will to confront House Calonar. The warlords are too weak to fight off the Black Duke's men, and Calonar has proven that his promise of protection is worthless."

Tomas turned to Donato. "Sir, thank you for the meal. I suddenly find myself very tired."

The innkeeper nodded. "Of course, Tomas. You have said, I think, more than enough to give us pause. Fiametta will show you to a room we prepared for you."

The young man nodded his thanks and turned to follow the pretty girl upstairs. At the door of the commonroom, before turning to climb the steps to the rooms above, Tomas stopped. "Let me say this one last thing, gentlemen. Trust in God. These are dark days to live through. But history is a study of dark days, one right after another, and I'm sure that the people living in each of those times wished that they had seen more peaceful times. Remember this, though. It is in times like these that the smallest choices can echo forever. Holy Mother Church tells us that God has a plan and that He loves us. Trust that someday there will be someone who can stand up to men like the Black Duke. Someone who can unite us, and allow us to choose between the evil and the good, not just the lesser of two evils."

Cecilia was dressed in a silk dress that did little to conceal her shapely figure. She slid with a sensuous grace onto Tomas' bed and sat before him, a smile suggesting things that should have made the shy girl blush. Tomas ran his eyes over the form of his childhood friend, appreciating every change time had brought upon her. No longer the boyish figure of infancy, Cecilia's body had bloomed into near-womanhood, with curve of hip and breast and a hungry gaze that spoke eagerly of adult concerns.

The two embraced each other and kissed. Soft at first, tentative, but soon their mouths opened in hungry moans. Tongues and hands explored each other's bodies as they both fell to the bed. Cecilia moaned as Tomas pulled at her dress, rational thought giving way to an instinctive need. With her gown pulled around her waist, the man ran hands and mouth along her exposed flesh, running his embrace up until he held her face in both hands and kissed her with such force that the small, thinking part of his mind warned of hurting her.

Rather than backing away or even whimpering at the rough treatment, Cecilia moaned her encouragement and dug her fingernails into his back, responding to his force with her own. Her heat rose to consume his. Pausing then in surprise, the shepherd was pushed onto his back by his lady, who straddled his waist. Already undressed for sleep, Tomas' body fell victim to Cecilia's desire. She kissed and bit, teased and licked, bringing shudders of both pain and pleasure to Tomas. She moved lower, never once pausing or showing the slightest hesitation.

In the moment when the young man felt his woman reaching a goal for which they both hungered, rational thought intruded from the quiet part of Tomas' mind: Cecilia was very shy, almost painfully so, especially while making love. So, who is this?

Tomas sat straight up in the bed provided him by the overly-generous Donato. He was covered only in sweat and his pulse was racing. The young man looked about in the dark and, through the evening drifting through the window Tomas had left open, saw that he was, indeed, still at the inn on his quest to find Cyras Darkholm.

Then he realized that he still had a woman's face planted in his lap.

"Hey!" Tomas cried, trying desperately to squirm out from underneath his unexpected company. With enough force that he feared the bruise he would enjoy in the morning, the young man landed on the hard wood floor with a thud. It was at times like these that he was glad of the many stories his father told him of the necessity of maintaining one's composure in combat and other tense situations.

Fiametta leaned over the edge of the bed, not bothering to cover her half-naked form. "Something's wrong," she sagely guessed.

"Well, yes." Tomas replied, trying unsuccessfully not to note how remarkable her nude form looked by the glowing light of the waxing moon. Fortunately, the rational part of his mind was working furiously to exert control against instinct and desire. "What are you doing in my room?" Tomas demanded.

Fiametta looked around the disheveled bedding and her own body, which still glistened with sweat. "What do you think?" she replied.

"Who told you it was acceptable to just sneak into a man's bedroom!?! Into a man's bed!?!"

The young woman ran a hand lightly over one breast. "You didn't seem to have a problem with that a moment ago," she purred.

"Yes, well, that..." Tomas sputtered, trying to find some kind of moral high ground. Looking about, he found none. "I thought you were someone else! I thought I was having a dream!"

Fiametta nodded, "I know. You kept calling me Cecilia. That's all right; I don't mind you thinking about a different woman. After all, I was thinking about another man."

The shepherd shook his head, hoping to perhaps get some blood moving in that direction. "That's not it!" he snapped. "I don't want to think about another..." he stopped. "Wait, who in Underworld were you thinking about?"

The innkeeper's daughter sighed and laid back on the bed, reveling in her fantasy. "He was here last week, from the north. He was the one that was trying to convince Father and the other elders to ally with Duke Calonar."

Tomas stared at her with a sudden lack of lust. The rational part of his mind was now fighting against a new surge of emotion having nothing to do with lust. "Who was he?" he demanded.

Fiametta nearly writhed on the bed, lost in the memories. "A knight. He rode into town on a magnificent black warhorse, dressed in shining armor. He spoke with such power, yet he was so gentle. I tripped on the stairs and would have fallen, but he caught me and held me. His grip was so strong, so firm, but had softness too. He had quiet dignity. He never gave an order, not even to me, a lowly serving girl. When Father introduced me to him, he took my hand and lightly kissed it. Oh God, he was incredible!"

The young man rolled his eyes. "Did he have a shield?"

Fiametta nodded, still lost in the memory.

"What was the heraldry?" Tomas demanded.

"The what?" she asked dreamily.

"The picture on the front of the shield, the colors."

"I told you," she sighed, "he was a knight loyal to Duke Calonar. The shield was blue and gray."

"And the emblem on the shield?"

Fiametta sat up and shrugged. "I think it was divided in two sections, along the middle. The top part was gray and the bottom was blue. In the middle were..."

"Two crossed, four pointed diamonds, the front one silver, the back white," Tomas finished.

The girl nodded. "How did you know that?" she asked.

Tomas looked very carefully at Fiametta, no longer caring about her state of undress. "Fiametta," he said carefully, "what was the knight's name?"

"Eigenhard." she replied. "Rogan Eigenhard."

With an oath, Tomas jumped to his feet and pulled his clothing straight. With a purpose born of vengeance, the young man began gathering his few remaining possessions together in preparation to leave. With a look out the window, noticing the faint pre-dawn light, Tomas yanked the door leading to the hallway open and marched out.

From the room behind, Fiametta called out, "So does this mean you don't want to...?"

Tomas was beyond hearing or caring what that fool of a girl had to say. His only thoughts were of the man who had murdered his father. One week, he thought to himself. Just one week earlier and I would have been here at the same time he was. If I hadn't stopped so damned early each night! If I hadn't walked so damned slow! If I hadn't lost that damned horse!

Having heard some of the commotion coming from upstairs, Donato emerged from the back hallway that led to the rooms his family used. "What's all the fuss?" he demanded, holding a candle above his head. "What's the emergency?"

Tomas marched straight up to his guest, hand resting on his sword. Donato noticed the placement of his guest's hand and the look of murder in his eyes and took an involuntary step back. The young man moved to face the innkeeper, barely a breath between their two noses.

"Is there something you wanted to tell me?" Tomas demanded.

Donato put down the candle on the nearby front counter and slowly reached for a mug of water behind it. "Yes," he whispered. "Eigenhard was here, only six days ago. He stayed in the room directly across from the one you slept in. His horse stayed in my stables, and he had the very same meeting you had, at the same table, with the same men."

"You chose not to tell me because...?"

The innkeeper poured himself a small cup of water and another for Tomas. Looking into the cup, Donato answered. "For fear of what is now happening. I like you, young Master Tomas. I cannot explain why. Perhaps you remind me of myself when I was still young and opinionated. I knew the moment anyone told you about our previous guest..."

"GUEST!?!" Tomas roared.

Donato slammed the cup down on the counter. "Yes! Guest! As you so eloquently reminded us last night, Tomas, this village is, and shall remain, neutral. That means we do not, have not, and will not take sides in this conflict! You are welcome here, as is your enemy. So long as you do not bring about any violence in my establishment you are welcome to stay just as long as you like, and Eigenhard brought none. In fact, Tomas, Rogan Eigenhard was much more civil than you are being just now. Never once did he raise his voice or stand over us in judgment or demand that we act one way or the other. He came, made his Duke's offer, told us how to reply, and left."

"You liked him," Tomas shook his head in disgust.

"I found him civil, courteous, and generous. He never made any demands or even spoke a single unkind word." Donato noticed his daughter trying to sneak down the stairs and disappear into the back rooms. Turning back to Tomas he fought not to sneer. "And he did not take advantage of a young girl's infatuation."

"Which way did he go?" Tomas demanded.

"And if I tell you, what? You'll go after him? He was mounted and you are on foot. There is no chance you'll ever catch up to him. What will you do, Tomas? Chase him on foot to the ends of the earth; all the way north to the Northern Keep? What will you do?"

"Get very uncivil if you don't tell me which way Eigenhard went," he replied quietly.

It hung there, between the two men, for several moments. Finally, Donato shook his head and sighed. "East," he said. "Eigenhard went east, towards Gioconda."

Without another word, Tomas turned and left the inn, leaving the town and the people to whatever fate they would make for themselves. Several hours later, once the hills had blocked any possible glimpse of the village, the young man had a deeply troubling realization. Twice now, he had failed to save a town. Once he failed in Nunzio, storming off in a huff before seeing that the people were convinced not to lose their souls in a deal with the Black Duke, and again he failed, in the same moment, when he decided to abandon the reason for his trip to Velaross. Should he successfully pick up Eigenhard's trail in the Holy City before he told the Church what had happened to Railing, he would leave the souls of the people of Railing to their fates so as to pursue his father's murderer.

Many failures, no successes. This quest was not shaping up as Tomas had hoped it would.

Chapter 14

Tomas had been traveling for over a month… nearly two, he realized. In that time, he had long since developed a set pattern of how he spent the average day, giving himself at least an hour or two to locate a suitable campsite. After learning how close he had come to facing Rogan Eigenhard, however, he had cut down on the time he spent ensuring a comfortable night. Despite the frequent nights in which he was forced to eat more of his dwindling rations and make do without a fire for lack of finding sufficient wood, Tomas found contentment in his hatred for Eigenhard, and the focus his hatred gave him, the warmth it filled him with. Luckily, the worst of the winter chill had passed, and the warm breeze hinted at an early Spring.

This rage was dangerous, the rational part of his mind knew. Rage was what led good men to do evil things. At night, when the darkness pressed in all around him, Tomas could often imagine Alexia chastising him, warning him against the path he was on. But rage could be useful as well; rage could lead someone to seek justice. More than anything else, the young man wanted justice for the Emperor, for Railing, for Pelsemoria, and for his father. The Church often warned that there was a very fine line between justice and vengeance, but Tomas was past caring. Finally, after so many years, he was on the trail of the man most directly responsible for so much evil in Lanasia. Rogan Eigenhard would die for his crimes; whether that life would end by the blade of Tomas' father or some other means, the shepherd swore he would not rest until his father was avenged.

Again, the young man was surprised by just how much he missed the company of Alexia. There was no doubt in Tomas' mind that his Sylva friend would have had answers to all his questions, answers that would seem so sensible and simple that he would have felt foolish for not having thought of them himself. If only she were there now, to smile and point out the foolishness of the situation he got into back in that inn. She would have laughed at him without bruising his ego and tell him why it was that he had fought against the lustful girl. As it was, Tomas was alone on the road to vengeance, with only questions clouding his mind.

These very questions occupied Tomas' mind as he continued his journey. They were thoughts that, incidentally, led him out of the darkness of vengeance, if for only a few hours at a time. Eventually, it was these thoughts that still turned through the young man's mind as he left behind the rolling vineyards and grasslands of Nunzio behind, entering the broad plains and endless farmland of the Kordenel Counties.

It was while he searched one day for a suitable sight to make camp for the night while traveling through the woods that bordered Gioconda that Tomas came into view of as odd a pairing of men as he had ever seen. The younger of the two was a giant, easily a head taller than the tallest Human and covered in such a thick coat of blonde hair that it stuck out of every opening of his thick clothes but still did little to hide a powerful physique. Tomas had never before seen an Uldra; his only knowledge of that terrifying race came from books. His shoulders rose, merging into a head without benefit of a neck. He wore no armor, yet his fair complexion seeded as solid as stone, even catching the early Spring sunlight as would a mountain side. His books had often spoke of the power, the unwavering presence of the barbaric mountain-men. Now, in the actual presence of an Uldra, Tomas realized his books had done them little justice.

The lumbering behemoth seemed to shove aside the air as he moved about the small camp on impossibly thick legs. As was befitting such a monster, he was dressed in the thick black leathers and furs so favored by the barbarian Uldra. What face there was visible behind the shrub-like beard and eyebrows displayed a nose that could, quite possibly, knock down a tree with the slightest sneeze. The giant's deep black eyes, like twin pits into the deepest mineshaft, though lacking that gleam of intellect so common in the more civilized folk of the south, nonetheless easily spotted Tomas' approach.

Turning to his comrade, the Uldra grunted, "Company, Boss." Tomas would later swear that the monster's voice was so deep and powerful that the shepherd did not so much hear as feel it as the sound rolled over the young man.

"Boss," in this case, seemed to be an irritable man of late middle-age dressed in what had to be the shoddiest, most worn out wizard's robes Tomas had ever seen. The blue of the robes had long since surrendered to time and faded to gray. There were so many tears, frayed edges, haphazard mending, and even burn marks that it was a wonder the entire thing did not simply disintegrate. Since the Arcane Guild had been headquartered in Pelsemoria before the death of the Emperor, Tomas had seen more than his fair share of magical adepts. In fact, his tutors had always made a point of teaching the children how to read the marks that wizards of the Guild used to identify themselves to the citizens of the Republic. The colored inseam on the ends of the sleeves, the runes sewn into the leather belt, and the colored braid worn on the right shoulder, all these marks Tomas had learned how to read.

The shepherd looked closely but could see no Guild runes on this old man's faded robes, nor could he make out any sign of color on the frayed sleeves. Strangest of all, the old man wore no braid, the badge showing rank and years in the Order. It was, of course, possible that in the chaos following the collapse of the Republic, some of the wizards of the Guild had gone rogue. With the death of the Republic and the destruction of Pelsemoria, the Arcane Guild, though technically still the governing body for all adepts in Lanasia, had never really recovered from the loss of their Headquarters Tower. Tomas had heard the authority of the Triumvirate did not extend far from their new base in Frostfront. As a logical result, many of the spellcasters who had once been respected members of the Arcane Guild would now freely violate the ancient rules set down to control all those adept in magic.

If this being was, in fact, a rogue wizard and he meant Tomas any harm, the young man was most likely as good as dead. There was simply no way for any man, no matter how powerful, to withstand a wizard's magic. Sir Ironheart had even warned his knights that, should they ever be forced into combat with a wizard, they must "strike first, strike quick, strike sure." No doubt the Uldra bodyguard was meant to intercept any threat against his master long enough for the wizard to bring his craft to bear.

Tomas wearily put his hand near the hilt of his father's sword, his mind racing with any possible escape from this dangerous situation. If the wizard wanted a fight, then by God this shepherd swore he would give one. The wizard in question, however, was busy rummaging through an incredibly worn out traveler's bag. In fact, the old mage did not seem to even hear the announcement, much less be aware of Tomas' presence.

The Uldra tried again. "Hey, Boss!"

Still either not hearing or ignoring, the wizard put his hands on his hips in irritation and said, "Nek, have you seen that newest copy of the prophecy I made?" he asked in annoyance. "I could have sworn I put it in here."

"No, Boss, but you might want to know that..."

"I tell you," the mage interrupted, digging deeper into his bag. "I hate traveling! I can never find anything!"

"I know, Boss, but..."

Digging back into the small bag all the way up to his elbows, the rumpled wizard rambled on. "When I'm in my tower, no problems! I need something, it's right where I left it! Out here I might as well be a first year student in the Academy!"

"Boss, I really think you..."

By now up to his shoulder in the small bag, the mage snapped, "Bottomless Bag my bent wand! Impossible to find what you need to find in the blasted things! Don't know what I was thinking when I made it!"

By now Tomas had relaxed somewhat. The befuddled old man seemed to be little immediate threat.

"Boss," the Uldra rumbled.

"Don't know why I bother with these things. It's not like I need them!"

"Boss," said with a little heat.

"That young man could be here any time now, and I need to know what to expect!"

"Boss!"

"How am I supposed to steer this kid in the proper direction when I don't know the direction?"

"Boss!!" By now the leaves were shaking with the power of the brutish Uldra's voice.

Giving up on the sack, the spell thrower shook his head and said, "Well, I guess I'll just have to improvise. It's not like I haven't done that often enough to..."

"BOSS!!!" Birds for miles in all directions took terrified flight at the explosion of sound.

Whirling around, the wizard raised a finger to the Uldra. "Don't you take that tone with me you overgrown ox! I can hear perfectly fine! Don't forget that I'm in charge of this…" suddenly spotting Tomas, the wizard smiled and gestured him closer.

"Excuse me," Tomas said, consciously keeping a distance. "I didn't mean to interrupt; I just hoped to share your fire for the night."

"Not at all, not at all," he replied warmly. "Nek, why didn't you tell me he was here?"

Nek rolled his eyes. "Sorry, Boss." he sighed.

"No excuse. None at all." Turning back to Tomas, the wizard began a detailed inspection of the young man, from about three inches away from his face. The old wizard's bright green eyes seemed to take in every bit of Tomas, from his hair to his shoes. "Hum; indeed; oh no, this just won't do. How am I supposed to work with this?" He paused then, his gaze locked on Alexia's pin, the closed golden rose resting on Tomas' collar. The wizard let his eyes slide up, into Tomas' own, and his gaze narrowed. His head then snapped sharpy back, as though he had been slapped.

Confused beyond all measure of the word, Tomas replied, "Uh, sorry."

Rubbing the side of his face, the old man muttered "Sneaky bitch." He sighed then, and shook his head. "So, it finally happened." He looked again at Tomas' eyes, though with less intensity. "And she just had to have her way, one last time."

Desperate to escape, Tomas tried backing away very slowly, careful not to make direct eye contact with the old man. "Well gentlemen," he said carefully, "I would really like to continue this interesting conversation, but there's still some daylight left so I'll just be leaving."

"Well," the strange old wizard said, "I guess we're doing it the other way. Nek, if you would."

Moving with a surprising burst of speed, the giant intercepted Tomas almost instantly and gently, but firmly helped him find a seat near the fire.

"Look, I don't want any trouble," Tomas said in anger, "but I've got better things to do than sit here and listen to the ramblings of a madman and his pet giant. Now, if you'll excuse me." Tomas rose to leave.

Nek helped him back to his seat.

"Dammit! Keep your hands off me, you great lummox!"

Again, Tomas rose and again, Nek helped him to his seat.

"That does it!" he roared.

As Tomas' hand went to his sword hilt, the wizard calmly said, "Tell me, Tomas, are you in that great a hurry to find Rogan Eigenhard?"

"I'm not looking for Eigenhard! I'm looking for Cyras Darkholm!" he cried in frustration. Doing a double take Tomas said, "Wait, how did you know my name?"

Ignoring the question, the old man asked, "Cyras Darkholm? What do you want with Cyras?"

"… I'm going to ask him a question."

"What question?" the mage asked with great interest, his bright green eyes getting even brighter.

"I really don't see how that's any business of yours."

"Try me," he smiled.

"Alright, I plan to ask Cyras how the Black Duke can be defeated."

"Cylan Calonar?" he asked surprised. The old man shook his head with a smile. "Sorry Tomas, but Cyras won't do a thing about Calonar."

"You're sure about that?"

"Of course."

"And how can you be so sure?" Tomas demanded.

The old mage laughed, "Because I'm Cyras Darkholm."

Tomas stared in open-mouthed shock at the Trickster-Mage. Nek brought over a drinking horn. "You'll need this," he said.

The young man wordlessly took the horn and raised it to his lips. A thick, viscous slime touched his tongue, causing Tomas to gag. He looked to the Uldra, struggling to find his breath. Nek just smiled and said, "The good stuff."

Leaving Tomas to enjoy the Uldra brew, Nek then walked over to the small cooking fire that had a pot resting near it. Drawing three plates from a pack lying on the ground, the giant prepared the meal and handed a plate to Cyras before putting one on a log near Tomas and settling down himself. "Just for the sake of argument," Tomas said, after clearing his throat several times, "what makes you think you're Darkholm?"

Cyras looked up from the wooden plate that held his dinner, a simple stew that smelled delicious, and replied, "Well, that is the name my mother gave me shortly after I was born."

Sensing a headache approaching, Tomas rubbed his temples. "No, I mean, what proof do you have that you are Cyras Darkholm?"

"Would you like a demonstration?" he asked maliciously.

Quickly raising his hands up Tomas yelled, "No! No, that's alright; I'll take your word for it."

"Good, in that case we can get to more serious matters." Handing his plate to Nek, who took that and the other dinnerware to a nearby creek, the possible Cyras reached into a small case at his belt, unrolled a crisp new scroll, and began to read to himself.

"What's that?" Tomas inquired.

Without looking up, the Trickster-Mage replied, "A copy of Darrel's Prophecy."

Confused beyond all measure, Tomas insisted, "Didn't you say earlier that your copy of the prophecy was in your bag?"

"What would it be doing in that sack?" he replied irritably. "I have a perfectly good scroll case on my belt." Cyras looked up from the scroll and said, "Very well, then. Your part in the Prophecy is very complex, Tomas. You're mentioned as the Final Host, a title I'm still decoding. This much I do know; it's necessary for you to travel to the Northern Keep."

"What? Why? What?"

"Do you plan to interrupt me continuously," he angrily replied, "or will you just choose the most irritating moments?"

"Sorry."

Cyras irritably looked back down to his scroll and read from it. "'Within the dozen years following the destruction of the Capital shall the Betrayer marshal his forces and the Final Host be anointed. Journey then shall the Final Host in the company of the Heir to the Northern Keep, there to learn his trade. Upon the night the False Light is conceived shall the Betrayer strike with wind and ice, and the quest to the Western Empire shall begin. In this quest, through the actions of the Heir and the Final Host, shall one Scion be destroyed, that one to be chosen by the Final Host. Only then may the Inversion be revealed and the way opened for the Dark Empress' return.'"

Cyras looked up at Tomas, believing that any possible doubts would have been allayed. Seeing Tomas' look of utter, confusion though, the Trickster-Mage asked, "What, don't you understand?"

"Understand what!?!" the young man snapped. "That was pure gibberish! It didn't make any sense at all!"

Cyras sighed, shaking his head. The Trickster-Mage seemed utterly disappointed in Tomas. "For someone supposedly educated, who is supposed to be so important over the next few years, you certainly aren't very bright." The Trickster Mage looked intently at Tomas. "Have you heard anyone in history referred to as 'The Dark Empress?'"

"Of course," Tomas shrugged, "Kelinva, Dark Empress of the Xeshlin…" The Shepherd blinked. "Wait, you said something about the Dark Empress returning."

Cyras nodded and smiled. "Ah, the sight of a young mind being opened. Yes, Tomas. The final line in that passage warns of the Dark Empress, Kelinva's return."

Tomas stopped, a memory surging forward. "Storm clouds to the south… Xeshlin raiding again…" he muttered, remembering Alexia's warning and the attacks on the survivors of Pelsemoria.

Cyras said nothing. He just waited.

"The Xeshlin are returning." This was not a question. The shepherd's very soul recoiled at the though. "Another invasion, another horror."

"And this time," the Trickster Mage confirmed, "no Heroes of Fate to stop them. Which makes your quest to the Western Empire so important."

"Look, you don't have to be insulting; I'm just saying this 'prophecy' of yours is too vague to understand. There are just a few indirect claims that could apply to nearly anyone."

"Of course it's vague. All true prophecies are vague. If they were clear and easy to understand, then people could just read it and know what will happen."

"Isn't that the point? Isn't a prophecy supposed to tell you what will happen?" Tomas asked, rubbing his head again.

"Of course not!" Cyras replied in surprised. "Where did you get that idea?"

"Then what is the point of a prophecy?"

Cyras shrugged. "To reveal truth, not facts."

The young man blinked. "That's ridiculous."

Cyras raised his finger in triumph. "Exactly!"

Tomas looked over at Nek and asked, "Is he serious?"

Nek shrugged, "You never know."

The young man put his face in his hands, praying silently for the world to stop spinning. "I just don't understand," he said. "I feel like an imbecile trying to understand long division."

Cyras moved over and patted Tomas on the shoulder. "Well, it's good you can admit that. True wisdom only begins once you can admit to your own stupidity. You're on your way, lad!"

Looking up with dead eyes at Cyras, Tomas said, "You know it's funny. Somehow that doesn't make me feel any better at all."

"Good! Outstanding!"

With a confused look on his face, Tomas asked, "Are you even listening to me?"

Standing up, Cyras moved to this bedroll. "Well, it's starting to get dark, best get some sleep."

"I'm not tired."

"Tomorrow we'll see about getting you to the Keep."

"I don't want to go to the Keep."

"Feel free to borrow the extra bedroll."

"My hair is on fire."

"Don't worry about the watch. Nek will take care of that."

"I find myself oddly attracted to you."

"Pleasant dreams."

Once the Trickster-Mage had rolled into his blankets, Nek moved over to Tomas and dropped an extra set of blankets in his lap.

"Is he always like that?" Tomas asked.

Nek smiled. "No. Most times he doesn't talk to people at all. Feel honored."

"I feel confused." The shepherd shook his head and looked up at the emerging stars.

The Uldra patted Tomas on the shoulder. "Do yourself a favor," he rumbled. "Don't try to figure out what's happening right now. Don't try to think of a way to talk the Boss out of his decisions, and don't try to run away. All three lead to the same thing."

Tomas looked far up. "What's that?" he demanded.

Nek dropped onto his own bedding. "You wake up with a headache."

Chapter 15

In the morning, Tomas tried once again, despite Nek's advice, to convince Cyras that he had no business going north. "So Cyras," he began as he saw the old wizard beginning to rouse from his blankets. "What kind of wizard are you?" The shepherd thought it best to broach the subject delicately, engaging the troubled spell-caster in light conversation before moving to the heart of the matter.

The old man yawned and stretched, looking about as if having trouble remembering how he had gotten there. He looked for a few moments at Tomas then nodded, obviously once again clear on his location. "What?" he asked.

"Your school of magic," the young man said. Tomas pointed towards the lack of coloring on the inseam of Cyras' tattered robe. "You aren't wearing the traditional marks of a Guild wizard. I was just wondering what kind of wizard you are."

"My own," the wizard answered.

"I don't understand."

"That's fairly obvious."

"What do you mean your own? Your own what?"

"What did you ask?"

"I asked you what school of magic you study, what kind of wizard you are."

Cyras nodded as he stood. "And my answer?"

"Are you saying that you're your own kind of wizard?"

"If you knew the answer, why did you ask the question?"

Tomas blinked. "I didn't know. I still don't."

"You just said the answer."

There must be many accidents by people around Cyras Darkholm, Tomas decided. The feeling of dizziness just does not stop. "Cyras, I asked you and that was your answer."

"So, if I answered your question, what's the problem?"

"Your answer doesn't make sense!"

"Neither does your question."

The young man actually screamed in frustration. "Fine, Cyras. You win. My question makes no sense."

"You certainly enjoy repeating me, don't you," the old man noted as he sat down against a tree.

"I'm just curious what school of magic you study, you damned senile old bastard!!"

"Mostly divination, but I'm fairly competent in all schools."

Tomas stopped. "Oh," he said, feeling foolish. "So, does that mean that you're an aquamancer, a water mage?"

"No."

"But you just said that you mostly study divination. Every diviner I've ever met was an aquamancer."

"I never said I was a diviner."

The shepherd thought he was beginning to understand just how it was that one must frame a question for the Trickster Mage. He was actually warming up to the conversation. "Alright," he said, rubbing his hands together. "You want to play this game, I'll play."

Cyras snored.

"Wake up!!" Tomas roared.

Cyras opened one eye in irritation. "Now what?" he demanded.

"The school of water is the one of intuitive thought, correct?"

"Yes," the old man sighed, trying to settle himself in for a nap.

"Then are you a master of water magic?"

"Yes, of course."

"So, you're an aquamancer."

"No, I'm not."

Tomas nearly shook in rage. "But you just said that you've mastered the school of water! A wizard can only master one school right?"

"What gave you that idea?"

"That's the rules!"

Cyras apparently thought that was funny since he started laughing. "Who made these rules?" he finally said through his laughter.

"The Arcane Guild," Tomas replied.

"And what made you think I was a member of the Guild?"

"Then you aren't sanctioned by the Guild?" the young man asked. "You're a rogue?"

"No, I have Guild sanctioning."

"You just said you didn't!"

"No, I didn't."

"Why are you being so difficult?" the young man demanded. "Do you enjoy driving people insane?!?"

"It does pass the time."

"What kind of evil old bastard are you?"

"Why is it you ask every possible question except the one you really want answered?"

The young man glanced about nervously. "What does that mean?"

"You planned to make some pointless conversation with me until you worked up the nerve to ask me for permission not to go to the Northern Keep."

"I planned no such thing," Tomas lied. "I was just making conversation."

The Trickster-Mage rolled his eyes. "I suppose you'll continue to pester me until I answer all these pointless questions of yours."

"What's so pointless about trying to get to know a little more about you?"

"Why would you want to?"

"You're one of the most famous people in history! You've seen more than most people even dream of. You're the most powerful adept in the world."

"Do you know every adept in the world?"

"What? Of course not!"

"Then how do you know I'm the most powerful?"

"That's what the stories all say."

"Do you believe everything you read?"

"I suppose," Tomas replied.

Cyras quickly grabbed a piece of parchment and scribbled a message on it with a quill pen he retrieved from inside his sleeve. Handing the message over to Tomas, the old man settled back down against a tree and closed his eyes. Looking down at the note, the shepherd could only laugh. It read, "You should leave him alone and let him take a nap." For whatever reason, Tomas stood and left Cyras in peace, somehow knowing that he would only learn what the Trickster-Mage wanted him to know.

"Does he ever listen to anyone?" the young man asked of Nek as the brute cleaned the dishes from the morning meal that his master had demanded. "Does he ever really answer anyone's questions?"

The Uldra paused in his departure preparations, thinking for a moment. "He listens to everyone. Of course, nobody has ever changed his mind, but he listens. And he did answer your question; you just didn't understand what he was telling you."

"Do you understand what he was saying?"

"No, but then, I wasn't the one he was talking to."

"Well, I don't have the slightest idea what he was saying."

"Maybe you weren't listening properly."

"What's the point of listening to someone that is going out of his way to be vague?"

The giant shrugged. "He might say something funny."

"I think you've been around Cyras too long."

"It has been a long time."

Tomas sat down on a log. "How long?" he asked.

Nek stopped and stared off into the distance. He thought for a very long time before answering. "I don't remember. Me and the Boss have been moving ever since he showed up in my village, saying he needed some muscle."

"You don't even talk with much of an accent anymore," he noted. "Where's your village?"

"In the valley of *Tsits*. It's about a month's journey west from Draila."

Tomas snorted. "You're a long way from home."

The giant shrugged.

"Why help him?"

"You youngsters always take a long time to figure out the truth."

"What's the truth?"

"Happiness is knowing who you serve, and why."

"Well, you know who you serve, but why?" the shepherd demanded.

Again, Nek shrugged. "Because he needs me."

"Well, I don't serve anybody," Tomas declared.

"Are you happy?"

"Not right now."

"Maybe you should find somebody that needs you."

"Like a wife?"

The Uldra shook his head. "Like somebody that needs you."

"Well, if you've been with him for so long, then do you know what kind of wizard Cyras is?"

"He already told you. He's his own kind of wizard."

"I still don't understand."

"You think of wizards the way the Guild has told you to think. Just like you think about non-Humans the way the Church has told you and the way you think of the Boss the way history told you."

"So how should I think of him?"

"However *you* think you should think."

Tomas shook his head. "I just want to know which school of magic he belongs to. Which color would he wear?"

Nek finished putting the dishes away and rubbed his massive chin in thought. "Well, by Guild law, he could wear any color."

"What do you mean?"

"Well, he's mastered every school and the Guild gave him the rank of Archmage, so I suppose if he wanted, he could wear any color he likes."

"How in the world did he manage to master all the schools? I was always taught that when you start learning one, you couldn't learn others."

Nek shrugged. "He can do just about anything he sets his mind to."

They were both quiet as Nek finished his cleaning. Finally, Tomas stood and sighed. "Is there any way I could talk Cyras out of this?" the shepherd asked.

Nek gave the young man a look that spoke volumes.

"What if I just say no and leave?"

"Do you think that would stop him?"

"I'm stuck with this aren't I?"

Nek nodded, saddling Cyras' horse. Stopping suddenly, Nek's eyes went wide, scanning the entire grove.

Tomas also looked about the trees, his hand going to his sword hilt. "What is it?" he asked.

"Druug," he hissed.

"What!?! Where?" At the Uldra's announcement, the young shepherd's pulse quickened to such a pace that he feared his heart would explode from his chest.

"In the trees, three of them."

"Do you have a weapon?"

"Don't need any," Nek strode forward, flexing his hands in anticipation.

Tomas, obviously the less experienced of the pair, ran over to Cyras. "Cyras!" he yelled, shaking the old man's slumbering form.

Hearing Nek battling the Druug, Tomas grabbed Cyras by the shoulders and shook him violently, screaming, "Cyras!"

Finally coming awake, the wizard groggily looked around. "Huh? What? Is it time to go? Oh good."

"No Cyras!" Tomas shouted, his desperation growing as the sounds of the fight drew closer. "Nek is fighting some Druug! You've got to help him!"

"Alright, alright. Just calm down," he said, rummaging through the pouches at his belt. "Now, where did I put that sulfur?"

Giving the Trickster-Mage up as a lost cause, Tomas turned to rush to Nek's aid as, with a thunderous roar and a sound akin to a boulder being split, Nek's unconscious form was hurled out of the patch of trees he had entered, toppling several in the process. As Tomas watched, open-mouthed in near terror, the Druug finally revealed themselves. Standing even taller than Nek and smelling like an open cesspool, all three of the grey-skins carried the crudest of clubs, their huge muscles displaying ample evidence of the extreme damage they could inflict. Tomas could easily make out the army of lice that moved about on each of the coarse-haired monsters. Over-developed lower jaws housed tusks dripping with drool. The yellow eyes of the monsters did not show even the faintest glimmer of intelligence, only a burning hunger and seething hatred. Three of the beasts emerged from the tree line, any one of which was easily capable of breaking Tomas in half with one blow. Now, all three looked at him.

A deep rumble the shepherd thought could be either a growl of the throat or a growl of the stomach rolled through the all too small distance separating Tomas from the Druug. The hair on the back of the young man's neck stood straight up at the sound, primal fear tearing through his soul as every instinct told him to run, to save himself from these awful predators. Even as Tomas was on the verge of throwing down his sword and fleeing, each of the monsters began throwing looks over at the bumbling Cyras. It seemed as though to Tomas he could almost hear the silent argument raging in the animalistic minds of the towering monsters. They had already defeated a strong foe. Their hunger for violence had been sated. Now they found two types of prey before them. Should they first kill and devour the younger and seemingly stronger of the two, enjoying one last fight before gorging on blood, flesh, and fear? Or should they perhaps let go this younger meal and enjoy the older, easier kill?

Grimly stepping between the trio of Druug and Cyras, Tomas, with his father's blade held at the ready in his hands, resigned himself to his fate. Had he been alone, there would be no doubt that he would have taken the advice of Mariano and fled. But something deep within the young man's soul, something even more primal than the desire for self-preservation, a new instinct took over. So long as Tomas Fidelis drew breath, he swore silently if only to himself, no harm would befall a weak old man. "Now would be a really good time for that demonstration you offered last night!" he urgently called over his shoulder.

"Nearly there," the befuddled old wizard announced.

The three Druug, sensing the resolve in Tomas, hunched down slightly at the shoulders and made ready. "Anytime now, Cyras!" Tomas cried.

"One minute, one minute," the Trickster-Mage replied angrily.

"We don't have it!" he nearly screamed as the green-skins each lowered themselves to one hand and tensed, ready to pounce. The stink of the brutes brought tears to the shepherd's eyes, and he trembled as death touched him on the shoulder.

"You know," Cyras said calmly, "patience *is* a virtue."

Sighing with resignation, Tomas squared off with the largest as it raised its trunk-sized club above its head and charged, leaping through the air in massive strides. So this is it, the young man thought to himself; this is how I go out, using my father's sword to fight three monsters, dying to defend a senile wizard. Oh, well. Roaring what he hoped was a decent battle cry, the shepherd raised his sword and ran forward. If he must die, then he would go down swinging.

Just as Tomas and his grey-skinned adversaries were about to collide, the young man and misfigured beasts all paused as they felt the ground shake beneath them. Turning in unison, both Human and Druug were stunned as a mounted warrior exploded from the trees, wearing a leather vest of splintmail and wielding a one-handed sword, its hilt and crosspiece unadorned. The warrior wielded it with one hand, the other keeping a tight grip on the reigns of his horse, and held the blade at the ready with apparent ease and skill. The knight wore no surcoat, and his shield was strapped to his saddle, instead of on his arm, so Tomas could make out no colors or heraldry. He wore no helmet, but instead had a leather headband in the style of a northlander with an Uldra rune stamped on the center to hold back his flowing red hair. The knight's horse was black, with a long black mane and tail, and was well-muscled and obviously powerful.

The warhorse thundered towards the trolls as the warrior roared a battle cry that even the monsters found intimidating. Mounted as he was upon what had to be the meanest-looking warhorse Tomas had ever heard of, the knight closed on his targets faster than a man could see. Stabbing at the first Druug with a mighty attack, the knight drove his short blade through the neck of the first monster. He then reared his charger in once the mount had passed the mortally-wounded grey-skin, ripping his sword free and sending the beast to the ground in a flood of ichorus blood. The great warhorse reared up and, using that leverage, slammed his forelegs back into the earth, raising his hindquarters and kicking the wounded Druug with such force that the monster's back snapped with a loud crack and was sent flying into the nearby creek.

The two remaining Druug raised their clubs and, roaring in fury, attacked. The knight, not pausing for even an instant, drove his hulking mount directly at the charging beasts. Skillfully parrying a clumsy swing from the left grey-skin, the knight retaliated by stabbing at the monster's throat, inflicting a vicious wound that brought a bloody flood of black ichor from its mouth as it collapsed dead. Even as his rider dispatched the one, the warhorse stopped the other by the simple means of ramming his head into the monster's gut, forcing the air from its lungs. Rendered helpless and vulnerable, the Druug could only gape as the warhorse reared again, kicking with his forelegs and caving the beast's head in.

With all the monsters destroyed, the warhorse reared flamboyantly, kicking his legs in a victory dance as the northland knight roared, "Dammit Stick, calm down! You almost threw me!" Prancing around and neighing his eagerness to continue the all too brief battle, Stick oriented on Tomas and snorted, making the sound as a man would muttering a threat and an insult. "Don't think that's a Druug, Stick," the warrior noted while dismounting. "You know, it's a shame you can't fight as well as you can dance."

Stick just flicked his ears in annoyance and dismissal of his "master."

"Alright!" Cyras suddenly said, "I'm ready." Looking around the carnage he asked, "What happened to the Druug?"

"Punctual as always, I see," the northlander noted with only the slightest hint of sarcasm in his voice. The warrior grabbed a rag from one of his saddlebags and wiped the ichorus Druug blood from his one-handed sword before sheathing it in the scabbard belted to his waist. He seemed to Tomas to be nearly glowing with satisfaction after the fight, his eyes dancing and a slight grin decorating his unshaven face as he wiped the sweat from his brow. He was solidly built, though by no means overly muscular, and he had a light step that belied the weight of his armor. He walked with a stride full of confidence but somehow no arrogance, crossing the small distance separating himself and Cyras and taking the old wizard's hand in greeting.

Cyras looked at him sternly. "You're late," he grumbled, throwing the mixture in his left hand over his shoulder and detonating a tree with a thunderous explosion of blue fire.

"Didn't realize I was on a schedule," the knight replied evenly, the destruction obviously coming as no surprise.

"You should know full well that you're due back at the Keep before next winter."

Rolling his eyes, the Northland knight sighed, "How would I know that?"

"Is says so right here in the Prophecy!" Cyras replied, waving the scroll.

"You mean the prophecy you won't let anyone else see?" The warrior walked back to his horse and removed his leather gauntlets, rubbing his hands and pulling a waterskin from one of his bags; a flash of light from the knight's hand briefly drew Tomas' attention to the small signet ring the northlander wore. With a glance to the waiting warhorse, Tomas noted that there was another blade strapped behind the warrior's shield, this one a longsword. The second weapon looked much like the first, with an unadorned cruciform hilt and a simple steel pommel.

"Exactly!" the wizard snapped.

Shaking his head, the knight pulled a waterskin from his saddle and splashed some water on his face. "Cyras, did it ever occur to you that you might get a much more positive reaction out of people if you just give them a better idea of what is going on and what you want from them?"

"Did it ever occur to you that since I'm the only one with access to the Prophecy, maybe you and that daughter of mine should occasionally trust me?" the Trickster-Mage retorted.

Confused to the point of physical illness, Tomas interrupted the two, trying to head off a futile argument. "Excuse me!" he yelled, startling the other two, "but shouldn't someone take a look at Nek? He got hit pretty hard."

"I wouldn't worry," Cyras said without looking at his henchman. "Nek is pretty hard to kill." Indeed, even as Cyras spoke, Nek stirred from the collection of lumber he was buried under, only a small bruise on his left eye the evidence of his being hit with enough force to knock down a stone wall. The Uldra nodded a greeting towards the northland warrior before moving to check on his horses.

"What about you?" the knight asked Tomas, looking him over. "Any wounds?"

"No," Tomas answered, sheathing his sword, "You took care of them before they got close to me."

The knight looked at the young man's blade as Tomas put it away. "Interesting choice in weaponry," he noted politely. "Although, to be honest, can't remember the last time I saw someone outside of the Legions using one." He glanced at the shepherd's shoulder, which was left bare by the simple sleeveless tunic he wore. "And you don't have the mark of the Legions."

"It was my father's."

The knight nodded in understanding. "Your father served?"

"For many years. He willed it to me before he died."

"Sorry."

The young shepherd shrugged. "It was many years ago."

"That was a brave thing you did, defending Cyras."

Tomas blushed, embarrassed at the praise from an obviously capable warrior. "It was nothing," he said.

The knight drew his own blade, checking it for any damage from the battle before sheathing it again. "Actually," he said, "it really is rare in these days for a man to step into certain death for someone else, especially for someone as notorious as Cyras Darkholm."

"You two know each other?" the shepherd guessed.

"Much better than I'd like," he laughed. "How long have you two known each other?"

"I've known of Tomas for years," the Trickster-Mage declared.

"Actually, we just met yesterday," Tomas corrected.

The wizard rolled his eyes. "That doesn't mean I haven't known you for years."

"You just met him and you were willing to die for him?" the knight asked, clearly impressed. "You've got a rare kind of bravery, kid, or maybe an even rarer kind of stupidity."

Tomas' embarrassment grew to nearly intolerable heights. None of his peers or teachers ever gave him such minor, yet earnest praise. Let alone mixed with such an immediate sense of camaraderie.

"What's your name kid? How did you come to be traveling with Cyras?"

"His name is Tomas Fidelis," Cyras said, packing his things back up in preparation for departure. "He's your new squire."

"Excuse me?" the knight and Tomas said in unison.

"I will tolerate no argument in this," the Trickster-Mage snapped. "Critical events will be put into motion very soon, and I need you both ready for what lies ahead."

"Cyras," the northlander said in exasperation, "for once, would you please drop the cryptic nonsense and just tell me flat out what in Underworld is going on!?!"

"No."

"No!?! What do you mean no?"

"You should know by now that I have reasons for everything I do, and I always get my way in the end so you might as well accept my decisions."

"Excuse me, Cyras," Tomas interrupted, "but I have no intention of being anyone's squire. I have a quest of my own you know. No offense." This last said to the knight.

"None taken," he replied. "Believe me; I know how frustrating it is dealing with Cyras." The knight turned back to the old wizard. "Besides, I'm in the middle of a... diplomatic trip. I'm due in Velaross next month, and don't have time for another of your wild errands."

"I don't even know why I'm bothering to stand here and argue," Tomas said. "Sir Knight, I wish you well; Nek, have a nice life. Cyras... seek help." As the shepherd was turning to leave, Darkholm's face split into malicious grin.

"Why, Tomas," the Trickster-Mage said in an overly friendly voice. "You want so badly to face Rogan Eigenhard, why would you just walk away from him?"

Realization dawning on Tomas' face, he turned very slowly and faced the knight, then moved to the far side of the warhorse, Stick, and took a good, long look at the heraldry on the shield.

"What are you talking about now, Cyras?" the knight demanded.

Cyras only smiled, clearly reveling in anticipation.

Speaking very slowly and evenly, Tomas asked. "What is your name, northlander?"

Looking, if possible, even more confused, the knight answered, "Rogan Eigenhard, of House Calonar." Tomas looked up, the shield bore a field divided in the middle, gray on top, blue on the bottom, with two four-pointed diamonds in the center, the front one silver, the rear, white, both surrounded by a golden circle. It was the heraldry of House Calonar.

Chapter 16

Tomas launched himself at Eigenhard, screaming obscenities and swinging his father's sword. The mercenary drew his own sword, easily countering the shepherd's frenzied attacks. The Northlander had little difficulty in parrying each clumsy swing, disarming Tomas without causing any more harm than a twisted wrist. Unfortunately, losing his sword so easily only infuriated the young man even further, forcing him to attack with his bare hands. Eigenhard, clearly more experience, easily defended himself without having to resort to a killing blow. The shepherd's attacks were crude, and the mercenary had little trouble blocking them, but he was obviously losing patience. Throwing his left shoulder into Tomas' gut, Eigenhard grabbed his opponent's leg with his free hand and lifted, flipping him over and sending him cursing and rolling into the dirt. With quick movements, the mercenary removed his sword belt and tossed the belt and scabbard aside.

Regaining his breath after much gasping and clearing his dizziness as quickly as he could, Tomas leapt again at Eigenhard, his hands going for the knight's throat. The warrior knocked both hands away and struck with lightning speed, again knocking out his breath. Following up, he grabbed the shepherd's arm and twisted it around, spinning around behind his back, pinning the arm.

"Cyras!" Eigenhard cried over screams of 'Assassin! Terrorist! Murderer!' "Cyras! Stop this kid before he forces me to do something!"

Tomas put his right foot back between the mercenary's and spun out of the arm-lock, quickly following up with a punch just below the northman's splintmail vest. As Eigenhard back-peddled to get some room, fighting to regain his breath, the shepherd lunged forward again, driving a fist into his enemy's face. The sudden pain shocked them both, and, acting purely on instinct, Eigenhard spun on his heel and drove his elbow in to Tomas' back, then reached back with the same arm, grabbed his neck, and heaved, sending his opponent rolling again over his shoulder and across the ground. "Dammit, Cyras!" the northman roared. "Do something!"

Without warning, even in the midst of preparing to launch yet another attack, Tomas stopped dead in place, held as though in amber. He looked about with his eyes and desperately tried to make his body obey, but remained frozen in place. Tomas could breathe, but not speak. His blood pulsed and his mind raced, but his body was frozen.

"Took you long enough," Eigenhard panted at Cyras. The knight gently put his hand to his nose and winced at the pain, clearly more annoyed at having let the blow land than the pain.

"It wasn't me," the Trickster Mage noted. Cyras walked over and looked intently at Tomas, though seemed to keep a careful distance. "I suppose… Fate intervened. As she often has." He gestured Nek back from where the giant had moved to take Tomas to the ground. "Nek wouldn't have allowed that to proceed much longer anyway," the Trickster-Mage said. "He disapproves of casual violence."

"You call that casual violence?" Eigenhard demanded, checking his nose for blood. "Wait, if you didn't freeze the kid, then who…?"

"Of course it was causal," Cyras replied, clearly ignoring an unwanted line of conversation. "You could have killed Tomas at any time, so there was no real danger."

"You have got to be the most cold-hearted son of a bitch who's ever walked the face of Arayel."

"Thank you," the Trickster Mage replied humbly.

Shaking his head and turning back to Tomas, Eigenhard's face took on a sad continence. "Let me guess," the knight said sadly, "this kid's from somewhere around Pelsemoria."

"The capital itself," Cyras confirmed.

Looking into Tomas' eyes and seeing the fire of pure hatred, Eigenhard turned back to the Trickster-Mage. "And he's lived in misery the last ten years hearing my name as the cause."

"As a matter of fact, he lost his father during the attack on the Emperor and the Elector Council. You remember his father, don't you? He was that Praetorian who Tienel Greysoul cursed."

"I remember," The knight replied grimly. "God, he's that man's son?"

"Would you like to know what he saw his mother do the night you and Kyla were first intimate?"

"I can imagine," Eigenhard sighed, rubbing his eyes in apparent shame. "Said he was on a quest. I assume it's to kill me?"

"Oh no," Cyras laughed. "His quest was to find me."

"Why would anyone want to find you?" Eigenhard asked flatly.

"The pleasure of my company, perhaps?"

Eigenhard threw the Trickster-Mage a look and said, "Yeah, I'm having a lot of trouble believing that."

"You've let my daughter's opinions influence you for far too long, you know."

"The point, Cyras! Why was this kid trying to find you? What's he doing here? For that matter, what're *you* doing here? Now?" The mercenary paused. "And what did that?" he asked with a jerk of the head toward the still-frozen Tomas.

"He wants me to help him defeat the Black Duke," Cyras replied casually.

Eigenhard looked right at the Trickster-Mage. "Why am I having so much trouble assuming you said no?" he asked.

"Probably because I didn't."

Taken aback the knight said, "Cyras, Calonar is your best friend! Are you trying to tell me you promised to help this kid!?!" Eigenhard demanded.

"That's right."

"Are you insane!?!"

Cyras shrugged, "Possibly."

"You're going to help this kid overthrow Calonar?"

"Of course not."

Shaking his head as if hit again, Eigenhard roared, "You just said you would!"

"No I didn't," the Trickster-Mage said calmly.

"Dammit Cyras! Will you give me a straight answer!?!"

"Probably not."

Eigenhard leaned in close to Cyras. "You know I *could* kill you," he muttered.

"No, you couldn't," he countered.

"Are you going to tell me what's going on?" Eigenhard asked evenly, but then stopped. "Strike that, are you going to tell me what I have to do?"

"Eventually."

"What would you do if I just bit you on the face?"

"React badly."

Hanging his head, shoulders slumped in defeat, Eigenhard sighed, "I give up."

"Good, I love winning."

"Just like your daughter."

"I've tried telling her we have much more in common than she wants to admit."

"Will you tell me what can?" Eigenhard nearly begged.

"Certainly," Cyras agreed amiably.

"Then please do so."

Cyras pulled a wine flask from his belt and took a long drink, then offered it to Eigenhard. Seeing that the Trickster-Mage was preparing to be cryptic, the knight took a long drink. Handing the wine flask back to Cyras, who tied it back on his belt, Eigenhard said, "I believe you were getting to the point."

"There is a major conflict coming Rogan, one that will threaten all Lanasia, perhaps even Arayel itself. A great many forces are in motion, including Ramalech itself. You will play a critical role in what is to come." The Trickster-Mage gave Eigenhard and even look. "I assume my daughter's husband has received reports of the Xeshlin's activity?"

The mercenary nodded.

"A prelude." Cyras paused, narrowing his eyes. "Or, perhaps, you should understand it as a search, a probe."

"What are they probing for?"

"Kelinva."

Eigenhard stopped, so stunned by the news as to nearly be as frozen as Tomas. Then he asked, "The Dark Empress has returned."

"In a manner." Cyras moved to a large rock and sat. "The Coven that has ruled the Xeshlin since their failed Invasion has begun seeing signs and having visions. As," he rolled his eyes, "amateurish as their divinations are, even they couldn't miss what's coming."

"The Dark Empress returns," Eigenhard guessed.

The Trickster Mage nodded. "All of Davenor is being mobilized. The Coven has searched their continent, examined every girl-child born in the last two centuries."

"Kelinva isn't there?"

Cyras shook his head. "Upon the death of her mortal body, Kelinva used her Soul Magic to reincarnate, but something… intervened." This last, the Trickster Mage said with a wicked glint in his eyes. "The Dark Empress intended to be reborn and almost immediately reclaim her rule of the Xeshlin in the name of her master, Ramalech. Instead of being reborn as a Xeshlin girl-child, though, Kelinva's soul was… let's call it: rerouted."

"Where?"

"Where it needs to be."

"Can you… will you get any more specific?"

"I'm afraid not, to both questions."

Looking over at the still frozen Tomas, who was obviously listening to every word despite his rage, Eigenhard sighed. "What about him?"

Cyras glanced at Tomas. "Darrell's Prophecy makes brief mention of him in connection to a critical series of events. He will join you in your travels for a time, help you with what's to come."

"Cyras," Eigenhard said wearily, "this kid has been raised on stories of the evil of House Calonar. How can I take him north? He'll lose his mind."

"Perhaps, but regardless of your reservations or his, Rogan, Tomas Fidelis will be traveling with you, and you must return home, immediately."

"And what's to keep him from killing me in my sleep?" Eigenhard demanded.

"I will emplace a geis, ensuring he will be unable to physically harm you or leave your immediate area," Cyras said in a consoling manner. "Don't worry; the big mean teenager won't hurt you."

"What am I supposed to do with him? Take him on a nature walk!?!"

"As I already said, return to the Keep. Introduce Tomas around, let him meet Calonar. After the Harvest Festival, the two of you will go to Tordenia and meet with Emir Balshazzar."

"Balshazzar? Cyras, he's led a war against House Calonar for ten years! He's hated the King even longer."

"Meet with him Rogan, see what he's been up to."

"And then?" the knight demanded.

"You'll know what to do then," the Trickster-Mage assured him.

"What will *you* be doing while I'm running all over Lanasia?"

The Trickster-Mage turned away from Eigenhard, looking into the sky with the first somber expression on his face the knight could ever remember seeing. Tomas recalled Alexia, looking in nearly the same way as Cyras did now, with a vacant expression through time as much as space. Though, Tomas realized, Alexia had always looked to the south; Cyras looked to the west. "I'll be handling a bigger problem," the Trickster-Mage said in a soft voice.

"And that would be...?"

Somber gave way to irritated, clearly Cyras' usual mind-set, and the Trickster-Mage stood from the stone upon which he had been resting. "The Harvest Festival is in just under nine months Rogan, and you still have a long ride ahead of you. I suggest you stop wasting my time and yours with pointless questions and go."

Without another word, Cyras, aided by Nek, mounted his horse, and departed west. The Uldra, after throwing a wave of farewell to Eigenhard, hurried to follow on foot.

Once the mismatched pair was out of sight, Tomas dropped to the ground with a surprised yelp. Picking both his sword and himself up, he renewed his assault on Eigenhard. Then, as he was about to renew his attack, Tomas' muscles locked, preventing any movement except away from his target. Seeing this, Eigenhard grunted, "I guess that means the spell worked."

"I'll kill you!" Tomas snarled.

Eigenhard, turning his back on the shepherd, went to Stick and pulled a waterskin from his saddlebags. "You were listening to Cyras same as me," he said after a long drink. "We both know you can't. Like it or not, kid, we're stuck together."

"This spell can't last forever! As soon as it ends, so do you!"

"Then, we have something to look forward to." Eigenhard replaced the waterskin and mounted Stick. "We should get going."

"I'm not going anywhere with you!"

"Then how are you going to kill me?" Cutting off Tomas' next statement, Eigenhard raised his hand. "Look, kid, I know you were raised on stories of the evil Black Due and that I'm no more than his hired sword, so I don't hold any of this against you. Like it or not, and I pretty much hate it, Cyras used some kind of spell to tether us to each other, so let's just get one thing straight right now."

The mercenary crossed and put his nose only a breath away from Tomas' face. "You can't kill me. Even without Cyras' spell, you have about as much skill with a sword as a baby. I've fought and beat some of the best out there. You don't even rank in the top one hundred people who want to kill me. I have to take you back to the Keep. Hopefully, the King can talk some sense into you. If he can't, at least he should be able to break this enchantment and we can be free of each other.

"Now, we have a lot of distance to cover and not a lot of time. I like peace and quiet while I travel, so shut up! Cyras left a horse behind, so get on and let's go!" He turned then and mounted Stick, grabbing the reins and settling himself.

"I would rather walk than accept help from a spawn of Ramalech!" Tomas said stiffly.

"Are you talking about me or Cyras?"

"Both!" Tomas snapped.

Eigenhard laughed, "Well, you're right about one of us, at least."

Spurring Stick, Eigenhard galloped off, leaving Tomas to struggle onto the back of the horse Cyras had left for him even as the Trickster-Mage's geis began pulling at him.

Chapter 17

Tomas' resolve to not speak to Eigenhard held true for some time. He rode along with the mercenary in total silence in the five days it took them to reach Gioconda. From time to time during their silent trip, the young man tested Cyras' geis. Whenever Eigenhard looked distracted or unobservant, whenever his back was to Tomas, the shepherd would reach for his father's sword, intent on vengeance. Even that initial act, though, was denied to him; the Trickster-Mage's spell locked Tomas' muscles the moment the young man made the slightest murderous movement. Each time, Eigenhard would glance at his unwanted companion and shake his head.

The voice in Tomas' head that had of late spoken with Alexia's voice told him to keep an open mind. The young man recalled a conversation he and his good friend had about how extreme times could force a man into acts he would otherwise find distasteful. Tomas wanted to listen to that voice; he wanted to keep his mind open and try to understand what may have forced a loyal colonel to savage an entire town. The situation the young man now found himself in, however, prevented this.

Tomas' silence was finally broken upon their arrival to Gioconda. The view ahead helped more than a little, since the Skani Straights was one of the truly great natural wonders of Arayel, especially highlighted in the setting sun. The massive cliffs bordering the Straights stood hundreds of feet high, with the thundering surf crashing against either side in a constant warning to respect the sea. The natural scientists of the University of Pelsemoria had believed the Straits had once been an underground river linking an inner sea with the ocean. Following the great devastation of the Disaster at Nassinalia, the land above the hidden river had collapsed, creating the great passage that was both feared and respected by all the sailors of Arayel. The tang of salt air hit the young shepherd and drew him home to Pelsemoria as it once was with a massive harbor and teeming trade. True Gioconda was in no way comparable to the wonders of the Capital in its glory, but the small harbor and cobblestone streets still did much to raise Tomas' mood. It was a bustling city, despite the chaos the Republic now suffered, with active commerce evident from far outside the community. In fact, the only sight marring the town of Gioconda was the sight of the many armed mercenaries patrolling the streets, ever watchful of any threat.

Tomas looked on at the gravel beaches laying beyond Gioconda, one on each side of the Straits, which marked the only points at which a vessel could make safe harbor. The Skani Ferry could be seen even from high atop the cliffs, pulling into Giaconda's port, opening its ramps and letting loose a number of travelers and merchant caravans. If the young man's memory served, the ferry would wait two hours before making a return trip, plenty of time to reach it and arrange passage.

Tomas voiced his surprise once Eigenhard turned north at the edge of town rather than continue on towards the harbor. "I thought your path went through the Holy City?"

"No point in going that far out of the way," the mercenary replied.

"You have a problem with Velaross?" the young man asked his enemy.

"I have a problem with all religious fanatics, and that city is full of them. Besides, Cyras warned us to reach the Keep as soon as possible; we don't have time for any side trips."

"Well, I need to speak to someone in the Church," Tomas insisted.

"Spiritual problems?" Eigenhard guessed.

"More like worldly ones," the shepherd replied.

"Like what?"

Tomas threw the mercenary a look of hatred. "My problems are none of your damned business!" he spat. "Like it or not, Eigenhard, we're going to Velaross!" The young man spurred his horse forward and set off at a gallop. The horse leapt forward and sprinted nearly ten feet before some invisible force pulled Tomas right out of his saddle.

Rogan rode up to where Tomas sat in the grass where he was trying to find some shred of his dignity. The mercenary watched as the riderless horse turned around and walked back. Looking down at the young man, he grinned. "So, what was that about needing to go into Velaross?" he asked.

"Go to Underworld."

Eigenhard shrugged. "Suit yourself. Cyras obviously gave me the reins for this little trip, and unless you can give me some kind of reason for putting up with all those bells and the stench of all that incense, we're heading straight for the Keep."

Tomas thought furiously about it as he delicately remounted his horse. Wither it was his own pride or simply not trusting Eigenhard, the young man kept his mouth shut. The warrior shrugged.

The two reluctant companions headed north along the Eastern Highroad towards Alvaro, neither speaking for three days. On the fourth day of their journey along the Highroad, Tomas finally ended his silence as the two sat in the early evening waiting for the light to finally fade and watching the stars come out. Looking into the small campfire, the young shepherd threw Eigenhard for a loop with a sudden question. "Why did the Black Duke choose you for his heir?" he asked.

"The King didn't choose me," the mercenary finally answered after a long pause, stirring up the fire and adding some wood. "His daughter did."

Looking confused, Tomas asked, "Calonar had his daughter choose his successor?"

Eigenhard shook his head. "Kyla didn't choose me as a successor to her father's House. We fell in love and got married. Everything else was secondary."

"But you will rule the Northlands once Calonar dies."

Eigenhard grunted.

"Considering the size of the Black Duke's lands, I would think any man happy at the thought."

"Have you ever led men into combat, kid?"

"No."

"Ever ordered the death of an enemy?"

"Of course not!"

"Ever killed a man in cold blood for no other reason than you know he'll eventually cause misery to others?" The young man threw a meaningful look at his enemy. The mercenary rolled his eyes. "You haven't killed me yet," he muttered.

"What does this have to do with anything?" Tomas demanded.

Eigenhard sighed. "Kid... Tomas, the very worst thing you can do to a man, worse than killing him, burning his crops, or slaughtering his family, is to make him responsible for the life of another."

"That doesn't make any sense," Tomas said, shaking his head.

"Every single person in the world, no matter his rank or position, all have one thing in common."

"What?"

"A life. Every man, woman, and child has an entire life full of dreams, hopes, desires, successes and failures. Everyone knows other people and interacts with them daily. When you take responsibility for another person, you take responsibility for all that and more. When a man dies, he leaves a hole in the world, a hole that can never be filled. His passing means there will be people who are lessened. A commander, a mother, a king, and an assassin all share one thing in common; they all take responsibility for another's entire life, and everything connected with that life."

"What does this have to do with you succeeding Calonar?" Tomas asked.

"Cylan Calonar is one of the greatest men I've ever met. By taking on the title of king, he's accepted responsibility for each and every life in his domain. He works tirelessly to ensure his people have every possible chance at happiness and prosperity. No sane man in the world would threaten even one citizen of Calonar's kingdom, since doing so means calling down the wrath of the man himself."

"Somehow," the shepherd snarled, "I doubt that everyone under the Black Duke's protection is kept safe."

"True," the mercenary replied. "There have been failures. We aren't perfect, kid. Sometimes the bad guys win, no matter how hard we fight."

"A fact with which I am very familiar," Tomas replied primly.

"You know, the King *has* offered protection and aid to the people of Pelsemoria. You really can't blame us for everything that's happened to you."

"Why not?" he demanded. "I was in the palace the day you and your minions attacked. I saw what happened."

"I doubt you saw it all, kid."

"And I suppose you'd be willing to tell me what really happened?"

Eigenhard shook his head. "No point," he replied. "You wouldn't believe me anyway. *I* was there and I don't believe it. But if it's any comfort, that day has haunted me ever since."

"Why would the greatest victory you've ever handed your dark master haunt you?"

Again, the mercenary shook his head. "Because that wasn't my greatest victory. But it was right up there with my greatest defeats."

"You're afraid, aren't you?" Tomas asked suddenly. "You're afraid you'll fail as king, and the people will suffer because of your failure."

The knight closed his eyes. "Yeah," he sighed.

Tomas laughed. "So, the great terrorist, Rogan Eigenhard, is afraid of something after all."

Pulling apart the bread that was the main staple of their meals, irritation showing on his face, Rogan looked at Tomas. "Listen, kid, only a fool thinks he's immune to fear. The Church Knights like to claim they're immune to fear. The Xeshlin like to claim they control fear. Hell, there are monks out there who say they've conquered fear. But I'll tell you something: each and every one of them is deluding themselves. Fear is a man's constant companion. Fear is what makes us close our doors at night. Fear is what makes us obey our leaders, and fear is what keeps a warrior alive. I feel fear every time I go into combat. I'm afraid someone innocent will get hurt. I'm afraid if I fall my wife wouldn't survive my death. I'm afraid what my death would mean to House Calonar. Mostly, though, I'm afraid that finally I've met an opponent who's better than me.

"Fear will keep you alive, kid. Fear will drive you to act when otherwise you wouldn't. Any man who truly feels no fear would have little reason to keep breathing. You think my having fears is surprising or even funny? Laugh all you like, kid. But remember something. The difference between a hero and a coward isn't that one feels fear but the other doesn't. The difference is: a coward let's his fears rule him, a hero will use his fear to drive him forward."

Saying nothing more, Rogan finished his meal, then unrolled his blankets and climbed in them, leaving Tomas to sit for some time longer, the knight's words echoing in his mind.

Chapter 18

The next two weeks passed without serious incident or significant conversation. The two men traveled along the Eastern Highroad as the old highway made its way north towards the great city of Alvaro. Despite the distance they were able to cover each day, however, the journey seemed endless. Eigenhard continued in his attempts to draw conversation out of Tomas, more from boredom with the uninteresting sights of the flat farmland of eastern Lanasia than any real hope of success.

Eigenhard laughed somewhat ruefully one day, sparking a new argument as they passed through a farming village.

"Something funny?" Tomas demanded.

"I was just thinking of how I'm supposed to explain you to the King," Rogan replied. He paused to hand a few coins to an old soldier, sitting with his rusted spear in front of a small chapel.

"Why would that make you laugh?"

Eigenhard nudged Stick back into a trot. "Because I know that, even though I've got no idea of what to do with you, the King will listen for a few minutes and give me an idea that I'll feel stupid for not thinking of myself."

Children began running out to watch the passage of the two travelers. The adults mostly ignored them, especially once it became clear they would not be stopping at any of the local shops. "I still don't see what's so funny about this situation," Tomas insisted. "I don't understand why Cyras Darkholm would force me to travel all the way to the Northern Keep. If he's allied with the Black Duke, why not just kill me or turn me aside from my quest?"

"That's assuming Cyras *is* allied with the King," the mercenary pointed out, waving at a couple of kids who cheerfully tried to get their attention.

"Aren't they?"

Eigenhard shifted in his saddle, brining an annoyed snort from Stick. "Well in all honesty, I've never really understood how the King and Cyras feel about each other," he said. "I'm pretty sure they're friends, but I don't think I've ever actually seen them do any of the things that friends usually do. They're almost never in the same place at the same time, and when they talk about each other, it's usually with irritation or resignation."

"Then what makes you think they're friends?" the young man asked contemptuously.

One of the nearby children tossed a wooden ball at Eigenhard and the mercenary caught it. He smiled and tossed the ball back. "Well, they haven't killed each other," he said.

"There are a lot of people in the world that haven't killed each other," the shepherd pointed out. "That doesn't mean they're friends."

"Haven't met many wizards, have you?"

"What's that supposed to mean?"

Rogan shifted again, ignoring his mount's irritation. "Don't ask me to explain why, but for some reason, the first thing two wizards of the same power do when they run into each other is fight. I can't count the number of times I've seen some spell-slinger enter a town just to challenge the local fastest wand."

"I've noticed mercenaries are the same way," Tomas pointed out.

"Some," Eigenhard agreed. "But when two mercs fight, they don't' usually blow up the town around them." The mercenary waved goodbye to the village children when they reached the edge of their community, then turned back to the road ahead.

"Powerful men wanting more power," Tomas muttered, his hand absently tracing the edge of the golden rose pinned to his collar.

"What?"

"Something a friend once told me," the young man said. "Powerful men want only more power. Anyone with the same power is a threat."

The mercenary nodded. "That's about the best explanation I've ever heard," he said. "Was this friend the one who gave you that pin?"

Tomas snatched his hand away from his collar. "That, Eigenhard, is one of many things that are none of your damned business."

Rogan shrugged. "I was just trying to be polite. I mean, a man wearing women's jewelry could lead to some nasty rumors. I was just giving you the benefit of the doubt."

"It isn't women's jewelry!"

"Whatever you say, kid."

Their arguments continued off and on through their journey north. These discussions often became so heated that it was only the power of Cyras' geis that prevented blood loss. Distracted as he was with debating everything Eigenhard said, Tomas barely even took notice at first when the two of them reached the Kazic River, the border to the Alvaro Dukedom. The Unity Bridge was a symbol of the newly-formed peace after the Uldra Uprising, both a literal and symbolic connecting of the disparate territories into a single, united Republic. The newly-enthroned House Majestos made an effort to bring together the three dominate races of Lanasia in the bridge's restoration: with Uldra practicality, Sylvai artistry, and Human ingenuity. Although first built by the Sylvai, the original bridge had fallen during the unending destruction of the Uldra Uprising. Once that conflict had ended and Humanity took power, a program of restoration began. One of the first project was Unity Bridge. Made of grey stone and inlaid marble, the bridge stretched across the Kazic River with its sixteen arches representing the sixteen noble Human Houses of the early Republic. A pair of towers, each topped with bronze domes, guarded the opposite sides of the bridge. Twin rows of statues stood sentinel along the bridge, alternating with the heroes of the Sylvai and the Uldra represented. The restoration of Unity Bridge was an icon for those who believed the people of Lanasia could live in peace and travel safely from one territory to the next.

One look at the now-demolished bridge reminded Tomas that this dream was almost certainly dead.

Eigenhard stared at the signs of violence and shook his head. "Warlords," he muttered. The bridge itself had huge, gaping holes scattered across its length. One large section near the center had given way completely. At either end were collections of bodies, partially covered by carrion-birds. The stonework was scorched by recent fire and the famous statues were all destroyed. The domes on either guard tower had been stripped, looking now like pock-marked skulls. The towns on either side of the river were still aflame, with the only sound carried on the wind being the ungrateful complaints of carrion-feeders.

Tomas fell from his horse and wretched. Even more than the stench of murder, the sight and sound and smell confronting the young man reminded him of Railing. "Why?" Tomas demanded, tears standing in his eyes at the destruction of the bridge that had stood for centuries.

Eigenhard shrugged. "To make life difficult for their enemies. To prevent someone else from controlling the bridge. To make a point. Right now, every warlord with territory around here is scrambling to secure what they've got and prevent anyone else from doing the same."

Tomas rose to his knees and stared unblinking eyes at the tragedy before them, one more scar on his young soul "That bridge has stood since the Majestos Dynasty. A thousand years! The people weren't warriors, just merchants and tradesmen. What's the point?"

Eigenhard looked at Tomas. He then nodded towards the smoking corpse of a bridge. "That is the point," he said softly. "Brutality for its own sake. When your army is made of men who've forsaken oaths, you have to give them some… entertainment."

"Entertainment?" Tomas demanded.

The mercenary shrugged. "Rape, plunder, arson. This is how bandits stay together. And for all their talk of the Republic or their warrior-oaths, that's all these warlords really are anymore."

"What now?" Tomas asked in an empty voice, remounting his horse.

"There's a shallow a few miles upriver. We'll ford there and, once on the Alvaro side, we can move back to the highway." He turned Stick off the broken Highroad to begin a side trip west. "It's a bit out of the way and the rapids can be a problem, but there's no helping it."

"Amazing how often one's sins come back to haunt them," the young man noted, following the mercenary away from the shattered bridge.

"Are you talking about my sins or yours?"

"I wasn't the one who killed the Emperor," Tomas reminded his enemy. "I wasn't the one who caused the destruction of the government, and I wasn't the one who unleashed the warlords."

"Would you believe neither was I?" the mercenary asked.

"Unlike the fools you trick into obeying your master, Eigenhard, I know the truth. I've watched Pelsemoria suffer for the last decade because of you. I've seen good, loyal men fall under the blades of the warlords or be enslaved by the Xeshlin. All the misery and suffering you and the Black Duke are supposedly fighting all started the day you and Kyla Calonar unleashed the Madness on us!"

A pained look crossed Eigenhard's face. He sighed and shook his head.

"Did I strike a nerve?" Tomas asked. "Is it possible there's some hint of remorse in your soul?"

The mercenary stopped his mount and stared at the turbulent Kazic River in silence, his eyes tracing across the foaming whitewater upriver towards the calm shallows ahead. After a time, he rubbed his eyes. "Kid," he said, "there are a lot of things in my life I'm not too proud of. There have been times when I've stopped and taken a look around and couldn't remember how I'd gotten to where I was. There are faces that haunt me at night, and memories threaten to drown me everyday.

"There are a lot of things that I've been accused of doing that are so untrue they make me sick. Unfortunately, there are also some things I've done lately that, if they aren't completely true, have some basis in truth. We didn't intend for the Madness to happen. But Kyla and I *were* responsible for it."

"How?" the young man demanded. "How did you make it happen if it wasn't intentional?"

"No, not today." The mercenary gathered up Stick's reigns and made ready to continue their journey. "I've had enough guilt for one day."

"You don't think I have a right to know?"

Eigenhard paused. "Alright. I'll tell you how it happened, but not today. Ask me again after we leave Alvaro, and I'll tell you."

"I won't forget that promise," the shepherd swore.

"I don't think you will."

Frostfront
Wasteland of the Exiles
Clayton
Bilela Sea
Jarek
Alvaro
Janoah
Klemens
Gracia
Benois
Zaka Sea
Thioda Woods
Kemael
The Ruins of Castle Roseland
Blue River
White River
Cosma River
Castle River
The Ruins of Ccmploa Tusiu
Illiqom River
Concsma Highway
Tulu River

III

The Alvaro Dukedom

Chapter 19

Eventually the reluctant companions realized that, in order to gain some measure of peace during the long journey north, certain topics were best avoided. Unfortunately, with the topics of philosophy, politics, ethics, history, and current events under the "best to avoid" list, that left little to talk about. Both men silently agreed not to discuss the butchery they had discovered at Unity Bridge. Nothing could be done for the people murdered, their homes destroyed or the historic bridge violated; speaking, therefore, seemed only to keep alive the tragedy. In the end, the weather was their only safe conversation piece.

"The Alvaro Dukedom has always had the best growing seasons in the Republic," Tomas noted, looking about the many farms and cattle ranges covering the vast valley housing the Twin Rivers.

"The breadbasket of the Republic," Eigenhard nodded. "It's amazing how much food the farms around here are able to produce. With such a mild summer and so much water, though, it really is no wonder."

"This region was always considered the easiest assignments amongst the Legions. Many officers considered this area for retirement."

The mercenary laughed. "Yeah, it's no wonder King Calvino was so quick to lay claim to these lands after Pelsemoria fell."

"*King* Calvino?" the shepherd demanded.

"That's right. Dukedom no longer. Now it's the Alvaro Kingdom. Calvino crowned himself not too long after King Cylan did."

"Seems like everyone is calling themselves kings these days," the young man noted sourly.

"What was anyone supposed to do, kid? Was Lanasia supposed to wait around for all the minor nobles of the Republic to finish fighting amongst themselves over who was supposed to be the next emperor? And what about when Pelsemoria was destroyed and the government dissolved? Lines of communication broke down,

Legions disbanded or went rogue, and the entire infrastructure of the Republic collapsed. Someone had to take control."

"Someone like the Black Duke?"

"Who else had the power to enforce peace in the Northlands?" Rogan demanded. "Balshazzar and Nicolas were busy in their own lands. Parano can't even maintain control over the Endless Sands. The south was filled with dozens of warlords, and Velaross sat around praying for a miracle. Who else was going to step up and make things right?"

"Make things right?" Tomas repeated in scorn. "How did the Black Duke make anything 'right?' The warlords still have dominance in the south. People are still starving. Civil war between all these self-declared kingdoms is imminent! The Xeshlin have almost free reign in the south! How are things 'right?'"

"It's only been a decade, kid. It took most of the Majestos Dynasty to put Lanasia back together after the Uprising. Do you think someone can just snap their fingers and make everything better? Change takes time, no matter who's in control."

"And what gives Calonar the right to be *in* control? He has no legitimate claim to any royal authority. For that matter, his noble standing was even in question when Pelsemoria was destroyed."

"What claim did Sharl Majestos have when he claimed the Redwood Throne?"

The shepherd shook his head. "Sharl Majestos was a hero of the Uldra Uprising. He was one of the leaders of Velaross and helped build the Trifold Treaty ending the war. And he didn't *claim* the throne; he was elected to it by the Congress of Races."

"And the fact that he had control of the largest surviving army had nothing to do with it, I'm sure," Rogan mumbled.

"At least he was of noble blood."

"Ever heard of General Naronor Calonar?" the mercenary asked.

"Of course I have. Everyone knows the Black Duke is descended from the commander-in-chief of the Sylvai military during the Uprising. So?"

"Well, according to Church's own records, Naronor Calonar was a cousin of Annakarala, the last Sylvai empress. That means General Naronor Calonar was of noble blood, as is his descendant, King Cylan Calonar."

"Sylvai rank became meaningless after the Battle of Lake Tragedy," Tomas snorted.

"Don't you mean the Battle of Lake Victory?"

"Whatever. What's your point, Eigenhard? You can't seriously believe that some ancient title gives the Black Duke the right to name himself king."

"Kid, my point is simple. No, I personally don't think the King's right to an ancient title means anything. On the other hand, I've never had much use for noble titles anyway; a man's actions should say who he is, not some rank he puts in front of his name. Not the accomplishments of his father and grandfather."

"What gives Cylan Calonar the right to be king is the same thing that gave Sharl Majestos the right. Both men stepped forward when there was a need and tried to fix things after the world had gone straight to Underworld."

"At least you're honest," Tomas conceded. "You don't even try to make a legitimate claim to power. Your master just took it."

"If there was any alternative, kid, he wouldn't have."

The look Tomas gave the mercenary said plainly that he did not believe that.

Because of their detour upriver, it was another three days before the pair were staring at the high walls of Alvaro, rising up from the banks of the Twin Rivers. The traditional home of House Calexto, sitting as it did at the border of so many different cultures, displayed a truly cosmopolitan style. The marble of Velaross rested alongside the wood and brick of the Northlands. The wide avenues of Pelsemoeria passed beneath the wide roofs and projective facades of Frostfront. Merchants and scholars walked and chatted with clergy and nobility. All that seemed good in Humans was on display in the city before them. The smells and sounds coming from the city ahead seemed untouched by the disintegration of the Republic.

As they slowly crossed the bridge spanning the Twin Rivers, Tomas recalled his history lessons of House Calexto. In the years following the Uldra Uprising, House Calexto had worked without rest to rebuild their city and the surrounding farmlands. When Chclodocar Majestos made his historic call for unity, the Calexto family had been among the first to swear fealty. During the Xeshlin Invasion, the Calexto House Guard had fought valiantly against the cursed slavers of Davenor to give time for the people of Alvaro and the surrounding villages to escape into the Northlands. Along with

Houses Parano and Balshazzar, Calexto was considered one of the great powers of Lanasia.

"After his father was killed in Pelsemoria," Eigenhard was saying, adding his own version of recent history, "Calvino Calexto took over as head of his House. After Cylan Calonar was crowned king, Calvino did the same. Right now, House Calexto controls all the land along the Gemino Rivers along with Janoah. He's got shipbuilders working night and day to build enough of a fleet to lay claim to the Zaka and Hilita Seas, but the pirates are giving him some problems. His House Guard is strong enough that none of the warlords have been able to push much past Kamael and Thioda Woods, but the constant fighting is starting to drain his treasury. If Calvino's not careful, in a few more years he could run out of money and his soldiers will abandon him. After that, the warlords will probably overrun the area."

"Whose side is he on?" Tomas asked.

"His own." the mercenary snorted, nudging Stick forward as the line advanced. "Calvino has made little secret of the fact that he thinks he should be the next emperor."

"Well House Calexto *did* have a seat on the Electors Council. They could make a legitimate claim to the Redwood Throne."

Eigenhard laughed. "They did make a claim, about eight years ago. Parano and Balshazzar immediately disputed it and Czar Nicalos announced that Kessia was finished with the Republic."

"What about the Black Duke?"

"The King realized at that point that the remaining nobles in the Republic were too busy squabbling over a non-existent throne to get the job done. It was at about that time he decided to abandon any chance to rebuild the Republic."

"So how does Calvino feel about your master?" Tomas asked with thoughts of treachery in his mind. He looked ahead to the city gate and the guards; perhaps, the shepherd thought, his salvation could lay under the yellow and black banners of House Calexto. After all, the young man reasoned, surely such a wealthy and power family would have wizards in his employ to sever the mystical chain currently around his neck.

"Right now, Calvino is more worried about the warlords to the south than anything House Calonar might do. He's also been trying to get his economy fixed and to do that he's trying to establish trade rights with the Keep and Ironheartshaven. With his money and armies stretched so thin, Calvino is trying to be everyone's friend." This would include, Tomas realized, avoiding any unfortunate incidents with the heir to House Calonar.

When the two finally reached the large gate that would grant them entrance to Alvaro, Tomas could not help but be impressed. The walls stood hundreds of feet high with battlements evenly spaced and visible sentries manning their positions. The gates themselves, though raised, were nonetheless impressive with thick iron bars and barbed spikes giving an image of impenetrable strength. Having seen the generally unimpressive mercenaries on his long journey north, the young man had expected more of the same here in Alvaro; to his great surprise, the yellow and black-clad soldiers who stood guard in defense of their city looked every bit as professional as any Legion of the Republic army. Standing clean shaven and proud without a spot of rust on their breastplates or a single tear on their yellow and black tabards, the House Guard looked to be the kind of professionals who Tomas had feared were forever vanished from Lanasia.

With only a few brief questions from the soldiers at the city gate and a warning to obey all local laws, Rogan and Tomas were waved forward while the guard and his men approached the next group in the line, a wagon team bearing what looked to be grain. Eigenhard led Tomas through the gate and into the cobblestone streets of Alvaro. The young man looked about, noting with a tug of his heart more than a passing resemblance Alvaro had with Pelsemoria. The architecture of the Republic had been dominant in most of her major cities, with marble pillars set around the entrances to most buildings and broad gardens scattered throughout the city. In the distance the bells of a Church rang, calling for afternoon prayer.

"Homesick kid?" Eigenhard asked.

"The home I miss no longer exists," he replied darkly. "It was destroyed by evil men."

There was nothing the mercenary could say to that. The two rode on in silence with Eigenhard watching about, alert for any danger, and Tomas staring up at the statues that adorned the various plazas and the many buildings that all shone with the grandeur of a lost Republic. The shepherd noted as they rode that the robes and mantles of Pelsemoria seemed to be falling out of fashion in favor of the styles common to Velaross- the light tunics, hose, and cotes.

Alexia had warned him that change was inevitable but seeing his home being forgotten so soon saddened the young man all the same.

Seeking to distract himself from such gloomy thoughts, Tomas decided to pick a fight with Eigenhard. "So where are we really going?" he asked.

"What do you mean?" the mercenary replied.

"Well, I doubt you came to Alvaro just to buy supplies, and you've said a few times that we're in a hurry. It would have been faster to ride around the city then go to through it."

"Actually, I really do want to resupply, but you're right; we could have gotten supplies in any roadside village."

"Then why lose the time coming into the city?"

"There's been some tension between Alvaro and Frostfront over the last few years. We've gotten reports about a few skirmishes being fought along the Cosima River. The road we're taking cuts north to Jarek then upriver to Drailia. I want to check in with the embassy here to get the latest news. The last thing we want is to ride straight into a war."

"Embassy?"

"House Calonar has sent representatives to a few of the major cities in the Northlands and to as many as possible throughout eastern Lanasia. The idea is to have someone close at hand of each of the new rulers who can speak for the King without having to send messengers half way across the continent."

"The Black Duke is planting his agents in every city in Lanasia?" Tomas asked, the thought chilling him to his soul.

"Don't make it more than what it is, kid. King Cylan just wants someone in every kingdom to expedite trade negotiations and improve relations with the Keep. Nothing more."

Alexia had warned him of this, the shepherd realized. She had said the Black Duke wasn't planning to conquer Lanasia with armies or powerful magics. "And is there one of these embassies in Frostfront?" he asked.

"Sure."

That was it. A war for no reason between two cities that could not afford to fight; both of which just happened to sit on Calonar's southern border. "Was Calonar planning to send aid to Alvaro?" Tomas asked.

"What do you mean?" Eigenhard look confused.

"You said King Calvino was running out of money and that he wanted to rebuild his economy. Was the Black Duke planning to help him?"

"We help anyone who asks. If Calvino wants our help, they we'll give it. If he needs money, then we'll look into buying his exports. If he needs food we'll send some."

"And if he needs soldiers?"

"We won't fight a war for him, but if he's being attacked without provocation and asks for help, we'll probably help."

That was it. Like some devious machine, the final piece fell into place and suddenly Tomas understood. The Black Duke was not going to invade central Lanasia. He did not need to. He had his agents stir up war between the young kingdoms until they could no longer support themselves, then he would send all the food and money they needed. He would send his soldiers to help "protect" them. In time, his soldiers could just take control and there would be no one to object.

Was that what happened to Railing? Tomas wondered. Did they accept help from the Black Duke, only to be forced into accepting his rule once his soldiers were in place? It was a plan so simple, yet so insidious, and so like House Calonar. To conquer a Republic without risking a single one of his soldiers, that was the method of the Black Duke. And there was nothing anyone could do to stop him; the plan would take time, but it would work.

"Not if I can help it," the shepherd muttered.

"What?" Eigenhard asked.

Tomas said nothing. He rode on and thought.

Chapter 20

The embassy of the Black Duke was a large complex of buildings set only a few streets from the castle of House Calexto. The buildings themselves were wood and stone, resembling more the architecture of the Northlands than the Republic with high-arched rooftops and shuttered windows. A large stone wall separated the buildings from the rest of the city and the blue and grey liveried soldiers of House Calonar could be seen guarding the only visible gate and on the various balconies and rooftops.

Noting the soldiers, Tomas could not help but shake his head in disgust. "Your embassy doubles as a barracks?" he demanded.

Eigenhard rolled his eyes. "Would you begrudge us some security?" he asked pointedly.

"And how much 'security' does your ambassador require?" the young man asked. "A hundred men? Two hundred?"

"Twenty," the mercenary said flatly. "Each of our embassies is manned by twenty soldiers as long as there's a local garrison that's agreed to help in case of any emergency. That's not counting the hundred or so staff of cooks, clerks, house-hands, and other workers."

Nearly two hundred men, Tomas thought. Twenty in uniform, identifiable to the local populace, another hundred and seventy who can blend in.

The two guards stood tall with hands firmly gripping their Northland poleaxes, eyes weary of the approaching riders until they identified who it was that approached. The younger of the two made a motion as though to bow, but his older comrade stopped him with a nudge. "Visible or invisible this trip?" he asked.

Eigenhard smiled somewhat ruefully. "Hopefully invisible this time," he replied.

The soldier nodded and called for the iron gate to be opened. "In that case, welcome to Alvaro... sir."

"What was that all about?" Tomas demanded once they were inside the courtyard and the gate was closed behind them.

The mercenary shrugged. "After the coronation, the King made me commander of the House Guard. Most of the men I've worked with over the last decade know I like to keep a low profile when I travel. Most times when I enter a city, I like to just slip in and slip back out. If I can keep quiet who I really am, I don't have to sit through a dozen or so ceremonies of people lying about how honored they are that I'm visiting."

An aging northlander with grey shot through his braided red hair and a slight limp in his massive stride walked through the open doorway ahead of them and down the few steps, meeting Tomas and Eigenhard in the center of the small courtyard. Despite the warmth of the day, he was dressed in a thick green robe. It was surprising to Tomas how little he was surprised when he noticed the sword belted at the man's waist. After all, what else did he expect of a servant of the Black Duke? "Your Highness," he rumbled in a deep but friendly voice through a thick red beard. "I wish I could have known you were coming. I would've had a meal and some drink prepared."

Eigenhard dismounted and clasped the northlander's hand warmly. "It's good to see you, Oskar. You've been well?"

The large man laughed and patted his stomach. "This post has been a little too good to me, I think. But at least the wife isn't complaining as much anymore."

"How is Mathilda? I heard she was delirious when you got this post."

"She's happier than I can ever remember. The summers are warm and the winters short. She says she misses the forests of home now and then, but mostly she just busies herself with being pregnant."

"Again?" Eigenhard asked.

"And again," Oskar confirmed. "It's so blasted peaceful around here there's little else to do!"

"How many is that now? Eight?"

"She gave me a ninth last autumn and is already starting to spread again." The giant shook his head and glanced down at Tomas, who had dismounted and made an effort to keep some distance between himself and the large northlander. "And who is this?"

Eigenhard looked over and sighed. "This is a very long story named Tomas," he replied.

"Trouble?"

The mercenary nodded. "Trouble named Cyras Darkholm. He did something to the two of us. Now we're stuck together until we can get it undone."

"Anything I can do?"

"I don't think so. Whatever Cyras did this time, only the King or maybe Esha can undo."

"So you're headed home then?"

"As fast as we can. I was only planning to stay the night and maybe steal some supplies from you."

Oskar put an arm around Eigenhard's shoulders and led him and Tomas into the large house. "My home is yours." the northlander declared. "For as long as you wish, you and your little friend are welcome. I'm sure Mathie will want to have a dinner tonight in your honor."

"How could I say no?" Eigenhard asked. "But I was hoping we could wash some of the road off first."

Oskar led Eigenhard and Tomas into his large house to his private study. Much like the outside, the interior of the house was built of stone and wood, with narrow hallways and large rooms adorned with bearskin rugs and intricately carved wooden furniture. The ambassador's study was crammed with numerous full bookcases and several tables littered with dispatches and maps of the various regions of Lanasia.

Upon their arrival, Oskar had poured all three of them cups of Northland mead before flopping into a chair. Eigenhard followed suit and drank deeply before questioning his agent over the state of affairs in and around Alvaro. To the mercenary's obvious dismay, his ambassador relayed dire news.

"The problem is Jarek," Oskar had started.

"Jarek?" Eigenhard replied in disbelief. "There's nothing around that town except farmland and mills."

"And gold," the ambassador finished.

"They found gold?"

Oskar gestured to a large map of the Alvaro Kingdom, which included the land surrounding the Miryam River. "Apparently, a few hunters found a large deposit in one of the streams that runs through their woods. The farmers were finished with the spring planting anyway, so most of them headed into the forest and started poking around. So far, they've found at least five different deposits. Pretty big ones, at that."

"And Calvino wants it," Eigenhard guessed.

"He immediately laid claim to the town and the forest," the ambassador confirmed. "He moved a few hundred troops in and 'offered' them the chance to join his kingdom."

"What did they say?" Tomas asked.

"They never got the chance to respond," Oskar replied. "The commander of the Calexto forces gave the town council a week to consider their response to Calvino's offer. Three days later the other half of this little tragedy arrived."

"Warlords?" Eigenhard asked.

"Frostfront."

"That's bad," the mercenary noted.

"You don't know the half of it," his ambassador confirmed. "Frostfront arrived with double Alvaro's numbers and a few wizards. They claimed to be there to defend Jarek's independence."

"How bad was the damage?" Eigenhard asked.

"Damage?" Tomas asked with a confused look.

"Two armies with that much gold at stake?" the mercenary snorted. "Only one way for that to end."

Oskar drained his cup and poured himself another, offering Eigenhard and Tomas some as well. It was then that the young man realized that he had not as yet drank any. One taste was enough, by far, the sweetness almost overwhelming him. "The battle lasted for two days," the large Northman said as he refilled his master's cup. "By the time they were done, Jarek was in pretty bad shape. The few surviving Alvarans retreated back here and Frostfront reinforced their positions."

"So Jarek is free," Tomas noted. "It sounds like good won in the end."

Both Eigenhard and Oskar gave the shepherd looks of equal scorn for his comment. "Let me guess," the mercenary said. "Frostfront has announced they'll maintain the garrison to defend against future aggression from House Calexto?"

"Yup," Oskar confirmed.

"That sounds like a good thing," Tomas remarked.

"And they've already sent their own workers to start mining the gold?" Eigenhard continued.

"The workers were only a few days behind the soldiers."

Tomas shook his head in confusion. The mead he had drunk was starting to cloud his thoughts a bit. "Wait," he pleaded. "I thought you said Frostfront was defending Jarek's independence."

The large Northman laughed a short, brutish laugh. "Oh, they are. Jarek is as free as a bird. They're also as poor as one. Frostfront has made sure to point out that the farmers and woodcutters had no official claim to the gold and that the deposits are well outside the borders of their town, fields, and mills. Thus, the wizards have laid claim. They have also said that the damage to the town was regrettable but unavoidable. It is also the responsibility of the townspeople to make their own repairs. Since Jarek is so poor, most of them have just moved out to the farms."

Eigenhard shook his head in disgust. "And they're just glossing over the fact that, with the Republic gone, there's no such thing as an 'official claim.' Trust the wizards of Frostfront to pick and choose which laws to maintain. So where do things stand now?"

Oskar traced a line with his finger along his large map of Lanasia from Alvaro to the small town of Jarek. "Calvino has dispatched three battalions to blockade the town. Word is Frostfront has already dispatched more soldiers to relieve the siege and secure the gold."

"So Alvaro and Frostfront are going to war?" Tomas asked.

Eigenhard stood and stared hard at the large map. "Neither of them has the soldiers for a war this big," he grunted. "How're they doing it?"

"You might want to sit down before I tell you," the ambassador warned.

"Just tell me," the mercenary sighed, rubbing his temples in preparation of the bad news.

Oskar pointed to Velaross. "Calvino has found an ally."

"The Church!?!" Tomas started.

"House Calexto has always had strong ties to Velaross," the Northman said. "And Calvino is very dutiful in his tithing. He's already promised that he'd remember his duty to the Church once the current matter has been resolved. The Lords Cardinal have issued a proclamation supporting House Calexto's annexing of Jarek. They've dispatched several hundred Church soldiers and four companies from the Knights of Duty. Most of the noblemen around the Holy City have sent their younger sons along as well, hoping for a land grant."

"Frostfront's response?" Eigenhard asked.

"The Triumvirate has made an alliance with House Aziel in Otylia. Baron Duriel has dispatched a large force to reinforce the wizards."

"Two huge armies marching to the same place," Tomas noted in horror.

"With the people of Jarek caught in the middle," Eigenhard sneered. "And no one cares about what happens to the town or the people. How long before the two armies meet?"

"Velaross' forces have already left home; they should be here within two months. After that, it's a three-month trip to Jarek. Frostfront had to wait for the spring thaw. Their army hasn't been able to leave Frostfront until sometime around now, and even then it'll still take months to reach Jarek."

The mercenary stared hard at the map before him and nodded. "So, Alvaro gets there first, overruns the Frostfront force already there and has more than enough time to build fortifications and bring in reinforcements before worrying about the other army. Have the warlords taken advantage?"

"Not yet," Oskar replied. "As a matter of fact, most of the warlords are staying quiet right now."

"That won't last. When those two armies hit each other, they'll destroy everything in and around Jarek, including each other."

The Northman nodded. "And no matter who wins, the loser will have too much invested to back out, so they'll send more, pulling forces from the south, giving the warlords free rein."

"The other kingdoms will get pulled in; the warlords will either take sides or take territory from the weakened nations which will force more fighting to force the warlords back south."

"Jarek could start it," Oskar muttered. "We've known it was coming for a long time now. This could be it."

"Could be what?" Tomas asked.

"Open war, kid," Eigenhard said flatly. "Ever since the Republic collapsed, all the fighting has been small-scale; just skirmishes and raids, no pitched battles. But everyone in Lanasia has been quietly getting ready, gathering strength for the day the Umbral break loose and the whole continent burns."

"Which would give the Xeshlin the perfect opening for another invasion," Oskar pointed out.

"One catastrophe at a time," Eigenhard muttered. "Is there any chance to head this off?

"I don't see how. If we send our own army, Frostfront and Alvaro will see it as us trying to get the gold for ourselves and attack. If we send mediators to Jarek, they won't be listened to. Those commanders out there have their orders and will carry them out."

"Who's in command out there?"

The ambassador consulted several parchments that lay on a small table beside the map. "Captain Gaius Paulus is in command of the Alvaro forces already at Jarek. He was in the Legions until Pelsemoria fell, then he and his company joined the Calexto House Guard. Colonel Gerard Minton is commanding the Velaross army that's massing in Janoah. On the Frostfront side, you've got General Yousha out of Otylia commanding the relief force and an archwizard called Radha commanding the forces already in Jarek."

Eigenhard paused a moment. "Minton? Any relation to the old Lenora prefect?"

"His cousin. Another Legion officer who looked for better employment when Pelsemoria fell. He's a little green, but was in one of the last graduating classes of the Military Academy."

"And Radha, is she the same one who...?"

Oskar nodded glumly. "The same. She's still got a price on her head in Velaross."

"So, a well-trained strategist versus an amoral firemage."

"And it's getting worse every day." The ambassador slumped back into his chair, shaking his head and frowning.

Eigenhard stared up at the vaulted ceiling, searching through his thoughts for any ideas. "Would meeting with Calvino help?" he finally asked.

"I don't see how," Oskar replied. "Whoever ends up in control of Jarek will have access to one of the largest gold deposits ever uncovered outside of the Ulheim. Calvino needs money, and he sees this as a gift from God. Right now, the only way to stop this war is to send in our own army, which will only antagonize both sides against us."

"Is it only the gold that motivates him?" Tomas asked.

"What do you mean, kid?" Eigenhard asked.

"If it's only money that motivates Calvino, then perhaps he could be bought off."

The mercenary shook his head. "There's no way Calvino would settle for less than that entire deposit."

"But what about the cost of this war?" the young man insisted. "How much will it cost House Calexto to maintain an army, fight Frostfront, defend against the warlords in the south, and rebuild enough of an infrastructure in Jarek to see a return on mining the gold? If Calvino settles for a lesser amount now, he could actually come out with more than if he fights this war."

Eigenhard shared a long look with Oskar. The two seemed to exchange several unspoken comments before finally speaking. "I guess this means I'll have to talk with Calvino," the mercenary said.

Oskar nodded. "And it'll have to be an official visit. If there's any stink of a secret agreement between the Keep and Alvaro, Frostfront will never go for it."

"Is there any way to get in to see Calvino quickly?"

"I can get you in. Calvino's been asking for aid from the Keep since this mess got started."

"Let's do it then."

Chapter 21

Tomas and Eigenhard, both dressed in the finery of court, rose to Calexto Palace. The young man had been expecting a fortress, recalling from his schooling the stories of the great Sylvai fortress that had formed the core of what would one day become Alvaro. Instead, he stared in confusion at the new construction. Atop the bones of the fortress, abandoned centuries ago, a new, utterly impractical palace was being built. It looked to the shepherd as though some unfinished noble country house had been dropped onto a military fortress.

Seeing his companion's look of distain, Eigenhard laughed. "The new home of House Calexto," he said, nodding towards the nearest scaffolding. "They even call it the 'New Palace.'"

"But…" Tomas said, "why?" Nothing of the old fortress and new palace matched. What remained of the old Sylvai construction was the grey stone of the region. Thick walls and battlements meant to project strength. The Calexto palace, though, was all graceful arches and delicate masonry, buttressed by imported wood.

The mercenary shrugged. "Rich people like fancy things."

Once having passed through the highly-ornamental gates, the two had dismounted and been escorted by a very thin chamberlain to the throne room where the king had been waiting. Tomas was little impressed by the obvious efforts of the Calextos to improve the grandeur of their new throne room. Large candelabras lined either side of the long hall but were clearly of lesser manufacture than what would be expected in any fine city of the south. The black and yellow carpet that led the path to the raised dais of the king was clearly of decent, if somewhat inexpensive, manufacture. A few clerical desks sat against a nearby wall, looing as though they had been only recently moved and arranged into some kind of formality. The throne itself was a large chair that served well as a throne, but actually looked as though it may be more appropriate at a dining table.

Much like the throne room around him, King Calvino Calexto was less than impressive. The Alvarans in general tended to be much shorter than northmen, more so than the people of Pelsemoria with leaner frames and darker hair to match their olive complexions and dark eyes. King Calvino seemed to take these attributes too far, however; he was very short, only a little taller than a child, and his thinning hair was deep black, matching his sunken eyes. The thick ermine robe he wore seemed much too big for his boney frame, not to mention impractical in the Alvaro spring heat. The scepter he held in his hands looked to be uncomfortably heavy, despite its lesser metals.

From the moment of their arrival, Eigenhard had made clear that House Calonar would not support House Calexto in any military action. That said, the mercenary was quick to assure the overly nervous king that House Calonar would also withhold any support for Frostfront. In truth, Eigenhard directed his proposal as much to the overwhelmed-looking king as he did to the small group of advisors standing near the throne. These men and women, fine lords and ladies of the court who wore expensive clothing and dripped expensive jewelry, were watching the representative of the powerful House Calonar wearily. One in particular, a lady of fine, delicate features and hair of midnight black, introduced as Ombretta, seemed determined to derail Eigenhard's argument. The lady stood at her king's side, one gentle hand on his shoulder, and frequently leaned in to whisper in his ear.

Rogan had been careful to propose Tomas' plan slowly and carefully, emphasizing to King Calvino the political and military dangers of open war, while emphasizing the economic threat to the advisors. Eigenhard spoke carefully and evenly, taking pains to repeat important points. Despite the appropriation of his idea, Tomas did not seek to upstage Eigenhard, nor did he interrupt. However, as the meeting continued, and Eigenhard's every argument was met with a counter, Tomas' suspicions continued to rise. King Calvino's eyes never seem to register what Eigenhard was saying, and only when the Lady Ombretta whispered in his ear did the spark of an idea shine forth.

Tomas stared closely at the dark-haired lady. There was something... The young man could not articulate the proper thought, the proper description. She was normal enough, for a woman of wealth and status. Her clothes were conservative, as most were in this province. She wore expensive jewels and fine cosmetics. Something, though. Some part of her felt... wrong. A though appeared in the back of Tomas' mind, like a whisper on a spring breeze. He ran an idle finger along the golden pin on his collar, the rose with its petals just beginning to open, and glanced at the pendant hanging from Ombretta's neck, balanced between her breasts. It was a large black pearl, very dark and yet catching the light. As Thomas stared and the whisper from his mind considered, he finally noticed it: the light was not reflected *by* the black pearl, the jewel itself *produced* the strange gleams of light.

The shepherd moved forward, ignoring the looks of warning from Oskar. He leaned and whispered to Rogan the same whisper that had begun in the young man's own mind. Eigenhard, to his credit, did not wave off his unwanted companion, but instead listened. He nodded then, slightly, and continued his argument.

For his part, although some of the other advisors seemed increasingly open to what Eigenhard was proposing, the Lady Ombretta was openly hostile and King Calvino was struggling with the notion that peace was preferable to war. "Prince Rogan," the monarch said in a thin, weak voice after another whispered consultation, "we cannot admit to understanding how giving up our legitimate rights to the gold deposits around Jarek could be more profitable than keeping them."

"Your Majesty, surely you are aware of the cost of maintaining your army in the field for any length of time. A cost born mostly by your taxpayers," this last was said pointedly to the advisors. "Now, you must not only pay for your own army, but for the soldiers Velaross has sent as well." Eighenhard glanced at Oskar and accepted an offered mead-horn and skin. "Forgive me, your majesty," he said then. "In my haste to discuss this matter, I overlooked the basic courtesies of court." He raised the horn and skin. "I have a gift from House Calonar, a fine clover mead." He stepped forward, smiling, to present his gift.

Eigenhard was nearly within arms reach of the king before the guards stopped him. The knight smiled again and offered a half-bow, giving his gifts to the guards for presentation to the king. Calvino waved for his official taster to first sample the gift before trying it himself. "Delicious," the king noted happily, waving Eigenhard closer.

The knight stepped closer, slowly, deliberately, careful not to appear threatening in any way. In fact, Eigenhard made a point of not approaching the king himself, but moved closer to the advisors, and the Lady Ombretta. "I'm glad you enjoy it, your Majesty," Eigenhard said. "So few people outside the Northlands get to enjoy our national drink." He looked then to Lady Ombretta, who was staring hard at Eigenhard. "Would you care to try some, my Lady?"

The noblewoman shook her head slightly. "Thank you," she said in a voice so soft it may as well have remained a whisper. To Thomas ears, her accent seemed strange. Not typical of that part of Lanasia, but close. "Oh, come now," Eigenhard insisted. He collected a small goblet from a nearby tray and poured some of the mead in. Raising the cup, he offered it to the Lady Ombretta. "Surely you wouldn't refuse a stately gift?"

The Lady's lips made the slightest twitch, as though to frown, but maintained their empty smile. She bowed slightly and accepted the cup. It was then Eigenhard struck. His hand lashed out, faster than the eye could follow, and snatched the black pearl pendant.

There was a flash of black fire and the crack of Umbral thunder. The circle of royal advisors were hurled back, their fine clothes burnt. The king and his throne were knocked aside, and Eigenhard was stumbling. The air became putrid with brimstone. The light streaming in from the windows dimmed, and it felt for a moment as though the entire world would shatter.

What was the Lady Ombretta had changed. Her long dark hair was now ghostly white. Her beautiful face was twisted in a snarl of hate, further marred by jagged scars running from temple to chin. Her once-glorious eyes were now dull red, like dried blood. Those eyes seemed to fill with heat, with pulsing rage. The creature hissed at Eigenhard and pointed a hand, curled like a predator's claw, and spoke words in a language like the breaking of ice.

Rogan Eigenhard tried to curse, but his body twisted backwards, his arms and legs splayed in a parody of human movement. He tried to resist, but found no purchase. He should have fallen, but his twisting body remained upright, held by the false-Ombretta's mystical attack.

Then, Oskar lunched at the false-Ombretta, roaring in Northland fury. The great man had no weapon, having come unarmed to their audience with the king, but instead made to throttle the creature attacking his prince. The false-Ombretta turned her burning, hate-filled eyes at this attacker. She released Eigenhard and turned, speaking a cracking word, and sending Oskar flying.

The Calexto House Guard, shaking off their surprise, tried to attack. Each of the men, armed with ceremonial spears and wearing chainmail, took only a handful of steps towards the false-Ombretta before they began screaming in agony. The pale creature, now floating just above the stone floor, had made an intricate gesture and spoke words of frozen power. The armor and helmets of the House Guardsmen had frozen, steaming in the warm air, but burning and crushing the men like ice drawn from some hellish winter lake.

With a roar much like Oskar's, Eigenhard leapt to the attack. The mercenary wrapped his arms around the false-Ombretta and heaved, bodily throwing her to the floor and pinning her there. The creature in his arms twisted and writhed. Her colorless hair lashed at Rogan, drawing small lines of blood. Her thin limbs reached back, impossibly dislocating from their sockets to claw at the Northlander. Despite the pain and the blood and the impossible writhing, still, Rogan held on. "Little help!" he snarled.

The idea presented itself from nowhere, from a silent place in his mind. Tomas was acting on the thought without a care from where it came. He sprinted to the side of the damaged throne and picked up the discarded scepter. Not knowing how he recalled the fact, he knew how to use this as a weapon. Bashing the scepter against the floor, Tomas knocked free the decorative jewels and gold flake, exposing the cold metal beneath. Some vague memory of childhood, of stories and near-memory, told him the value of iron.

The shepherd then lunged across the room, to where Rogan still desperately clung to the false-Ombretta. "Eigenhard!" Tomas snarled, raising the scepter. The mercenary glanced, saw, and understood. At the last moment, he rolled aside, exposing the magical creature to the shepherd's attack. Tomas swung with all his young strength, smashing the iron scepter down onto the false Ombretta's head. There was a flash of released power, of magic unchained. A crack of thunder sent Tomas and Eigenhard both rolling across the stone floor, to lie near each other, panting and blinking, trying to force their thoughts into rationality.

And then all was calm. The world righted itself. Tomas blinked away stars in his sight and breathed deeply clean air. He glanced over and gratefully accepted the help as Rogan puled the young man to his feet. "Next time," the knight grumbled, "keep your damned observations to yourself."

The pair looked to the Lady Ombretta. Her body was twisting even further, as though her fingers and arms were trying to fold in on themselves. Her fine dress was scorched with frozen heat, looking as though it had been burned years ago and was now crumbling to dust. The body seemed to drain of all moisture, cracks appearing and dust disappearing into the slight breeze. Her buring red eyes sank into their sockets and the colorless hair withered.

Oskar limped over to where they all stood, watching this strange, accelerated decay. "Nekalan," he growled.

"What?" Tomas asked.

Parano House Guards, those few who still breathed, were gathering, looking down at the crumbling body. King Calvino himself had recovered, shaking his head as though to banish an unwanted dream. "She was a Nekalan," he gasped. He then looked around. "How long?"

Oskar knelt and pushed at the crumbling body. "Years, from the looks of it."

"What is it?" Tomas demanded.

Eigenhard grimaced. "Xeshlin death magic." He looked to King Calvino. "Lady Ombretta was probably murdered years ago and replaced with… this. How long has she been one of your advisors?"

Calvino held a kerchief to his nose. "Five years," he replied.

Oskar stood and nodded. "And I bet she came up with sending your army north?"

The king nodded. He shook his head again and walked away, to the other side of the room. Eigenhard, Oskar, and one of the king's older advisors joined them. Tomas followed, but kept his distance.

"The Xeshlin want a war," Eigenhard insisted.

The king nodded. "Indeed. And I fear they shall have one."

"You can end it here and now."

Calvino shook his head. "We may be too far gone. We have already invested much in this new gold deposit. To leave it now…"

Eigenhard shook his head. "Even if you defeat the forces of Frostfront, which is doubtful, and the Arcane Guild doesn't send another force, which is even more doubtful, it will take months to build the necessary facilities to mine the gold. Add to that the danger of having your army weakened fighting Frostfront." He looked hard at the king. "Have you heard of the Xeshlin raids to the south?"

Calvino nodded.

Eigenhard rubbed his eyes. "I've gotten… reports, that they're looking for something."

"For what do they search?"

He glanced at Tomas, who shrugged. "We've heard that the Xeshlin believe Kelinva will soon be reborn, somewhere in Eastern Lanasia."

"The Dark Empress," Calvino gasped.

Eigenhard nodded. "The raids and their other activities," he looked at the crumbling monster, "are all just in preparation of Kelinva's return."

One of the Calexto advisors stood forward. "From where does this information come?" he asked.

Rogan hesitated. Again, he glanced at Tomas, who could only shrug. "From Cyras Darkholm."

"The Trickster-Mage?" another advisor snorted.

Rogan held up his hands. "Look, I understand Cyras' reputation. Hell, I've suffered it myself. But," he held up a finger, "has anyone ever heard of any story, any legend, any rumor, of Cyras Darkholm *lying?*"

The ideas struck Calvino and his advisor with obvious force. They knew Eigenhard's words were true, no matter how much they might wish it was not so. In all the legends surrounding the Trickster-Mage, one fact remained constant: Cyras Darkholm never lied. He would confuse, he would conceal, he would misdirect or just refused to answer. But the Trickster-Mage never lied.

"As you say, Prince Rogan," the aging advisor said. "The kingdom faces great peril. No matter the reason, the Xeshlin clearly desire us weakened. Civil war could erupt at any moment and the south is still beset by banditry and their vile raids. My king's economy is greatly weakened; we need a new source of revenue. If we cannot get the money we need from Jarek, then from where can we?"

"Alvaro produces a great deal of food, my lord," Eigenhard replied. "The growing season here is much longer than in the Northlands. King Cylan will agree to buy whatever excess food your farmers have to sale at a reasonable price." He glanced towards the other advisors, still struggling to recover from Lady Ombretta's transformation. "We will do the same with your fishermen and your herdsmen. We will also accept merchants from Alvaro at our fairs."

"But this will only provide money for our merchants, farmers, and fishermen," the king objected. "How will these trade rights provide our government with the funds we need?"

"Taxes, your Majesty. House Calonar will send our own merchants to Alvaro, and they will pay whatever reasonable taxes you require to do business in your great city. You may tax the farmers and fishermen who sell to us. Your businesses will make greater profits, and your government will gain the funds it needs."

"But what of the gold in Jarek?"

"It can still be yours, sire," Tomas noted, stepping forward. "In a manner of speaking. Instead of sending your miners to work the streams, why not let the people of Jarek do the work? They found the gold; why not let them mine it? Once they do so, they will still need a market to sell the gold, and Alvaro is the closest city. The only cost you need suffer is to maintain a small security force in Jarek."

"What would be the purpose of this force?" the king asked.

Rogan smiled a strained smile. "Sire, the same gold that nearly brought Alvaro and Frostfront to war will draw in the warlords of the south, perhaps even the Xeshlin themselves. Without proper protection, Jarek would be raided time and again. With your soldiers there, the mercenaries would not dare attack." He glanced at Tomas, seeming to read the shepherd's mind. "And the people of Jarek would be protected from any other... interested parties. They maintain their independence and freedom, but do business with you. Your men would also be able to monitor the mining process, ensuring that nothing illegal or immoral occurred."

"We do not see why House Calexto should bear sole responsibility for guarding the miners if we do not have exclusive rights to them," the king insisted.

"You will not, your Majesty. Frostfront will also be required to send a security detachment. Frostfront will bear half the cost of maintaining security, the people of Jarek would retain their freedom while working to mine the gold and Alvaro would profit from the gold miner's work. The Xeshlin plot to bring war to Frostfront and Alvaro will, instead, bring you together, make you stronger. Surely this is an agreeable proposal."

Calvino returned to his throne, placing a hand on the singed and overturned chair, considering. He looked to each of his advisors who nodded in turn. Finally, the king nodded. "So it shall be, Prince Rogan. So long as Frostfront agrees to the same terms you proposed here today, so shall we. Jarek may keep its independence so long as they mine the gold and agree to trade fairly with our merchants. Most importantly," he said with a glance towards the crumbling ruins of Lady Ombretta, "the Xeshlin will be thwarted."

After exchanging only a few more empty courtesies, Rogan and Tomas were granted the king's permission to leave. "You want to explain how you knew she had an enchantment on her?" Rogan asked softly as the small group walked through the crowded street of Alvaro.

"I don't know," Tomas admitted. "She just seemed... wrong."

The knight glanced at his unwanted companion, grunting. He said nothing else on the subject.

Chapter 22

The next morning, a pre-dawn messenger reported that the king had prepared a ship to speed them on their journey north. So, as the sun's first rays hit the rooftops of Alvaro, Tomas and Rogan boarded the ship and stood at the bow watching the city of House Calexto slip away.

"You're awful quiet this morning," Rogan noticed as the two enemies stared out at the white sand beaches and tall cliffs bordering the Zaka Sea.

"Complaining?" Tomas asked.

"Are you kidding? This is the first peace and quiet I've had in weeks."

"Then why ask?"

The northlander shrugged. "Seems to be something on your mind," he replied. "Might help if you spoke your peace."

"Every time you or I speak our peace, we end up arguing for days," the shepherd pointed out.

"True. Of course, there's not much else to do at sea than talk."

"I wouldn't know."

"First time, huh?"

The young man nodded. "My father often spoke of taking me on a trip to one of the distant territories, but we never made it further than Railing." Thought of the dead town caused a deep sadness to well up in Tomas' heart. It had been months now, he realized. Months had passed since that entire community had been destroyed. The birds and rats had surly feasted on the bodies. The buildings, he realized, would soon start to crumble as time began its work in erasing what had once been a vibrant, peaceful home to so many.

"That's a serious cloud you've got hanging over your head all of the sudden," Rogan said, turning away from the calm beaches and clear waters to watch the deckhands go about their work.

"Do you care?" Tomas asked, genuinely curious.

"I might," the northlander replied. "We'll never know unless you talk about it."

"I was just remembering."

"Looked more like regretting."

The shepherd also turned away from the perfect scene before him, instead walking across the deck to look out at the Zaka Sea. The water was clear and bright, but its emptiness matched the mood in the young man's soul, and he felt some comfort in it. The beaches looked warm and pleasant, with birds and surf working constantly to bring some unwanted cheer to Tomas' heart; but the sea held the quiet solitude and uncaring serenity that more accurately matched the shepherd's soul.

Rogan joined his unwanted companion and gazed out at the water as well. They stared at the surf slowly pushing in against the land only to retreat, regather, and try again. The endless conflict between seemingly-unmovable land and ever-changing sea was beautiful. Seabirds sang as the danced amidst the waves. The rising sun shone like golden sparks upon some ancient forge. The wind caught at the ship's rigging and lent its strength to their course ahead.

Tomas notice none of this, though. In that moment, his mind filled with the many failures and tragedies he had experienced, pushing in on him again and again. Sorrow pushed at the young man's heart, and unshed tears glittered in his unblinking eyes. Looking out at the Zaka Sea, Tomas could see only unending suffering.

"Want to talk about it?" Rogan asked.

"To you?" Tomas snorted.

"Not many other options, are there?"

"Did you ever read the stories about the Heroes of Fate?" the shepherd asked after a long pause.

Rogan crossed his arms over the deck railing and leaned over, resting on them. "Sure. When I was a kid and my parents wanted me studying the subjects they thought I should be learning, I'd read about the Heroes instead. I don't know of many kids that haven't at least heard some of the tales."

"Do you know what I loved most about the Heroes of Fate?"

The northlander shook his head.

"They always knew what they needed to do. There was never any indecision. They were destined from birth to be great heroes. From the time they first gathered together and fought the rogue priests Leria and Lar Nenic, to uniting Lanasia against the Xeshlin Invasion, they never had any doubts about their duties or what they should be doing.

"Did you know there was even a prophecy about their arrival?" he asked suddenly.

Rogan nodded. "Hence the name. What was it, two hundred years before the Walking Death broke out?"

"Three," Tomas replied. "Three hundred years. The Emperor's Seer fell into a trance and spoke the names of each of the Heroes of Fate, saying that when Death and Disease walked Lanasia, Heroes would arise and bring light to the world, forcing back the Dark Empress."

The northlander glanced at Tomas. "You've got the words memorized?"

"They were inscribed on the Great Amphitheater. Right above the northern entrance was an engraving of all seven of the Heroes with those words beneath them."

"I wish I could have seen that," Rogan said. "Which of the Heroes was on the engraving? The group changed a few times."

"Sir Talius Ironheart, Knight of Justice and leader of the Heroes of Fate. Father Mortimus Dominus Euginus, priest and defender of the Faith. Khaine, Walker of the Sylvai. Tienel Greysoul. Samantha, warrior-woman of the Gunrsvein. And…"

"And Cylan Calonar, warrior-wizard of the wilderness" Eigenhard finished. "He *was* one of them, you know."

Tomas shrugged. "He wasn't the first of the Heroes to turn to evil," the young man pointed out. "Khaine betrayed the Republic and retreated to Wildelves Wood, slaughtering all the Humans within its borders. Tienel Uskera destroyed the holy city of Adama and murdered more than half the Holy Knights."

"Well, I might argue the interpretation of Khaine's actions, but there's no arguing what Tienel Greysoul became."

"My mother used to tell me that if I didn't say my prayers every night, the Greysoul would steal my shadow."

Rogan smiled. "Back when I was a kid, there was an old stablehand who told stories about Tienel swallowing the souls of the unborn. Supposedly, he lived out in the woods where the light couldn't hurt him. We said that he came out on nights of a new moon and darkness covered the land, to feast on the hearts of wicked children."

Tomas nodded. "In Pelsemoria, we said that he lived in the sewers and catacombs. The priests told us that he came up on nights when the shadows were long."

"I don't know anyone who wasn't afraid of Tienel Greysoul when they were a child," Rogan confessed. He then turned to his troubled companion. "He doesn't talk much about it, but the King has hinted that Tienel eventually made some kind of deal with Ramalech for the secret of Shadow Magic. That's when he reappeared and..."

"And what?" Tomas asked.

Rogan shook his head. "Bad memories, kid," he replied. "You have yours, I have mine." The northlander then looked at his unwanted companion. "So, what does this have to do with what's bothering you?"

The young man's hand drifted again to the golden rose pined to his collar. "There's been so much death," he whispered.

"These are bad times," Rogan pointed out. "But things will get better. Only a question of time. No matter how bad life gets, it always gets better eventually. It's the way of things."

"I left home to help my people, to try and change things for the better. But ever since I left, I've only seen more death, more tragedy."

"Easiest thing in the world to give up and go home. I don't think anyone would fault you for that. Takes a really rare kind of person to see the things you've seen and keep trying."

"A friend said something very similar."

"The one who gave you the pin?"

Tomas nodded, his hand absently going once again to the golden rose resting against the pulse on his neck, its closed petals offering some comfort to his young soul. Not much, but some.

"Family, friend or lover?"

"A friend I loved like family."

"Those are the worst," Rogan said, looking back out over the waves. "With any normal friend, you can just let them go and remember the good times. With a lover, you can keep them in your heart and never really have to say goodbye. But a friend close enough for you to love... No easy way to let them go; shouldn't even try.

Rogan leaned against the railing and crossed his arms over his chest. "A friend can tell you when you're wrong. A lover can help you make things right. A friend is a part of your life and a lover part of your heart. A friend you love exists in such a deep part they become an attachment, permanent as the air. When we lose them, there's a hole in the world that can never be repaired."

"Are you a poet as well as a mercenary, Eigenhard?" Tomas asked.

The northlander shrugged. "Just call it like I see it, kid."

"I miss her," the young man said softly. "She always knew what to say. She had all the answers."

"Always a great person to have around. Someone who's got all the answers, that is."

"So, what's the answer?" the shepherd asked. "How do I go on?"

Rogan thought about it for a few moments before answering. "I met this tribe over in Maka," he said, "the great western continent. They said, 'no one ever really dies, so long as they're remembered.' There's always going to be that empty feeling whenever you think of her; the trick is to understand she's still here. She lives in that empty place in your heart. It only feels empty because you can't help but think of her not being right next to you. When you realize she's still with you, that empty feeling starts to fill."

Tomas turned and started walking towards the aft cabins, where a small room had been set-aside for him. "I need a nap," the young man said.

The shepherd entered the cramped cabin and stood for a moment, thinking about his lost friend. He remembered the soft hood she always had pulled up. He remembered the feel of her hand on his arm and the soft comfort of her words. Most of all, he remembered the sound of her laughter filling the woods they had traveled through together.

He's right you know, Tomas could almost hear Alexia say as she would have put a hand lightly on his shoulder. *I'm still here, and I always will be.* The young man glanced in the small mirror Oskar, the Black Duke's ambassador to House Calexto, had provided. He studied the small golden rose that he wore against the pulse of his neck. Tomas smiled at the delicate flower with its petals that looked as though they were just about to open.

Chapter 23

The ship made its way along the coast towards the Janoah Passage. Tomas' mood brightened noticeably in their two days aboard King Calvino's vessel. His thoughts often drifted to the time he spent with Alexia, though they did not remain too long. He thought often of the soft advice his friend had often given and how it applied to the many facets of his life. Alexia had a deep, profound wisdom, Tomas knew. It was a great shame she had been forced out of loyalty to her life-long friend Raven to serve the Black Duke.

When their ship approached the southern docks of Janoah on the early afternoon of their second day aboard, the young shepherd approached the bow where Rogan stood, looking out at the large shipyards. For more than a mile on the western side of the Janoah Passage, the skeletons of ships lay in their births. Acres of sail and miles of rigging rested in storehouses in orderly miles behind the construction yards. The air was filled with the barks of organized overseers, the casual curses of laborers, and behind it all, the alluring call of the waiting sea. Their approach slid past the shipyards, to the eastern side of the Passage, where the shipyards have way to commercial docks, the sounds of haggling, trading, taxing and other commerce replacing those of construction.

Tomas's eyes rose. The Janoah Passage was, so far as the young man knew, the tallest waterfall in the world. The mighty cliffs rose from the surrounding countryside, Janoah and House Calexto on the left and Velaros and the Church on the right. The city ran the length of the great wall, an irregular series of buildings that marred the natural horizon. Rogan looked up as well and grunted, "one more scar."

"Scar?" Tomas asked.

"Your school teachers never taught you how this was formed?"

"The Disaster at Nassinalia," the young man replied.

Rogan nodded. "I've heard a few... 'intellectuals,'" this he said with unmasked derision, "who tried to claim the Disaster never happened, that it was just some natural even like an earthquake or volcano." His cold, northland eyes looked to where the Hilitia Sea funneled into a great crack, then spilled down, forming a heavy fog as it blew out to join the Zaka Sea. "You think you can take one look at that and call it natural?"

Tomas studied the ugly fissure, realizing Rogan was right in calling it a scar. "It looks like something tore the planet." Indeed, the cliffs themselves did not look like ones naturally formed, but rather as though, in the moment the scar had formed, earth had risen up in an impossibly-flat wall. "How do we get up there?"

"The switchbacks," Rogan nodded towards a jagged-appearing trail that ran back and forth, up the Janoah side of the Passage. Along those switchbacks, Tomas could see whole mule teams making their slow way up, burdened with the spoils brought to the harbor below.

"That looks like it takes awhile," the young man noted grimly.

"Well," the knight snorted, "unless you can fly, that's the only way up."

"Get moving you overgrown jackass!" Rogan roared at his stubborn mount.

They had unloaded from the House Calexto vessel and reached the base of the switchbacks with no difficulty. Once there, Rogan and Tomas had been required to wait an hour, as the men who monitored the crisscrossing passage signaled for up-bound traffic to halt in favor of down-bound. The unlikely duo waited at a nearby shop, getting a lunch of roasted pork and bread. They watched as mule-train after mule-train came down, the harness bells joining the orchestral cacophony at the base of the Janoah Passage. Finally the handlers waved their brightly-colored signal flags and rang a heavy bell, announcing that up-bound traffic could resume.

Rogan and Tomas mounted and moved into the queue. The problem appeared when, after handing a few coins to the signaler, the two men guided their horses to the switchbacks. It was at that moment that, after taking only one look at the steep trail and clearly doing some math of distance and elevation, Stick shook his head and turned away.

The dark warhorse absolutely refused to be moved. Rogan tried kicking at his middle, but Stick only bumped against a post, knocking his rider off. The knight, trying to ignore the riotous, and growing, laughter from the assembling crowd, grabbed Stick's ear, intending to twist his mount into subservience. The prince of House Calonar screamed and flinched back, bleeding a little from his fresh bite wound.

Tomas stared at Rogan, narrow-eyed and plotting, and Stick, glaring and unmoveable. The young man then leaned in his saddle towards the signaler. "How do you get the mules to climb?" he asked.

The signaler, leaning against one of his bright signal flags, just shrugged. He then put his fingers to his lips and let fly a shrill whistle. An assistant moved to the stalled queue and brough forth a team of horses and their handlers. Each of the mounts wore blinders.

Tomas shook his head, glancing at the sinister dark warhorse. "I'm not trying to put those on him," he muttered.

"No need," the signaler replied, gesturing for the horses to begin the climb. A confused moment passed, and then Stick perked his head up and glanced around. His previously hate-filled gaze fell on the team of horses, all of which, Tomas realized, were female. The dark warhorse let out a heavy, eager breath, and happily trotted up to the rear of the horses, even as they began the climb.

Tomas nudged his much more obedient horse over to the fuming Rogan. "Need a hand?" he asked politely.

The northlander offered a few choice insults and hurried to catch up to his enthusiastic mount.

At the top of the switchbacks, after Stick neighed a sorrowful farewell to his climbing companions, Rogan and Tomas made their way to the nearby dock registry. There, the northlander identified a ship flying the blue and grey of House Calonar and led Tomas to the appropriate dock. Once the identity of Calonar's heir was established, the captain of the *Blue Lady*, as he declared his ship, immediately set about preparing for their departure. Within three hours of their arrival to Janoah, not including the hour and a half to negotiate the climb, the two men were once again at sea, this time in the Hiltia Sea heading north along the coastline. Despite the Rogan's urgency, the captain, a dark-skinned man named Ahmed who Tomas learned was from the Endless Sands, assured his master that it was too great a risk to cross the open ocean.

"I'm sorry, but unless you want to risk getting killed by a *hili'aya*, we can't cross the open sea." Ahmed wore clothes that reflected the most current trends, with a perfectly sized tunic colored a deep red that matched the hat he wore cocked off one side of his head.

"*Hilt'aya?*" Tomas asked nervously. "What's that?"

"Sylvai word for waterspout," Rogan translated.

Ahmed laughed, throwing his head back and letting his long dark hair flow freely about his head. "Actually, it translates better as 'a voyage of beauty and pain.'"

"Is he kidding?" the shepherd demanded.

"Exaggerating maybe," the northlander replied. "But no, not kidding."

"What's a waterspout?"

"For some reason, this area has them all the time," Ahmed replied, stroking the thin beard that framed his lean face. "It happens when there's a strong wind that starts circling around in a tight vortex. That wind starts sucking up everything in its path. When they're on land, it's a tornado. When they're on the water, they suck up water. When the waterspout breaks apart, the water drops down again."

"So, what happens if one of these waterspouts hits a ship?" the young man asked nervously.

Ahmed laughed again. "Well, we get sucked up and dropped back down again... in several pieces."

"Don't worry, kid," Rogan said, throwing a dark look at Ahmed. "Even though they happen a lot in this sea, they almost never strike near land."

"What causes them?"

"Nobody really knows."

Ahmed made a gesture across his heart, as though protecting it. "We know," he said in a darker tone and with a glance along the coastline. "These waters are cursed."

Rogan shook his head. "Just legends."

Ahmed signaled for one of his men to take the tiller and gestured Tomas over to a table where he had several charts laid out and held down with weights. "Judge for yourself, my young friend. This was once a great valley, surrounded by mountains. But after the Disaster at Nassinalia, when the world was nearly destroyed, the sea came rushing in and covered the land. Many people lived in this valley; it was a beautiful place of vineyards and towns. And then, in just one day, the oceans rose and drowned them all."

"Lot of places were drowned," Rogan snorted, standing at the rail. "Or buried or burned or whatever else. Half the world died in the Disaster."

"The mountains became islands and the valley became a shallow sea" Ahmed continued, ignoring Rogan. "You can see the ruins beneath the waves: homes, shops, farms. They're all just tombs now.

"There's strange weather here; storms appear and disappear without warning, currents shift constantly, and ships disappear without a trace. This is a haunted place, a place of great power where Arayel rarely tolerates intruders."

"Knock it off, Ahmed," Rogan snapped. "It's a sea with weird weather. Quit trying to scare the kid and get us to Clayton."

The sailor bowed slightly with a grin on his face. "As my prince commands."

"Is that it?" Tomas asked as he looked out at an imposing range of mountains lining the coast. The tips of their jagged peaks were covered in snow despite the coming summer, and the setting sun cast a red glow on the slopes, as though they were drench in fresh blood.

Ahmed nodded grimly, his hand firmly on the tiller. "Yes. Somewhere in those mountains are the ruins of Ctharaq Turin."

"The greatest slaughter in history," Rogan muttered.

"And turning point of the Uldra Uprising," Tomas added in a soft voice. The shepherd looked grimly on the site jagged peaks, skeletal fingers reaching for peace that would never come. His eyes ran along the harsh mountains and let his mind drift through the horror that unfolded there.

"Not that they knew it at the time," Tomas noted. "At the time it was just another battle. It wasn't until word of the slaughter spread through the Sylvai Empire that Humanity became fed up with dying for the Sylvai and abandoned them."

"Shame it took so many deaths for our ancestors to realize they were fighting someone else's war," Rogan grunted.

"Not my ancestors," Ahmed pointed out. "My people had abandoned any imperial foolishness centuries earlier."

"I've been meaning to ask," Tomas said. "How does a tribesman from the Endless Sands come to be a sailor for the Black Duke?"

"My brother and I had a falling out with our tribe," the captain replied. "We decided it would be best to seek fortune and adventure in other lands."

"Fancy talk for being exiled," Rogan muttered.

"Well, if you want to be rude about it," Ahmed sniffed.

"How close are we going to get to the ruins?" Tomas asked.

Ahmed scanned the horizon, a weary gaze given the calm waters. "That's the trick to sailing these waters," he muttered.

"I don't understand."

The captain pulled free his hat and wiped his brow with a small cloth. "You have to find a safe passage between the threats."

Tomas looked around, shielding his eyes against the setting sun. "Threats?"

Ahmed nodded towards the cliffs on one side. "Too close and we risk a rip current."

"Rip current?"

"Another problem of this haunted sea that surely has some reasonable explanation, right your highness?" he lightly asked Rogan.

The northlander just rolled his eyes.

"What is it?" Tomas asked.

"The sea will be calm, predictable," Ahmed explained. "And then a sudden force grabs you and pulls you down and in a random direction. Often they go out, further to sea, but they can also go in, right into the cliffs."

"They're strong enough to move a ship?"

Ahmed grimly nodded. "And they're particularly strong here, near the ruins of Ctharaq Turin." He pointed then, towards the red cliffs. Tomas looked. For a moment, the young man could not tell what the sea captain was pointing to, but then his eyes identified the grisly scene. Scattered along the cliffs, trapped along the jagged rocks like dead insects trapped forever in amber, were the broken, rotting husks of innumerable ships. Tatters of sails and rigging fluttered in the light breeze, as though waving to the *Blue Lady*; though, whether they were waving the ship away or beckoning it to come closer, Tomas could not tell.

"So many," the young man whispered.

"Anyone foolish enough to draw close to Ctharaq Turin," Ahmed agreed.

"So why not go out further?" Tomas asked.

Ahmed said nothing, only making that same protective gesture over his heart and nodding towards the open Zaka Sea. Tomas looked, and again initially saw nothing. He finally heard and felt, more than saw, the threat. The sea remained calm, but small swirls became distinct if one looked at a single spot long enough. Little swirls, here and there, disturbing the air and the water for only a moment. It was hard at first for Tomas to notice against the sea pushing endlessly against the cliffs, but a soft tone slipped along the waves with each whirl. A song of lament, of misery, and of welcome.

"What is it?" Tomas asked in a choked whisper.

"Nothing," Rogan insisted, not looking out at the waves.

"Something," Ahmed argued. He reached out and turned Tomas' head away. "Best not to look too long," he advised. "Men have been known to listen too long, and go looking for the source."

Rogan grunted something unintelligible and headed towards the bow.

Tomas followed along behind the northlander, keeping silent until the two had some measure of privacy on the busy ship. "You don't believe in spirits?" he asked.

"I believe in leaving things alone," the mercenary countered, sitting down in the shelter of the bow. "Nothing to do about it, so why bother at it?"

Tomas was quiet for a while, standing and looking out at the cliffs and the dead adorning them. "I haven't forgotten your promise, you know," he finally said in a soft voice.

"What promise?"

"You said once we were gone from Alvaro, you'd tell me how you caused the Madness."

"Oh, yeah. Honestly, I'd just forgotten."

"Well, now you remember. So how did it happen?"

Rogan took a deep breath. "My wife, Kyla, is the Sister Superior to the Lady of Light."

"I know," Tomas replied. "The old Sylvai pleasure cult. Everyone knows she was imbued with great power by her pagan goddess."

"I don't know if 'imbued' is the right word," the northlander said. "More like she generates it. She believes in her goddess with all her heart. She does have power, no denying that. Kyla can make people around her feel different degrees of happiness and pleasure. When we first met, she tried to use that power on me, but I resisted. She considered it a challenge and started going out of her way to seduce me. I didn't much care for the thought of being her plaything, so I kept right on resisting. I'd just started serving her father, and I've never thought it was a good idea to get involved with the boss' daughter. But, eventually, she won me over; we fell in love and got married."

"I don't see how this has anything to do with causing an entire city to descend into Madness," Tomas said pointedly.

"I'm getting to it. The first night Kyla and I slept together, things... happened." He took another deep breath. "Kyla has the ability to make people happy, to amplify their... I dunno, joy. Because of this, her life has always been about making people happy. My wife is one of the most selfless people I've ever met. She gives without any thought of reward or cost to herself. But there was a... limit. Kyla was raised as an only child, and there was always a little bit of... selfishness to her generosity. Kyla was always so worried about making everybody *else* happy, but only because it made *her* happy. When we made love that first time, she felt love, genuine, selfless, love. For the first time in her life, she wasn't thinking of herself. She was feeling love: mutual compassion with another person.

"Kyla and Esha have tried to figure out exactly what happened, but apparently there was some kind of magical... thing that happened. In one moment, Kyla both experienced this overwhelming emotion at the same time she was... you know."

"No," Tomas argued flatly. "I don't know."

Eigenhard rubbed the back of his neck awkwardly. "Well, when she and I... I mean... I was her... you know... her first."

"She lost her virginity."

"Yeah." Tomas was surprised to see the Northlander actually blushing. "Anyway, after losing... you know. After a little while she... got... she had a... you know. It was the first time she... achieved." Rogan was blushing furiously now. "Anyway, in that moment, she lost control over her power and it washed out over the entire city. Her natural ability to enhance happiness was sort of... amplified. Everyone in Pelsemoria felt what she was feeling at that one moment. Everyone felt not only intense passion, but also more base... that is, more physical... more primal... desire."

"I saw men raping women," Tomas said in a flat voice. "I saw women sleeping with men other than their husbands. I saw a priest attack a nun."

The mercenary shook his head. "Kid, some people don't know the difference between love and lust. A lot don't care. Some people are incapable of love. Some people take advantage of a moment of weakness to indulge themselves and then regret it later."

"Eigenhard, I saw *my mother*, the same night after my father was killed, sleep with the father of my best friend!"

"Did they love each other?"

The young man stomped up to the warrior and glared up at him, Darkholm's magic locking his muscles for the first time in weeks. "If you ever question my mother's loyalty or virtue again, this magic will not save you!" he snarled.

Eigenhard held up his hands. "I'm sorry, kid. I didn't mean to suggest anything improper, and I'm not trying to make excuses..."

"Yes you are!" Tomas snapped. "You're trying to justify what happened! You're trying to make it sound like something other than what it was! You gave in to the advances of a dark priestess and unleashed her power on my home! You caused the Madness not out of love, Eigenhard, but out of lust!"

"Kid..."

"NO!" the young man barked. A few House Calonar sailors could not help but overhear the exchange, but Eigenhard waved them back. "No more explanations or justifications! You know, I was almost ready to believe the stories about you were exaggerated, Eigenhard. Now I think I know the truth. You are innocent of what you're accused of. You're not the heir to the Black Duke. You're not his chief enforcer or the commander of his forces. You're just his hired sword! You're nothing more than a common mercenary and the plaything of the Black Duke's whorish daughter!"

Eigenhard exploded up from his seat, his own muscles locking up even as his hands went for his enemy's throat. Veins bulged at his temples and murder was in his eyes, but Tomas was unafraid. What he had suspected for many weeks now had been confirmed. "You're under this geis as well," he said with satisfaction. "Cyras made sure you couldn't harm me any more than I can harm you. Darkholm wants me to reach the Northern Keep safely."

A thought occurred to the young man then, and he did not even attempt to hold back his laughter. "Well, Eigenhard, it looks like you're fulfilling your role as errand-boy again. Darkholm made sure you'll take me to the Northern Keep and he's used his magic to make sure you don't fail." The shepherd shook his head and turned, putting his back to his enemy before making his way casually back towards his cabin. He paused only long enough to say over his shoulder, "You're pathetic."

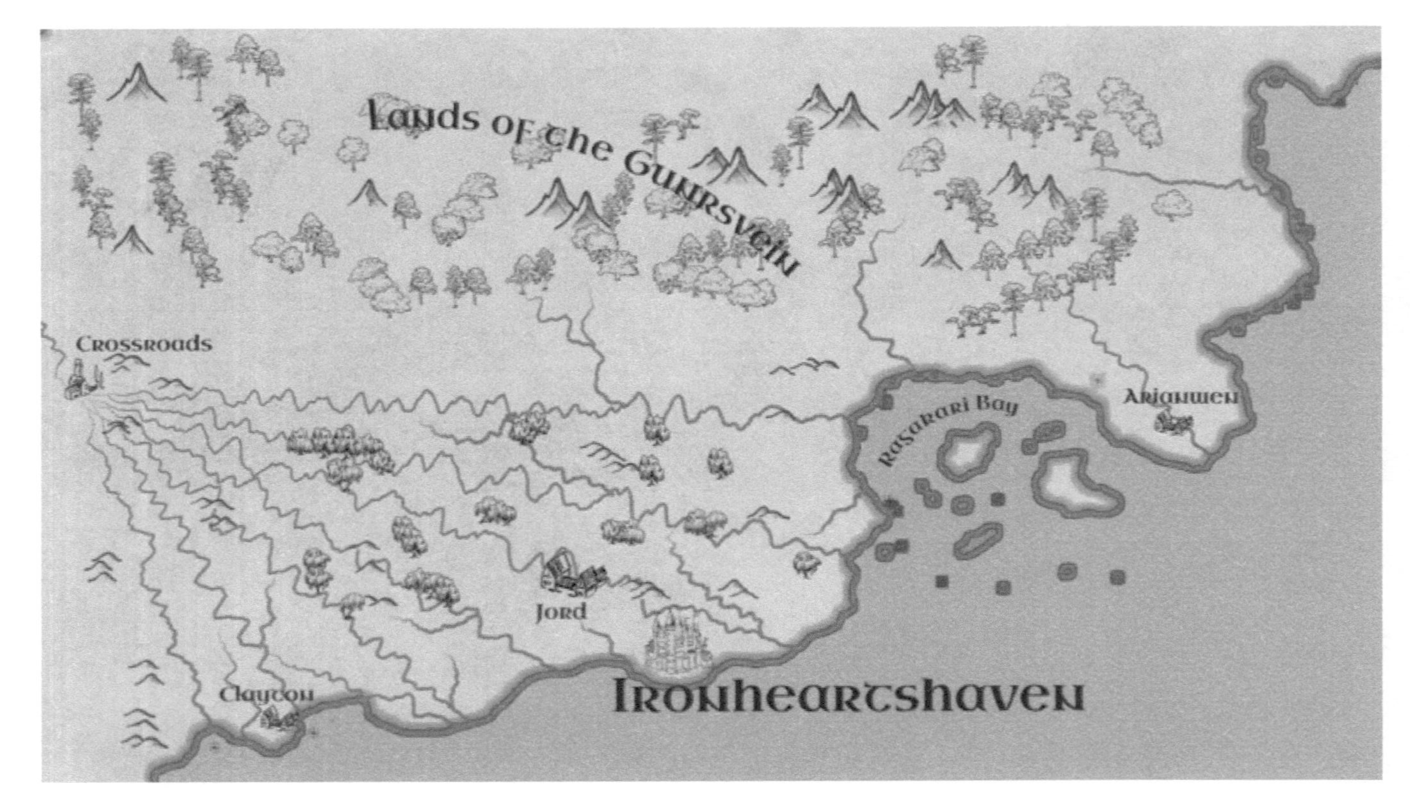

Lands of the Gunnsvein
Crossroads
Rasarari Bay
Arianwen
Jord
Claytou
Ironheartshaven

IV

The Ironheart Province

Chapter 24

Only a handful of words passed between them over the next two days. Although Tomas tried to avoid or further antagonize Eigenhard, it took the rest of their voyage aboard the *Blue Lady* for the mercenary to regain his temper. For as long as they were at sea, the mere sight of Tomas, laughing and joking with the crew, was enough for the warrior's muscles to lock under the power of Darkholm's magic. By the time Ahmed waved goodbye from the wharves of the small, mud-choked town of Clayton, Eigenhard had reached a point in which he no longer wished to kill the shepherd on sight, but was still in no mood for conversation.

The ferry they employed to go upriver was a simple barge, with a wide-open deck that gave the two enemies more than enough space apart to maintain their fragile peace. While Eigenhard spent the trip tending to the animals and cleaning his equipment, Tomas spent the time in casual conversation with the ferryman piloting their course upstream.

This region, Tomas knew, was navigable only by its residents. The Ironheart Province was a maze of rivers, streams, lakes, and ponds that shifted each spring. With the sun's return, a torrential thaw poured from Ulheim, overflowing the banks of the Oolaug River and reshaping this expansive delta. For centuries, this region had protected the tribes of the Gunrsvein from the civilized armies of the south. Those brutish ancestors of the Northmen living in the tundral forest of the far north could use the interconnected riverways to pilot their small ships to sea to trade, raid, and explore as they saw fit. Even through the history of the Republic, these lands retained their wild nature, resistant to the civilization from the south.

With the expansion of the Republic north, though, came a need for some reliable method of traveling the dense swamps at the mouth of the Oolaug. The great leader of the Heroes of Fate, Talius Ironheart, founded his city on the coast of the Hilita Sea, and dedicated his loyal knights to the defeat of the Gunrsvein. With the help of House Calonar, a Great Causeway was built and the raids of the barbarians reduced. Eventually, the Elector Council recognized the creation of this new province, in honor of the leader of the Heroes of Fate. Despite this, though, the people who made their homes in the waterways around Ironheartshaven remained willful.

Eventually the maze of winding streams and ponds through which they traveled united into a single river and finally their barge reached a small docking area resting at one of the many hostels that lined the Great Causeway. This highway was the Republic's answer to their dependance on local boatmen. Although Ironheartshaven and House Calonar were content with the independence of the locals, the Republic desired order and control. Stretching for leagues from Ironheartshaven, all the way into the valley beneath the Sentinel Mountains, the Great Causeway was a mighty stonework rising hundreds of feet above the sluggish waters of the Oolaug's many tributaries. Using the same architectural principles as the aqueducts the Sylvai Empire once built, Republic engineers had constructed a wide, flat roadway supported by hundreds of arches. Broken only by the evenly-spaced on- and off-ramps, the Great Causeway was a constant line, a road of stony civilization marking the border to the barbaric Northlands.

Tomas stood for some time staring at the stone highway raising above the water level and stretching to the horizon. It nearly brought tears to his young eyes when the shepherd saw that the great highway, began in the time of the Majestos Dynasty, was not only still intact, but heavy with traffic.

"Who maintains it?" he asked one of the oarsmen.

"Ironheartshaven," the worker replied. "They send a lot of goods to the Keep along the Causeway, so they need keep it in repair."

"Time to go," Eigenhard grunted as he saddled his irascible warhorse and led the way off the dock. The mercenary gave a few more coins to the ferrymaster before beginning the climb up the gently sloped ramp that led onto the Great Causeway. Tomas followed along, eager to ride out along this marvel of Human architecture.

Riding as they were along the safety of the Causeway, it took only another week for the pair to cross the Ironheart Province. The stonework angled almost imperceptibly downward, offering the gentlest decent. They rested briefly once the Causeway finally reached the ground along the now-constant banks of the Oolaug and became instead just another well-maintained highway. They then continued at their moderately fast pace. The open plains of the valley eventually gave way to forests and hills. The weather of early spring was pleasant, though still carried the chill of the Northlands winter. The usually awoke to grey clouds, clinging to their morbid frost. These typically only yielded to the spring sun in grudging breaks, brief openings to allow a renewing warmth in, before closing again in a sullen attempt to extend the winter's cold.

Three more days passed as the two traveled up along the Oolaug River. Through the entire trip, Eigenhard never resumed in his attempts to convince Tomas that House Calonar was, in fact, a force for good and that Kyla's Madness was some kind of horrible misunderstanding. It was clear that Tomas' words aboard the *Blue Lady* had angered his enemy, which caused the shepherd little concern. Eigenhard was also clearly trying to put those words behind him, with great difficulty.

The pair passed from one village to the next. Tomas noted in surprise that Eigenhard had covered his shield and hid any other obvious marks of House Calonar. The northlander seemed to prefer anonymity as they pushed deeper into his homelands. He paid full price to each innkeeper, and made no demands for accommodation for his exalted rank. He rarely offered his name on the rare occasion it was asked, and usually made some half-hearted lie. The commoners did not recognize him, of course, seeing only some country knight and his companion.

The peacefulness of the region gradually pressed itself into Tomas' mind. His entire trip had been marred with one tragedy after another. The lynching of Alexia and burning of Raven's body by an angry mob. The destruction of Railing, of the destruction of Unity Bridge. The sacking of so many small villages and towns. The imminent war between Alvaro and Frostfront. Tomas' quest had been filled with seemingly unending suffering and death.

But now, that same story seemed to have shifted. The villages through which they passed were peaceful. Children's laughter filled the air with the warm promises of happy kitchens. Tradesmen and merchants haggled. Only spares soldiers wearing the blue and grey of House Calonar appeared on the streets, and even then, made effort to be unobtrusive to village life. Songs of fellowship filled the tavern halls, and it seemed to Tomas that every doorway and open windowsill was filled with springtime lovers.

Two weeks passed before they reached the edge of the Ironheartshaven Province and the boundary to the Northlands. They were riding up a small hill, following the cobblestone highway on its course parallel to the Oolaug River, and just as they reached the top, the whole sky seemed to relent. The clouds of this unending winter at last gave way, blowing off to the south and west. A bright blue sky shone down, warming the earth. Tomas could not help but pause at the hilltop, closing his eyes and taking in the welcome, albeit tardy, arrival of springtime to the Northlands.

Tomas was about to mention the change in weather to his unwanted companion, to make some gesture of peacemaking, but the look on Eigenhard's face stopped him cold. The mercenary's eyes were locked on a shoddy collection of buildings set in the center of the valley below them, a sneer of utter contempt marking his tanned features. Following the gaze, Tomas peered intently at the object of his enemy's interest.

"I don't recall a town or village being on any map of this area," Tomas noted.

"It isn't supposed to be here," the mercenary replied.

Seeing the uneven, mud-chocked streets, Tomas said, "It certainly looks poor."

"More money in that town than the Republic Treasury."

"If there's so much money, why is it so run down?" Tomas pointed out the many tents, pavilions, ramshackle sheds, and even buildings formed from ruined walls. "The only complete building seems to be that large complex in the center."

"Smoke and mirrors, kid; all a show. People who come here go out of their way to be unnoticeable."

"What is this place?" Tomas demanded.

"Only name it's ever had is Crossroads. Single largest site of smuggling and black marketeering in all Lanasia. In this town, kid, everyone and everything is for sale. Only question is the price. Murder and mayhem are the two biggest forms of entertainment here."

"If it's so bad, why does the Black Duke allow it to stand?" the shepherd asked suspiciously.

Not taking his eyes off the town, Eigenhard grimaced in memory. "You know, I asked him that very same question once."

"What did he say?"

"'This kind of thing will happen,'" Eigenhard almost unconsciously drew himself erect in the saddle, his voice going deep and low. "'As it stands, we can watch and ensure things don't get completely out of hand.'"

"You mean your 'great and noble king' not only allows this place to exist but approves of its existence?"

Rolling his eyes, the mercenary said. "Look, kid, as long as there have been laws, there's been law-breakers. As soon as something is forbidden, it's desired. There will always be people who want everything they can't have, so there'll always be those who specialize in getting things to people that they can't get legally.

"House Calonar has the resources to obliterate this place, but the king understands that, as long as we know about it, we can limit what they do. As soon as Crossroads is raised, they'll just set up shop again someplace we don't know about."

"I guess I never thought about it like that," Tomas grumbled.

Eigenhard did not to push the issue. Instead, the knight said, "Alright, kid, listen up. I've got to go down there, and I'm betting that Cyras' spell won't let you stay up here."

"I thought you hated this place?"

"I do."

"Then why go in?" Tomas asked.

"Cyras was hinting at something big happening. It's a fair bet that whatever it will be is already disrupting trade; that means someone, somewhere, is losing money. Anytime money is involved, you can bet Crossroads knows."

"It doesn't sound that safe."

"It's not," Rogan grunted. "So while we're in there, you stay close to either me or Stick. If something happens, cut and run. This town can kill anybody."

"Sounds like fun," Tomas said sourly.

Chapter 25

Once they entered Crossroads, Eigenhard had them both dismount. "Less chance for a crossbow to get a clean shot," he explained. Walking the horses towards the central complex, the mercenary's eyes were everywhere. His bearing and attitude, not to mention the sword, clearly conveyed the message that it wasn't worth the trouble of giving him a hard time. Tomas, trying desperately to grow eyes in the back of his head, twice had to smack away someone's hand as it reached for his money pouch. At one point as the two made their way through the twisting streets, back alleys, and dead-end roads of the town, they had to pause as a fight between a man and woman, both naked from the waist up and each armed with straight-bladed daggers, exploded out of a building.

"What in God's name is that?" Tomas demanded. He winced when the large, red-haired woman grabbed the brutish-looking man's head and slammed it down upon her upraised knee, then drove that same knee into his crotch.

Eigenhard shrugged. "Domestic dispute." The man wrapped his arms around the woman and drove her to the ground. They spun together out of the street and into an alley, where more sounds of brutish violence followed them.

"That looked a lot worse than a 'domestic dispute!'"

"Welcome to the Northlands, kid. Life's a lot harder up here. Summers are short and winters are hard. Even before the Republic collapsed, its law was all but non-existent up here. The 'civilized men' of Lanasia never much cared about these people. Between the climate, the terrain, and the Gunrsvein, life in the Northlands is all about living."

"Doesn't sound like living to me," the young man insisted.

"To each his own, kid. To each his own."

Tomas continued to be shocked at the scenes of violence and barbarism on display throughout Crossroads. He maintained constant vigil all around him, looking about in anticipation of an attack and his hand never far from the hilt of his father's sword. The shepherd's only real trouble came when, out of the overly busy street, a beautiful woman with auburn hair appeared in the crowd. She had soft, pale skin and a classical yet sultry beauty that turned most heads in the busy street. Her black satin outfit enhanced, rather than concealed, her very feminine curves, curves that pulled with swaying tides every eye in the street.

Even as Tomas watched, mouth agape, the woman prowled up to him, using every part of her sultry body to draw his eyes from the low-cut neckline of her thin blouse to the intoxicating lines of her nimble legs. Running a finger lightly over Tomas' lips, the woman pressed every inch of her corruptive curves against the young man, pinning him in a most pleasurable way against his horse. "Come by the tavern," she breathed into his ear after staring deeply into his eyes with pools of brown emotion, causing shivers to run throughout the shepherd's body. "We could... talk."

Winking at Tomas, the woman in black turned and started sauntering away until Eigenhard grabbed her by the back of her neck and turned her to face him.

"Oh, hi Rogan," she said in a bright, cheery voice. "I didn't see you standing there."

"Althaea," the knight grunted, holding out his hand expectantly.

Smiling sweetly, Althaea pulled Tomas' money pouch from her extremely low cut, but quite full, blouse. "Hey!" Tomas said indignantly.

Taking the pouch, Eigenhard tossed it to Tomas and released the woman. Rubbing her neck, the shapely thief walked beside the mercenary as he resumed his course. "So, how have you been?" she asked brightly.

"Fine," he grunted.

"How are Kyla and Aebreanna?"

"Fine."

"How's the Temple?"

"Fine."

Althaea jumped in front of Eigenhard, blocking his path. "You're not still mad about your birthday present, are you?" she asked.

"No."

"Would you like to talk about it?"

"No."

"Would you like to come back to my place?"

"No."

"Then can I borrow your young friend?" she asked matter-of-factly.

"What!?!" Tomas started.

"No!" Eigenhard barked, losing his patience.

"You're no fun." Althaea pouted, absently tracing a finger along the neckline of her blouse.

"I can be lots of fun," he said, brushing past the shapely thief. "But I save my fun for my wife." A great deal of emphasis was put on 'wife.'

"You know, for a man who married the Sister Superior of the Lady of Light, you sure are stiff."

"You have no idea," the knight muttered.

"What?"

"Nothing," he grumbled. "Don't you have anything better to do?"

"Not really," she said, casually picking a man's pocket as she brushed by him. The unfortunate man leered at Althaea and ran his eyes along her body, noting with appreciation her overly friendly smile and wink. He did not, however, notice his purse disappearing behind her belt.

"Find something."

Althaea threw a sultry look back at the red-faced Tomas. "I already have," she said.

"Althaea," Eigenhard said.

"Yes?" she replied innocently.

"Go away."

Tomas cleared his throat. "I thought you wanted information."

"So what?" the knight snapped.

"Well, your friend here seems to be, uh... Well, she might know something."

"Oh, yes," she purred. "I know a lot of things."

"Kid, I'm not indulging your teenage lust for the sake of some information."

Tomas shrugged. "You did say you only came here because of Cyras' warning…"

Eigenhard let out a breath explosively. Turning to Althaea, the knight grabbed her arm and led her to one of the many nearby alleyways. He glanced at Tomas and jabbed a thumb back towards the street. "Keep watch," he grumbled, more to Stick than the shepherd, Tomas suspected.

"Need a little privacy, do we?" the young man asked teasingly.

"Shut up, kid," Eigenhard pushed the nubile thief up against the wall and looked deep into her eyes.

Althaea smiled and licked her lips. "Now this is more like it," she purred.

"Don't get any ideas, woman. Like the kid said, I just need some information."

Tomas, being unable to tear his eyes from the beautiful Althaea, should have been paying attention to the street; fortunately for the young shepherd, Stick was much more professional. A cutthroat who was sneaking up behind the inattentive Tomas suddenly screamed in pain and ran off. Tomas spun in time to see blood coming from the criminal's neck and Stick licking his lips. "Thanks," he told the horse.

Stick flicked his ears and finished cleaning his mouth.

"Has anything unusual been happening around here the last few months?" Eigenhard was asking Althaea.

"By what standards?" she smiled.

"Don't get cute," he muttered. "This is important."

"Yes, the boy did say something about a warning."

"That's right. Cyras Darkholm has popped up again; you know what that means."

Althaea ran a finger along her collarbone. "Trouble…" she breathed. "I like trouble."

Eigenhard leaned in. "The Keep could be in danger. Your home."

Althaea glanced about the alley. "This is my home now, thanks to that little temper tantrum of yours," she pointed out.

"Do you have any information for me or not?"

"I might," she replied, running a finger absently along her lips.

Eigenhard shook his head. "What do you want?"

In response, she again ran her eyes up and down the knight's thick, muscled body. "Besides that!" he snapped.

Althaea shrugged. "What else have you got?"

"Look," he snapped. "I know you're not interested in money, and I know you're not interested in power. You're still in good standing at the Temple, and you're welcome in any city or town under House Calonar's control, including back at the Keep. It was *your* decision to leave in the first place. I can't bribe you or appeal to your sense of patriotism, so just what do you want?"

Althaea shrugged. "I want you to ask me nicely," she replied in a voice dripping with sweet sincerity.

Eigenhard raised an eyebrow. "What does that mean?"

"You've never been very nice to me, Rogan. I've tried being friendly. I've tried being polite. Nothing I do seems to make any difference to you. You still treat me poorly. If you don't want to sleep with me, that's fine. After all, it's your loss. But even if you don't sleep with me, that doesn't mean that you have to be so mean to me all the time. If you want my help, all you have to do is ask me nicely."

The warrior stared hard at her for several seconds. Finally, he stepped back and nodded. "You're right. I haven't been very polite. I'm sorry. I've just... this isn't an easy time. I'm sorry."

"Do you want to talk about it?" she asked with genuine sympathy.

Eigenhard let out a breath explosively. "No, I don't think so. I just need to stop being as childish as the people around me. I would, however, appreciate it if you didn't keep coming on to me. In return I'll try to start being a little… nicer. Now if you do know something about a threat to the Keep, please tell me."

Althaea patted the knight on the cheek and smiled. "There now, do you see? That didn't hurt at all."

"Are you going to talk or not?" he muttered.

"Yes I am," she laughed. "You want to know if something out of the ordinary has been happening. Well tell me if you think this is out of the ordinary. Every merc I know has stopped working."

"What? With all the wars on, there are none working?"

"That's right. Right now, Crossroads is full of the worst, most dangerous of the scum of Lanasia, and none of them are looking for work."

"Meaning they've already found it," Eigenhard guessed. "Who?" he demanded.

Althaea shrugged. "Sorry, I don't know. They're all spending different kinds of money, though. I've seen Uldra silver marks and gold thrones, old Republic denarii, those new plebeians Calonar is putting out, and the deckets that Parano and Balshazzar are using. I've even seen money from Tramaya."

He thought a moment, then looked at Althea. "What about copper ingots? Any Davenorian coin?"

She shook her head. "No Xeshlin money of any kind."

"Almost like someone was trying to hide their origin."

"You know, sometimes you can be very quick, despite what people say."

Eigenhard shook his head. "I don't like it. A merc army right on our doorstep with plenty of money to spend and no urge to find work. Something stinks."

The beautiful thief waved a hand over her face. "Yes well, you did pick a fragrant place to have this little conversation."

The knight looked her dead in the eyes. "Thank you, Althaea. Talking to me won't cause you any trouble, will it?"

She laughed. "Don't you worry," she said with a kittenish twinkle in her eye. "Like I said, I like trouble."

"Well, if things get too dangerous here, you should come home."

"That's all right. I actually kind of like it here. Life is never dull in a place like this. Besides," she added, "maybe if I find out anything useful, you could come back and have a visit."

"You never stop, do you?" the knight muttered.

She laughed again, a sound that filled the air with predatory joy and earthly delights, as she languidly stepped out of the alley. "Let me know if you ever change your mind."

"Goodbye, Althaea."

The sensual woman rolled her eyes and slid off, her curves turning every head once she was back in the street. "Give Kyla my love," she called. "Bye Stick."

Stick neighed lustily.

"What did she do that annoyed you so much?" Tomas asked as the knight rejoined him and led them down a different street.

"Drop it, kid," Eigenhard grunted.

"I could always call her back and ask her," Tomas suggested with a malicious grin.

The knight growled. "Althaea used to be a Sister of the Lady of Light."

"Yeah." Tomas looked again towards Althea. "Yeah, that tracks."

"She'd been tying for years to convince me to... uh... engage in... extra-marital... relationships. Well on my birthday about three years ago, my wife and I were... together. Kyla got up and left at one point, saying she needed to freshen up. Anyway," the knight said, as though breaking himself from a brief trance, "while I was laying in bed, I was suddenly rolled onto my back as my wife climbed on top of me, at least that's what I thought. Now, once you marry and come to know your wife's... tendencies, you definitely notice when something's wrong. I reached over to that heatless torch thing Remm invented, and when the light came on..."

"It was Althaea," Tomas finished.

Rogan nodded, grimacing.

"So how did your wife feel about this? Assuming you told her."

"I didn't have to tell her. It was her damned idea!"

With a perplexed look on Tomas' face, the young man stopped in the street. "So... your beautiful wife is encouraging you to be physical with another beautiful priestess. And that's... bad?"

"Look kid. I love my wife dearly and I have no doubt regarding her loyalty. I would do almost anything to please her, and believe me, I've done some damned strange things. But I'll be damned if I'll be the passing entertainment of some lustful priestess!" the knight snarled.

Hearing the words, Tomas was suddenly reminded of his own experience with Fiametta, the daughter of the Nunzio tavernkeeper. The young man had also been unpleasantly surprised by an unwanted late-night visitor. For a single, incredibly uncomfortable moment, Tomas could almost hear Alexia insisting that he had found something in common with Rogan. The shepherd quickly shook off the unwanted thought. Rather than risk any further bonding, he was content to let the matter drop. "So, where to now?" he asked.

"The tavern," Rogan replied, pointing towards a collection of buildings just ahead. "Anyone with business in Crossroads goes to the tavern, sooner or later."

"And how dangerous is the tavern?" the young man asked.

"Makes the rest of the town look like child's play."

"Sound's interesting."

With that the knight turned to tie Stick's reigns to the posts lining the front entrance of what looked like some kind of nightmare cross between an inn and a prison. The buildings were huge, with three wings visible at the front and more behind the street, and a second story with shuttered windows covered with metal grills. The stables sitting on the first floor of the left wing were also barred, with heavy locks visible even from a distance on each stall door. Some rough music and singing could be heard from the doorway, which conspicuously lacked actual doors, and the sounds of violence and drunken revelry were obvious even over the din of the crowded street.

Eigenhard began climbing the wooden stairs that led to the front doorway, still fuming.

Tomas' voice brought the knight back to reality. "Aren't you afraid someone will steal our horses if we just leave them tied up out here?" he asked.

Eigenhard shook his head, giving Stick a mixed look of affection and irritation. "I'm not that lucky," he answered, smacking the horse on the rump.

The knight did not notice the man until he was right on top of him. Of all the disreputable character Tomas had seen since entering Crossroads, this one was by far the worst. His scraggly blonde hair stuck out in various places, looking as though he had been hit repeatedly by lightning. The only color in his sickly pale skin was from a bad outbreak of acne and the scars older ones had left behind. He could not have bathed since the last rainstorm, as the stench surrounding this near-animal was so thick it was almost a taste. He was dressed in a horrid clash of colors and had a voice that only varied from a nasal whine to a drooling leer. He did not see Rogan until the two nearly collided.

"Senen!" Eigenhard roared tearing his sword from its scabbard.

Throwing his hands up in surrender, the rodent tried desperately to duck behind a support pillar for cover, shrieking, "Rogan! Wait! I give up!"

With a roar of fury, Rogan obliterated the pillar, sending Senen and a great deal of lumber flying into the street. Seeing his doom in the warrior's eyes, Senen jumped onto a nearby horse and, kicking the startled owner, fled. The knight whistled to Stick, and the beastly warhorse immediately snapped the rope holding him and galloped towards his rider. Rogan leapt onto Stick's back without the horse slowing and thundered off after his target, cracking the air with a torrent of obscenities. Tomas frantically remounted his own horse, struggling to catch up before Cyras' geis simply started dragging the young man after the pursuing knight.

Senen tried desperately to lose his pursuer, guiding his horse throughout the maze of twisting alleys and narrow streets that criscrossed the town. His maneuvers were pointless, though, as Rogan and Tomas remained fixed behind him, steadily closing. Senen's course finally left the relative safety of the town and entered instead a nearby series of gullies. After an eternity of flight, twisting from one jagged path to another, cutting through broken vegetation and forcing his frothing horse to jump crevasses, Senen's route ended before a steep cliff. He could only whimper, frozen in terror, as Rogan thundered up and, without stopping, flew from his saddle, slamming into his target. The two were forced to the ground by the impact, Senen hitting the ground hard enough to force the breath from his lungs. Unfortunately for him and heedless of the weight of his chainmail shirt, Eigenhard rolled with the fall and was back on his feet in half a heartbeat, sword in hand. Striding over, the warrior grabbed Senen by the front of the shirt and lifted him clear off the ground. Senen lost control of his bladder.

"Are you scared?" Eigenhard grinned evilly.

"Y-Y-Yes!" Senen sobbed.

"Good." The warrior raised his sword, but then paused. He dropped the blade and struck the man he held in the face with just his leather-gloved fist. Again and again he reached back, holding Senen aloft with one hand and beating him with the other. Even once the man was half-dead, coughing up blood and begging for his life, Eigenhard only beat him that much harder.

Tomas could only watch in frozen horror as, his rage finally sated, the northland warrior dragged Senen by the throat towards the nearby cliff as he weakly kicked and begged for mercy. Finally, Tomas yelled, "Eigenhard, stop!"

His face unchanged, the warrior tossed Senen over the edge, holding the man by his scrawny neck. Seeing his doom at hand, Senen screamed in mindless terror. There was nothing but open air around the man and a wall of stone that led only to a chasm below filled with the growing shadows of day's end.

Calmly and carefully, Tomas dismounted and walked towards Eigenhard. "You've told me that all the stories I've heard about you and the Black Duke are false," the young man said. "You've tried to convince me for weeks that you and Calonar are men of honor and justice. Are you just going to murder a helpless man? Is this your honor, Eigenhard? Is this your justice?"

The knight said nothing, only stared at Senen with burning eyes and clenched teeth.

"If you drop that man, you prove me right. If you kill this helpless man, in cold blood, then you prove you make yourself judge, jury, and executioner whenever it suits you."

"You weren't there, kid," Rogan said finally, staring into Senen's terrified eyes. "You didn't see the bodies."

"Tell me."

Eigenhard snarled and pushed Senen to the ground at his feet. "I was in Drailia," the knight said, towering over the still cringing man. "Two years ago. We were returning from a relief mission to a mining town. They'd suffered some landslides.

"The local authorities had been investigating a series of child murders and asked for help. I waited outside the school for days until I saw this… parasite lure a young boy into his carriage. I lost him in the crowd.

"Kyla was with me; she did an augury. She led me and the town watch to an old granary. When we entered, we found this thing with… He was nude, the boy too. Before he'd started… pleasuring himself… with the boy, he had… used a knife to open… the boy was still alive but we couldn't…" Tears blinded Rogan at the memory.

Taking a deep breath, the knight continued. "We couldn't save the boy. His wounds were too serious. Nearly killed this pig on the spot, but Kyla insisted we take him into custody. There were other missing children. We had a diviner lead us to Senen's hideout. We found the children… what was left of them. This monster was sentenced to death by fire."

It was several moments before Tomas was able to speak, the horror of what Rogan told him threatening to overwhelm the young shepherd. "If he was sentenced to death, why is he still alive?" Tomas asked.

"Good question." Rogan faced Senen and smacked him in the face. "How about it, you waste of skin? How did you escape the dungeons?"

Trembling and even paler than usual, Senen shook his head, his mouth pressed firmly shut. Leaning in very close, Eigenhard snarled, "You *will* talk! So help me you'll talk or…"

"You'll only kill me anyway!" the rat screamed.

"Probably right," the knight agreed.

"Something big is coming, Rogan!" Senen cried desperately. "You need what I know! The Keep itself is going to be attacked!"

"When!?!" he demanded, violently shaking the criminal. "How!?! Who!?!"

"I want your word, Rogan! I want your word that if talk, you'll let me go!"

The warrior snarled, "There is no way in…"

"Eigenhard," Tomas interrupted, finally able to speak through his horror at what Senen had done. "Cyras warned you about this. Althaea warned you about this. You can always hunt him down later, but right now his information is worth more than your satisfaction."

Struggling desperately to control his rage, Rogan finally conceded. "Talk fast," he growled.

"It was Balshazzar. The Emir of Tordenia. He hired some group who called themselves the Bellonari."

Rogan had stiffened at the name, just slightly, but enough that Tomas noticed. "The what?" he asked.

"Later," the knight shook his head slightly. He then leaned again towards the sniveling Senen. "Why would Balshazzar hire… why would he pay to free you?"

"It wasn't just me. Those Bellonari freed everyone in the prison. These were bad men, Rogan, the nastiest mercenaries and cutthroats in all Lanasia; most of them were about to get sent to Ubelheim. These guys cost a fortune to hire, just for one, but they're worth every copper piece and Balshazzar hired them all. Also, the Bellonari were being led by a wizard."

"A wizard?" Eigenhard asked.

Senen nodded. "I was never told his name, but he was tall and thin. He had brown hair and was well-kept, like a noble. He shook when he walked, and he talked with a soft, hissing kind of voice. He was educated, too; he used a lot of big words and talked down to everyone. And whatever else he was, he wasn't Guild affiliated. He wore no marks or robes, but his face had markings all over it."

The knight leaned in close with a hungry look in his eyes. "Marks?" he demanded. "Tattoos or scars?"

"Both!" the criminal insisted. "They were designs like tattoos, but carved into his flesh."

"Anyone you know?" Tomas asked.

Rogan squinted his eyes and grunted. "Question is: where would Balshazzar get the money to hire a rogue wizard… these assassins, and the deadliest mercenaries in Lanasia?" Rogan mused. "He barely has enough to pay his standing army."

"He has a lot now," Senen said. "More than you could believe. Balshazzar's people are spending money like it falls out of the sky. Gold. Silver. Precious stones. And there's something else, Rogan, Balshazzar has an ally."

"Who?" the knight demanded.

"I don't know. Nobody knows. Whoever it is, he's the one pulling the strings and supplying all the money."

"What about you?" Tomas asked. "What part do you play in all of this?"

"Balshazzar's agents told me to come to Crossroads. I'm also supposed to find every one of Rashid's agents in the area and send their names back."

"How do you know how to find Rashid's agents?" Rogan demanded.

"Balshazzar's people told me."

"How in Underworld do they know!?!" the knight roared.

"It's that ally of his Rogan! Whoever it is knows everything about Calonar and his forces."

"He has a man on the inside," Tomas suggested.

Rogan grunted. "Is that it?"

Senen nodded.

The knight grabbed the weasel's face. "Who!?!"

He whimpered and tried to shake his head. "I don't know! Nobody knows! Only Balshazzar!"

Rogan dropped Senen with a sneer, and he went aside to consider the information. The sniveling coward made a move briefly to try and run, but Stick's hulking presence was more than enough to quell any thoughts of escape.

"Do you really think that's all he knows?" Tomas asked walking up beside him.

"I'm surprised he knew that much," the knight replied.

"What's a Rashid agent?"

"Later. Right now, we have to figure out what to do with him."

"You gave your word," the shepherd reminded him.

With a growl, the knight crossed back, retrieved his sword, and picked Senen off the ground. Tomas made to intercept but Rogan held up his hand, signaling him to wait. "Listen to me," he growled, looking deep into the pedophile's eyes. "Listen as if your soul depends on what I say. No matter where you run, no matter where you hide. No matter the friends you think you have or the protection you think can buy. None of it matters. I will find you.

"You live, Senen. Today, you live. Tomorrow, who knows?"

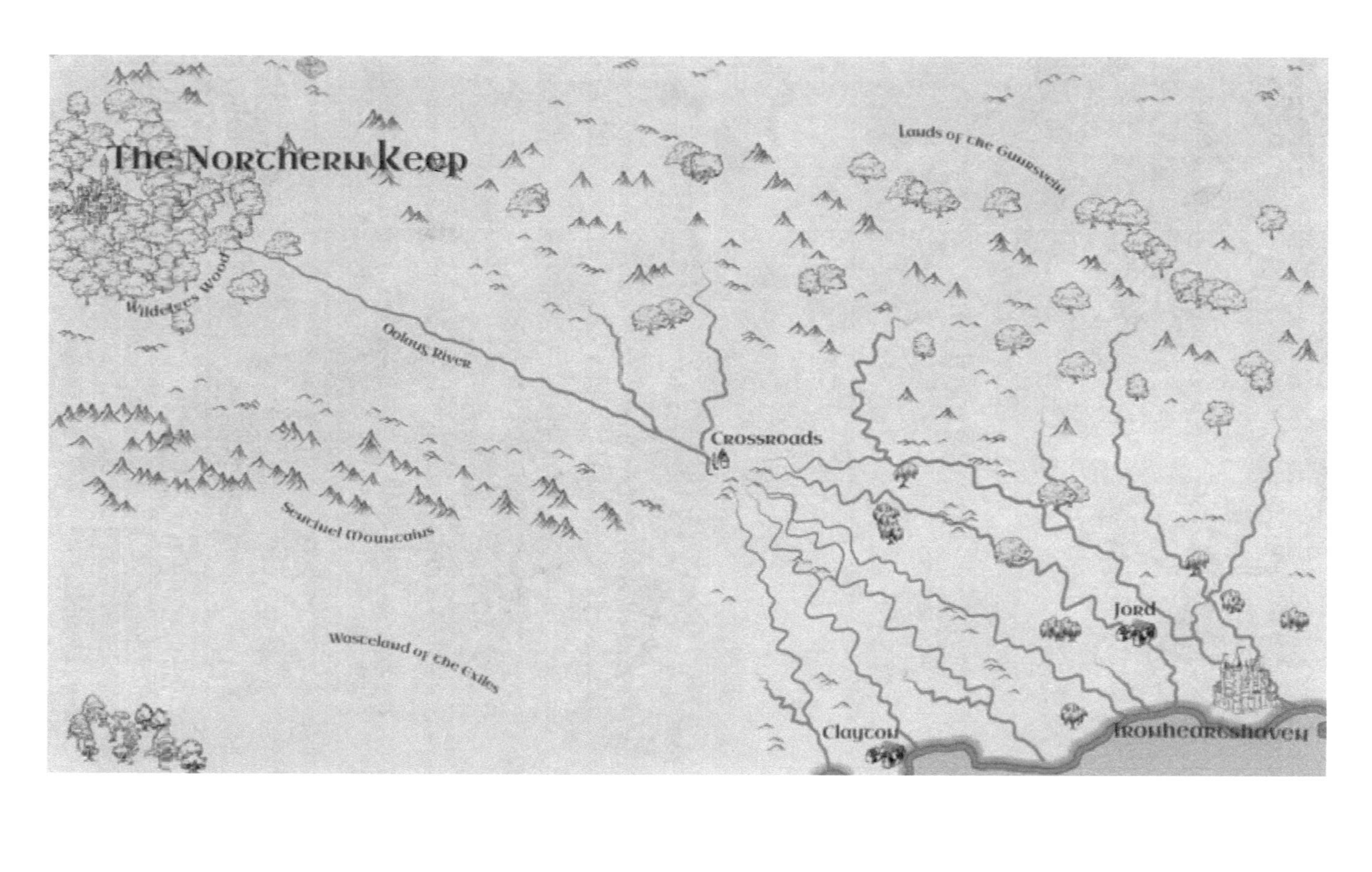

The Northern Keep
Wildeyes Wood
Oolnus River
Sentinel Mountains
Wasteland of the Exiles
Lands of the Gunnsvein
Crossroads
Jord
Clayton
Ironheartshaven

V

The Northlands

Chapter 26

A month of hard riding was needed for the unlikely duo to crest one of the numerous hills of that region and finally to catch sight of Wildelves Wood. Although they traveled hard, following the road that ran alongside the Oolaug River, stopping only once the sun had set in a local inn, and rising again with the dawn, still the road seemed unending. Their meal breaks lasted only long enough for their horses to rest before they were off again. The worsening news gathered on their journey seemed to press at Eigenhard. The northlander grimaced and muttered to himself often, clearly turning over the growing threat to his master, the Black Duke. The Xeshlin grew more bold in the south. Alvaro and Frostfront remained at the precipice of war. And now, their trip to Crossroads revealed that an army of mercenaries was gathering at the edges of House Calonar's domain. A force, Tomas recalled, that included some mysterious Brotherhood that Rogan feared.

The northland warrior was obviously relieved when, at last, the two of them caught sight of Wildelves Wood, home and sanctum of House Calonar. The forest was massive, with massive trees pressing together as though in protection against the civilized world. The Oolaug River flowed out from the center of the great Wood, seeming to Tomas to be in a great hurry to leave the cursed forest. The bright spring sun could not seem to penetrate the ancient wood, leaving a blight of cursed shadows upon Lanasia. Wildelves Wood was the traditional home and seat of power for House Calonar. For centuries, holy knights, inquisitors, and mercenaries had entered that forest, seeking to put an end to the evil of the Black Duke's family; of these, no survivor escaped the trees. Some said the wood was, in fact, a portal to a dark realm, a borderland into some hellish world of nightmares. And within the heart of that foreboding place was the greatest den of evil: the Northern Keep.

"Any way I can talk you out of taking me in there?" the shepherd asked Eigenhard.

The knight glanced at his charge. Rogan had not spoken since the two had left Senen sobbing at the cliff's edge. The hardened warrior seemed subdued by the encounter with the child killer. For himself, Tomas did not know what to make of the encounter. Senen had obviously been a vile sort of creature, exactly the kind known to inhabit the cold, bleak Northlands. Still, despite his crimes, there could be no doubt that Eigenhard had brutalized the helpless man. Eigenhard, it seemed to Tomas, was a study of contradictions. On the one hand, he had beaten Senen half to death; on the other, he had honored his word to release the criminal in exchange for information. Despite his dismissive attitude towards the thief Althaea, the knight was quick to swallow his pride to learn what she could tell him. There could be no doubt in the young man's mind that Rogan Eigenhard was his enemy. The man was a murderer and served an evil lord. There would one day be a reckoning between them. The only doubt in Tomas' mind was just how many of Rogan's acts were genuine and how many were exaggerated for his benefit. "Don't tell me you believe all those stories about boogeymen and evil Sylvai?" the knight snorted. Eigenhard shook his head. "You know," he mused, "I used to think that a kid would be lucky to grow up in a city like Pelsemoria. Always figured there'd be no better place in the world for someone to get an education."

"What changed your mind?" Tomas asked, still nervously eyeing the forest ahead.

"Despite your education, you're still just as superstitious as any villager."

The young man pointed at the Wood. "That place is cursed," he declared. "Pagan shrines, dark magics, monsters hidden in perpetual shadow. That place is a breeding ground for evil. Hell, if for no other reason, men should avoid that place because of the Sylvai warlocks, to say nothing of the Northern Keep."

"Speakers," Rogan corrected.

"What?"

The knight pushed Stick forward into a slow walk down the hill. "Sylvai don't call their spellcasters warlocks; they call them Speakers."

"What about Sylvai who joined the Guild?" Tomas demanded. "They were called wizards."

"They're called wizards by Humans," Rogan corrected. "To a Sylvai, if someone uses magic, he's a priest, a speaker, or a Xeshlin."

"'The Dark Ones," Tomas translated with a slight shudder. "I heard all their females make packs with demons and cast dark magics."

The knight shook his head. "Run into a couple Xeshlin over the years. They're not much different than Sylvai…" Rogan looked around nervously, then leaned in a bit towards Tomas. "Just don't point that out to any Sylvai." He then straightened in his saddle. "Just like their cousins, Xeshlin females have all the magic, males are workers, warriors, servants. It's just the coloring that sets them apart."

"Pure white," Tomas agreed, thinking back to the lessons from school. "No color in their skin or hair, and eyes like burning blood."

"Plus all the slaving, demon-worship, and generally-bad attitudes."

Wanting to change the subject from the many horror-tales of the Xeshlin Invasion of centuries ago, Tomas said, "If their spellcasters are Speakers, what do they call Human wizards?"

"*Lin'al'en'al'a.*"

"And what does that mean?"

Rogan laughed again. "'One Who Acts Instead of Thinks."

Tomas looked suspiciously at the knight. "Are you making fun of me?" he demanded.

"Wish I was. It's a little pretentious, but to be honest, I've never met a Sylvai who wasn't. Doesn't mean you can't like them. Just means you'll never like them as much as they like themselves."

The knight led Tomas and their two packhorses further down the road, eventually reaching a bridge that looked to be recently constructed.

"I didn't know the Republic bridged the Oolaug," the young man remarked as they approached the bridge. A small house rested to the side against the bank of the great river. Smoke came from the chimney, and the smell of freshly baked bread made Tomas' mouth water. The laughter of children came from behind the home, and a mother's voice floated through the valley, singing of home and family. The house, though of stone and straw, nonetheless had the look of a home and made the shepherd suddenly sick for Pelsemoria.

"They didn't," Eigenhard replied as the two of them rode towards the large stone bridge. "The Republic never gave a damn about the people of the Northlands. As long as the tribute was paid, a second thought was never sent our way."

"Then who built the bridge?"

"Whoever lives in that house. After the Republic collapsed, the king set up a new program to loan anyone enough money to construct bridges and maintain roads. Since then, we've had work done throughout the Northlands."

"But what would a man get out of building a bridge here?" the shepherd asked.

"The toll," Eigenhard replied. "Anyone who wants to cross the bridge has to pay a small toll."

"Toll bridges are illegal on Republic highways."

"This isn't a Republic highway anymore. That family maintains this road, including that bridge. Why shouldn't they get something out of it?"

An older man with a large frame and many scars who had been carrying wood around his house stopped when he saw the travelers. The gruff man walked to the door to his home and, after a muttered conversation with the woman inside, reemerged carrying a poleaxe. He carried the long weapon with experience, the speartip held at chest-level of a riding man. Although he did not bear the mark of the Legions on his shoulder, the man carried himself nonetheless as a man trained for fighting. He approached wearily but then stopped and looked hard at Rogan's face. The heraldry on the knight's shield was still hidden from their passage through the Ironheart Province, so the man stared hard at Rogan's face. Then, he bowed, his poleaxe held nearly at attention. "For you, my prince, no toll."

Eigenhard nudged Stick forward, handing over a few coins to the man. "It's your bridge, and everyone should pay the same."

"My prince, I couldn't..."

The knight held his hand up. "I insist."

The bridge keeper again bowed low. "Thank you, your Highness. It's an honor for you to use my family's bridge."

"I'm just grateful you finished it," Rogan replied. "Afraid we'd have to ford, and that river can get pretty cold this time of year."

"My lord, if it's not an imposition, my family would be honored to meet you."

A brief shadow crossed the knight's face. "Sure. No problem at all." As the toll-taker turned to retrieve his family, Rogan sighed and removed the cover from his shield, letting the spring sun catch the blue and grey heraldry of House Calonar. The northland prince placed the shield on his left arm and turned Stick so the heraldry faced the cottage door.

Despite Rogan's obvious discomfort with the situation, he and Tomas were introduced to the entire family. The wife, Hannah, positively gushed over meeting her prince and offered to cook him a feast. Rogan politely refused, insisting they were urgently needed back at the Keep. The children, though obviously thrilled to meet their prince, seemed even more excited to meet Stick. The mighty warhorse took their petting and the many treats they snuck to him with equanimity, obviously enjoying the celebrity Eigenhard wished to avoid.

Within only a quarter of an hour, Tomas and Rogan were saying their goodbyes. "I know this is probably nothing, my lord," Raegin, the owner of the bridge said, "but a small group of men crossed the bridge just this morning. They asked whether you had passed by here. They seemed to be expecting you."

"Which way were they headed?" the knight asked.

The bridge keeper pointed further down the same road upon which Rogan and Tomas traveled, the one that made straight for Wildelves Wood. "That way, your Highness. They didn't seem to be in any great hurry, either. And my lord, they were armed."

Rogan handed a gold coin to Raegin. "Thank you," the knight said. Turning to the waiting family he smiled and waved. "Thank you all." Without another word, he led Tomas across the bridge at a gallop, not slowing down until they were out of sight of the cheering family.

"Must be hard to be so famous," Tomas mused once Rogan finally slowed down.

"Could do without it," the mercenary replied. He settled the shield in place and loosened his shortsword in its scabbard.

"Still, it must have some good points."

"If there are any, I haven't seen them," Rogan paused to pull his helmet free from its carrying-loop at the back of his saddle. Removing the leather headband he typically wore, the knight set the helmet in its place.

"Expecting trouble?" the young man asked.

The knight shrugged slightly, his eyes intently scanning the horizon. "Just cautious."

Tomas was about to reply when, without warning, Eigenhard's eyes went wide. The knight swore and tore his shortsword from its sheath, pushing Stick into the young man's horse. The shepherd grabbed his reins and tried desperately to hold on to the rearing mount and so missed Eigenhard deflecting a crossbow bolt with his quickly-raised shield. "Look out, kid!" he roared, spurring Stick further down the hill just as fast as the warhorse could move.

"What is it?" he demanded.

The knight slammed his visor down and roared, "Ambush!"

Two more bolts flew towards Tomas but fortunately sailed high, giving the young man a chance to spur his own horse after Eigenhard and duck down, almost forgetting to draw his father's sword along the way. Rogan was swearing venomously as he reached the bottom of the hill and spotted the attackers. Without pausing, Eigenhard angled Stick's course straight at a small thicket from which suddenly emerged five men. They wore a variety of well-maintained armor, from several regions in Lanasia. Their raised weapons similarly reflected a variety of origins, as did their features. Seeing the knight charging straight at them, they men showed no fear and little surprise, instead bracing themselves for the charge. Two set the butts of their spears into the ground, the points level with Stick's chest. Behind this improvised line, three more readied weapons, two carrying swords and one a vicious battleaxe. No matter this formation. Rogan roared a battlecry and Stick thundered straight ahead.

Tomas tried to keep up with Eigenhard, but his horse, though slightly larger, could not match Stick's speed. That sleek warhorse seemed just as eager as his rider to engage their opponents. When Rogan closed to within twenty feet of the bandits, though, Stick suddenly fell forward into the ground, letting a squeal of surprise and pain emit before hitting the dirt. Eigenhard flew out of the saddle, twisting in mid-air and, taking the landing on his shield and shoulder, and rolled to come immediately back to his feet, already set in a fighting stance with his sword held high and his shield at the ready.

Thinking the advantage theirs, the ambushers surged from the thicket. Their attackers uttered not a single battle cry, instead moving with a chilling and silent competence. With a sneer of contempt, Eigenhard side-stepped the first attack and spun, coming around behind the second attacker and stabbing into the man's lower back, beneath the breastplate. The first bandit stumbled, obviously taken by surprise by the knight's fighting style, and fought to keep his balance; unfortunately for the man, he stopped dead in front of an enraged Stick. The warhorse had recovered nearly as quickly as his rider and stepped over the improvised tripline, snorting and rearing, ready for vengeance. He rose on his back legs and lash out with his forehooves at the screaming man, crushing the attacker's skull.

Tomas reached the battle just in time to see the doomed man crushed beneath Stick's fury. The warhorse seemed content, for the moment, to continue stomping the dead man into the earth, so Tomas left him to his amusements. Eigenhard himself seemed to need little help, however, as he danced amongst the bandits, easily deflecting their attacks and launching an attack himself when the opportunity presented. Eager to engage himself, disregarding the voice of warning coming from the back of his mind, the young man dismounted and ran towards the fight, his father's sword held aloft.

Leaving his compatriots for easier prey, one of the attackers broke off and met Tomas' charge, blocking his swing, ducking low and spinning. Before the young man could react, he found his feet kicked out from under him. Landing hard, Tomas was forced to roll along the ground as his opponent thrust, again and again, at where he lay. Finally, the warrior put his foot down, blocking any escape and raised his blade, eager for the kill. "Die!" he hissed.

Suddenly, Eigenhard's shortsword erupted from the man's chest. "You first," the knight grunted, ripping his weapon free of the dying man. Sparing only the briefest of glances down at Tomas, Rogan said, "Ground's no place for a fight, kid."

The shepherd looked over Rogan's shoulder and pointed. "Look out!" he yelled.

With barely a backward glance, Rogan raised his shield over his left shoulder and blocked one of the incoming attacks, the battleaxe penetrating the shield's steel by a fraction. With his shield entangled with the axe and the axeman trying to leverage his strength against Rogan's the knight was vulnerable. The second of the last two living bandits swung his blade low, cutting through Eigenhard's splintmail leather vest and drawing a spurt of blood from the northland prince.

Roaring in fury, Rogan barreled forward, shoving both men back and knocking free the axe from his shield. After that initial outburst, however, the knight's strength in his left leg gave out and he stumbled. Seeing an opening, the warrior on Rogan's right launched several, lightning-fast sword strikes, eventually forcing the knight's blade from his hand. Eigenhard tried backing away using his shield to defend, but the wound he weakened him, and the knight fell briefly to one knee before rising again to a faltering defensive stance. With victory only a killing-blow away, the two remaining ambushers advanced on Rogan, still acting as though they feared him and circling to either side of the northlander. The knight stared at the men without the slightest trace of fear on his face, lifting his chin in defiance.

"Rogan!" Tomas barked, tossing his father's sword. The knight caught it in mid-air and pivoted on his good hip, slashing one of the raiders across the face with the very tip of the gladius. Without pause, Rogan thrust with terrific force, plunging the shortsword into the man's chest and yanking it out again. The shining gladius, the pride of the Republic Legions and the honor of Tomas' father, punched through the bandit's breastplate as though it were only linen. Rogan kicked the dead man free and spun to face the last threat. The final attacker launched several strikes which Eigenhard fought to stay ahead of. The knight tried to use his shield, but the wound on that side betrayed him, draining the strength from Rogan's shield-arm and forcing the northlands prince to rely only on the gladius of Tomas' father. Though well-maintained and well-designed, the sword of the legions was no match in a duel against the heavier Velarossi longsword. With one final swing, the bandit swung will all his might and great over-head attack. Rogan had no more strength to raise his shield, and so he raised the gladius. With a sorrowful chime, a mournful relenting to the inevitable, the blade of Tomas' father broke, and Rogan was forced to the ground.

Panting with exertion, the bandit stood over the knight, reveling in his victory. "The great Rogan Eigenhard," he grinned. "The Brotherhood doesn't forget, traitor." The warrior raised his longsword but then stiffened. Turning with a look of utter surprise on his face, the killer was shocked to see his own blood covering Rogan's shortsword in Tomas' hands.

The shepherd snarled, pulling the blade free and stabbing again into his opponent's neck, this time forcing the blade all the way through his enemy and sending the man tumbling to the ground. There, the man stared at Tomas in shock as his his body limply twitched and his life's blood poured onto the grass.

Rogan dropped to the ground and lay back in the tall grass against the hill, panting with a mixture of pain, relief, and exhaustion. Glancing up, he shook his head. "Took you long enough," he sighed.

Tomas shrugged, breathing heavily. "Had to find your sword."

Chapter 27

They made camp on the leeward side of a nearby hill, neither wishing to travel any further that day. Being uninjured, Tomas did most of the work to clear a spot, gather wood, and make their dinner. The knight sat against his saddlebags, tending to his wound as best he could, holding a heated knife to the wound before tying it with twine. Handing Rogan his plate, Tomas sat down across their fire.

They ate in silence for a while. Neither looked up to the night sky as the stars peaked out. Neither glanced at the rising moon, smiling her benediction on a new season of hope and renewal. Neither mentioned the dead men, lying scattered in the field on the opposite side of the road, where they awaited the lonely rot all vile men deserved.

Finally, for reasons unknown, Rogan suddenly shook his head, tearing a chunk of bread, chuckled. "I notice you came through without a mark."

"Actually," Tomas primly corrected, "I've got a rather nasty bruise on my butt."

"Oh, heavens! A bruise, you say? On your butt? But however will you think now?"

Tomas wrapped a slice of cheese with his own bread and took a bite. "I guess that means I'll have to be content with thinking at your level for a while," he said through a mouthful.

Rogan grunted, eating a few more bites. "Still," he said reluctantly, "not too bad a job today, all things considered. You even managed to save my life."

The shepherd shrugged. "You can't win them all, I guess." The shepherd winced then, just slightly, and swallowed his food. Not looking at the Northlands prince, he then said, "As I recall, you saved me as well. I'd say we're even."

They sat quietly for a while, eating their meal. A gentle breeze had picked up, blowing in from the east and carrying the faintest hint of warm bread and home. The breeze pushed away any hint of the fallen bandits. Finally, Tomas smiled. "That was pretty good the way you caught the sword in mid-air and cut that one guy," he noted.

Rogan nodded. "Yeah, I liked that. Always feels really good when you manage a move like that. Just wish to God I knew how I did it."

"You mean that wasn't planned?"

"No," the knight laughed, taking a long drink of water. "No move that good is ever planned."

They both ate in silence. Once they were done, Tomas packed up the remaining food and unrolled his blankets. Rogan looked over and sighed. "Sorry about your father's blade, kid."

Tomas reached into his bag and pulled out the hilt. There was now only a small piece of blade still attached, terminating just above the golden eagle. The young man had tried to find the rest, but the tall grass had hidden it too well. "It's alright," he said, putting it back into his bag. "It really wasn't very practical, anyway."

"You know, when I first started out, I used someone else's sword."

"Father's?"

"Uncle's." The knight looked up towards the distant peaks of Ulheim, small on the western horizon and tiny, barely visible through the dense forest only a mile away. Even in the fading light of the hard day, the great mountains still reflected the memory of dusk from their snowy peaks. "A pretty good sword, but there was something about it that just didn't feel right."

"What?" Tomas asked.

"Couldn't tell you. No weapon I used worked just right, until I met Fang here," Rogan hefted his sheathed shortsword. "After that, everything just worked."

"Fang?"

"Everything needs a name," the knight shrugged.

"What about the other?" the young man asked.

Rogan glanced back at where the longer, two-handed longsword rested against his shield. "That's Talon. They were gifts from someone I was very close to back home."

"Why two?"

The knight shrugged. "Well for one, it never hurts to have a backup." He nodded to the bag containing Tomas' broken sword. "Also, Fang is meant to be used with a shield like I did today."

"I guess it's important to find a weapon that suits you," Tomas noted.

"Important to find a style first. Find a fighting style that feels right and get the equipment to match."

Tomas lay back on his blankets and stared up at the stars and the soft moonlight, waiting for sleep to come. Rogan did likewise. "So just who were those guys?" the young man asked.

"What do you mean?"

"That wasn't a random attack. Those weren't highwaymen. They were professional soldiers. That last one called you by name."

"Would it surprise you if I've got a price on my head?"

Tomas shook his head. "'The Brotherhood doesn't forget,'" he said, quoting one of the attackers. The young man looked evenly at the knight. "I'm not stupid, Rogan."

The knight thought for a few seconds, staring up at the emerging stars, his gaze seemed to linger on one constellation in particular, barely visible through a few stubborn clouds. Obviously, the question sparked memories in the warrior, memories that he would perhaps not have wanted to share.

"I'm not going to let this go," Tomas warned. "I think that if there's a chance that whatever *you* did to these people could get *me* killed, I have a right to know."

Rogan shook his head. "Don't worry," he said. "There won't be another attack anytime soon. They never have two groups operating in the same area."

"They?"

The knight sighed. "They're called the Bellonari."

Tomas thought for a moment. "The group that freed Senen?"

"Apparently," Rogan agreed. "They're an order dedicated to Bellonar."

"What's Bellonar?"

"An aspect of Ramalech. 'She who brings war and bloodshed.'" He shifted, trying to find a comfortable position against his wound and his memories. "Originally, the Bellonari were a Sylvai warrior lodge, dedicated to worshipping their goddess of war and martial prowess. Sometime during the Uldra Uprising, the lodge was… perverted, corrupted. They turned to the worship of Ramalech during the worst of the Uprising under the leadership of Kelinva, the Dark Empress. She twisted the lodge into a cult more interested in sacrifice and slaughter than in martial prowess.

The knight sighed. "Anyway, after the Uprising, and Kelinva was banished with her followers to Davenor, everyone thought the Bellonari were gone as well."

"But, they weren't?" Tomas guessed.

Rogan shook his head. "They became a secret society. Funny thing is, during all those years of Human rule, the Brotherhood was... corrupted, back to its original intent- a lodge that venerated the old Sylvai goddess of war and martial prowess. They traveled to every city, every remote village, learning everything they could about being a warrior.

"By the time they returned to Lanasia, they knew some serious tricks. Ever since, they've hidden themselves from the Church and most of Lanasia by posing as mercenaries and bounty hunters. The Brotherhood has amassed incredible wealth from the jobs that they take, and they've used that money to build temples in secret locations throughout Lanasia, maybe the whole world. There's one home temple somewhere, but only the most senior members of the order know the location."

"You were one of them," Tomas guessed. "That's where you learned how to fight the way you do. That's how you know so much about them. You joined these Bellonari."

The knight nodded. "I'd been working as a mercenary for a few years and, after a battle I barely remember, I was recruited. The Bellonari offered to train me, provide contacts for steady work, and take me to anywhere in the world I wanted to go."

"They broke their promises?"

Rogan laughed. "Oh, no. They kept every one. I was given a master and taught to fight in the ancient styles. I learned swordsmanship, mounted and dismounted combat, strategy and tactics, even how to fight magical adepts."

"So, what was the problem?" the shepherd asked.

Rogan rubbed his eyes. "I'm not sure when. Rumors... half-truths. I've heard that sometime in the last two hundred years or so, things began to change. The Brotherhood slowly turned back towards the darker arts of combat. They started working with people... well, with really bad people. There's some kind of schism in the Brotherhood; in-fighting between the traditionalists, who want to master war as a higher art, and the others, who want power for its own sake.

"After a couple of years, when I was just about finished with my apprenticeship. I was tested by the others."

"Tested?"

The knight nodded. "They assigned me to a routine kidnapping. They partnered me with a real low-life, a true believer in all the bloody-goddess bullshit. We were supposed to snatch the daughter of a minor nobleman and hold her for ransom. The client who hired us was specific that he wanted the girl raped and beaten while being held."

"Sounds like a nice guy."

"I had a problem with the whole situation to begin with, but to make it even worse, our client forgot to mention that the daughter was only nine years old. So, I refused. But my partner wanted to go through with the job. Real professional, that one. We had an… argument."

"With or without weapons?"

"With. We made so much noise on the roof of that nobleman's house that his guards found us. During the fight, I was separated from my partner, and he thought he saw me cut down. When he returned to the Brotherhood, he reported my death. That gave me enough time to run. I've been running ever since."

"They obviously don't still think you're dead."

"No, they don't. After I joined House Calonar, it was impossible to keep my name quiet, and the Bellonari have come looking. They can't get anyone inside the Keep, so they have teams moving around the edge of the forest waiting for me to come out."

"So, every time you leave the Northern Keep, you get attacked by these guys?"

"No; they don't have anywhere near the numbers for that. I've only been attacked three times in the last decade."

"You're going to have to do something about them, you know," Tomas noted. "If the Bellonari are as under-handed as you say, if this corruption is spreading, then sooner or later they're going to try something to get you away from the safety of Calonar's forces, and then they've got you."

"Believe me, kid, that thought passes through my head at least three or four times a day. Problem is, I have no idea where any of their temples are, and the only people I knew that might tell me are either dead or in hiding."

"You don't know where any of their temples are? I thought you used to be one of them."

"That's how the Bellonari have survived for so long. They only tell you what you need to know. I was only ever shown one temple, and we destroyed that one not long after I joined House Calonar."

"What makes you worth all this effort?"

"I know them," he replied. "I know their tactics and their teachings. I know what they're doing and who they worship. The Bellonari will never allow any man to live who knows their secrets but doesn't obey their commands."

"So, what are you going to do?"

The knight shook his head. "I don't know. We've been looking for years, but we don't have a single lead. I guess I'll just have to keep surviving the attacks until someone thinks of something."

Tomas shook his head. "Great plan."

"You have a better one?"

The shepherd shook his head. They were both quiet for some time after that. Rogan had little desire to relate any more of his time among the men that now were trying their best to kill him, and Tomas really did not want to ask. The fact that the man that was thought of as the worst terrorist in the world was actually on the run from the worst terrorists in the world gave Tomas a great deal to think about. Both men climbed into their bedding, neither saying a word as they looked up at the night sky. The moon was nearly full, the wind was calm, and the stars bright. It was a peaceful sky, one that lent itself to quiet contemplation.

Finally, Rogan found the words that he had been searching for since his argument with Tomas all those weeks ago. "Kid?"

"What?" the young man replied.

"It was our fault."

Tomas looked at the knight. "Could you be a little more specific? A lot of things are your fault."

"The Madness."

The shepherd stiffened. After a few moments he said, "Yes, it was."

Rogan's eyes roamed the stars overhead. "No matter how we try to justify it or explain away what happened, it all boils down to the fact that we lost control and an entire city paid for our mistake."

"Is that an apology?"

"I won't insult either of us by thinking words will ever make up for what happened. It's one of the reasons we've been sending help to your people."

Tomas stared at the mercenary. "Help? What help?"

Rogan shrugged. "Money, food, supplies, medicines. We've sent everything we thought we could sneak in without your knowing."

"You'll forgive me if I have a little trouble believing the Black Duke has been secretly helping the survivors of Pelsemoria."

The knight looked at Tomas, and without expression on his face he said, "You have approximately three hundred people living in the old Sylvai Quarter. The only remaining military is a single company wearing the regalia of the Praetorians."

"How?" the young man demanded.

"After the collapse of the capital, Velaross recalled all the churchmen in the city. Everyone went except one shamed priest, a man who renounced his vows and lived in poverty. About a year after the death of the Emperor, Cardinal Alton met secretly with that former priest. He convinced the priest we were the good guys and enlisted him to receive and distribute the supplies we could get in and coordinate with our military maneuvers in the area."

"You had your army there the whole time?"

"Kid, why do you think any of you survived? You're three hundred people surrounded by thousands of renegade soldiers, bandits, warlords, slavers, and who knows what else. We stopped everyone we could, but every now and then a raiding party would get though, mostly because the Praetorians kept fighting us."

"Father Conrad," Tomas whispered the name in shock.

The knight nodded. "A good man. Risked his life every time he met with one of our teams. In fact, one of my missions in the area was to find out what happened to our last team sent into the area. They disappeared. We assumed they were caught and killed. That's what I was really doing when we… met. The diplomatic stuff was only a cover."

The shepherd felt as though he had swallowed a lump of lead. "Sylvai Walkers?" he asked, fearing the worst. "And a… a priestess with them? A speaker?"

Rogan glanced at Tomas and nodded.

The shepherd closed his eyes, fighting the tears. "They were lead by someone named Raven… and… Alexia." It was no longer a question.

Again, the knight only nodded.

"They died," Tomas reported. "The Practorians and… they died."

Rogan stared for a time at his unwanted companion. He said nothing; he only stared. Then, "Like I said, nothing we can do will make up for the Madness. We're helping as much as we can, but it's getting harder, more dangerous. The warlords are getting closer to the capital, and you're just too damned far away for us to keep giving you clandestine aid." He turned back to his consideration of the stars. "Not to mention the danger in just trying to send in supplies to a group that hates us. Worse, the Xeshlin are escalating their operations in that area. When the day finally comes that one of those raiding groups gets though to your people…"

The two were quiet then. They both sat for a time, and then they lay back into their blankets. There were no words at that time that could convey what either of them was thinking

"Hey, Rogan," Tomas finally said.

"Yeah, kid?"

"Thanks for saving my life."

"You're welcome. Thanks for saving mine."

"You're welcome."

They were both quiet again for a long time.

"I still hate you, you know."

End

Tomas and Rogan's
Journey Continues in:

The Northern Keep

ABOUT THE AUTHOR

William Price Jr is a teacher of writing and literature.
Having published numerous short stories and poems, he still
searches for truth amidst his many made up stories. He lives
in New Hampshire

www.ingramcontent.com/pod-product-compliance
Lightning Source LLC
Chambersburg PA
CBHW022127310726
48972CB00007B/2238